JOY
Hell's Handlers Book 7

D1565860

Lilly Atlas

Other books by Lilly Atlas

No Prisoners MC
Hook: A No Prisoners Novella
Striker
Jester
Acer
Lucky
Snake

Trident Ink
Escapades

Hell's Handlers MC
Zach
Maverick
Jigsaw
Copper
Rocket
Little Jack
Joy

Join Lilly's mailing list for a **FREE** No Prisoners short story.
www.lillyatlas.com

Table of Contents

Life, death, trauma, healing; the Hell's Handlers have been through it all over the past year. They've conquered old enemies, acquired new ones, and struggled through devastating upheavals. So far, they've come out on top, knocking down challenges by focusing on one essential ideal: family above all. With Copper at the helm, the Handlers are a patchwork family of bikers who will fight to the death for what they've created.

And after all they've survived over the past three hundred and sixty-five days, the Handlers are ready to lay down their weapons, pick up their drinks, and coast through the holidays with nothing but joy in mind. But as often happens with life in an MC, Christmas takes a back seat to club drama.

As the year rolls to a close, the men and women of the club will experience new life, new chapters in love, and plenty of new beginnings. But not everything is sparkly and bright as dangerous enemies threaten the tight-knit group of rough and rowdy bikers. Will twenty-nineteen end in tragedy, or will the club once again emerge victorious in time to find a little joy for the holidays?

JOY

Lilly Atlas

Chapter One

VIPER

The cringe-worthy sound of repeated retching jerked Viper from a deep, restorative sleep. He shot to a seated position, immediately aware of the absence of his better half who'd fallen asleep in his arms some hours ago.

With a heavy sigh, Viper dropped his head and allowed himself one moment to buck the fuck up and muster the incredible amount of strength needed to endure what he'd find when he walked into the bathroom. To be the man his wife needed. Who'd have thought, after all he'd been through in his life, after all he'd survived, overcome, and fought for, he'd end up as nothing but a terrified coward?

Certainly not him.

But then, he'd never been faced with a battle like this one. A battle where pain, suffering, heartbreak were inevitable, even if he and Cassie emerged victorious.

Another heave followed by a tortured groan had him jumping out of the bed and sprinting to the bathroom.

There was no victory here, not when the uphill climb was fraught with so much torment.

"Baby," he said as he walked into the lit bathroom to find the love of his life clinging to the toilet with a white-knuckled grip.

God, he was a selfish fuck, worried about his own misery when Cassie was the one fighting for her life. Literally. And had she complained once? Had she whined, cursed the universe, or screamed at the injustice of it all until her throat was raw?

Fuck no.

Cassie was stronger than all the men in his MC combined.

But he'd sure raged, and cursed, and told the universe to go fuck itself on more than one occasion. He'd just made sure to do it out of earshot of his wife.

Without moving a muscle, Cassie said, "I'm sorry I woke you," in a dry, raspy voice. Her throat had to be raw as fuck from all the vomiting she'd done in the past twenty-four hours.

"Woman," he said, injecting a growl into his voice. Normally, the grizzly bear impression would have had Cassie giggling and rolling her eyes as it had for all the years they'd been together. She knew when it came to her, he was far more a kitten than a ferocious bear. The woman had owned him heart and soul since the moment he first laid eyes on her back when she was in her twenties and in a desperate situation. "Didn't I make you promise to wake me before you ended up riding the porcelain bus?"

She let out a feminine grunt, then threw up all over again. Viper winced as her thin body heaved and jerked with the strong force of the abdominal contractions.

The worst part of this for him was how useless he felt. He strode forward then sank to his knees, gathering up her long silver tinged hair into one hand as he rubbed her back with the other. That was it. All he could do. Hold her hair and stroke her skin as she weathered the storm.

Her flannel pajamas were soft beneath his palm but did nothing to conceal the bony feel of her spine. The amount of weight she'd lost recently would be alarming if they didn't have more frightening medical concerns to focus on than the drop in pounds.

Cassie blew out a shaky breath. "I think I'm done for now." She shifted to her ass, letting her back rest against their deep soaking tub.

Viper reached up to flush the toilet, then assumed his position next to her, gathering her into his arms.

"Thank you," she said, piercing his heart with the sweet words.

He snorted. "Thank you? For fucking what? I can't do jack shit, beautiful."

"I know you wish you could do more," she said, voice thick with the need for sleep. "But you have no idea how much you do. This right here, you holding me, climbing out of our warm bed in the middle of the night to comfort me, calling me beautiful when I couldn't feel further from it, those things take away so much of the agony. They make me smile, make me feel loved, still wanted."

There he went, whining again like a little bitch while Cassie wasted no time jumping in to soothe him. Shit. "Baby, I've wanted you every minute of every day since I met you. And I will every day for the rest of our lives." *Please let that be a long, long time from now.* "Never doubt that."

"Even that time I called you a stupid, motorcycle-riding monkey?" she asked, humor lacing her voice. "Not sure you wanted me then."

Viper threw back his head and laughed. Even at her maddest, that was the meanest insult she'd been able to come up with. "Even then."

"Huh," she said. "Guess you must love me almost as much as I love you, huh?"

"More, baby." After a few more minutes of sitting on the cold tile floor, his tailbone began to ache. Even though he could sit there forever, absorbing the soft weight of his wife against him, she had to be feeling it too. And she needed to sleep. "You ready to try and get a few more hours in?"

She nodded against his chest. "I want to take a quick shower first. I'm gross."

"Baby, in the morning. These bouts always make you so tired you can barely stand."

She looked up at him, eyes still so green after all their years together, but now they were tinged with pain. Pain that was always present these days. God, he'd do anything, fucking anything to take it all away from her.

"You'll hold me up. You always hold me up."

"Damn straight, beautiful."

He stood, then helped her to her feet. As predicted, she was a weak, unstable mess. After brushing her teeth with his arm firmly around her waist, she started to draw her nightgown over her head.

"Let me," he whispered, working the silky fabric over her head as he helped keep her steady.

"I'm so scrawny," Cassie whispered as she turned to face the mirror. "Look at me. Skin and bones." She cupped her breasts, no longer full and perky as they'd once been, shaking her head.

She sounded so dejected.

Viper flipped the water on in the shower, stripped out of his sweatpants, then fit his body behind hers, staring into her eyes in the mirror. For the first time since the initial crying jag after her diagnosis, Cassie looked seconds from shedding tears.

She was right about being extremely skinny, she'd lost nearly twenty pounds since being diagnosed with lymphoma, twenty-pounds she didn't have to spare, but her beauty hadn't faded a bit to his eyes.

"My hair is starting to fall out too," she whispered, choked up. This was the first time she'd expressed concerns like this to him and Viper's heart literally broke.

"Baby," he started.

Joy

Cassie shook her head, eyes glistening. "I'm sorry. I know these are stupid things to worry about right now, it's just…" She sighed.

"It's just what, Cas?"

"It's just hard enough with the chemo, and exhaustion, and the feeling like shit all the time, and the constant fear. On top of it all I have to look like a hairless skeleton."

From behind her, he cupped her breasts, lifting the much thinner and less firm flesh than they'd both enjoyed throughout the years. Flicking his thumbs across her nipples, he smiled at her soft gasp. "Yes, you've lost a significant amount of weight. And you will probably lose your hair, we were warned about that, but, baby—" he pressed his erection into her low back, "—it isn't physically possible for you to not be beautiful. Or for me to not react to your body. It's just who you are, a gorgeous woman, inside and out."

The tears finally escaped her eyes. "You have to say that. You're married to me."

He snorted. "You think so? You know how many men out there go looking for it elsewhere because they aren't attracted to their wives after more than twenty years of marriage? We've both seen enough fucked-up couples to know I don't have to say shit just because you're my wife. I say it because it's true. And if you don't believe my words, believe this," he said, nudging her with his erection once again.

Her hand flew to her mouth as a sob burst from her. She spun, wrapping her thin arms tight around his waist as she finally, finally allowed herself a moment of sorrow and grieving for all the changes in her life. Hot tears hit his skin and flowed down his chest. Steam filled the bathroom, cocooning them in warmth, and dampening his skin along with her tears.

"Let it out, baby," he said against her head as he rocked her back and forth. "I've got you, Cassie, and I won't let go for anything."

After a few moments, the tears ceased and she sagged against him, completely spent. "Come on, beautiful," he said, maneuvering her into the walk-in shower. Keeping one arm around her waist, he washed her as best he could with one hand, then killed the water. Holding her up was easier than it probably should have been, considering she was a grown woman. Another testament to how frail she'd become in such a short time.

"So tired," she whispered against his chest as he wrapped a large towel around them both.

"I know, baby. Good thing is we don't have to do shit this weekend, and last week the nausea started to subside by the third day, which is tomorrow."

"Got the baby shower, Sunday," she muttered, sounding so near sleep he decided to forgo new pajamas.

"Shit, I forgot about that. You can—"

"Don't even think about it," she said, a little piss and vinegar coming out now. "I'm going to Izzy's baby shower if I have to crawl there on my hands and knees."

There was his feisty girl.

He chuckled then guided her to the bed. "Yes, ma'am."

Cassie snuggled under the covers. "Ahh, that feels good. And for the first time since Thursday, I don't feel like I'm going to puke."

Finally. He slipped in beside her and pulled her into his arms. With their future hanging in the balance, he didn't plan to miss a minute of having her as close as possible.

"Don't you think it might be time to tell them?"

Cassie fell silent. Then, just when he thought she'd fallen asleep, she said, "No. Not yet. Izzy's due any second now, and Christmas is next week. Holly struggles this time of year since her birthday is always a reminder of the sister she lost. And something is bothering Shell, I just haven't figured out what yet. It's not the right time to lay something as heavy as this on them."

His woman was the definition of selfless. "And that's why they all love you so damn much, Mama V," he said. "You take care of each one of those chicks as though they were your own."

"Mmm, they are mine."

"Yeah, but, woman, do you have any idea what they're going to do to me when they find out you've been keeping this quiet for months? They're a vicious bunch of bloodthirsty bitches, and once that baby is out of Izzy, all bets are off. She'll kick my ass, no questions asked."

With a soft chuckle, Cassie huddled even deeper into his embrace. "Just want all of us to enjoy Christmas together without the sadness of cancer ruining the mood. This might be my last, and I'm not going to spend it being gawked at with pity and watching my girls cry for me."

Her last Christmas? Jesus Christ, Viper's heart had never hurt as much as it did right then. He wanted to deny it, tell her there was no fucking way this would be her last Christmas, but they both knew the words would only be that...words. They had a very real enemy attacking them from all angles.

They were fighting her cancer with every weapon in modern medicine's arsenal, but both knew there were no guarantees in life. They'd both seen and survived too much to view the world through rose-colored glasses. But that wouldn't stop them from fighting like hell to survive this. And as they battled, Viper would grant her every wish, and make sure she knew just how much she was loved.

If that meant getting his ass kicked by Izzy, so be it.

His ol' lady was going to have the merriest fucking Christmas of her life.

Chapter Two

SCREW

Screw blew into his hands then rubbed them together, trapping the heat of his breath. The move warmed him for about ten seconds, but then the cold took over again. So much for being a tough biker who didn't need gloves.

What the fuck was taking her so long?

Shit couldn't have gone better. Even Mother fucking Nature got her ass in gear to make this night go exactly as he'd planned. As he'd been planning for months. And if all continued to coast along as expected, Screw would be buried balls deep in Jazz within the hour.

No woman could resist all the stops he'd pulled out tonight. And this particular woman would be spreading her legs and begging him to fuck her.

Finally.

Jazz had the privilege of being the first woman—first person —to ever turn him down flat. And stick to her guns. That meant she was also the first woman to receive genuine effort from him. For fuck's sake, he'd been working on her for months. Anything more than twenty minutes of work was out of his norm. Sure, his track record wasn't one hundred percent right out the gate, but even those who turned down a night in his bed initially were easily swayed. A few heated looks, casual-yet-anything-but touches, and some whispered dirty words had the women and men falling into Screw's bed without much effort.

Just as he liked it.

He liked to fuck, and he liked to fuck often.

And hard.

And dirty.

Shit, just thinking about fucking had him growing hard. He needed to rein that shit in if he wanted to convince Jazz to spread for him. The usual tricks wouldn't work with her, and if she caught him rocking a boner out the gate, she'd be more apt to knee him in the balls than give them a lick or a tug.

A flash of light out of the corner of his eye had him turning just in time to catch Jazz's small SUV pull into the driveway of the two-bedroom house she'd been renting for a little over a year.

He studied her for a moment as she sat behind the wheel of her car, staring through the windshield. Though the dark kept him from making out her exact features, Screw knew exactly what expression she wore in that moment. Lips compressed, face a mask of seriousness, eyes on the wrong side of sad. If anyone needed a good fucking, it was Jazz.

Lucky for her, Screw was up for the job.

Literally.

And he'd be willing to give it to her all night if that's what it'd take to unwind and relax her. Hell, maybe she'd even laugh and start to enjoy his company. Most people thought he was a trip.

Not that liking each other was a requirement of a good fucking. Sometimes, the best fucks were born of mutual hatred.

He blinked, nearly having missed his cue as she opened her car door. Dragging her feet as though she was exhausted, Jazz meandered toward the short walkway leading to her front door.

The moment her boot hit the concrete, Screw pressed a button on his phone—everything worked via fucking Bluetooth these days—and Jazz's entire house lit up with the hundreds of colorful lights he'd strung all around.

"What the..." She stepped back, gaze roaming over the front of her home. A laugh of delight bubbled out of her as her hand flew up to her mouth.

That sound, that unfiltered bit of happiness had Screw freezing in place. Had he ever heard that honest pleasure from Jazz? Sure, she had fun with her girlfriends, even with his brothers, and she knew how to enjoy herself, but she'd always come off as guarded to him. Constantly protecting herself by remaining somewhat aloof.

Something shifted inside him. An unfamiliar ache formed in his chest at the thought of her going home to an empty house so close to Christmas.

And every other day.

Not that he really knew for sure she went home alone. For all he knew, she had a man or two on the side. He frowned as the ache in his chest twisted into an ugly ball of...something. Certainly not jealousy because he didn't know the meaning of the fucking word.

Fuck, the cold was killing off his brain cells. Time to get this show on the road.

To focus on the fuck instead of whatever the hell had short-circuited in his mind.

Jazz glanced around as though suddenly realizing someone had to be responsible for the decorations to her home.

"Screw," she said as their gaze connected, voice falling flat.

So much for instant gratitude and thanks via sex. No matter, he wasn't above working for it.

He shot her the grin that tended to leave a trail of panties in its wake. Part cocky, part playful, part inviting, but all promise of sexual satisfaction. "Hey, gorgeous."

She looked absolutely adorable with a long black quilted jacket, a gray wool scarf around her neck, and a matching hat topped off with a fuzzy poof. The tip of her slender nose had already turned pink from just a few moments in the cold. Hopefully, it wouldn't be long before she invited him in, though he wouldn't mind having to warm her ass up.

"Did you do this?"

He nodded.

She gazed back at her house. He'd hung lights all along the roof, through a row of bushes across the front of her house, and in the two trees she had on her front lawn. "Must have taken you all day."

"Nah, not too long."

Six hours.

When she turned back to him, her smile had disappeared, and her mind seemed to be running on overtime. "Why'd you do this?" Still no pleasure in her voice.

Why had he done it? Well, that was easy. He tilted his head and waggled his eyebrows at her.

Jazz laughed. She continued laughing until she realized he hadn't joined her. Then her eyes bugged. "You're serious?"

"About what?"

With a wave of her gloved hand, she indicated the house behind her. "This. *All* this. You seriously spent your day hanging Christmas lights on my house just so I would sleep with you?"

"Ah, no. I was not angling for any sleeping here. But I was hoping for a few solid hours of fucking. Maybe one hour for every hour I spent decorating your house." Sounded like a pretty fair trade-off to him.

Jazz pinched the bridge of her nose. "Jesus, you're something else."

"Thank you."

"That's not a good thing." Now that the shock was gone, her voice had flattened yet again. "I don't get you, Screw." She threw up her hands, then paced five steps away before walking back toward him. "Why go through all this trouble just for sex? It's not like you're hard up. You get laid more than anyone I know."

He frowned. "You say that like it's a bad thing." Who the hell didn't like sex?

"Can you be serious for one minute? Like, give me sixty seconds of your time where you're not mouthing off some smartass remark or trying to get me naked."

He had nothing to say to that. Sure, she'd been turning him down at every pass, and he'd been laying it on thick, but he'd thought that was part of the fun. Part of their game. This cat and mouse foreplay thing they had going.

"I'm not going to sleep with you, Screw."

Apparently, he'd been dead wrong. "I already said—"

Jazz held up a hand. "You only made it twenty seconds. I know you said there'd be no sleeping." She pointed over her shoulder toward the house. "You know this is like boyfriend shit, right? The kind of thing a guy would do if he was actually interested in a girl. In dating her, spending time with her, starting a relationship. Wooing her or something."

"Wooing?" His eyes widened, and he stepped back as he sputtered. Dating? A relationship? Was she fucking crazy? "Whoa, woman, keep that filthy talk to yourself," he said with a laugh that didn't quite feel right.

The soft huff that left her was full of disbelief. "Let me make myself very clear, Screw. I'm not going to have sex with you. Not going to fuck you, not going to blow you or let you eat me out. I'm not even going to invite you into my house to warm up because I know your fucked-up mind would turn that into some kind of victory. Have I covered everything?"

"That mean you're willing to jerk—"

"Jesus!" she yelled. This time, she marched ten steps away and stayed there, hands on her hips as she stared at the house. A chirp came from her phone, which she dug out of her pocket. He didn't have to see her face to know she paled at the sight of whatever was on the screen. The tense set of her shoulders and her small gasp gave her away.

"What's wrong, babe?"

"Nothing that concerns you." Jazz sighed then shoved the phone back in her heavy coat's pocket. "I want you to stop this." Her voice wavered but she cleared her throat and tried again. "Stop hitting on me, and please don't do something like this again. Your games were silly and only mildly irritating at first, but I'm so over it now. Go to the clubhouse and you'll find at least three Honeys willing to fuck you the moment you walk in the door. Stop wasting your energy and just leave me alone. Please."

The genuine misery he heard in her voice had Screw biting back the snarky comment at the tip of his tongue. For the first time, he realized what he'd considered fun and games might not be so to Jazz. Finding out what she'd read on her phone took a back seat to his own annoyance.

"You're serious?"

Her harsh laugh grated his ears. "About not fucking you. Yeah, Screw. I know it's hard to imagine there's a person in this world who might not want to sleep—have sex with you, but it turns out it's true."

Anger burned in his gut as he marched forward. "Fuck that," he said. When he reached her, he grabbed her shoulder, spinning her back around. "I mean, are you serious about wanting me to leave you alone?"

Her shoulder fell, but she looked him straight in the eye, unwavering. "I want you to listen to me when I tell you it's not going to happen. I want you to back off. I don't understand what you're hoping to get out of this game."

"What I'm hoping to get? Well, babe, I'm hoping to come. Was planning to make you come as well. Quite a few times." Let Miss High-and-mighty chew on that one.

"I come just fine without you, Screw."

Say what? Fuck, now all he could think about was Jazz, naked in her bed alone as she played with her clit and thrust a thick dildo inside her pussy. He groaned. "How about we take fucking off the table, and you just let me watch you get yourself off?"

"You really can't take anything seriously, can you Screwball?"

"Hey! That's not true!" He took plenty of shit seriously. His responsibility to his club. His job at Zach's gym. Hell, he even took coming seriously. Very fucking seriously.

But aside from that, she was right. It'd been how he'd gotten his nickname after all.

"Maybe we can try it this way. I'm not looking for a man to make me come. Been there done that, and as I said, I manage just fine on my own."

Screw clenched his teeth. Why did the thought of the men who'd fucked her in the past make him want to strangle each and every one of them with a strand of Christmas lights?

"I'm looking for a man. A real man to be in my life. I don't want a guy who's gonna walk out the door with his pants unzipped because taking the time to do them up would mean sticking around too long. And let's face it, Screw, the idea of anything resembling a commitment is the last thing you want."

Well, she had him there. Just the idea of being someone's *man* gave him fucking hives. Still, something about the idea of walking in the door after work to Jazz had that odd feeling blooming in his chest once again. Since he had no clue what it meant besides having eaten something bad, he fell back on his typical M.O.

Snark and wit. Worked every time.

With an exaggerated shudder, Screw shook his head. "Jazzy, Jazzy, Jazzy, I'm crushed." He slapped a hand over his heart and staggered back as though she'd stabbed him. "Shoulda just mentioned all that monogamy shit right of the bat. Nothing kills my boner faster."

"Screw…"

He tossed her a cocky grin and winked. "Ain't a thing, babe. Gonna take your advice though and head to the clubhouse. Find myself a Honey. Maybe two. Hell, maybe I'll jump in on one of my brothers lays. Never know what the night will bring. You have fun with BOB, though. Hey! Maybe I'll find a Bob of my own." Another wink, then he was striding toward his car.

"Screw," Jazz called after he'd made it halfway across her lawn.

He turned.

"Thank you," she said. "For all this. It couldn't have been easy." Finally, a genuine, though small, smile from her.

One that pierced his chest for unknown reasons. Unknown and intolerable. "Ain't a thing, babe. Mind if I drive by with my nightly conquest? Show 'em a little Christmas magic? Maybe it'll earn me a second round. Or even a third."

She didn't so much as crack a smile at that one. In fact, her face fell so far it nearly slid into the snow.

It was a low blow, but no one took the shit he said seriously. Besides, she had no interest in fucking him, so she shouldn't care if he paraded a whole bus full of easy women through her front yard. He sure as hell didn't give a fuck.

At least that's what he told himself as his conscience tried to make him feel like an asshole.

He'd parked a few houses down from her to avoid being spotted before she arrived home. As he drove past her house, he couldn't help but notice her staring after his car, still standing in the middle of her front yard.

Whatever. She sure as hell had no right to be upset about anything he'd said or anything he planned to do for the rest of the night.

Though if that was the case, why the hell did he feel like he wanted to vomit at the thought she might be angry with him?

Chapter Three

SHELL

"All right, I think we are pretty much set then, don't you?" Shell asked as she gazed across the booth at two of the most important women in her life, Toni and Stephanie. As friends, they'd come a long way in the past year or so. At first, Shell hadn't been thrilled by Stephanie's involvement with Maverick, at least after it had been revealed the other woman worked for the FBI. Fear for the club, fear for Copper, kept her a little cold initially, but now? After experiencing first-hand Stephanie's loyalty to both Maverick and the club, Steph considered her a treasured friend.

More than a friend, really. Each of the club's ol' ladies had become her chosen family. Sisters of the heart. And one of their sisters was about to add another little one to the next generation of Handlers. Hence the baby shower planning meeting.

"Yeah," Toni said. She and Shell had become instant friends almost from the moment they'd met when Toni took over the diner she'd inherited from her parents. The diner Shell worked at. "I've got the food and drinks covered. Ernesto agreed to cater for us. Holly is on desserts, of course, and she's going to be running the show, day of. Shell, you and Chloe have decorations covered. Jazz is bringing the mommy-to-be around two, and our dear brave Stephanie here has come up with some games to play."

Steph rolled her eyes as Toni and Shell snickered. "I'm having a hard time picturing Izzy playing any game that doesn't involve beating someone bloody, but I'm giving it my best shot. Actually, since her due date was yesterday, I'm really hoping she'll just go into labor before the shower."

Izzy was going to make a...interesting mother, to say the least. A kick-ass tattoo artist who also happened to be an underground MMA fighter—though not for the past nine months—Izzy wasn't exactly the PTA-joining, minivan-driving type. In fact, the pregnancy had been an astounding shock in the first place. Despite her less than maternal ways, Izzy was truly a phenomenal friend and all-around amazing woman. Shell had a feeling boy or girl, Iz was going to raise one incredible kiddo.

"Um, excuse me, Miss Toni?"

All three women turned toward the timid voice coming from the slip of a girl who stood near their booth, staring at the ground.

Toni's expression softened, and she shifted to face the young teen. Her ratty sweatshirt hung off her small frame, and she wore jeans with torn knees. Not the fashionable kind, the old and worn kind. "Lindsey, what did I tell you about dropping the Miss?"

The girl shrugged her slight shoulders. Hanging in straggly strands down her back, her long auburn hair would be gorgeous if it had a good scrubbing and someone to style it properly.

Shell's heart squeezed at the sight of the girl. She'd appeared at the diner a few days ago asking for a job. Since she was only thirteen and under the legal working age in Tennessee, Toni's hands were tied. But of course, Shell's compassionate friend found a way to help the girl without officially hiring her. She'd given her small jobs, taking out the trash, wiping tables, refilling napkin holders, and after each task had been completed, Toni gave the girl a meal and a little bit of cash.

Shell's first thought was that the girl was a runaway and the authorities should be contacted. Toni had been reluctant but eventually agreed to call the sheriff's department. Before they'd had the chance to place that call, Lindsey had sworn up, down, and backward she did not run away from home. She claimed to just be from a poor family and had begged them not to call the police.

Toni seemed to believe that about as much as Shell did, but Lindsey's insistence on having a home limited their options. Toni hadn't wanted to call the police regardless of Lindsey's wishes. If it turned out the girl wasn't lying, the cops would most likely call in child protective services, which wasn't always a good thing. They needed more information before they acted, but details about herself were not something Lindsey dished out.

"You all finished with the trash?" Toni asked softly when it became apparent the gun-shy girl wasn't going to speak again. Due to a rough past of her own, Toni had a soft spot for all troubled teenagers, but this girl seemed to have wormed her way into Toni's heart more than most.

"Yes, ma'am." Lindsey still hadn't glanced up from where her tattered sneaker rubbed at a small scuff on the tiled floor.

"Oh no, ma'am is even worse than miss. Just Toni. Please."

Lindsey nodded without looking up. She seemed as taken with Toni as Toni was with her, but she shut down when in a group. Or around men. So far, Shell hadn't seen any signs of physical abuse, but she certainly had the skittish nature of someone who'd been mistreated.

"Well, thank you for coming around again today, Lindsey. You really saved me a lot of time and made it so I could get some other work done." Toni dug a few bills out of her pocket and held them out.

Finally, Lindsey peeked up at Toni with a small smile on her face and two pink cheeks. "Thank you, ma—uh, Toni," she said, snatching the money and holding it in a tight fist as though someone might try to snatch it from her at any point. Would they? Was that this poor child's reality? Clinging to the lifeline of five dollars?

Whatever the reality of her situation, Lindsey seemed to be struggling just to make it through each day. Hopefully, Toni would be able to break through the girl's wary exterior soon and provide more help than a few hot meals and a couple dollar bills. If she had a family in need of assistance, Toni would most likely move heaven and earth to provide it. If it turned out Lindsey was a runaway, well, Toni would probably let the girl move into the diner.

"Will we see you again tomorrow?"

Back to focusing on the floor, Lindsey nodded.

"Great. And, Lindsey?"

The girl tensed but gave Toni her attention.

"You have my phone number if you need anything, right?"

She nodded.

"Anything. At any time. And I mean that. I hope you'll use it if you need it."

"Thank you," she whispered, then scurried out the front door.

"Gosh, that poor child," Stephanie said, a hand pressed to her chest.

With a sigh, Toni nodded, her brown eyes following the girl as she darted across the parking lot. "Tell me about it. I'm trying to get some more information out of her, but she's pretty locked up. She swears she isn't homeless, but I'm worried. Do you think she's lying, Shell?"

"I don't know. Something seems off. Just breaks my heart." Shell said as she tried to envision how difficult life would have been as a young teen on her own. It'd been hard enough surviving without help in her early twenties.

Across the diner, Shell's own daughter let out a squeal of laughter as she sent her Barbie doll diving over the edge of a table. Shell couldn't imagine a future where she'd kick Beth out of the house or one where Beth felt the need to run away. No, that little girl knew just how loved and cherished she was, no matter who she became or what she did. Hopefully, there was someone out there who felt the same about Lindsey, and if not, she had no doubt Toni would work her magic on the girl.

Shell's lips curled as she watched her child entertain herself. Without thinking, her hand automatically moved to rest on her stomach. Though Beth was conceived in a traumatic manner, she'd been a blessing in ways Shell never could have imagined. And now that they lived with Copper, her daughter finally had the father she'd been denied for the first four years of her life.

Since moving in with Copper near six months ago, Shell—and Beth, for that matter—had never been happier. The man was attentive, affectionate, protective, and sexy as all get out. Shell hadn't known one woman could have so many orgasms and still function.

Life was great.

Perfect, really.

Well, it had been until yesterday…

"Hello? Shell? Earth to Shell, come in Shell."

She blinked. Toni's form morphed into view as she waved her hand in front of Shell's face. Her face heated. Both Toni and Stephanie were staring at her with expectant gazes from across the booth. "Sorry, uh, what did you say?"

Steph laughed. "Well, we said a lot. First, we asked if you were bringing Beth to the shower. Then when you didn't answer, we asked if you were listening. When you still didn't answer, Toni said she saw Copper running around the parking lot naked. When that didn't even get your attention, we gave up. You good, girl?"

"Sorry, got lost for a second thinking about Lindsey. No, Beth and Copper are going on a daddy-daughter date tomorrow afternoon. I think I heard something about *Frozen II* and a big tub of popcorn."

Toni pressed a hand over her heart. "Aw, he's the cutest. Who the hell would have thought that giant, gruff, beast of a man would be the best daddy in the world?"

Joy

Shell smiled. She'd known. Of course, she'd known. How else could she have fallen in love with the man?

"Speaking of daddies," Stephanie began, which had Toni groaning up at the ceiling.

"Please, if this is some sex story about you calling Mav daddy, just stop now. We don't want to hear it. There's not enough bleach in the supply closet to scrub an image like that from my brain."

Shell giggled as she nodded. "She's right, Steph. We love you, we love Mav, and we love that you're all out there with your sex life, but there's a limit to what our ears can handle."

Face red, Stephanie tried to scowl, but her mouth couldn't turn down since she was laughing as well. "That's not what this is." She paused, tilting her head. "Though you give me ideas. Anyway, I was just gonna ask who you think will be next?"

"Next?" Shell asked as she glanced over at Beth again. Her daughter still happily played with her dolls while munching on the French fries Toni had made her.

"Yeah, next on the baby train. Next to get knocked up. Next to repopulate the earth." Steph sipped her coffee.

"Okay, I think we get it," Toni said as she shook her head. "Well, we all know it's not gonna be you." She shot a pointed look in Stephanie's direction.

"Nope. Not me. I'm uber careful about that shit. Babies scare the tar outta me. They're all tiny and vulnerable." She shuddered.

Shell snorted. "They're actually a lot harder to kill than you'd think." She shot Steph a wink.

"Well," Toni said as she waved her hand back and forth. "It's a dumb question anyway because we all know it's gonna be you, Shell."

"What? Me?" she squeaked. "Why do you say that?"

"Uhh, because you're an awesome mom, you love kids, and you've mentioned a few times that you want a sibling for Bethy."

"Not to mention your ol' man is an old man," Steph said as she shoved a ripped off chunk of muffin in her mouth.

"Thanks," Shell said in a droll tone as her stomach fluttered. This conversation hit a little too close to home.

Toni bumped Steph with her shoulder. "He's not *old*, he's just *older* than Shell. The man is still sexy AF and probably will be when he's eighty."

True. So true.

"Well, we'll see," Shell said, pasting a smile on her face. It felt forced, fake.

"Yeah, we'll see all right," Steph said with a laugh. "We'll see you get all big when you grow a monster-sized mini-Copper inside you."

Despite her unease, Shell managed to chuckle. "We haven't talked about it much actually. I'm still taking the pill, so…" She shrugged, hating the lies.

But she wasn't ready to voice the truth.

"You're crazy. That man can't wait to knock you up." Steph shook her head. "I give it until March. If you're not carrying prez junior by March, I'll…"

"Ohh, this could be good. You'll what?" Toni said, turning her interested gaze on Steph.

"Yeah, what are you gonna offer me, Steph?" Shell waggled her eyebrows.

"Well—"

The bell above the entrance jangled. Glancing at her phone, Toni said, "Who is that? Zach isn't supposed to be here for another forty-five minutes." She stuck her head out the side of the booth to get a better view of the door then stiffened. "Shit," she whispered.

"What?" Shell asked.

Across the booth, both Toni and Steph grew rigid and tense. Who the hell could it be? Shell stood slightly and glanced over her shoulder to where three men dressed very similarly to their own men strode into the diner. MC cuts, biker boots, bandanas, chains.

But one very big difference—the Chrome Disciples patch on each of their cuts.

The one-percenter patch also caught her eyes. Same as the Handlers wore. But there were rules, an outlaw code of conduct, so to speak. And a biggie was not wearing colors in another MC's territory. To do so was considered an aggressive move. A show of force.

A shiver raced down Shell's spine. Copper was going to lose his shit.

"I'm sorry, gentlemen, we've been closed for a few hours," Toni said, voice steady despite her rapid blinking and rigid posture. "You're welcome to a delicious breakfast if you come back tomorrow during business hours."

When our men are here.

The unspoken words hung thick in the air.

Shell didn't dare move, terrified of drawing the attention of the other two bikers.

One of the men, the ringleader with an enforcer patch and a crooked Santa hat made his way to their table. Light brown, wavy hair hung from below the hat, reaching his shoulders. The biker had a nose that looked like it'd taken one too many hits in the past. His eyes, nearly the exact same color as his hair, danced with how much he enjoyed taking them by surprise. "Huh, would you look at this," he said with a smirk. "Ho...ho...ho..." His gaze landed on each one of the women as he spoke.

Clever.

"Ain't hungry. Why don't you scoot over, sweetheart," he said, placing a hand on Shell's shoulder. She fought the urge to shove his long, dirty-nailed fingers off her.

Swallowing, she caught Stephanie's eye. Her friend gave the subtlest of nods, so Shell scooted to the very inside of the booth, losing his touch in the process. Her heart pounded, and her eyes fixated on Beth who'd crawled under the table she'd been sitting at as though inherently sensing danger. So far, her daughter remained quiet, and the bikers hadn't noticed her.

Thank God.

"The name's Crank," he said.

"There something you need?" Steph asked in a frosty tone.

Either she was really good at hiding her fear, or she was some kind of superhero, but she didn't seem scared at all, while Shell could barely stand to be in her own skin at the moment.

One of Crank's eyebrows took a slow climb into his forehead, and his face split into a grin. "Now is that any way to welcome newcomers to your town, blondie?" he asked. "Don't need nothing. Just came in to check the place out, seeing as we're new around here and all."

Steph cocked her head. The woman had balls, Shell would give her that. Thank God, Izzy wasn't there. She'd have been rip-shit pissed and was still unable to battle things out with her fists as she'd like to.

"You know you're in Hell's Handlers territory?" Steph asked.

Crank snapped his fingers as though a light bulb had just gone off in his mind. "You know, I had heard something about that. And I heard this place is run by one of their ol' ladies. Guess that'd be you, huh?" he said, shifting his creepy gaze to Toni.

When she did nothing more than stare him down, Crank looked between Shell and Steph. "You two club property as well?"

Shell followed Toni's lead, leaving her mouth firmly clamped. If she tried to speak, her voice would probably come out as a terrified squeak. Keeping her gaze off Beth proved near impossible, but she didn't want Crank to follow her line of sight with his own eyes. His two buddies stood next to their booth but had their backs to Beth and hadn't noticed her yet. They needed to keep it that way.

"All right, I can see you're not chatty bitches, so let me just lay shit out for ya. I'm looking for your president. Got some shit to discuss with him. Don't suppose one of you bitches belong to him?"

A cold wave of fear washed over Shell. This time, when she caught Steph's gaze, the unspoken *keep your mouth shut*, came through loud and clear. Christ, what would this guy do if he knew he not only had access to the president's ol' lady but his kid as well? She swallowed a painful lump in her throat.

"Sorry to disappoint you," Steph said with a shrug. God, the woman was cool as a freaking cucumber. "You'll have to find him on your own."

"Too bad," he said, snagging the rest of Stephanie's muffin off the small plate. "Mmm, yummy. Maybe we will be back tomorrow." With that, he stood and stepped out of the booth, following his buddies who were already near the door. "Well, who's this?" he said as his attention landed on Beth.

"No!" Shell shot out of the booth, as did Stephanie. Steph grabbed her shirt and yanked her back. Acting on pure maternal instinct, Shell immediately began to struggle against her friend's hold. The need to have Beth in her arms felt like a beast inside her clawing its way out.

"Calm down," Steph whispered harshly against Shell's ear. "He won't hurt her. He's just feeling shit out."

With her heart running wild, Shell nodded but stayed ready to attack if necessary. Badass bikers or not, she'd rip all of them to shreds if they laid a finger on her daughter.

"What's your name?" Crank asked as he crouched to a squat, peering under the table into Beth's hiding spot.

She frowned and shook her head. "You're a stranger."

"Very smart. Your mom taught you that, huh?" he asked as he looked over his shoulder at Shell.

"Yes. She said don't tell my name to strangers."

"Well, how about this, I don't need to know your name, but I do need your help. Your mommy's right there, so it's okay."

Shell wanted to scream at her daughter to stay quiet, but would that only make things worse?

God, how she wished her ol' man was there at the moment. She'd agree to any damn thing he wanted if he'd just appear.

Beth frowned. "Okay," she said.

"Do you know who the Hell's Handlers are?"

Beth shot him a wary look. "Yes. I know all of them."

"How do you know them?"

"They are my family," she said with a small smile as she seemed to forget the rule of not talking to strangers. "My daddy is in charge. He's the president!"

Out of the mouths of babes. Shell's eyes fell closed as her stomach hit the floor.

"Thank you, you've been a big help. You tell your mommy you deserve a treat, okay?"

Beth crawled out from her spot under the table. Crank extended a hand, and Beth happily took it. Shell's eyes nearly fell out of her head. They'd be having another conversation about strangers only this time it'd be ten times more serious.

One of Crank's men hovered by the exit while the other moved toward the hallway leading out of the dining area. Had they been dumb enough to try to run, their exits were blocked. Steph still held Shell's arm, and Shell could feel Toni's presence behind her, still near the booth.

"Mommy, did you hear that? Can I have a treat for helping the man?" Her eyes held a hopeful light.

Shell opened her mouth, but nothing came out as all the saliva dried right up. Instead, she nodded at her daughter.

"Here, mommy," Crank said, extending his and Beth's joined hand toward Shell. "Come get your little princess."

"Calm," Steph murmured as she released Shell.

Feeling as though she was walking into a trap, Shell stepped forward until she could reach her daughter. Sweat slicked her palms, so she rubbed them on her jeans. Instead of handing Beth over, Crank leaned in and whispered against her ear. "I want to talk to your ol' man." He held up a folded slip of paper between his second and third fingers, then stuck it into the front pocket of

Shell's jeans. The moment his hands touched her, she stiffened and squeezed her eyes shut. "Have him call me." Then he pressed a lingering kiss to her cheek before passing Beth off to her. "Don't recommend he waits too long."

"Be seeing ya," he said as he strode for the door. The men with him trailed right behind.

As soon as the bell rang out, indicating their departure, Shell's knees buckled. Thankfully, Steph had rushed over and shoved a chair under her ass before she could hit the ground.

"I'm not explaining it over the phone, Copper," Steph said into her phone. "Just get to the diner now." There was a pause in which Steph shook her head. "No, I promise your girls aren't hurt or in danger. Just freaked. But we've got some shit to tell you. Okay, see you soon." Steph hung up then looked down at Shell. "He's on his way. Zach too."

Shell just nodded, but Toni blew out a shaky breath then said, "Thanks, Steph. You are one cool customer under pressure." As she spoke, she scooped Beth up and carried her toward the kitchen. "I think this calls for some ice cream, what do you think, Bethy?" Her voice quivered, but she seemed to be holding up.

God love the woman for realizing the need for a distraction.

"Is that my treat?" Beth asked.

"Um, sure!"

They disappeared into the kitchen, leaving Steph and Shell alone. "You okay?" Steph asked.

Shell released what felt like a gallon of air. "Yeah, uh, I think so. Guy just scared the shit out of me." She ran a hand through her hair, needing something to do with herself.

"Yeah," Steph said, keeping her attention on the parking lot. "Never ends, does it?"

"Doesn't seem to." Saying the words out loud had a profound sadness rising up in Shell.

As they waited for the cavalry to arrive, her gaze drifted toward the kitchen. Just when they crawled out of the darkness, new storm clouds rolled in.

Lilly Atlas

Her hand fell to her stomach.
There better not be a hurricane on the horizon.

Chapter Four

STEPHANIE

Stephanie stepped through her front door and released what felt like the first breath in hours. After Copper had rushed to the diner—then blew through like a freakin' hurricane—she'd had to recount what happened no less than ten times. With each retelling, she'd laid out the encounter with Crank, and the edges of her nerves had frayed a bit more. Hiding the tension and fear from Copper's assessing glare hadn't been an easy task, but she'd tried her hardest. Last thing she wanted was for the prez to have to call Maverick in from work because she'd turned into a basket case. She'd had to promise Copper a dozen times she'd fill Mav in, then have her ol' man call his prez as soon as he got home from work. Mav had been on a sensitive job, requesting no contact unless an extreme emergency. While what happened at the diner sucked, no one was hurt or in any true danger, so technically not an emergency. Steph worked hard to prove to Copper that Mav didn't need to be interrupted.

She'd been a federal agent for Christ's sake. Trained to handle far worse than that little spectacle at the diner. But, fuck, it'd been hard to keep from freaking out. Even hours later, she felt the lingering effects of fear. A quivering stomach, headache, and shaky limbs.

Her nerves tumbled and rolled around in a mess of anxiety. The most recent enemies of the club were rotting away in hell where they belonged, but they didn't get there without wreaking havoc on the MC first. No one knew that better than she and Mav. Except maybe Chloe. All three of them had been tormented and tortured by the last gang to mess with the Handlers

Rest in misery, motherfuckers.

Stephanie would be lying if she didn't admit the thought of another MC harassing the men and women who'd become her family didn't freak her right out. Now that she knew first-hand the depravity of some men and the ease with which they could inflict pain on others, she'd become far more skittish than she used to be.

Though she worked her ass off to hide it from her man.

Shaking out her tingling fingers, she pushed the events of the morning out of her mind. There'd be plenty of time to discuss what happened with Maverick later. Now, all she wanted to do was locate her man and spend some quality time getting lost in him before she had to burst their happy bubble. Copper could yell at her later.

No one could lift her mood quite like Maverick and his snarky personality. Especially at this time of year. Turned out, Mav was a Christmas freak, and he'd been bouncing around like a little boy for weeks.

Come to think of it…why was the house so quiet?

Steph frowned as she headed down the front hallway toward their festive living room. Ever since he'd swallowed his last bite of Thanksgiving turkey, Mav had been driving her insane, constantly blaring Christmas music. Who the hell would have guessed her pierced, inked, and sex-crazed biker would be such a Santa nut? She hadn't walked through the door to a quiet house since the first of December. And she'd seen his truck in the garage, so…where was the ridiculous man?

Joy

As she made her way through their overly decorated house, she couldn't help but smile at all the ludicrous Christmas crap they owned. In true Mav fashion, he'd adorned their entire tree in what he lovingly called *pornaments*, complete with a light-up butt plug ornament, a ceramic Rudolph doing an elf, and of course, a fully nude Mrs. Claus riding the jolly ole guy straight to heaven. Their house was littered with naughty Christmas trinkets that really captured the meaning of the season.

At least for her man.

And then there were the gifts. Christmas pre-game presents as he called them. First, she'd found a gift bag with some sexy Santa themed lingerie waiting for her on the kitchen table, then a porn DVD complete with horny elves and other horrifying yet merry characters. But the piece de resistance was the candy cane vibrator he'd given her last weekend. That one Steph totally got behind. Literally.

"Babe, you here?" she finally called out after she'd searched the entire first level.

When he didn't reply, she started up the stairs. Mav had been pulling some long working hours recently. Maybe he'd fallen asleep. When she reached the top of the carpeted steps, Steph hung a right toward their bedroom. Left would lead to the office and guest room.

Actually…

She spun and headed toward the office. This wouldn't be the first time he'd passed out on the small couch in their shared office. And last time, she'd woken him in a very pleasurable way.

Smiling at those spicy memories, Steph stepped into the office only to come to a dead stop. She let out a half snort, half laugh as she covered her mouth. "Oh, my God. You're out of control."

"I love that you think of me as your god, baby," Mav said with a wink. "But I'm just a mere mortal. Though parts of me do seem to possess god-like powers. As you well know."

This time, she just snorted.

Seated on their charcoal leather love seat, naked except for miles of ink, sat Maverick, legs spread, and hard cock in hand. Only since it was mid-December, it wasn't a normal naked and horny Maverick. It was the Christmas version complete with Santa hat, blinking light bulb necklace, and mistletoe belt. Around his waist, a red and white striped cloth belt closed at a buckle which extended to an arched wire where some mistletoe dangled. His reclined position had the plastic plant bobbing directly over his cock. The cock he worked up and down this his fisted hand. The cock leaking with precum.

Stephanie couldn't help it, she started laughing even as her body flared to life. The sight of her man sans clothes did it to her every time. Ridiculous props and all. Before him, she'd considered herself a normal woman with a typical sex drive. Now, thanks to the hot and randy biker on the couch, she was a borderline nymphomaniac. All he had to do was peel off his shirt and bare those lean, ropy muscles covered in tattoos, and she was ready to burn her panty drawer.

"You know, I've heard it's bad luck if you don't kiss under the mistletoe," he said, giving her a sexy grin as he continued to stroke his tattooed erection in long, slow pulls.

"Is it?" Gaze rooted to where he pleasured himself, she bit her bottom lip. Watching him get himself off could be a fun time, but that cock was hers, and she'd be the one to enjoy it tonight.

"The worst luck."

"Well," she said, slowly walked toward him. "We don't need any of that."

"Strip," he commanded as he tugged on his length.

Steph licked her lips, which had him groaning. "You sure that's what you want me to do first?"

"Fuck yes," he said, voice strained, hips punching up into his hand. "Want to see my tits."

Mav was a jovial guy. He joked around like no other, had the raunchiest sense of humor, and generally viewed life as one big playground. Of course, living with him, Steph saw another side of him, the real Maverick. A protective, loving, and fiercely loyal man who would saw off his own leg for those he cared about. Still, he wasn't as much of a macho, possessive alpha as some of his brothers. Until it came to the bedroom. When it was just the two of them, lost in their own sensual and intimate world. Then he was all *mine this* and *mine that*.

Steph fucking loved it. Because she did belong to him. He owned every part of her, body, heart, and soul just as she owned him in return.

She stripped off her sweater and the cami underneath, leaving her in the bright red bra she'd purchased just to feed his Christmas addiction.

"Damn, woman," he said, circling his thumb and forefinger around the base of his cock. "You get hotter every day."

Steph smiled. She loved how much he wanted her and never failed to let her know it. How he could make her feel like the sexiest woman alive with just one look and two sentences. "Your tits all you want to see?"

"Fuck no," he said. "Wanna see my pussy too. Wanna see it all. Show me what belongs to me, baby. Then I'll show you how I play with my toys."

A shiver ran through her, the most delicious kind. Her panties were already wet and all they'd done was chat while she watched him jerk himself.

With a little wiggle, Steph worked her jeans down her legs and kicked them off right before toeing off her socks. As she straightened, she pressed her lips together to keep from smirking.

Mav had no such control. He barked out a laugh the moment his gaze connected with her panties. A red thong to match the bra, with the words, "If you can read this, I've been naughty," scrawled across the crotch.

His gaze met hers. "Fuck, I love you, Stephanie," he said, all clowning gone from his voice.

Even though by now they'd said it countless times, those words never failed to send a thrill coursing through her. Her nipples tightened and her sex practically dripped with arousal. This was more than an I love you for wearing playful and silly underwear. It was an I love you for seeing *him* and being the partner he needed. This was serious Maverick, and he was intense and rough.

Serious Mav made her heart pitter-patter.

Serious Mav fucked like no other.

"Come here," he said, eyes smoldering. "Come sit on Santa's lap."

Steph took three steps forward. She could have toyed with him a little. Teased him and watched his eyes flare as she played with herself, but her need rivaled his, and she'd only be denying what she really wanted. What they both needed.

When she reached the couch, instead of sitting on his lap, she dropped to her knees and placed a chase kiss to the tip of his dick. Precum coated her lips. One lick of the salty fluid was all it took to have Mav groaning and yanking her from under her arms.

"Fuck it, changed my mind. I can't take that today."

Landing with a knee on either side of him, Steph rubbed her soaked pussy up and down his length. Mav's head fell back as he hissed out a curse, neck muscles cording with tension. "Fuck, baby, how'd you get so wet already?" He sounded like he'd been chewing rocks.

Still grinding on his steely shaft, Stephanie placed her lips next to his ear. The position put her tits right in his face, and he wasted no time burying his face between them. "You made me wet. All I have to do is look at you and I'm drenched. Don't you know that, Mav?"

"I know it," he said as he kissed and nipped his way across the tops of her breasts, making shivers trail down her spine and goosebumps pop up all over her skin. "That's one of the many reasons you're so goddammed perfect for me."

Joy

Steph smiled, running her hands through the back of Mav's hair.

"Can't wait, baby. Need inside this gorgeous body now."

"Well," she said as she lifted a few inches up and grabbed his cock. He groaned through clenched teeth. "I think we've already established I'm ready for you."

Panting now, Mav speared two fingers into her. "Yeah you are." He scissored his fingers, opening her, and together, they joined their bodies. "Fuuuck," he drew out as she slowly descended on him. "So fucking hot."

Yeah, her sentiments exactly.

"Love you, Steph," he said as he grabbed her ass in one hand and banded the other arm across her back. Tight. She could barely move on him, he held her so close. "You're fucking everything to me. You know that, right? That you're my world?"

She nodded, unable to speak around a constricting throat. They were a demonstrative couple both in words and actions, but this seemed over the top even for Maverick. He pressed his lips to her neck before resting his forehead there. Whatever had him in this intense and extra loving mood, she didn't care, she freaking loved it.

She closed her arms around him as well, one across his upper back and the other clutching his hair, holding his forehead pressed to hers. With their chests pressed together, she swore their hearts beat as one. Never before had Stephanie felt so connected to another person. Warmth filled her as they stayed still and quiet like that for a few moments. She closed her eyes and just absorbed the incredible sensation of being loved and protected. But the peace didn't last long, Stephanie's sex clamped down on him as the need to move tore through her.

"Mav," she said, sounding desperate and needy.

She jerked her hips, trying to get some leverage to fuck him properly, but he didn't release her, didn't even lessen his hold.

"Like this," he whispered, gazing into her eyes. His own shone with emotion and adoration.

"Baby," she whispered as love for him nearly made it impossible to breathe.

"I know," he said.

Stephanie sucked in a breath, forcing her body to calm as much as was possible, given her level of arousal. The steadiness in Mav's gaze held her captive. The house could burn to the ground around them, and she'd never even notice. With tiny upward thrusts, he rocked his pelvis into her. Stephanie mimicked his moves, grinding down on him and rocking against him as well. While it wasn't close to the furious pounding she'd come to crave, this position did amazing things for her clit.

Not to even mention she'd never felt more connected to the man she loved. She had no idea how long they stayed that way, pressed against each other, gazes locked, and bodies moving as one.

The climb to the top was different than she'd ever experienced. A slow, steady glow flared in her core, heating her from the inside. She shivered, lost in the connection to this wonderful man.

"I love you too, Maverick," she whispered.

His eyes flashed with deep passion as he gripped the back of her head with one hand, never releasing the way he crushed her to him. He fused their mouths together, and they kissed exactly how they made love, lazily, a languid exploration and mating.

When the orgasm claimed her, it wasn't an explosion of pleasure, but a rolling wave that started low in her gut and undulated out through her limbs, cresting again and again.

When the need for air grew too great, she ripped her mouth way, "God, Maverick," she cried. "So intense." Her body trembled as the climax grew in size and strength.

All of a sudden, Mav's arms clamped even tighter around her. He sunk his teeth into the side of her neck and groaned as his body began a rhythmic convulsion of release. "Jesus," he said once his arms had finally slackened.

"Yeah." Stephanie grinned down at him. He had this dopy, drunk glazed-over look in his eyes. "That was intense."

He stroked a hand up and down her spine as he nodded.

Stephanie frowned. Where was the snarky Maverick quip about his prowess? "You okay?" Maybe he had already caught wind of what happened at the diner and it had him reeling. Though even if that were true, this subdued, reflective mood wasn't his style.

"Yeah, baby, I'm perfect. You ready for your next Christmas Pre-game gift?" There it was, the mischievous twinkle he'd had since December kicked off.

With a laugh, Steph rolled her eyes. "What is it this time? Red Rudolph's nose pasties for my boobs? Or maybe an apron with a naked elf and 'Santa's little helper' written above the penis?"

Mav threw back his head and laughed. "Shit, woman, you've got a future in naughty greeting cards or something. You know that?"

"Mmm, my dream job." She held out her hand. "Okay, lay it on me."

Mav reached over to the desk where a flat rectangular box she hadn't noticed sat wrapped in gold paper with a green bow. It had the look of a box of chocolates. Hmm, that she could get on board with even if they were shaped like body parts.

She gave it a gentle shake. "What is it?"

Mav barked out a laugh. "You ask that every time. If you would just open it, you could save your breath."

"Good point." Steph tore into the paper. She'd never admit it to him, but this little pre-game gift tradition was the best thing ever. Even if the gifts were one hundred percent ridiculous. Okay, fine, that vibrator wasn't ridiculous. It had actually served her quite well. That aside, knowing Mav thought of her enough to buy all these quirky trinkets made her feel so damn special.

As the gift was revealed, Steph smiled in triumph. "Chocolates! I knew it." The box boasted Santa shaped chocolates with liquor fillings. "And it's not even perverted. Look at that!"

"No, but they've got booze, so if you eat them all, it might lead to all things perverted." Mav waggled his eyebrows.

"True. Let's start now." What woman didn't love her some chocolate?

She opened the box. Where to start— "M-Maverick?" Her hands shook.

"Yeah, babe?"

"Um, w-what is this?" The words came out whispered so low it was a good thing his ears were less than a foot away. Because she'd lost all her air and her throat had gone dry.

He chuckled. "This?" he asked as he picked up the sparkly platinum ring resting in the very center of the box where a chocolate treat used to lie. "Well, this is a ring, baby."

She opened her mouth, but no words came out. He'd rendered her completely and utterly speechless.

Her heart raced so fast she grew dizzy.

As he lifted her left hand, Maverick said, "We met under the worst of circumstances. But from that horrifying experience, came the best thing to have ever happened to me. You, Stephanie." His voice cracked. "You're fierce and loyal. You love hard, and protect those you care about. You've fought for me, and played with me, and become my life. I want you to do all those things for the rest of our lives. And in return, I want to make each day for you better than the one before it. I love you with an intensity I didn't even know existed." He cocked his head and gave her his customary teasing grin, but his eyes held a suspicious shimmer. "Let's lock this shit down, baby. Will you marry me?"

By now, tears streamed down her face, and her hands shook so hard, she'd never be able to hold onto the ring. Instead, she extended her trembling fingers and let Maverick slide the glimmering round solitaire on.

She couldn't tear her eyes away from her hand. Like any woman in love, she'd hoped for this someday but figured it would take Maverick years to warm to the idea. Never had she imagined their second Christmas together would be celebrated as an engaged couple.

Still seated inside her, Maverick began to harden again.

Stephanie gaped at the incredible ring circling her finger. If she had her way, it'd never come off. With a grunt, Mav shifted, and she suddenly found herself on her back.

"Let's celebrate," he said.

Finally finding her voice, Steph said, "But I haven't given you an answer yet."

His snort had her chuckling. "Like you could say no to all this." He leaned down next to her ear as he started to thrust. "Not when I fuck you so good."

Well, he had a point there.

"Even though I know the answer, I still wanna hear you say it," he said as he powered into her, no longer gentle, but a possessive animal claiming its mate.

As his cock stroked over her g-spot, Stephanie's back arched off the couch. "Yes!" she cried out. "Yes, Maverick, yes!"

"Damn straight, baby."

Best Christmas ever, and the holiday was still days away.

"Hey, how'd your meeting with the girls go?"

Just like that, Stephanie's soaring mood plummeted. Shit, now she had to ruin their day with club drama.

Chapter Five

COPPER

Copper stared at the slip of paper with ten digits scrawled across it. The note had been forced upon his woman, scaring her and his daughter while in a place they'd always felt safe. He clenched his fists and ground his jaw. The risks to his club never seemed to fucking end.

In the month since he'd married Shell, he'd really been feeling his age. Not that forty was old by any adult's standards. Maybe it wasn't *his* age he was feeling, but Shell's. The sixteen-year age difference had never been more apparent than it was today.

He was tired. Both his brain and his body.

And Shell never ran out of steam. She always seemed to have boundless energy for him, the child he'd claimed as his own, and the rest of their friends and family.

He loved that woman with every fiber of his being and wanted her beside him at all times. That hadn't changed and never would, not even after he took his last breath, but at times he felt selfish. Like he'd cheated her out the life she could have, and maybe should have, if she'd married a man her own age.

Instead, she'd tied herself to a crusty biker who spent his life on the wrong side of the law, putting out fires and battling enemy threats. The events of the past year had been weighing heavily on his mind over the last few weeks. As he watched Jigsaw and Izzy come to the end of her pregnancy, the idea of adding to their family had been at the forefront of his mind as well. And not necessarily in a way that would make his wife happy. In fact, the more he considered it, the more he became uncertain about the idea of more children.

And then today, it was as though all the worries in his mind materialized. His fears had been driven home when he got the call from Stephanie about the incident at the diner.

Without having any information about or contact with this new club, Copper knew in his gut they were going to fuck shit up for the Handlers. What if the worst happened and they took him out? How could he look at himself in the mirror knowing he'd be leaving Shell to survive on her own with a baby and a small child? He couldn't.

Fuck, that wasn't even the worst. The worst would be something happening to Shell or Beth. Or any other child they might bring into the world. His thinking wasn't melodrama. Toni, Stephanie, Chloe, even Izzy had been reached by the club's enemies. Chloe suffered the worst fate, requiring a long healing period and receiving both physical and mental scars that would never fully heal. The same could happen to Shell. Or their children. The notion horrified him to such an extent, he knew he had to do anything and everything to prevent those possibilities from coming to life.

Though he feared he might break his wife's heart in the process.

Before he could delve into that issue, he needed to find out what the fuck was going on with the men who'd visited the diner. The Chrome Disciples Motorcycle Club. Not one he'd heard of, so he'd had Mav do a little digging. Nothing the security expert found eased the knot of tension in Copper's gut. In fact, it'd had only coiled the ropes tighter.

The president of the CDMC went by the handle Blade for obvious reasons. The man served ten years for aggravated assault with a deadly weapon. A switchblade, if Mav's research was accurate. Most of the club's ranking officers had served time for various crimes, manslaughter, arms trafficking...rape. That last one had the hairs on the back of Copper's neck standing at attention for the past few hours. He was no fucking boy scout. Hell, he could have been arrested for assault with a deadly weapon or manslaughter. Fuck it, he could have been arrested for murder one if he'd been caught eliminating some of the club's enemies. He was of a firm mind that his club had done the world favors by ridding it of the scum it had, but rape? There was no fucking justification for that shit.

He didn't want the motherfuckers who'd committed those crimes living in his town, harassing his club's women, or fucking up the Handlers' businesses. He rotated his neck right and left. As a loud crack reverberated through the room, he blew out a breath. Time to deal with this shit.

Steady as an ox, he punched the ten digits into a burner phone. One, two, three rings, and then, "The fuck is this?"

"Think that's my question," Copper said to the deep rasp on the other end of the line.

The man, Blade, he assumed, chuckled. "Irish accent. Must be Copper, President of the Hell's Handlers Motorcycle Club.

"It's Blade, right?"

"I see you've done your research. Impressive."

Copper grunted. "Not sure what you've heard about me, but I'm pretty sure it wasn't that I'm a fucking idiot."

Another laugh from Blade, this time longer and louder. "No, I've heard you're a mean motherfucker. And that you're possessive of your town. That your club has killed off more than a few who threatened your reign as king. Even heard a rumor you offed the town sheriff."

Not true. Though the club had run him off with threats to his life. But the sheriff, crooked as he'd been, also happened to be the father of an ol' lady. So, Copper had refrained from killing the man. Some of his deputies hadn't been spared the Handler's wrath, however.

Why deny it? Whatever got this guy to leave. "That what you plan on doing? Moving in on my kingdom?" As he waited for the answer, Copper gazed out the window at the leafless trees making up the winter woods. As usual, this time of year, his urge to ride his motorcycle through the mountains peaked. Something about being unable to ride had the need skyrocketing. Too bad the forecast called for fucking snow.

"Well, I guess that all depends on how well you play with others," Blade said.

"Not too fucking well," Copper said.

"Then we may have a problem."

Fuck.

"You are setting up shop here in Townsend?" Copper asked.

"Close by is my plan."

"It's a shitty one."

"Hmm." Blade laughed. "I disagree. Location is prime. Lots of tourists, lots of…isolated areas. Easy to move through the mountains unseen. This is the perfect area to move my products between the north and south. No, this seems like just the spot to me."

His product? What was it? Drugs? Women? Guns?

"Lefty thought that too." If Blade was as clued into the Handler's dealings as Copper thought he was, there was no way the man didn't know all about the gang leader Copper and Rocket had killed. Lefty had been a rapist pig who traded kidnapped women like playing cards. Someone cut from the same cloth as Blade.

"Ah, but Lefty was stupid and greedy. I'm neither of those things, Copper. I'm fucking smart, and I know how to bide my time. I also have a very loyal club at my back. Heard Lefty couldn't pay a fucker to be loyal to him."

A soft knock on the door pulled Copper's attention from the window. Shell popped her head in but winced when she realized he was on the phone.

"Sorry," she mouthed then started to duck out.

Copper shook his head and waved her in. He continued to signal for her to come closer until she was climbing onto his lap with a guarded look. Normally he'd never allow her to be burdened with club shit, but he needed her close, and she'd already been tossed in this lion's den. "You willing to risk your devoted followers just to set up shop here? Because I'm telling you now in plain English, you're not fucking welcome."

Shell stiffened, but he ran a hand up and down her back. Maybe he should have let her slip out of the office.

"You know, *prez*," Blade said. "I think I am. My men are my army, and we'll fight to keep what we have and get what we want. Now, unlike you, I can play with others, so I'll leave the ball in your court. Either move over and let me in your sandbox or be ready for the mother of all dust storms. 'Tis the season, Copper."

The line went dead.

Copper gripped the phone, not even aware of how he'd nearly crushed it in his palm until Shell's gentle fingers pried his fist open with a soft touch. "Hey," she said, drawing his focus to her solemn face. She gave his beard a little tug. "Talk to me."

He shared with her often, not enough to have her up worrying at night, but what he needed to ease his weighed down soul. "It's not good," he said.

Her hands moved up, rubbing the soft hairs on his face. His woman loved the feel of his beard. Especially between her legs.

"Then you'll do what you always do." She spoke with such faith, such confidence in him he couldn't help but crack a smile.

"And what's that?" he asked as he captured her hand, turned his head, then kissed her palm.

"You'll fight with our guys until it is right."

"That could come at a high cost this time," he said as a heaviness settled in his heart. Still holding her hand, he pressed her palm against the left side of his chest as though her touch could somehow seep through his skin and bones and lift the weight on his heart.

Oddly enough, it did just that.

Shell tilted her head. "You think any one of your men would suggest something different? You think there's an ol' lady in the bunch that doesn't trust you and the club to protect them? We all want the same thing here, Aiden. And that's for our family to thrive. We can't do that if there's a threat to the club."

Sixteen years his junior. Just twenty-four years old, and Shell had more wisdom and maturity than most of his club combined.

"How'd I get so fucking lucky?" he asked as he tucked a loose curl behind her ear.

Shell shrugged. "The accent. It's the honey that drew this fly."

Instead of laughing and kissing her as she'd probably expected, he said, "I need to talk to you about something else serious."

"O-okay…" Shell answered, her eyes going wide and body stiffening. "Is something w-wrong?" She swallowed. "Are you okay?"

Fuck, he was an idiot. Of course she'd worry about him. He ran his hands up and down her arms. "Yes, babe, of course. Sorry. Didn't mean to scare you."

"Phew," she said with a small laugh, pressing a hand to her heart. "Okay, lay it on me."

"I—" The words died in his throat as he took in the sight of his smiling wife.

Fuck.

Fuck.

This was going to tear her apart. But it had to be done. It was the best, the safest, the smartest decision.

"I'm thinking it might be a good idea for me to get a vasectomy."

A barked laugh came from her, and she whacked his arm in a barely felt slap. "Okay, har har, very funny. What did you really want to talk to me about?" Then she rolled her eyes. "Is there even a real thing? Did I just get played, hard?"

He squeezed her hands. "Uh, no, Shell. This isn't a joke."

Immediately, as though someone flicked a switch, the light in her eyes died. "Wh—you're serious?"

"Yes."

"Wow, uh, I, uh…help me out here." Her mouth opened and closed as she struggled to understand his seemingly abrupt change of heart. But it wasn't abrupt. He'd been stuck on this for weeks.

"Toni was almost killed by Shark. Steph was kidnapped. Chloe raped. Fuck, even Izzy ended up in the hospital because of the club's enemies. I'm not invincible, Shell. If something were to happen to me—" Shell flinched, and he felt like the lowest piece of shit, but he held his ground. "I can't put you in a position where you might be left alone with a baby. And fucking Christ, Shell, if something happened to you or Beth…and to have more…"

Shit, he was barely making sense at this point, but the words weren't there. Putting a voice to his fear for Shell and Beth made it too fucking real.

She blinked, staring at him as though she'd never seen him before.

Giving her time to process, he remained quiet, though he wanted to shake a response out of her. Was this it? The end? When she'd slap him across the face, curse him, and run out. Was today the day she realized she could be with a different man. A man who could give her what she wanted?

All of that would be less than he deserved, yet the thought of having to watch Shell walk away from him had him clutching the arms of his chair so hard they creaked.

"I'm sorry," she said after a few moments. She climbed off his lap and paced, wrapping her arms around herself in a protective hug that had him itching to provide the comfort she needed. But he'd caused the pain and would most likely be rejected. "I'm just a little surprised." She stopped walking and stared at him with devastation written all over her face. The woman couldn't hide shit from him.

With a nod, Copper said. "I'm sorry to drop it on you like that. Outta nowhere. But it's this kinda shit that happened today," he said, pointing to the phone, "that makes me realize I'm right in this. More kids just aren't a smart idea, babe."

Shell swallowed then nodded. She pasted a smile on her face that wouldn't even convince a stranger she was happy, let alone the man who knew her inside and out. "I understand your concerns. But, Copper, it's almost Christmas. Let's get through the holidays, and then we can talk about this."

Shit, that grin was phony as fuck. Disappointing her gutted him, but Shell was a reasonable woman. She'd come around and recognize his judgment was sound. Intelligent. Safe.

"No point in revisiting it, babe. Shit's about to get rough around here. Can't be worrying about a baby while I'm fighting a war."

"It's that bad?" She stood in the middle of his office, looking so small and vulnerable.

"Probably gonna get there."

She pressed her lips together, then nodded. "Whatever you think is best, Copper. I trust you." Her voice grew flat. Lifeless.

After she spoke, she climbed back into his lap and rested her head on his shoulder.

She was there, saying all the right things, touching him as usual, yet Copper couldn't help but feel distance grow between them.

Even though he expected it, tried to plan for it in his head, he'd fucking crumble if she walked away from him. Shell was a good woman and an even better ol' lady. She'd stick this crisis out. Stand by him through the coming months and impending storm. If he were a better man, he'd free her now. Give her an out and a chance to live her life. But he was a selfish fucker.

She pulled back. "I'm gonna get Beth home. Think she's had enough for one day." After a quick kiss to his cheek, she hopped off his lap and hurried out of the office.

The fuck?

Not once since they'd gotten together had either of them walked out of the room without a real fucking lip lock. Even when they'd been pissed at each other or in the midst of a fight. A proper goodbye was just their thing. And now he got a peck on the cheek?

Was it the beginning of the end? Maybe. *Something* was off with his woman.

Something that could be a fiercer enemy than the Chrome Disciples.

Chapter Six

HOLLY

Holly glanced around the decorated clubhouse then let out a sigh. The place was an explosion of stereotypical baby shower decorations. Storks, elephants, rattles. Poor Izzy.

Speaking of the guest of honor, Holly caught sight of her and couldn't help her hearty laugh. Izzy sat sprawled in a chair Shell had done up to look like some kind of frilly throne complete with pink and blue streamers, tulle, and helium-filled balloons. Izzy's scowl left no doubt as to how she felt about sitting there, actually, about participating in this baby shower at all.

Yet, even with a sour face, the mom-to-be looked beautiful. She was one of those lucky women who only seemed to gain the baby weight in her stomach. The type that looked the same from behind with just a basketball under their shirt in the front. Now, Izzy's basketball was gigantic, but still… Holly would probably look like one whale had swallowed another when she got pregnant. And here was kick-ass Izzy who could still model workout wear if she wanted.

"You ready to rock this?" Jazz asked as she wandered over, holding a stack of paper plates. She looked adorable in tight black jeans and a long-sleeved teal blouse.

Holly rolled her eyes. "How exactly did I end up as emcee for this jubilant event?"

"You drew the short straw?" Jazz said with a shrug. "Actually, if I'm being serious, the girls wanted to give you something positive to focus on."

Ugh, stab to the heart. Holly tried to give her friend a smile, tried to block out the niggle of grief that worked its way under her skin. You'd think after so many years without her sister, this time of year wouldn't hurt anymore, but every birthday that passed only reminded her of her twin's tragically short life.

"Thanks," she said as she bumped Jazz's shoulder. "You girls are the best."

"We are, aren't we?" Jazz asked, giving Holly a cheesy grin.

"Yeah." And they were. Now her heart clenched for an entirely different reason. How lucky was she to have friends that cared enough to want to keep her mind off sadness? Very lucky.

"Well, I just do what I'm told, and I was told to come over here and let you know we are ready to start."

"Great," Holly grumbled. "You know, I'm pretty sure Izzy hates me. Maybe you should do this instead."

"Nope." Jazz popped the *p* and gave a totally unrepentant grin. "I can't stand being the center of attention. And she doesn't hate you. She's told you she likes you before."

"Well, I don't like being the center of attention either!" Holly said. Oh whatever, if Izzy already hated her, at least she wouldn't be losing a friend by emceeing a shower the expectant mother specifically asked not to have. "Ugh, fine," Holly said, digging down deep for her imitation announcer voice.

"You got this, girl," Jazz called after her, laughter in her voice.

"Hey, everyone," She walked to the center of the room as a hush fell over the ladies. "Thank you all for joining us today to honor Izzy. She is thrilled you all came out to celebrate with her."

"Lies!" Toni called out.

Izzy snorted and flipped her friend the bird.

This poor child was doomed.

"Okay, fine," Holly said with a roll of her eyes as she threw her hands in the air. "Izzy hates all this shit. She made us promise not to throw her a baby shower, but Shell got her to agree to allow one if and only if she went past her due date. Well, guess what, ladies?" Holly asked the crowd of mostly ol' ladies, a few of Izzy's repeat clients, and some friends from the gym. "Yesterday was her due date! So today, we party."

If looks could kill, Holly would be nothing but a smoking pile of ash right then. She had to admit a twisted part of her got some enjoyment out of torturing the woman who'd been the hardest sell since Holly started dating LJ. When they'd met, Holly's father had been their town's sheriff and extremely anti-biker. After much drama and heartache, he no longer lived in the state or worked in law enforcement. Even though Holly had proven over the past months that her loyalty lay firmly with LJ and his brothers, Izzy remained slightly frosty toward her.

Regardless of her discomfort in running this show, Holly was glad to have something to focus on besides her usual hatred of the Christmas season. With her birthday being Christmas Eve, this time of year, she tended to think of nothing but the twin sister she lost over a decade ago. Typically, she preferred to spend the holiday holed up in bed, licking her emotional wounds. But not this year. This year she had a group of pushy friends who refused to allow her to wallow.

Hence being the one running this shindig. That whole short straw thing was just a smokescreen. While she adored her girlfriends for trying to take her mind off her troubles, she could have done without this task. "We're gonna start right off with a fun game."

"Can I leave yet?" Izzy asked with a dramatic roll of her eyes.

"Did your water break?" Chloe asked.

"No." Yikes, that was a death glare if Holly had ever seen one.

Chloe either didn't notice or didn't care. "Then, you're not going anywhere until we've showered you with love, gifts, games, and sugar."

"Sugar?" Izzy perked up and started looking around. "I like sugar."

Holly shot Jazz a look then indicated the dessert table with a jerk of her head. Thankfully, her friend caught her drift. Jazz jumped up, grabbed a tray of brownies, and presented them to Izzy with a flourish.

"Mmmm," Izzy said on a moan as she bit into the ooey-gooey chocolate goodness. Holly smiled. Didn't matter how many times she fed her friends, their groans of delight made her day every damn time. As Jazz went to remove the tray, Izzy's hand shot out and pulled the platter from Jazz. "Mine," she growled, making everyone in the room laugh.

Jazz lifted her hands. "It's all yours, Mama."

With a hum of pure pleasure, Izzy looked to Holly. "I'm good to go now. What's the first game? And P.S., you're a sugar goddess."

The way to tame a pregnant Izzy was definitely through her stomach via way of her sweet tooth. Or teeth.

"Okay." Holly walked over to a rolling whiteboard Shell had borrowed from a teacher friend of hers. It had been covered with a sheet that Holly removed with a flourish.

"What the hell is that?" Izzy asked around a mouthful of brownie.

Holly laughed. On the board were twelve pictures of women's faces lined up in two rows. Each face was contorted in some twisted expression. "This is a little game called *Porn or Labor?* You each have a sheet of paper with the numbers one through twelve listed on it. Take a look at each picture and guess whether it's a photo of a woman in labor or a still from a porno. Got it?"

"Oh, my God," Izzy said with a shake of her head. "I should have known you bitches would make this awesome and not some lame vagina-fest shower."

"That's right, you should have," Steph said. "You know we wouldn't do you wrong, girl!"

An hour and a half later, the food had been devoured, games played, gifts opened, and Holly had laughed so hard she'd nearly peed herself—twice.

As she tossed the last of the plastic cups into a giant trash bag, the door to the clubhouse flew open. Screw burst into the room. "It's four o'clock. Times up, ladies. I need a fucking drink and some pus—Jazz," he said as he caught sight of the slender woman with the spiky black hair he'd been pursuing for the past few months. Pursuing unsuccessfully, she might add.

With a roll of her eyes, Jazz looked at Holly. "The first thing out of the man's mouth is how he's trolling for cheap pussy, and he can't imagine why I won't give up mine?"

"Cheap? Who said anything about cheap?" Screw asked, totally not giving a shit he'd been caught red-handed womanizing. No surprise since it seemed to be his favorite competitive sport.

Jazz huffed and strode into the kitchen, Screw hot on her heels.

A set of bulky arms closed around her from behind, and warm lips landed on her neck. She smiled. Oh, how she loved those strong arms.

"Mmm," Holly said as a shiver raced down her spine. "Um, I have a boyfriend. He's six-six, and he's a badass biker, but you know what?"

"What?" he spoke against her jaw right before giving it a nip that had her thighs clenching in anticipation.

"This feels so good I'm willing to keep it from him if you are."

LJ growled in her ear. "You think this feels good, wait until I get you home, spread you out, and bury my tongue in your pussy."

Her knees wobbled, but thankfully, LJ was strong as a freakin' ox, and he kept her from collapsing. Damn potent man. "I'm pretty sure my ol' man would have something to say about all that."

"You're goddammed right, he would. He'd have a whole lot to say. Like how sexy you are, and how you smell like heaven and taste even better." He grazed his teeth over her earlobe, and Holly nearly begged him to bend her over the closest table, friends be damned. "How was today?" he asked, and Holly knew he wasn't referring to the party.

As she ran her hands over his forearms, she said, "Today was a good day, LJ. A really good day."

"Good, sugar. I'm glad." He spun her and kissed the hell out of her right there in the middle of the clubhouse with his brothers filing in to begin an evening and night of partying, and the women finished baby shower clean-up. "Gonna be an even better night."

She smiled as he cupped her ass and pulled her even closer. "Oh yeah?" Even without his naughty promises, the night would be fantastic. Just being in LJ's presence filled her heart with happiness, leaving very little room for sadness and grief for what she'd lost.

"Yeah. Any night I get to spend inside you, then beside you is the best night of my life." His hazel eyes burned with an intensity that let her know his words weren't just letters and sounds strung together but had genuine feelings backing them up.

"LJ?"

"Yeah, sugar?"

"Take me home." The need to be naked and in his arms, surged higher than ever before.

He gave her a lascivious grin. "You need me so bad you're willing to risk the wrath of your girls by skipping out on clean up?"

And suddenly Holly couldn't have been happier they forced her to run the party. "Don't have to clean up. Those evil bitches made me emcee the whole freakin' thing today, but in return, I got out of clean-up duty."

"Well, shit," he said as he grabbed her hand and dragged her toward the door. "What the fuck are we standing around here for?"

Twenty minutes later, Holly found herself on her back with LJ shuttling in and out of her so hard, her bed smacked the wall with each forceful thrust. At some point, while he'd been working his very generous length into her, he'd scooped her legs up, and she was now bent so far in half, her knees nearly hit her ears. Not that she minded. The man could twist her into a damn pretzel for all she cared, as long as he kept bringing those earth-shattering orgasms, she'd be a happy girl.

"Jack," she said on a gasp as he drove her closer and closer to the edge of her favorite cliff. In this position, she could barely move, just hang on for the ride and take it at the pace he gave it to her.

"Go ahead, baby," he whispered against her ear, never losing the rhythm. "Take the leap. Let me see how gorgeous you are when you come." As he spoke, he worked one hand between their sweat-soaked bodies and pressed his thumb to her clit.

Her back arched, or tried to arch, as pleasure erupted throughout her entire being. "Jack," she shouted this time.

"I love you, Holly," he said, and then he was coming with her. They clung to each other as they bucked and trembled through the shared climax. Most of the time, she came first, and multiple times. Once in a while, it was him, but these moments when they reached the summit together were the most powerful experiences in her life.

Holly had no doubt LJ loved her, and the feeling was completely mutual. She hadn't thought it possible to feel so strongly for another human being. To not just want but need to be in their presence as often as possible. To have them at the forefront of her mind and want their happiness above all else. Even her own wellbeing. These days, she thought about LJ first in every decision she made, every dream she imagined. To hear someone else describe it, the way she felt sounded burdensome. But it wasn't. Not in the least.

It was everything.

The closest she'd come to sharing a connection like she had with LJ was the bond she had with her twin sister, Joy. Part of Holly felt shame in thinking her link to LJ was more significant than that of her twin sister, but it was the truth. Maybe, had Joy's life not been cut so tragically short…

All of a sudden, tremendous despair gripped her, surprising her with its strength. A strangled sob tore from her throat, and she shoved LJ's shoulders, needing to escape before she completely lost it.

"Sugar?" he said, those hazel turning a deep green as they always did when he worried.

"S-sorry," she managed to grind out. "I-I d-don't know w-what-what's—"

"Shhh."

Tears poured from her eyes as he gathered her into the comfort and protection of his strong arms. Intense sadness chased away the glow of satisfaction she'd been feeling, leaving a tight ball of anguish in her stomach.

What the hell was happening to her? Was she having a nervous breakdown?

"About fucking time," LJ whispered as he rocked her back and forth.

"W-what?"

Somehow, he'd maneuvered them so his back rested against the headboard with her cradled in his lap. With his arms tight around her, he gently rocked side to side in a soothing motion.

For the life of her, Holly couldn't seem to stem the torrent of tears. It felt like every ounce of happiness she'd ever felt was flowing from her eyes.

"Let it out, baby. Let it all out."

Sure, this time of year was hard for her, but that wasn't anything new. But it'd been years since she had such an overt emotional meltdown at Christmas time. LJ held her close until the worst of her sobs faded away.

With a hitch in her breath, she sagged against him. Totally spent, wrung out like an old sponge.

"Feel any better?" he asked as he began to rub her back.

"Not sure. I feel tired. And embarrassed."

"Hey," he cupped her face between his hands and gave her the most intense look she'd seen from him since the day she was injured by one of the deputies on her father's force. "You haven't been talking about it. Not about Joy or your parents. The pressure's been building and mounting. If I'm being honest, I'm not sure how you haven't exploded before now."

"My parents?" she whispered. Just saying those two words was like a dagger to her already bruised heart.

"Yeah, sugar. This time of year is hard enough for you. And now, it's the first Christmas without your family. Even though it was fucked up, it was still your world."

And there it was. The thousand-pound elephant she'd been forcing from her brain at every turn. Holly hadn't allowed herself to miss them, to think about how different things would be this year without the few traditions her family upheld.

Though her parents had been far from perfect as had her relationship with them, and though Christmas time had been difficult for her entire family, they'd still been there for each other the best they knew how. And they'd made some good memories. Things she'd looked forward to.

The stockings her mother still filled though her children were fully grown adults.

The butter cookies from the recipe that had been passed down from her great grandmother.

The homemade ornaments her parents had saved from her childhood.

All gone.

And not just for this year. For the remainder of her life. Blown away in a spectacular explosion of pain and betrayal.

"I haven't been letting myself think about it," she whispered as she ran a finger around LJ's nipple.

He grunted. "I know. And if there's one thing I've learned in all these months of therapy, it's that shit eats you from the fucking inside out if you don't let it free. Shoulda pushed you to talk before now."

"No." Holly shook her head. "I wasn't ready."

"Do you want to call them?"

She froze, staring at a photo of her and LJ that lived on the nightstand. They were on his bike with the Smoky Mountains making the most beautiful backdrop she could imagine. Huge smiles dominated both their faces. "No," she said. "I'm not ready. I'm not sure I'll ever be ready for that. Besides, I'm pretty certain Copper would skin you alive if you let me call them." She glanced up at him.

"Copper understands how complicated family dynamics can be."

Holly just nodded. What could she say to that? Complicated was too mild a word. "LJ?"

"Yeah, sugar?"

The up and downward stroke of his hand on her back lulled her into a boneless state. Her eyes drooped, and for the first time in weeks, the anxiety she hadn't even realized was present dissipated. "Thank you."

"Christ, Holly, don't you know?"

She met his gaze, still so serious. "Know what?"

"I'd move those fucking mountains just to see you smile," he said as he indicated the picture she'd been staring at. "Now, tell me about your favorite Christmas growing up, and I'll tell you all about Maverick's pornaments."

Holly laughed and finally felt a lightness in her soul. No one could have pulled her out of the deep end like LJ had. "I'm both intrigued and terrified."

"You should be more of the second."

With another laugh, Holly pressed a kiss to LJ's chest. For the next hour, she regaled him with stories of her and Joy at Christmas time. Before long, the anguish completely fled, leaving only the joy of being with the man she loved.

Chapter Seven

ZACH

"Pleasure doing business with you, as always," Zach said as he stood over the supine form of the loser who'd just made his final payment on a loan he'd taken from the Handlers.

Two weeks late.

"Fuck you," the guy spat out. His name was Quincy, and he was around Zach's age, mid to upper thirties, with a long blond goatee and a shiny bald spot on the top of his head.

Easy to spot since Zach had a good five inches on the guy.

"Don't know why you hada knock me the fuck down," Quincy grumbled. "I fucking paid you."

With a grin, Zach stuck the thick envelope in the back pocket of his jeans. Call him deranged, but he couldn't deny the zing of excitement that shot through him whenever he got to exert a little force to get the Handler's money back. Once the money was tucked away safe, he swung his trusty baseball bat off his shoulder and pointed it at the guy. "Quincy, you're fuckin' lucky that's all I did. If you hadn't caught Louie looking so dapper tonight, I'da taken a whack at a kneecap or two. You're two goddamn weeks late."

"I'm aware. You made that point two weeks ago when I didn't have the money, and you used that fucking bat to bust out the window of my car." He pushed himself to a seated position and scooted out from between Zach's legs.

Zach shrugged. "Don't know you why you guys are always surprised by this shit." He glanced over his shoulder at Quincy's beige Nissan Sentra, which had a piece of cardboard and about six yards of duct tape covering the rear driver's side window. "The rules are so fucking simple. When I come to collect, you pay. No matter what. If you can't pay in cash, I choose how you pay. So. Fucking. Simple."

As he spoke, Zach tapped Louie against the side of the guy's knee. "Let you off easy since it was your first time being late. If it happens again, I take my payment in pain."

Quincy's eyes shifted to the bat, and his face paled.

Zach couldn't help but chuckle. Louie had become his mascot of sorts. Zach never collected payments without his trusty Louisville Slugger in hand. Less clean up than a gun or knife, kept his knuckles from getting beat to shit every time he had to dish out a little motivation, and it was just plain fun to swing. But today, he'd given Louie the day off and used his leg to sweep this fucker on his ass. Last night, Shell's daughter, Beth, had painstakingly wrapped battery-powered Christmas lights all around the bat then secured them with about a mile of tape. It now blinked alternatively between red, green, and white. Zach didn't have the heart to undo it all, and he couldn't risk bloodying or breaking the lights. Not after Beth worked so hard to get Louie in the Christmas spirit.

Of course, Beth just thought he loved to play baseball…

"All right," Zach announced. "I'm tired of looking at you. Get the fuck outta my face. And, Quincy?"

The guy cast Zach a wary look. "Yeah?"

Zach crouched down until he was eye-level with the man. "Next time, and we both know there will be a next time because you can't stay away from those fucking ponies. But, next time?" He raised an eyebrow and tapped Quincy's cheek with Louie.

"Y-yeah?" Quincy said, finally seeming to realize the seriousness of his misstep

"Next time you fucking pay me when my money is due. Otherwise, it'll be a while before you can show your face at those races you love so much."

Quincy swallowed and nodded his head so fast the guy's tiny brain must have rattled.

"Good. Glad we understand each other. Now, you seen any bikers around the track or in town who aren't us?"

With a shake of his head, Quincy said, "No. You looking for someone in particular?"

For the past few days, yeah, he'd been looking for a motherfucker named Crank who gave his woman a fucking scare. But so far, none of the trees he'd shaken had dropped any fruit. Kinda seemed as though the Chrome Disciples had taken Copper's advice and split town.

At least he fucking hoped so.

"Nah, just checking on something. Merry fucking Christmas, Quincy."

Zach used the bat to push up from his crouched position. Without so much as a backward glance at Quincy, he strode to his truck, hopped in, and peeled out. He was ten minutes late picking up his ol' lady thanks to Quincy and his whining. Actually, he wasn't supposed to have been the one collecting the money in the first place. It'd been Screw's job, but his brother was busy working on some master plan to worm his way into Jazz's panties, so Zach had offered to stand in.

He'd never understand these idiots constantly borrowing money from his club and never being able to pay it back on time. Again and again, the Handlers raked in mountains of extra dough because these fuckers ended up paying double, sometimes triple what they'd borrowed.

Though, he should keep his mouth shut and be happy as their stupidity kept him eating and drinking the good shit.

The fifteen-minute ride to Toni's diner passed in a blink, and before he knew it, Zach was stepping into the building through the employee's back entrance. He waved off the prospect hanging out in case Crank decided he was in the mood for an omelet. The place had been closed for about two hours now, but Toni had asked him to give her some time to work on the week's payroll. She'd done well and would be able to give each of her employees a small bonus this Christmas.

The diner was church-quiet. Zach frowned as he stepped into Toni's empty office. "Babe?" he called out.

A noise from the dining area had him heading that way. As he stood in the mouth of the short hallway between the dining room and the two offices, Zach studied his woman. Toni was bent over a table, wiping it down. Over and over and over again. The thing was so spic-n-span, she could probably see her reflection in the gleaming table, yet she continued polishing it like it was filthy. Aside from the fact her ass looked delectable all encased in tight denim, the picture she made felt all wrong. Zach could see the tension in her bunched shoulders, as well as the deep frown reflected back at him from the front windows.

Something was troubling his woman, and that wouldn't do.

"Babe?" he said again.

Toni jumped slightly, then turned to face him. "Oh, hey, Zach. Sorry, I didn't hear you come in. Guess I lost track of time."

Now it was his turn to frown. Her normal greeting consisted of a radiant smile, a tit-crushing hug, and a hell of a kiss. Hell, she greeted her customers with more enthusiasm than she'd just given him.

"You all right, Toni?"

"What? Huh?" she asked, then shook her head. "Oh yeah, I'm good." She twisted the damp rag in her hands. "Just want to finish these tables, then I'll be ready to go. There's some fresh coffee if you want some."

He almost called bullshit, but maybe she just needed a minute to work something out in her mind. Instead of giving her grief, he poured himself a cup of coffee and sat at the counter.

Twenty-two minutes later, he'd watched her clean each table, reorganize the juice glasses behind the counter, then begin restacking coffee cups. Not once had she uttered a sound. In fact, Zach was pretty convinced she'd forgotten about his presence altogether. When she grabbed a fresh rag and returned to a booth she'd already cleaned, he'd had enough of watching his woman succumb to whatever was grating on her mind.

"All right, babe, you're done," he said from his spot on a counter stool.

Toni startled so hard, she banged her hip on the edge of the table. "Ow! Shit, Zach, you scared me." One hand went to her chest while the other braced on the tabletop.

He tilted his head and studied the beautiful face of the woman he loved. "I've been sitting here for twenty-five minutes."

With a nervous chuckle, Toni ran a hand through her light brown hair. "Yeah, I know. Sorry, I guess I was just in the zone."

Zach slid from the stool then walked over to the booth she'd been about to clean once again. When he reached her, he removed the rag from her hand and sat, pulling her down next to him. "Or you're stressing so hard about something you forgot I was here. This about the fuckers who came in here the other day?"

"What? No, I'm good." There was that nervous laugh again. This time it was accompanied by a really shitty attempt at a fake smile. "I'm not really worried about them. Probably just flexing their muscles, right?"

With a snort, Zach said, "Nice try, babe." Why the hell wouldn't she confide in him? Could she...no, it wasn't possible for her to be questioning their relationship.

Was it?

His stomach flipped, and suddenly, he had the urge to shake her and demand she tell him what was wrong. If she said she wanted out, he'd throw her down on the table and fuck her until she remembered exactly why they worked in every way possible.

She frowned at him. "What do you mean, 'nice try'?" she asked, mimicking his voice.

"Toni, I fall asleep next to you every night and wake with you in my arms each morning. I watch your beautiful face across the breakfast table. I stare at you while you're helping me in the gym. I can't take my eyes off you when I'm here and you're working. And whenever we're at home chilling with a movie, I spend more than half of it looking at you."

"Zach," she whispered as she stared out into the empty diner.

"I know you, babe. I know your smiles, and I know your frowns. I know how you look when you're happy, when you're fucking pissed, and when you're being pleasured so good, you can't do anything but scream." He rubbed at a line of tension that had formed between her eyes. "I know the face you make when you're stressed. So don't try to feed me a line of bullshit, babe, because I also know when you're lying. And you suck at it. What's going on?"

Toni sighed. After a few more moments of heart-pounding silence, she spoke in voice so dejected, it had him wrapping his arms around her and pulling her close. "Last weekend, this kid came by looking for work."

A few months ago, Toni began a program where she employed at-risk teens in her diner. She gave them a paying job, which not only took them off the street and away from whatever trouble they were sure to get into, but she also spent time career counseling, teaching basic skills for self-sufficiency, and being a friend to these kids. When possible, she coordinated with their high school counselors and became part of the team of adults working to better the kids' lives. After having spent her teen years strung out and dating a sadistic gang member, Toni knew first-hand how rough life could get for these kids. She'd save each and every one if she had the means.

"You give 'er a job?"

With a shake of her head, she said. "No. I couldn't, she's just thirteen. Her name is Lindsey. She swore she had a family, but after today, I think she's homeless. Maybe a runaway."

Laws in Tennessee prohibited minors under the age of fourteen from pursuing gainful employment.

Zach pressed a kiss to her temple. "So, what did you do?"

"Hmm?"

"Come on, babe. I know you. You wouldn't have just turned her away."

With a soft chuckle, Toni rested her head on his shoulder. "I had her take out the trash, then let her pick whatever she wanted off the menu."

"What'd she get?"

"A double bacon cheeseburger with extra fries and a chocolate shake."

He let out a low whistle. "That's big eating."

"Tell me about it. She's just a tiny thing too. Looks like she'd blow right over if she set her hairdryer too high." Toni frowned. "Bet she doesn't even have a hairdryer. Anyway, she ate all that food in under ten minutes. Zach, she had to have been starving."

Sadness gripped him. No child should have to live that way. And thirteen was still firmly a child in his mind. No matter how tough their lives were or how fast they'd been forced to grow up. They weren't equipped to navigate the world on their own or take on adult problems.

"She been back at all?" Zach asked, playing with the ends of Toni's shoulder-length hair.

"Every day."

He smiled. "And every day, you give her a simple task and feed her." God, his woman had a heart the size of the whole state of Tennessee.

She turned. "Zach, she has nothing. She's been here seven days in a row, and I noticed she wore the same shirt four of those days. She's dirty and rail-thin. But it's her eyes that got me."

"Her eyes?"

"They're so sad. More than sad, sort of resigned. Like she's just accepted the fact her life is shit and is plodding through each day without meaning."

"Why do you think she's homeless?"

"She let it slip that her parents died about six months ago," Toni said. Then in a move very unlike her, she averted her gaze.

Zach narrowed his eyes. "And?"

"And nothing," Toni said with a shrug.

Nice try.

With a snort, he grabbed her chin in a soft hold before turning her face to him. "And?"

Toni huffed out a sigh. "And I might have followed her when she left here today. She walked about two miles to that spot beneath the overpass where all those people with nowhere to go sleep at night. I thought about going after her, but she seems so skittish, I was afraid she'd take off running if I got too close."

Zach ran a hand through his hair as all the many ways she could have been hurt bombarded his mind. "Jesus, Toni, do you have any idea how dangerous it is down there?" And that was before the potential addition of a new one-percenter MC. He took a breath to rein in his frustration. She was tense enough, barking at her now would just ensure a fight she didn't seem to have the energy for.

Staring him dead in the eyes with a somber look, Toni said, "Yes, Zach. I do know how dangerous it is. Especially for a thirteen-year-old girl."

Fuck.

So much shit went on beneath that overpass. Most of the drugs that passed through Townsend were sold from there, and more than a few drug-related murders had happened over the years. More than their fair share of assaults, and God knew how many rapes occurred yearly. That spot was yhe very last place a vulnerable teen should be hanging out. No wonder his woman was all worked up. Toni was nothing if not compassionate, and she'd probably been obsessing over the girl since the moment she left.

"And now you've been beating yourself up all afternoon for not stopping her from leaving or dragging her back here."

Toni gave him a sad smile and nodded. Their gazes connected, but she immediately looked away again, and Zach finally figured it out. The real issue. What she'd been stressing about all day. God, he loved her and her heart that had an endless amount of love to share.

"Come on," he said as he nudged her out of the booth.

Toni stood and cast him a confused look. "What?"

"Let's go see if we can find her and convince her to come back with us. Someone might as well make use of our guest room."

Toni's mouth fell open and her eyes final lit up. "Zach," she said, "are you sure?"

"I'm sure."

"But-but it could be a for a while. I mean, if she doesn't have anyone else…"

Did she even realize how her eyes pleaded with him for what she was afraid to voice? If the girl had no one, Toni would want to offer her a permanent or at least long-term spot in their home. "I know."

"Zach, you need to think about this. We—we aren't even sure if and when we want our own children, let alone taking in a teenager who probably has a shit-ton of baggage. This might be really difficult. I want you to really think—"

"Babe," he said, shutting her up with a quick, hard kiss. "I've already thought. I'm sure about this." And he was. Yes, they'd discussed kids, and both decided to table it for a few years, but something about this just sat right with him. Knowing they could be saving a teen from the same fate Toni had suffered felt damn good. Plus, clearly Toni had already formed some sort of affection for the girl. Maybe she saw herself in the teen. He and his ol' lady were fucking blessed with amazing friends and chosen family along with two successful businesses. If they could share it with a kid who needed it, all the better.

"Thank you, Zach," Toni said, her voice catching. "I love you." She threw herself in his arms and squeezed the fuck outta him.

"Right back at ya, baby." As he peered down at her smiling face, he couldn't help the surge of love. "Let's go find your girl and make sure she has a warm bed and good fucking food for Christmas."

After making sure Louie was ready to rock and roll if necessary, Zach drove them to where she'd last seen Lindsey. Toni worried her lower lip and squeezed his hand with a death grip the entire ride.

"It's so cold tonight," she said as they pulled over to the side of the road fifty feet from the underpass. "She must be freezing."

Up ahead, two fifty-five-gallon drums blazed away with roaring fires. A few makeshift shelters constructed from boxes, plastic crates, and blankets lined the edges of the underpass while the majority of the occupants, mostly men, huddled around the fires. The thought of a thirteen-year-old girl living here turned his stomach.

"Ready?"

"I'm ready to find her. Let's go." Toni opened her door and started to step out.

"Wait," Zach said as he caught her wrist. "Most of these people are cold, hungry, and many are strung out. We have no idea who or what we're walking into, so I want a hand on me at all times. You grab my belt if I need both hands, okay? I need to know you're okay if I can't be watching you."

Wide-eyed, Toni nodded. When her gaze drifted to the men and women milling around, her shoulders slumped. He hated to add to her fears, but taking her there was risk enough, he wouldn't compound it by going in unprepared. People became unpredictable and dangerous when cold, hungry, penniless, and possibly jonesing for a hit.

"If shit gets real nasty, you come right back here, lock yourself in, and call Copper." He wasn't taking any chances with her safety. Grabbing Louie, he exited the car then came around to take Toni's hand.

Together, they strolled through the surprising number of individuals dwelling under the overpass. Over and over, they called Lindsey's name and asked the few people who'd give them the time of day if they'd seen her. Toni rewarded anyone who'd help them with a few dollars, but most people refused to even glance in their direction.

"Oh, God, that's awful," Toni said as she brought her forearm up under her nose.

"Stay close." The stench of weed mixed with marijuana and piss, making him want out of there in the worst way.

Toni's gaze fixed on a trio of men standing near a concrete pillar. One had a belt secured around his upper arm while he injected a needle into his vein. Another swiped at his arms as though brushing away invisible bugs. The third snatched the needle as soon as the first had finished and refilled it with liquid on a spoon.

"Oh my God," Toni said on a gasp. "He's using the same—"

"Keep moving." Zach circled his arm around her shoulders. "It's not our business, babe."

After a good fifteen more minutes of continued searching, Toni turned to him. "She's not here. Zach, she's not here." The high pitch to her voice let him know how close she was to panicking.

They'd—well he and Louie had—looked in every ramshackle shelter and under every blanket they came across to no avail. Lindsey wasn't there.

"What if something happened to her?" A cloud of white drifted from her mouth each time she spoke. "What if she's hurt somewhere? Zach, I never should have let her leave." Her cold hand gripped his with a crushing force.

Shit, he hadn't realized she didn't wear her gloves.

"Shh, babe, breathe." Rubbing her hands between his as he guided her back to the warmth of their car, Zach said. "We don't even know for sure she was staying here. She may have a home, Toni."

Her shoulders sagged, and Zach wanted to take Louie, run back under the bridge, and wail on someone until they coughed up information on Lindsey. But it'd do no good. Chances were high not a single person there even knew who the girl was. That place didn't exist for socializing. It was a place to hunker down during the long, frigid nights and nothing more.

When they reached the truck, Toni turned and slammed into him. He caught her with an arm around her back as his senses went on immediate alert for danger. The harsh sob that tore from her throat nearly wrecked him and had him relaxing his guard. Nothing had hurt or scared her. At least nothing out there with them tonight. This was her internal distress.

"Shh, babe, she'll be okay. She's come by the diner every day, right?"

Toni nodded against his chest.

"Okay, then we'll talk to her tomorrow. Find out where she's living and what help she needs. We'll make sure she knows she's welcome to stay with us even if she has a home. Because it sure doesn't sound like the fuckers she lives with take care of her."

"We?" Toni asked, but the word was muffled by his shirt.

He gripped her upper arms with a bit more force than necessary, resisting the urge to shake her. "Of fucking course, we. Shit, babe, don't you know by now that we're a team?"

Toni lifted her tear-stained face and finally gave him a smile. "Yeah, Zach, I know it. It's the best thing in my life." She shivered and the tip of her nose shone bright red from the cold. At some point during their embrace, she'd wormed her frigid hands under his shirt and used his skin to warm herself.

He kissed her, long and hard until she whimpered into his mouth and her nails curled into his stomach muscles. "Come on, baby. Let's go home so I can get you out of these clothes and warm you up."

She smiled against his mouth. "That sounds really nice."

Tonight, he'd do what he could to keep her mind from spiraling, and tomorrow he'd meet this girl who'd been lucky enough to capture his woman's heart.

Chapter Eight

CHLOE

Chloe inhaled the crisp, chilly air as she curled her hands around her large peppermint mocha latte. That's right; she'd sold out for a trendy seasonal coffee. And it tasted fantastic.

A sugar rush in a cup.

Some might call her crazy for lounging on a bench in the park on a day where the high had been estimated to only hit forty-five degrees, but ever since Chloe had begun frequenting more public and crowded locations, she'd come to this park to settle her mind and find quiet. Rocket knew where she was, and no one had seen a Chrome Disciple since they'd showed up at the diner, so her ol' man had *allowed* her to head to the park.

A peaceful sanctuary to breathe, regroup, and ensure she wasn't feeling panicky or overwhelmed, she'd developed the habit of spending time in the park after a particularly anxiety-producing task. And three hours in a crowded shopping mall less than a week out from Christmas certainly counted as anxiety-producing. Especially for a woman who'd been only a few panic attacks away from full-on agoraphobia about six months ago.

Since she'd gotten together with Rocket, and begun learning to fight from Izzy and Jigsaw, her ability to spend time in locations full of strangers had greatly improved. But that didn't mean the task was without its drawbacks. Exhaustion and frayed nerves being two of them.

So she came to the park to breathe the clean mountain air, soak up the sun, and revel in the peace, quiet, and precious feelings of safety in solitude. Rocket knew where she was and always demanded a text when she arrived, left, and returned home.

With the hustle and bustle of the holidays keeping her busy at every turn, finding time to quiet her mind had never been more important. It was more than a year ago now that Chloe had been kidnapped and violently assaulted, leaving her to think she'd never have a normal social life or healthy relationship again. While not everyone would consider falling in love with an assassin turned outlaw biker a healthy relationship, it certainly beat out what she'd been doing to control her panic before she met Rocket.

As she lifted the cardboard cup to her lips, a twig snapped behind her. Chloe whipped her head around in time to see a man emerge from the woods wearing black jeans and a black leather jacket. For a moment, based on the countless hours she'd spent around bikers the past few months, Chloe instinctively smiled at the newcomer. Then, her brain caught up to her eyes, clueing in to the fact this man was not a Hell's Handler.

Chloe sucked in an icy breath as a wave of fear crashed into her. Didn't matter how many times she trained with Jigsaw for a variety of threatening scenarios, instant terror remained her gut reaction. Once she took a breath and recalled her training, and that she could no longer be considered a weak, vulnerable woman, she calmed.

Somewhat.

Without a word, she set her cut down, stood, and forced herself to take one slow step away from the bench. Sprinting away would only highlight her fear, and if this man was predatory, make her the perfect prey.

"Sit down, Chloe," he said.

She stopped dead in her tracks as though she'd hit a brick wall straight on. He knew her name.

Was this the guy who'd showed up at the diner?

How did he know who she was?

Shit! With fight or flight impulses warring in her brain, Chloe turned until she was facing the man. He stood about fifteen feet away, with the bench her only barrier.

A Santa hat rested lopsided on his head. By no stretch of the imagination could the man be considered handsome. Maybe some years ago, before someone smashed his nose, rendering it crooked. The one ear she could see flared out from his head in a bulbous display of cauliflower ear. But what captivated her in the most terrifying way was the gleam in his eye. Totally opposite of anything she'd expect from a man impersonating Santa Clause, the guy's eyes shone with pleasure at her discomfort.

Chloe swallowed, caught somewhere between the intense desire to flee and the fear of being chased. Pursing her lips, she blew out a slow breath. The small trick she'd learned to avoid panicking barely worked. With each rapid beat of her heart, a thunderous pulse pounded in her ears. Giving in to the anxiety right then could be disastrous. She was strong. She knew how to defend herself. She could handle this.

Fuck yes, she could. She'd battled far worse and come out on top.

The small pep did the trick, curbing the immediate threat of a full-on freak-out.

"W-who are you?" she asked, internally cursing the tremor of her voice. As she'd done in the past, she channeled her inner Izzy and squared her shoulders. Who cared how petrified she was on the inside? This asshole wouldn't be allowed to see it on her face or in her stance. "I asked who the fuck you were."

"Oh-ho," he said with a laugh as he took two steps closer. "A feisty one. I admit I wasn't sure what to expect from you, Chloe. I'm pleasantly surprised it's not a meek little woman jumping at every shadow. Seems like you survived your…ordeal."

Not only did he know who she was, but he knew what had happened to her. How?

You're strong like Izzy. You're strong like Izzy.

"I'll ask one more time before I walk away. Who the fuck are you?"

"The name's Crank. Enforcer for the Chrome Disciples MC. We're new 'round here, but don't worry, you'll be seeing us plenty. I'm sure you'll be used to us in no time." As he spoke, he advanced on her until he stood directly on the other side of the wooden bench.

Oh, this was bad. Very, very bad. "This town is claimed by an MC," she said as though he hadn't heard it before.

"So I've been told." He rested his hands on the backrest of the bench. "Actually, my president had a little chat with Copper yesterday." He huffed out a laugh. "Not exactly a welcoming fucker, is he?"

"Depends on who's coming around. He was very welcoming to me."

Crank straightened and let out a laugh. The up and down leer he gave her had Chloe feeling as though her sweater and down jacket weren't adequate protection from his x-ray vision.

"I'm sure he was, darlin'. I'm sure he was." He licked his lips, taking his sweet time as he continued to undress her with his eyes.

"Hey," she snapped as she worked to fight the nausea. "Why don't we cut the shit. Just tell me why the hell you sought me out."

One dark eyebrow rose as a smirk tipped his mouth. "What makes you think—"

Chloe narrowed her eyes as she lifted a hand. "I said, cut the shit. Not sure how stupid the women you're used to being around are, but I assure you, I'm not one of them. So, tell me why the fuck you wanted to talk to me." No longer cold, the anger that had chased away her fear made her toasty warm.

He chuckled as though he found her truly amusing. Eyes still on her, he walked around the bench until he stood within touching distance. Almost without thought, Chloe curled her fists and slid her right leg back a long step. The fighting stance she'd drilled over and over with Jig and Izzy provided comfort.

"Retract those claws, kitten," he said. "Don't you want an answer to your question?"

No. She wanted nothing more than for him to disappear. Not only had he scared her and pissed her off, but now he'd ruined a place she'd considered her safe haven.

But the guy had a reason for being there. Whatever that reason was, she'd bet it was bigger than her. It had something to do with the Handlers, and Chloe needed to find out so she could relay the message to Rocket or Copper. After a breath, she relaxed her posture, letting her hands fall to her sides, but keeping them fisted.

"Speak," she said.

Crank pulled a cigarette of his pocket, lit it, inhaled, then blew out a long cloud of smoke. Chloe clenched her teeth as she waited. This was all a game, and one she refused to lose. He could make her wait, take his sweet time, there was no way in hell she'd beg him for information.

Finally, after another drag, he said, "Had to meet the woman Lefty lost his life over."

She forced herself not to react on the outside while reeling on the inside. How did he know? Outside Rocket's brothers, the only person who knew what had happened to her, the real story, was her brother Scotty. And even he didn't know the name of the man who'd kidnapped her, raped her, and had beaten here bloody, flipping her world on its ass.

So how did this guy, this random biker know details no one else did?

"I—" she cleared her throat. "I don't know what you're talking about."

"Oh, come on, Chloe. We were getting along so well. Let's not start lying to each other now. I know all about you. All about the time you spent in a certain motel room last year. And all about the man who rescued you."

She couldn't speak. Could barely draw in a chilly breath. Rocket's past was mired in secrecy and operations so confidential he couldn't begin to tell her about most. The man had been an assassin for crying out loud.

Chloe's mind raced as she tried to form her next words. Before she had a chance to speak, Crank said, "Just wanted to introduce myself, kitten. Met a few other ol' ladies at the diner the other day. It's nice to know how easily I can...get in touch with the Handlers' women."

A subtle threat?

"You know him?" she asked, finally finding a voice through the fear.

He tilted his head.

"Lefty."

A sinister smile curled his lips. "Picked up on that, huh? Guess you were right, you're not a stupid one."

He knew Lefty. Shit, what the hell did that mean? For her? For the club? Did he plan to somehow turn Rocket and Copper in for Lefty's murder? Or were his intentions even more sinister?

Lost in her head, she didn't realize he'd walked even closer until the words, "Let's just say we have some mutual business associates. I mean had. Right? Since no one has seen him in six months."

Shit. Shit, shit, shit.

"You have exactly three seconds to get the fuck away from her before I put a bullet in your fucking brain."

Rocket. Chloe's eyes fell closed as the fear leeched from her body. Rocket was there. He'd protect her, get them out of this unharmed. Of that, she had no doubt.

Crank snickered and stepped back, raising his arms to head level. "Saved by the killer," he said.

Chloe immediately took three giant steps back as her head whipped around. Where was Rocket?

"Walk to me, babe," he said as he emerged from the woods to her left, a long, black rifle perched on his shoulder. He looked about as comfortable holding the deadly weapon as she did carrying a purse. One strong finger caressed the trigger, and though he was a good thirty feet out, Chloe had no doubt he'd hit Crank right between the eyes if he tensed that digit just a bit more.

With her heart trying to leap its way out of her chest, Chloe walked to him. The entire trip, she could feel Crank's gaze burning a hole in her back.

"Left side," he said the moment she reached him. All business, Rocket kept his focus on Crank and his finger on the trigger. As she assumed the instructed position on his left side, opposite his gun, he asked, "He touch you?"

"No." She shook her head.

Rocket didn't speak again, but then, she hadn't expected him to. Over the months they'd been together, she learned he much preferred to wait people out, especially his enemies. Most people couldn't handle silence for too long, especially under the spotlight of Rocket's coldest glare.

Sure enough, after only a minute or two, Crank said, "You gonna fire or what?"

One of Rocket's shoulders rose then fell.

"Was just enjoying getting to know your woman. She's quite something. Love all that red hair. She like you to pull it when you're fucking her?"

Beside her, Rocket tensed but didn't react in any other outward way, and they were far enough from Crank, the guy probably didn't even notice a change in Rocket.

But Chloe did. Her man grew more lethal by the second. His insides had to be swirling with fatal rage. Something had to give, or she'd be witnessing a murder.

"She a screamer?" Crank asked next. "Bet Lefty knows the answer to that question."

Not nearly as stoic as Rocket, Chloe sucked in a sharp breath as her stomach flipped. She needn't have worried about the sound drawing further attention to herself because, for the first time since she'd met him, Rocket lost his legendary cool. He charged forward so fast, the barrel of his rifle rested between Crank's eyes before Chloe had a chance to react.

"Say his name again, motherfucker," Rocket barked as he jammed the gun against Crank's forehead.

On instinct, Chloe took a step forward, gaze darting around like a ping-pong ball. Rocket would not hesitate to end Crank's life right then and there. The park might be deserted now, but she doubted it'd stay that way if the loud crack of a rifle split the quiet afternoon. And was Crank even alone? If Rocket fired, would they be swarmed by Crank's men?

"Rocket," she called.

He didn't respond.

"You got a fucking death wish?" Rocket asked Crank.

The other biker just smirked. "You mean like Lefty? You the one who killed him?"

Though he didn't seem to have heard her, the sound of her calling Rocket's name must have done something because he was back to waiting Crank out.

Crank took a step back. "You folks have yourself a Merry Christmas. I'd love to stay and chat some more, but you know how it is. Gotta boost my inventory for the after Christmas sales."

Then, as though there wasn't a very well loaded gun trained right on him, Crank turned his back and strode into the woods, whistling as he walked. Both she and Rocket remained in place for long seconds until the shrill sounds of Jingle Bells faded into the distance.

Finally, Rocket lowered his weapon and spun toward Chloe. Rolling his right shoulder as though the static position of holding the gun had cramped it, he marched to her. The moment she was within reach, Rocket jerked her into his arms with no finesse. She hit his chest with a thud then lost her breath as his arms banded around her in a vice-grip.

Nothing scared her ol' man. He'd witnessed the worst of the worst and been a party to acts that made her shudder to think of. To have him bury his face in her neck and squeeze her like he feared she'd slip through his fingers if he loosened his grip had her own protective instincts rushing to the surface.

"Hey," she whispered against the side of his head as she stroked his back. The soft leather of his Handlers' jacket warmed her chilly fingers. "I'm okay, Rocket. Swear it."

"Fuck," he bit out against her skin. The warmth of his lips brushing her neck sent a shiver that had nothing to do with the cold down her spine.

"Who is he?"

"New club rolled into town a few days ago. They claim they're settling here."

"Oh, my God. Seriously? I thought he was just bullshitting me." She tried to step back, but he held her too tight.

Rocket lifted his head and nodded.

Her mind spun with all the possibilities. "What does that mean?"

"Not sure yet. Nothing good."

"He knew Lefty."

Rocket stilled. "He said that."

Chloe nodded. "Yeah. Said they shared business contacts."

"Don't know. Pretty sure he's moving guns. Scumbags tend to run in the same circles."

With dread settling low in her gut, she stared at the tree line Crank had faded into.

Pressing his forehead to hers, Rocket said, "Come on. We need to head to the clubhouse to talk to Copper."

"Okay," she whispered.

"But first…"

His mouth met hers in a bruising kiss that stole her breath and her mind. The temperature inside her coat shot to near boiling, and all she could think about was shedding the garment. And the rest of her clothing. Too bad they had a good few hours before they could head home.

"Fuck, you scared me, babe."

Chloe pulled her head back and got a good look at his serious expression. "Why did you come here?"

With a shrug, Rocket grabbed her coffee, then slung an arm around her shoulders and steered them toward the parking lot. "Not sure. My gut has been screaming at me all morning. Since listening to it has saved my ass more times than I can count, I never ignore it. Figured it would calm down if I saw you."

Well, she'd never ignore a gut feeling from him either. Who knows what the hell would have happened had he not shown up? "Remind me to ask Holly to make your gut a special treat. Think he deserves it."

The laugh that left him had her smiling and finally letting go of the tension. Took a lot to make her man laugh. He'd seen too many of life's horrors to be overly jovial. But every time he did it, his face relaxed and his eyes lit.

And Chloe felt victorious.

Too bad the triumph wasn't enough to drown out the undercurrent of fear Crank brought back into her life.

Chapter Nine

COPPER

Copper leaned back in his chair as he studied the men seated around his table. Men who put their trust in him. This time of year, the stress of leading his club in the right direction always sat a bit heavier on his shoulders. The Christmas season was meant for families, laughter, lightness, and love. That meant the club's businesses needed to be profitable to support the men and their loved ones. It meant they needed to stay off the cops' radar and keep any enemies at bay. A lot of pressure for one man.

Now, should he ask, each and every patched member of his club would inform him that the job wasn't his alone, but as president, he disagreed. It was one hundred percent his job to make sure the men were taken care of, whether that be financial assistance, by being kept out of prison, or by staying safe in general.

Call him a fucking sap, but this year, with Shell and Beth in his life in a new way, he wanted each and every day to be filled with nothing but smiles and happiness.

Now, however, a dark cloud had settled over his clubhouse, and it was unacceptable.

The men talked and laughed as they waited for him to begin the meeting. None of them seemed overly concerned by the appearance of a rival MC in town, but then, they had yet to learn what went down with Chloe just over an hour ago. After getting his woman settled in his room upstairs, a furious Rocket had burst into Copper's office with the story. Since hearing it, Copper couldn't rid the sour sensation from his gut. The itch at the back of his neck telling him shit was about to get fucking real, fast.

"All right," he finally said, straightening up. He'd take care of pleasant business first, before fucking up everyone's day. "Let's get rolling. Gonna start with Christmas. Dinner here at three in the afternoon. Gives you the morning to spend at home. Obviously, this isn't mandatory club business, but if you're sticking around town, our family will be here sharing a meal on Christmas Day."

"Fuck yeah," said Mav, who wore a holly green shirt with a Christmas nutcracker. Across the top, in block letters, it read, *Put your nuts in my mouth.* "Always a damn good time."

Copper smiled. Beth sure thought so. His little princess had each and every club member wrapped around her skinny little fingers. On Christmas, the girl made out like a bandit.

"Mamma V all set to cook?" Zach asked Viper as he rubbed his stomach. "She's got her work cut out for her if she wants to top last year."

The VP's face clouded, and he shook his head. "Uh, she's actually passed the torch this year. The rest of the ol' ladies banded together, and all claimed parts of the meal." As he spoke, he stared down at his hands.

Copper frowned. Mamma V hadn't missed cooking a Christmas dinner at the clubhouse once since Copper patched in. He made a mental note to check in with Viper following the meeting. Something had been off with the guy the past few weeks. He'd been missing phone calls, flaking on simple tasks, and generally in a subdued mood. He'd barely reacted to news of Chloe's encounter with Crank.

"Sure as hell hope Izzy didn't end up having to make part of the meal," Jig grumbled under his breath.

The comment had the room chuckling. Izzy was known for and excelled at many things. Cooking wasn't one of them.

"Nah," said Viper with the first smile Copper could recall seeing from him in ages. "Cassie ain't stupid. She's off the hook in case she pops anyway."

Jig made a show of wiping his brow in relief.

"Think Beth might be getting a little MC cousin before Christmas?" Copper asked Jig.

"Fuck if I know," he said with a snort. "About ready to pull that baby out myself, just to get my woman back."

"She has been a little...cranky," Mav said with a smirk.

"Don't let her hear you say that," Screw piped in. "I told her she was grouchy yesterday and she 'bout ripped throat out." He shuddered. "She was intense before, she's downright scary as fuck now."

They went around for a few moments teasing Jig and laughing. Copper fucking hated to drag down the mood, but it had to be done.

"Quiet it up. We got some serious shit to discuss for a few moments."

A hush fell over the room until Rocket said, "Chrome Disciples."

All eyes turned to him. Shocked eyes. Not once in the years he'd been in the club had he spoken up first. On anything.

"Chrome Disciples," Copper confirmed.

"We really concerned about them?" LJ asked with a frown. The big guy was the only man in the club larger than Copper himself.

With a heavy sigh, Copper rested his elbows on the table. "Not sure, to be honest," he said. "Don't know how much of what Blade or Crank have been saying is posturing and how much they're willing to back up with action."

"Gut feeling?" Jig asked as he ran a thumb over the scar on his cheek.

"Not good."

"Yeah," Zach said as he shifted forward in his chair. "I'm with you. I've put some feelers out with some contacts, prez." As enforcer, Zach had quite a few friends in low places. Men who owed him favors all over the state. "Finally got something worth reporting just before I got here."

"Tell me what you got."

"Looks like they're setting up shop in Walland. Reports are they purchased an abandoned warehouse and might be turning it into their clubhouse."

Walland. The next town over. So not Townsend, thank fuck, but way too close for comfort. Though his club could cause plenty of issues being just one town over, at least there wouldn't be an all-out turf war for Townsend. Copper rubbed his chin.

"We know what they're into?" Screw asked. He'd been working with Zach ever since he prospected, sort of a backup enforcer.

Here came the part he'd been dreading. "We're hearing guns. But Crank admitted he knew Lefty. Said they had some business associates in common. Know at least one of their guys did time for rape."

"Fuck!" said Jig as he slapped his hand on the table. His woman had been assaulted on Lefty's orders, not raped as Chloe had, but roughed up and choked.

Across the table, Rocket sat still, clenching his teeth so hard his cheek twitched. "He confronted Chloe when she was alone in the park."

"Shit," LJ whispered. "She okay?"

Rocket nodded. "Yeah, she's good. Just freaked her a bit. He knew details of her kidnapping. Not sure if this fucker is a trafficker, but he at least knows that world. Seems he does run guns. Maybe he's outfitting the fuckers who traffic women."

Copper needed to think. "I spoke with their president a few days ago. Guy goes by Blade. Seems smart, ballsy, and determined to settle in this area. He likes the tourist traffic and isolation of the mountains. Now, if the fucker wants to open a cat house or some shit, I don't give a fuck, but if he's gonna be moving weapons or women all through the county, we're fucked. That shit will bring some serious ugly to our little slice of the pie."

His brothers nodded, a few expressing their frustration with vulgar suggestions for Blade and Crank. All this shit was way too heavy for the week of Christmas.

"What's our play, Cop?" Zach asked.

Copper rolled his shoulders and cracked his neck. "Not sure yet. For now, I want you all to keep a close eye on your ol' ladies. Seems Crank likes to pop in on them to stir shit up. If you need a prospect or help looking out, let me know. Let's get through the holidays then reevaluate."

He cast a glance at Rocket. Of all the men, he was the one mostly to go off and act without authorization. Rocket had the skills to remove the Chrome Disciples for good, but they had to be careful. Enemies couldn't keep disappearing without the Handlers blipping on the cops, or worse, the FBI's radar.

"You okay with that?" he asked Rocket.

Though he looked mad enough to spit nails, Rocket nodded.

"Anyone you can check in with to get some more info?"

Again, he only nodded. Rocket had more connections than the rest of the club combined, but he didn't often call on them. Sometimes they came with strings attached.

"All right. Let's get outta here. Keep your eyes and ears open, men. Especially when it comes to your women. If I don't see you, have a merry fucking Christmas. Otherwise, I'll see you here on Christmas Day."

A lot of the guys got together Christmas Eve as well, but that wasn't exactly a family-friendly party. Now that he had Shell and Beth waiting at home, he'd be spending that night watching

Frozen with his girls and trying to convince Beth Santa would only visit if she actually went to sleep.

Not to mention he'd be working to keep his ol' lady from picking up on his fucking worries.

Who the hell would have ever thought he'd choose shit like that over a night of partying with his brothers, but he couldn't think of a better way to spend the night before Christmas.

As the men he wouldn't see until after Christmas wished him a good holiday as well, and filed out of the chapel, Copper tried to release the tension he'd been carrying since he received the call from Stephanie about the Chrome Disciples.

This had to be it, right? The last challenge he'd have to face this year?

What more could happen before the end of twenty-nineteen?

Chapter Ten

CASSIE

"Hey, beautiful, can I get you a drink?"

Mamma V looked up into the flirty face of Thunder, one of the prospects nearing his patch-in time. He was an attractive guy for sure. Funny, sexy, snarky. When he first began prospecting, he'd been working as a stripper, but recently gave it up due to scheduling issues with club business, though Cassie was pretty sure he still did some private parties on occasion.

Now, he worked at Zach's gym alongside Screw as a personal trainer. Good job for the guy, considering he spent all his free time working out anyway.

"Just a bottle of water, sweetie," she said.

"Water? Come on, Mamma V, it's Christmas. Live a little." He winked.

That's exactly what she was trying to do. Live a little. Actually, a lot. In no way was she ready to cash in her chips just yet. She had so much life left to live. For crying out loud, the guys were just getting started making the next generation of Handlers. How could she miss watching them fumble through parenthood?

"Just water."

"All right. One bottle of the hard stuff coming up." He reached into a small refrigerator behind the bar and grabbed a bottle of water. After uncapping it, he slid the bottle a good ten feet down the bar to her without spilling a drop.

With a laugh, Cassie said, "You've got some skills."

"You have no idea." Another wink. The guy gave them out like Santa distributed presents. To Thunder, flirting was just a primary part of his personality. She was pretty sure he didn't even realize he laid it on so thick with every woman he came across. Old or young, taken or single, they all got the patented Thunder wink and come-hither grin.

She took a small sip of the water, giving her stomach a chance to let her know if it was going to accept the liquid or not. When it didn't churn and threaten to expel the bit she'd taken in, she went for more. Finally, after days of crippling nausea, she'd been able to eat some toast at breakfast and keep it down.

Small victories were what her life was all about these days.

"You waiting on your ol' man?" Thunder asked.

"Yeah, he and I have something to speak to Copper about."

His eyes narrowed. Thunder was no dummy. He may not have been the most educated of the group, but he had street smarts and well-honed instincts. Made him a valuable asset to the club. "You guys good?" he asked, seeming to assess her with his gaze. "Ain't splitting up or nothing, are you?"

Cassie laughed. "No, sweetie. We aren't splitting up. That man wouldn't survive a day without me." Now it was her turn to wink.

"Know it," Thunder said as he wiped out a glass. "So does he. Hell, none of us would survive without you around here."

She smiled despite the ache in her chest at the thought of not being around. Somehow, she'd managed to avoid truly thinking about the very real possibility of her own death. Probably wasn't healthy, some kind of denial, but whenever she let the reality of her diagnosis sneak in, fear took over. The terror was so profound, she couldn't function. So, she'd learned to compartmentalize like a boss over the past few weeks. But then someone like Thunder would make an innocent comment, forcing her to face her own mortality.

She would. She had to. But not until after Christmas. If this was going to be her last December twenty-fifth, she wanted to enjoy it without fear and anxiety. "So what's new with you, Thunder?"

He studied her for a moment longer as though deciding whether or not to let her get away with the subject change. "Not much, babe, not fucking much."

She blew out a sigh of relief. "Come on, no special lady for the holidays?"

"Didn't anyone ever tell you all ladies are special?" *Wink.*

Cassie laughed. "Oh, you're good. I can see why you excelled at your job." Thunder had the magical ability to make each and every woman he came in contact with feel as though she were the queen of the world. That skill had to make him very effective in his former profession.

He tossed the damp bar towel in a dirties bin then leaned his forearms on the bar. "I'm working a bachelorette party tomorrow night. You're more than welcome to come by and see the real reason I'm so fucking great at my job."

Cassie's face heated. Even though she was more than old enough to be Thunder's mother, and his flirting was all in good fun, he still managed to make her blush. Despite all her years around the club, she'd never fully gotten used to the way the men were so blatant and free with their sex talk.

"Hey, beautiful," Viper said as he walked up behind her and circled an arm around her shoulders. "What was it you were offering to show my woman?"

Without thought, she leaned into her husband's body. The young bucks could flirt with her all they wanted; she wouldn't trade her old stallion in for all the sexy twenty-somethings in the world. Not for all the money in the world. Not even for a clean bill of health. She'd rather endure misery with Viper than even attempt life without him.

"Uh, nothing, VP. Just playing around." Thunder lifted his hands and took a step back, but his eyes twinkled with mirth.

Viper mock scowled. "Maybe play with someone your own age, huh?'

"Hey!" Cassie gave him a weak elbow to his still hard stomach. "You saying I'm old?"

With a shake of his head, Viper said, "Nope. Never, baby. Just don't want this fucker getting any ideas."

Thunder shrugged with a laugh. "Hey, I know when I'm out-manned. Wouldn't dream of poaching your woman, VP." He turned toward the shelves of liquor as the guys leaving church started yelling out drink orders.

"You ready?" Viper whispered in her ear.

She looked up at him. Ready for their world to change yet again? Hell no.

"You're sure about this?" His last out before they went in and made it official with Copper.

"Yeah, beautiful, I'm sure."

"I'm sor—"

He kissed her. "What did I tell you about all that?"

"You told me if I said I was sorry one more time, you'd return my Christmas present." Cassie rolled her eyes. Her husband would never carry through with that threat.

"That's right. And it's a good one, too, so keep that pretty trap shut, okay?"

She nodded. If this was what he wanted, and he was confident in his decision, then she'd back him one hundred percent. Every time. "Okay, let's do it."

Her handsome gray-haired man gave her his hand and helped her down from the barstool. How he managed to support her on the way to the chapel without making it look like she was weak, she'd never know, but she was grateful for it. Though they owed

Copper an explanation, she hadn't gotten in the headspace to tell the entire club about her diagnosis yet.

With his arm snug around her, they weaved through the men leaving the chapel. Each greeted her with a wave, hug, or kiss on the cheek, so it took long minutes to make it across the room. Copper still sat at the table in the chapel, rubbing his chin, lost in thought. "Everything okay?" Cassie whispered to Viper.

"Some shit going down. Nothing for you to worry about." When she cast him her well-practiced, *nice try* look, he chuckled. "I'll fill you in later. Promise."

Viper knocked on the frame of the open door. "Got a minute, Cop?" he said.

Copper jolted and straightened as though surprised he'd been caught unaware. "Yeah, come on in." He waved them in. When Cassie went to hang back, he said, "You too, Cass."

Not that she hadn't known she'd be welcome, but technically, un-patched members of the club weren't permitted in the chapel. That included prospects and women. Now, in reality, she'd been in there a number of times over the years, and Copper would never deny her entrance, but she wanted to give him the respect of understanding how the place worked. Little quirks she'd had to learn all about when she'd become Viper's ol' lady a lifetime ago.

"What's up?" Copper asked. "Sit, hon," he said to Cassie. "Haven't seen you in a bit."

His keen eye took her in, probably calculating how much weight she'd lost in the three weeks since she'd seen him. "Yeah, sorry I've been kinda MIA recently."

"You go to Izzy's shower? I didn't see you there."

"For a bit," she said as she settled into a chair opposite the table from Copper. Viper sat next to her and took her hand.

Copper narrowed his eyes. "Shit, why do I have the feeling you guys are about to tell me something I don't wanna hear?"

Viper sighed, and it was heavy with the weight of their burdens. Cassie wanted to cry for her strong man. Amazing didn't begin to describe the incredible care he'd taken of her since she'd gotten sick. He'd pulled out all the stops to not only make her feel better but be secure in the fact that he was right where he wanted to be. By her side.

Didn't keep the guilt at bay, but it made each day a little more bearable.

"Sorry, I've been less than reliable lately, prez," her husband said.

Copper's eyebrows drew down. "No apology necessary, Viper. I've always known I can fucking count on you. This club can count on you. Talk to me."

Viper cast a glance her way, and her heart clenched. She squeezed his hand while giving him a small nod. "Cass is sick," he said, voice catching on the word sick.

Copper's eyes widened and his gaze shifted to her. "Is it serious?"

"Cancer," she whispered with a nod.

"Oh fuck, Cassie." Copper's shoulders sagged and he ran a hand down his face. "Tell me."

After clearing her throat, she continued. "Lymphoma. I've had two rounds of chemo treatments so far, and they're pretty much wrecking me." Her nervous chuckle had Copper frowning as he shook his head.

"Why didn't you say anything before now? Shit, brother," he looked to Viper. "We coulda been helping out. I know the ladies would have made you an army of food and helped with anything you guys need at home."

Viper opened his mouth, but Cassie beat him to it. "That's on me. I asked him to keep it quiet for a while. I don't want to be responsible for ruining everyone's Christmas. I'll tell the club, I promise, but not until after the holidays. Please," she added since Copper looked like he wanted to argue.

He blew out a breath. "Fuck. You know Shell's gonna have my ass when she realizes I kept this from her, right?"

That finally had Cassie laughing for real. She folded her hands in front of herself. "I promise to take the blame."

With a snort, Copper said, "Won't matter, Mama V. You know that woman thinks of you as a second mother. And a grandma to Beth. She ain't gonna be happy to be kept out of the loop."

"I know how she thinks of me. And I know how much I love her and Beth," Cassie whispered. "Which is why I don't want to destroy their Christmas. You know this news would put a dark cloud over the day. Let them have it and be happy before they have to be sad."

"All right," Copper said after a moment. His voice sounded thick with sorrow. This was why she'd wanted to keep quiet. This blanket of despair that would be over all of them from now on. "I'll keep my trap shut on one condition."

Cassie raised an eyebrow.

"You tell me the moment you need anything. Any fucking thing, you get me?"

God, she loved this patchwork family pieced together with people from all walks of life, with difficult pasts and uncertain futures.

"We get ya, prez. Which brings me to the other reason we wanted to talk to you."

Copper shifted his attention to Viper. Cassie's heart beat so hard, she expected one of the men to hear it. This was the right decision; in her heart she knew it, but God, how she didn't want to hear Viper's next words.

Words she felt so responsible for and knew would hurt him, though he'd die before admitting it to her.

"I need to step down as VP."

Knife to the heart. Not everyone knew Viper's story. How he'd come to live in Townsend and be part of the Handlers, but it had been a long and hard journey for her husband. For both of them. They both loved this club, this life more than they could express. Walking away, in any form, had to be killing her man.

Copper didn't respond. No words, not so much as a flicker across his face. In fact, he stayed quiet so long, Viper began to squirm.

"Look, prez, I know this is the worst fucking timing with the Chrome Disciples—"

Copper stood and extended his hand across the table. "No explanation necessary, brother. You take care of yours, and the club will take care of you."

As her eyes threatened to overflow, Cassie looked away. The tip of her nose tingled, and she blinked the tears back. This family was everything to her and Viper.

"Thank you, Copper."

When she turned back, the two men were clasping hands across the table. Neither seemed eager to sever the connection.

"Position is yours anytime you want to come back to it, brother."

Viper shook his head. "No. I won't yo-yo like that. You give it to someone else, it's theirs for good. Won't snatch it back."

With a tilt of his head and a chin rub, Copper said, "Fair enough. You'll meet with me after Christmas to figure out how to restructure?"

"Of course."

Copper came around the table then, his hulking form approaching her. When he was within arms distance, he pulled her from her chair into a gentle but firm embrace. She felt so tiny in his massive arms. Copper had hugged her countless times over the years, and she'd always known his power, but now, standing in his strong embrace, she realized just how frail she'd become.

"What can I do for you?" he asked. Copper didn't make empty offers or give canned platitudes. If he asked what she needed, he meant it. And he'd do anything in his power to help.

"I'm managing right now," she said, absorbing the warmth and comfort of being loved by family. "Just be there for him,

Joy

okay?" she whispered against his chest, not even sure he'd hear her.

"Always," he whispered back.

"Thank you." Knowing Viper would be taken care of no matter the outcome of her illness provided a small measure of comfort. Should the worst happen, his family would gather tight around him and see him through the dark days.

After squeezing Copper, she stepped back. It was Christmas time, and she promised herself she wouldn't get mired in despair until after the holidays. "So, uh, Shell and Beth excited for Christmas?"

Copper let her have the subject shift. He leaned his hip against the table as he folded his arms across his wide chest. Cassie returned to Viper's side where her man immediately drew her back against his chest then wrapped his arms around her.

But something crossed Copper's face. A shadow of some sort, she'd never seen. Usually, the man lit up when he spoke of the two most important females in his life. Soon as she got home, she needed to make plans to check in on Shell.

"They are. You guys gonna make it for Christmas breakfast?" This would be the second year in a row Shell had invited them to join them for the Christmas morning gift opening and breakfast.

"We'll see. If Cass is feeling up to it, we'll be there," Viper said.

"No." She shook her head and resisted the childish urge to stomp her foot. Cancer had already taken so much from her. Her energy, her sex drive, Viper's position with the club. And now it was starting in on her hair. No way in hell would it take Christmas morning with her family away from her. "We'll be there, no matter what."

"Babe," Viper said, casting her a stern look. "You've got treatment on the twenty-third. You might not be feeling up to much on Christmas."

Cassie straightened her shoulders and looked Copper in the eye. "We'll be there," she said with force. Nothing was stopping

97

her from watching that sweet kiddo open her gifts. Not nausea, not intense fatigue, not…fucking cancer.

Chapter Eleven

JIGSAW

Jig eased back the covers and hauled his tired body up to sit on the side of the bed. Third night in a row, he'd stared at the ceiling for hours without so much as a hope of sleeping. By now, his eyes held a constant grit and his limbs hung heavy with fatigue. On top of it all, his brain refused to get in gear and work fast enough to make him effective throughout the day. He'd slogged through his business at the clubhouse, making mistake after mistake until he'd finally tossed in the towel, disgusted with his lack of concentration.

A glance over his shoulder confirmed Izzy snoozed away on her left side, facing him.

As she'd required for the past month or two, a pillow propped her swollen stomach so it lay in line with the rest of her body. Another between her knees helped her find some small measure of comfort, and a third behind her back, prevented her from rolling flat.

Fuck, he loved his woman. Loved that he was the only one to see her this way. Sleeping, vulnerable, guard down and heart open. To the rest of the world, she was a sassy tattoo artist, MMA fighter, and all-around kick-ass ball-buster. But to him, she was his Izzy. And his Izzy had a soft side she only revealed to him.

With a low grunt, he pushed up off the bed and shuffled down the dark hallway toward the kitchen.

Two a.m.

Shit.

He ran a hand down his face, pausing to finger the puzzle-piece shaped scar that served as a daily reminder of the fragility of life.

Bypassing the kitchen in favor of the den, Jig made his way toward their small liquor cabinet. A few swallows of Izzy's favorite Bourbon ought to dull his mind enough to squeeze a couple hours of shut-eye in before he had to get up and head back to the clubhouse.

After filling the glass well past the level of socially acceptable, Jig sat on the couch that used to be Izzy's but had become theirs over the past few months, as had everything in the house. The scenic view out their front windows called to him, tranquil and calming; in complete contrast to his internal turmoil.

He was about to become a father. Again. In fact, he should have been a father already. Izzy's due date had come and gone a few days ago, leaving her in a…delicate mood. His poor woman was losing her mind with the discomfort of being nine-plus months pregnant.

He, on the other hand, was losing his mind for a whole host of reasons, the newest of which was this fucking club pushing in on their turf. Just when life seemed to settle, shit got fucked again.

But even enemies weren't what had him wide the fuck awake. A deep-seated terror grew by the day, starting as a small niggle of discomfort and growing into a monster so big, he was drinking Bourbon at two in the morning in a desperate attempt to fall asleep.

Once before, he'd been in this exact position. Waiting on his woman—his wife—to deliver a child. His daughter. Fuck, Jig had been happy with his wife. A sweet woman whose tongue had never uttered a swear word and who could barely kill an ant, let alone best a grown man in an unsanctioned fight. She'd been a true southern bell. Sweet, rational, unassuming, and eager to please.

Basically, the complete opposite of the woman slumbering in their bed. The kicker of it was, he'd loved his wife. Truly loved the woman he'd married and planned to spend the rest of his life with. And fuck, did he love that daughter they'd created. The adorable little girl who'd been the spitting image of her mother and shared her kind, giving nature.

Fuck.

Jig took a sip of his drink as he stared out into the night. The moon hung high in the sky, illuminating the outdoors enough for him to make out the outline of the Smoky Mountains. Best feature of their house. Tonight, the view wasn't enough to take his mind off his worries. Neither was the Bourbon.

Two things were responsible for Jig's serious sleep deprivation.

Guilt and fear.

The guilt gnawed at him like a ravenous rodent, burrowing its way deeper and deeper by the day. He was not the same man who'd married Callie all those years ago. He was no longer her Lincoln. That man had died the day his wife and child were senselessly and brutally murdered. From Linc's death, a bitter, vengeful, and violent man was born. Jigsaw. And Jigsaw had fallen head over fucking heels in love with a tough woman who wasn't afraid of his darkness. A woman who allowed those aspects of his personality, even welcomed them. A woman who fucked him as well as she made love to him. A woman his first wife would have prayed for because she wouldn't have understood her.

Then again, Izzy sure as hell wouldn't have understood Callie, either. In fact, he was pretty sure his current woman would have hated his passive and docile wife. And that's where the guilt came from. Yes, he loved Izzy with everything he had, but somehow it felt like he was dishonoring his wife by choosing a woman she'd have been wary of herself. Then he felt as though he was dishonoring Izzy for having those thoughts.

Worst part of it all was that the man he was today would never have chosen Callie either. She could never have survived a relationship with Jigsaw. He'd have chewed her up and destroyed the light in her soul before spitting her out. He'd have dragged her down to the darkness with him.

How could that be? How could he have changed so much he could no longer visualize a life with the woman he'd promised forever to?

Christ, his head was fucked beyond reason.

In these quiet moments, when his mind wouldn't release its grip on him, Jig allowed himself to admit his feelings for Izzy were stronger than those for his wife. Well, maybe not stronger, but different. More intense. Consuming.

Fitting, since the woman herself was so much more of a force than his wife had been. Then again, so was he. Now.

The guilt haunted his soul.

Add all that guilt to the bone-chilling fear of losing what he now had, and it was a wonder he been able to keep from running outside and howling at the moon.

For the first time since the day his wife and child were killed, Jigsaw could truly say he was happy with his life. But now he'd ended up right back where he started. A woman. A child.

Would they be taken again? Would it be by the Chrome Disciples?

Was it his destiny to lose those he loved?

Another healthy swallow of Bourbon didn't produce any answers.

Shit, Izzy would probably kick his ass if she knew he was thinking these far-out thoughts about fate and fortune.

"Jig?" Her sleepy voice came from behind him.

"Fuck, babe, I didn't mean to wake you." She needed all the sleep she could get.

With a snort, she waddled over the couch and plopped heavily by his side. Instantly, her hand went to his bare thigh and his to her round belly. "*You* didn't wake me. My fucking bladder did. And now your spawn thinks it's time to play." Her head flopped back along the top of the couch. "God, I'm so ready to be done with this."

As proof of her words, their child kicked directly into his hand.

Another difference between Izzy and his wife. Callie had loved being pregnant. She'd reveled in the changes to her body and even the weight gain, whereas Izzy struggled with the inability to push her body to the max as she'd done prior.

In a move so un-Izzy, he blinked to make sure she was really the one next to him, she lifted his hand to her mouth and kissed his palm before returning it to her stomach. Once again, the baby inside nudged him. "You know it's not going to happen, right?"

"Huh?" He shifted to find Izzy's head resting against the couch, facing him. "What's not going to happen?"

"You're not going to lose us."

His throat thickened. For a few moments, they just stared at each other until the baby punted again.

A soft smile tipped Izzy's lips. "If you tell anyone I said this, I'll kill you in your sleep, but I'm really going to miss feeling your spawn moving around in there."

That statement did nothing to ease his tension. Only served to remind him of how amazing his woman was.

She must have sensed his distress because she placed her hand over his. "I mean it, Jig. Nothing is going to happen to us. We're safe, happy, and prepared for more of life's troubles than you were back then. I'm not Callie. Not that there was anything inadequate about her, but I can handle myself. I can protect myself and our child in ways most women can't. And you can protect us. Then there's the back up of your brothers. We're safe, baby. Safer than most. You don't need to worry about anything bad happening to us."

The scar on his face tingled until he couldn't ignore the prickles and rubbed it. Izzy caught his hand, pulling it down before she pressed a kiss to the raised skin of his cheek. "I want you to enjoy this," she whispered in his ear. "To enjoy being a father. Enjoy watching me fumble around as a mother. You can't do that if you're worried about what's lurking around every corner."

"How'd you know?"

Her rare sweet smile warmed him every time. "Because I know you, baby. I know how you think and how you stress."

God, she was killing him. Ripping his heart out and exposing every insecurity that plagued him. He should have known she was on to him and wouldn't let him stew in silence. Izzy confronted problems head-on with guns blazing. This conversation, so reminiscent of one they'd had months ago, when he first told her about his past, had some pressure finally easing out of him. Back then, they'd sat on this very couch, and he'd bared his soul for the first time. Izzy had said all the right things then as well.

"Nothing. Will. Happen. To. Us. I will fight with everything in me to ensure we get our happy ending, Jig. And you know this bitch can throw down."

He chuckled, as had probably been her intent. She could only handle so much intense emotion. "Fuck, Isabella, I love you."

She tilted her head as she ran her hand up and down the ridges of his abdomen. Since he never slept in anything more than boxer briefs, if that, the hardening of his cock wasn't exactly hidden. But Izzy made no move toward sex.

"You know that's okay, too, right?"

"What?"

"It's okay for you to love me as much as I know you do. It's okay for you to love a woman who is nothing like the woman you married. From what you've told me of her, she'd want this for you."

Jesus, was she a fucking mind reader? "I—" Fuck, what the hell was happening to him? He couldn't even fucking speak.

"You show me every day, Jig. And I know you. You're hard and lethal, with steel at your core. Different from what you've told me of the man you used to be. But he's not gone, Jig. He's still there. He's there every time you rub my aching back or surprise me with a milkshake. He's there when you make me dinner and let me ramble on if I've had a shit day. He's especially there when you wake up in the middle of the night and whisper in my ear that you love me."

She knew about that? He'd thought she'd been asleep all those times.

"He's there in everything you do, but it's okay that he's changed. It's okay that he's no longer Linc, but now Jigsaw. Life is basically us doing the best we can to manage the circumstances we've been given. And you were given far worse than most. What you went through would change anyone, baby. Anyone. So it's okay that you're not the same version of you. Callie would have wanted you to find love. She'd have wanted me for you even if she wouldn't have understood me. Because I love you, Jig. And I love her, Lincoln. I'll take care of you both, and your spawn," she said as she rubbed over her stomach, "with the fierceness of a lion."

Izzy was right. So right. Callie would have hated the anger and vengeance that had blackened his heart, but she'd have wanted him to find a woman to care for and take care of him.

He grabbed a handful of her long black hair and pulled her face to him. Most of the time, she kept the thick strands pulled back in a tight braid, but at home, she'd been leaving it loose more and more. Just the way he liked it. That silky waterfall of hair was one of his favorite things about her.

"I've never once doubted your ability to protect yourself or our child," he whispered against her mouth right before he took it in a scorching kiss.

Izzy moaned into his mouth.

"Thank you," he said, lips brushing hers. "I know there is a large part of you that doesn't believe this, but you're going to be an incredible mother."

Izzy's breath hitched, and she tried to shake her head, but he held her firm.

"You're going to be an incredible mother, baby. This kiddo won't care if you don't bake a million cookies or spend your days on Pinterest. You will love this child and teach them to love themselves. You'll encourage them and help them grown into who they are supposed to be."

"Jig…" Izzy's eyes filled. So rare for her, even though her pregnancy. Most of her wild hormones came out as irrational anger instead of tears.

"You're gonna be the most badass mother out there, because you give a fuck, Izzy. And you excel at everything you do."

"I love you," she whispered.

He smiled against her mouth as he moved in for another fiery kiss.

"But how the hell do you know what Pinterest is?" she asked right before their lips met.

Jig chuckled. "Holly told me all about it."

With a snort, Izzy said, "At least the spawn will have Holly for the cookie baking shit."

"Mm-hmm." He nipped at her lower lip before sucking it into his mouth.

"Ugg," Izzy groaned. "This baby needs to come out so we can go back to having a normal sex life."

The baby had moved low enough, Izzy was no longer comfortable with penetration. That sure as hell didn't mean he couldn't get her off, though.

With a laugh, he slid off the couch and onto his knees between her legs. Ignoring the ache in his hard as fuck dick wasn't easy, but if he knew his woman, she'd return the favor. And then some.

"Why are you laughing?" Izzy asked as she shifted her hips and allowed him to peel off her panties.

"Because you think you can have a normal sex life with a newborn."

The scent of her arousal hit him, ramping up his own desire to nuclear levels. He rid himself of his underwear then returned to his knees. Izzy's eyes lit at the sight of his rigid cock.

"Excuse me, but I'm pretty sure we are not your average parents. We'll still manage a rockin' sex life, bubba, trust me on that one."

He gripped his length and stroked, loving the way she licked her lips. "I have no doubt you'll give it your best shot."

With a bark of laughter, Izzy said, "Shouldn't you be spending a little less time on yourself there and a little more time on me?"

"Yes, ma'am."

"Ohh, ma'am, I like that," she said right before he took a long, slow lick through her drenched folds. "Oh, shit, God, yeah, I *really* like that. Do it again."

"Yes, ma'am," he said as Izzy's laughter turned into a low, drawn-out moan.

He ate at her like he was starving, which he supposed he was. Starving for everything their life had become, and at that moment, craving to hear her come. Her flavor dominated his senses, making his own need shoot through the roof. He sunk two fingers into her at the same time he wrapped a hand around his cock and tugged. As he pumped into her pussy, he licked her clit and jerked himself. He grunted as his balls drew up tight. Wouldn't take him long tonight. The combination of Izzy's flavor, his own rampant need, and the high emotional connection to his woman had him at the edge in no time.

"Fuck, I wish I could see you right now," she said, breathless as he fucked her with his fingers. When he sucked her clit at the same time, she let out a keening wail. "Jig," she screamed as her lips lifted off the couch, pushing her pussy into his face. "I'm gonna come."

He jacked himself like a madman.

"Oh, God. More, more, more. I'm so fucking close."

So was he.

He grazed his teeth over her clit while curling his fingers inside her and off she went. Izzy thrashed on the couch, groaning and thrusting her hips as she rode out the orgasm on his fingers. Two more tugs were all took for the white-hot pleasure to overtake him as well.

"Fuck," he growled as he rested his forehead on Izzy's damp thigh. He covered the tip of his dick, catching his release as it claimed him.

"Shit, did I need that," Izzy said. "It's like the best muscle relaxer in the world. My back doesn't hurt, and my feet don't feel swollen. Ahhh."

Jig stood and smiled at the picture a blissed-out Izzy made. With her hair a mess around her shoulders, she wore only a sports bra to contain her much larger than normal tits. Her eyes were closed, head tipped back, and a satisfied smile on her lips.

Jig placed a kiss on her distended stomach before heading to the bathroom to wash up. When he returned, Izzy lay sprawled in the exact same position. "Come on, mamma. Let's get you back to bed."

Without opening her eyes, she shook her head. "Don't wanna move."

Jig pushed an ottoman toward her, then lifted her legs onto it one at a time. Still naked, he dropped down next to her. Her head automatically went to his shoulder and his hand to her stomach. She wrapped her arms around his. "Think you can finally sleep?" she asked, voice husky with exhaustion.

"Yeah, baby."

"Good."

He kissed her head. "Thank you." Two simple words, probably not enough to let her know how much he valued her in his life. Tonight, she'd eased his mind and soul. For the first time in weeks, the fear had abated, and he no longer had the crushing heft of guilt on his chest.

"You don't have to, Jig. I love you."

"Love you too, Iz." He rubbed a hand over the mountain of her stomach. "Love you, spawn."

Her soft chuckle was the last thing he heard before falling into a deep, restorative sleep.

Chapter Twelve

SHELL

The doorbell rang, causing Shell to do a quick scan of her kitchen. Or rather the explosion of sugar, flour, and sprinkles that used to be her kitchen. If she'd been smart, she'd have taken Holly up on her offer to make the cookies for her and Beth to decorate. But no, she'd had to get all it's-our-tradition and insist on baking the cookies with Beth.

In the three hundred and sixty some-odd days between cookie baking sessions, she always managed to forget just how much of a mess they made. Otherwise, she'd never do this again. Kinda, like the way the pain of labor faded, allowing women to agree to have a second child.

Ugh, why did her mind always go there?

"I'll get it!" Beth screamed as she dashed from the kitchen. "Maybe it's Santa."

With a chuckle, Shell wiped her sticky hands on a dishtowel. "Santa doesn't knock on the door, silly," she called after her daughter. "He comes down that big old chimney. And you know not to open that door until I get there." She chased after the energetic five-year-old.

Thunder had been sitting outside their house since Copper left, but she still didn't want her child ripping the door open.

Beth dropped her hand from the doorknob and shot an innocent grin over her shoulder.

"Busted," Shell said as she approached the door.

"You're here. Can I open it now?"

"One second." She swiped her phone open, checking the security app. Cassie stood on the Santa welcome mat while Thunder remained in his car on the street. "Go for it."

After struggling with the deadbolt, Beth yanked the door open. "Mama V!" she squealed. "Even better than Santa."

Cassie gave Beth an indulgent smile. "Well, don't I feel special now," she said as she crouched down. As was her custom, she pulled a lollipop out of her pocket and held it out for Beth.

Her daughter's face lit as she reached for the treat, but then she thought better of it and looked up and over her shoulder at Shell. "Can I have it, Mommy? Pleeease?"

"Yeah, Mommy, can she have it? Pleeease?" Cassie said in an almost perfect copy of a whining kid.

"All right," Shell said as she rolled her eyes. "Lay off it, you two. You can have the lollipop."

"Yes!" Beth raised her arms in victory then snatched the lollipop from Cassie. As she turned and started to dash back into the house, she caught Shell's gaze then spun back around. "Thank you, Mama V," she said, throwing her arms around Cassie's waist. Then she shot off, charging into the house. "I'm gonna make you and Viper a Christmas picture!" she shouted as she disappeared up the stairs.

"Oh, to have even half her energy. Come on in, Mama V. Didn't mean to make you stand out in the cold." Was it her imagination, or had Cassie lost weight recently? She stood in a fluffy coat, shivering on the porch.

"Thanks, sweetie." Cassie pressed a kiss to Shell's cheek as she entered the home.

"Let me take your coat."

Cassie handed it over, rubbing her slender arms once the garment was gone.

"Can I get you some coffee or tea? Hot chocolate?" Shell asked over her shoulder as she stowed Cassie's coat in the front closet.

"Oooh, I'd love some tea if you'll join me. Warm me from the inside out."

Shell smiled. "Sounds perfect to me. Just pretend you don't notice the state my kitchen is in."

As they entered Shell's kitchen, Cassie let out a laugh. "I see you two were engaged in your traditional Christmas kitchen destroying."

"Hey, I told you to ignore that!" Shell filled the red tea kettle then set it on the burner.

"Sorry, Shell, I refuse to ignore the state of your kitchen. This is exactly how a kitchen should look at Christmas time." Cassie's tone grew serious as she met Shell's gaze across the kitchen island. "Have I ever told you what a wonderful mother I think you are, Shell?"

"Aww, Cass, thank you. And yes, you have. More times than you probably should."

She reached across the island and grabbed Shell's hand. "No, honey, I'm serious. You've never once let the circumstances of her conception color your treatment of her. Not everyone could do that." With a soft smile, Cassie looked around the house. "The home you've created here with Copper is perfect. I'm so happy you two found your way to each other. I've always loved you, Shell. From the first moment your mama let me hold you. You were two days old, chubby-cheeked, and bald as a cue ball. And for such a tiny thing, you sure could scream."

Both women laughed. "You're sentimental today."

Some unreadable emotion crossed Cassie's face before she shrugged. "Must just be the season. You've been through some shit, Shell. But none of it prevented you from being the sweet, loving mother you were always meant to be."

"Cassie…" Shell's voice thickened with emotion as she blinked back unshed tears. "Thank you."

"You're very welcome. Beth's a lucky girl. As any other kids you have will be."

Shell's face fell, and she lost the battle she'd been so fiercely fighting since the day Copper dropped his bomb. Tears exploded from her eyes.

"Shell? What's wrong, sweetie?" Cassie's eyes widened.

God, she must look like a crazy woman, bursting into random hysterics.

The tea kettle chose that moment to let out its ear-piercing whistle.

"Oh, gosh, I'm so sorry," Shell said as she dashed at her eyes while turning toward the stove. The gesture was useless. Now that she'd started, she couldn't seem to stem the flow of tears.

Cassie rounded the island then batted Shell's hands away from the stove. "I got the tea," she said as she turned the knobs to off. "You go sit."

With a heavy pit in her stomach, Shell did as instructed and made her way to the kitchen table littered with trays of cooling cookies. There was barely enough room for the two steaming mugs Cassie arrived with only a few seconds later.

Shell's tears still hadn't begun to abate by then.

After placing a mug in front of Shell, Cassie sat next to her but didn't say a word. She had that way about her. A quiet, calming presence that always had Shell unburdening her soul to the older woman.

"Copper wants a vasectomy," Shell said.

"And?" Cassie blew on her tea before taking a sip.

"And what?" Shell asked with a shake of her head.

"And tell me the rest."

With a humorless laugh, Shell said. "Are you a mind reader or something?"

"Nah, just old women's intuition." Another sip of her tea. "And…"

Shell played with her teabag, watching it swirl the liquid in the cup. Then she raised her head and gave voice to the words she'd yet to say out loud. "And I'm pregnant."

Cassie's softly spoken, "Congratulations, sweetie," and genuinely happy smile had the crying kicking up all over again.

"What am I gonna do, Mama V?" She shook her head. "This isn't what he wants."

"Oh, honey." Cassie scooted her chair closer and gathered Shell in a motherly hug

Once again, she had the feeling Cassie had lost weight. What once was a soft embrace felt much bonier than usual.

"He wants a baby, Shell. He's just scared."

Shell pulled back. "I don't know. He was pretty adamant about it."

"How far along are you?"

"Nine weeks," she said, then winced at Cassie's widened eyes. "I know. I'm running out of time. Second baby, I'm already starting to show."

One of Cassie's eyebrows journeyed upwards. "With as much as that man is on you, how has he not noticed?"

That finally had a real laugh bubbling out of Shell as her face heated. "I'm not sure. You know men can be pretty oblivious. But I won't get away with it for much longer."

"How are *you* feeling about having another child?"

She couldn't stop the slow grin from spreading across her face as her hand automatically went to her stomach. "It's like a dream come true," she whispered. "Having Copper's baby growing inside me. It's something I never thought I'd have. I wanted him for so long. And now, I not only have him, but we made a baby. I can't even describe how amazing it feels. But the timing...it's all off."

Cassie grabbed both her hands and squeezed. "Oh, honey, I'm so excited for you. Copper will come around." She frowned. "I'll kick his ass if he doesn't."

Both women laughed. The idea of Cassie taking on the mountain that was Copper would break the tension at any time.

"How have you been feeling?"

"Ugh." Shell rolled her eyes as nausea rippled through her stomach like it had been summoned by Cassie. "Pretty sick. It only started last week and thankfully, I've managed to only throw up when Copper has been out of the house, but it's really ramping up this week."

Cassie's hands flew to her hips. "Okay, that's it, missy. You're telling that man, and you're telling him today. He will not be pleased to find out you've been sick behind his back."

"I know. I just…" She shrugged. She was a chicken, plain and simple. The life they'd created for themselves grew better by the day. Shell thought she'd been in love with Copper for years, but now that she lived with him, the feelings had strengthened to something she couldn't even put words to. Love seemed too fragile and insignificant an emotion.

Or at least it seemed fragile now that Copper wanted different things than she did.

She'd found out about the pregnancy two weeks ago and had been working on a fun way to tell him. Until a few days ago when he shattered her anticipation.

The sound of her front door opening had Shell straightening in her chair. Cassie shot her a chastising look.

"Babe? That Cassie's car out there?"

"Yeah. We're in the kitchen having tea."

Ten seconds later, Copper's big form filled the entryway to the kitchen. "Holy shit," he said. "What the fuck happened? Were we robbed by Holly?"

Both women laughed, but Shell's felt hollow.

"Nah," Cassie answered for her. "You're ol' lady was just being the amazing mother she is." She winked at Shell, earning her a narrow-eyed glare. "Well, I gotta run home and feed my own man." Cassie stood then gave Shell a quick hug. "No time like the present," she whispered. "I'll see myself out."

As she passed Copper, she rose on her tiptoes and pressed a kiss to the side of his beard. "Twice in one day. Love you guys," she said, then disappeared.

Beth hadn't reemerged, and normally, Shell would call her down to see Cassie off, but there was nothing normal about this day. Not anymore. Not now that she planned to take Cassie's advice and get it over with.

Finally.

"How you doing, gorgeous?" Copper asked as he walked into the kitchen. He stopped right by her chair, looking down at her. "Lotta sugar in this room. You gonna share some with me?" He arched an eyebrow.

"I'm pregnant," Shell blurted then slapped a hand over her mouth.

Shit.

Shit.

Clearly, the pregnancy severed the connection between her brain and her mouth because she never would have spit it out that way had her brain worked. That was not the way to give Copper news he might not be enthused about, but once she'd gotten it in her mind to tell him, the words felt hot and sharp in her mouth, and they just jumped out.

They stared at each other. The stony expression Copper wore had nerves skittering beneath the surface of her skin. She wanted to rub the irritation away but stayed still, rooted in place.

"What did you say?" he asked, not a hint of excitement or even acknowledgment of what she'd revealed.

"I'm pregnant," she whispered.

A harsh chuckle escaped him. "This a fucking joke, Shell? Cuz it ain't funny."

Her breath hitched, and she shook her head as tears filled her eyes. "No. Not a joke. I'm nine weeks pregnant," she whispered.

"Nine weeks?" he spat out as he paced away from her. "Nine fucking weeks and you didn't think to tell me before now?"

"I was gonna," she said as she rose on shaky legs. "I was gonna tell you after I confirmed it at the doctor, which was the day…" She cleared her throat. "The day you told me you wanted a vasectomy." For the first time since they became a couple, Shell didn't know how to act toward Copper.

Should she go to him?

Should she stay away?

Should she talk or remain quiet?

Would he want her touch at that moment?

Never before had she felt insecure when it came to their relationship, and the emotion had her stomach churning.

"You're goddamn right I want a fucking vasectomy." He threw his hands up in the air, accidentally hitting a canister of flour which clattered to the floor in a white powdery cloud. "Jesus," he shouted. "What the hell were you thinking?"

The question hit her like a slap to the face, making her stumble back. "What?" she whispered, then her voice grew in strength. "What was *I* thinking?" Her laugh sounded ugly and bitter even to her own ears. "Pretty sure it took both us of us to put *your* child in me."

"You're the one who takes that goddammed pill."

The blood in her veins began to boil. Who the hell was this man wearing Copper's skin? It certainly wasn't her man. Her lover. Her husband. With a huff, she stomped around the kitchen island to the counter where she kept their medications. After opening so hard the door bounced back, nearly hitting her in the face, she ripped out the packet of birth control pills and whipped them at Copper. They hit his chest, causing him to fumble the plastic case, but he managed to hang onto them.

"Count 'em." She folded her arms, tapping her foot as she waited. Never in all the years she'd know him, had she felt this angry toward Copper. "I haven't missed a single one. But I did have a sinus infection a few months ago. Remember? The one I took antibiotics for. And I believe you were the one who wanted to risk it, knowing the pill could be ineffective. Remember that?"

She sure did. It'd been an epic night that most likely resulted in the pregnancy. Now it all felt tainted.

He tossed the pills on the counter without opening the pack. "Shit's heading south with the club, Michelle."

Michelle? When the hell had he ever called her Michelle? Was this supposed to be his way of distancing himself? "I know…" she said. When was *shit* not difficult with the club? Lately, it felt like they were constantly battling something or someone. "So, what are you saying?"

"Saying it's a bad fucking time to have a fucking kid."

A few more comments like that and he wouldn't need to schedule a vasectomy. She'd take care of it for him with a swift and debilitating kick to the nuts. "And what would you like me to do about that now?"

"Not goddamn thing you can do now, is there?"

She blew out a breath. At least he wasn't asking her to get an abortion. Because that was a conversation that could end them. "Look, Copper…"

Staring at him, she shrugged then averted her gaze. She had nothing. He didn't want this baby. What the hell else could she say?

As he ran a hand through his hair, he sucked in a giant breath then let it out slowly. Calming himself down. For the first time since she'd admitted the pregnancy, a small seed of hope bloomed in her stomach. Maybe he'd been too surprised to handle the news. Maybe he was about to gather her in his arms, apologize, then tell her he loved her.

"This was a fuck up," he said, and her knees buckled.

She grabbed the counter to keep from collapsing.

"A big fucking fuck up, but we're stuck with it now." He paced across the kitchen. "Fuck. Wish I'd had that vasectomy three fucking months ago," he said as though he was the only one in the room.

Well screw him.

Shell grabbed a rubber spatula off the counter. Her chest heaved with building rage as she hurled the utensil across the room at her stupid, pigheaded man. The damn thing bounced off his arm, probably feeling like being hit by a cotton ball.

"Ow! What the fuck, Shell?" He said, turning toward her.

She placed a hand over her stomach. "I'm sorry that the child growing in me, the child I was so excited about, the child that is half you and half me, is such a fucking mistake in your eyes."

He took a step toward her, hands out. "Shell, calm down. You probably shouldn't get so upset."

She laughed another one of those harsh sounds. "Now you're concerned about me? Don't worry, Copper, I'll take care of this fuck up all by myself. We already know I can handle it all alone."

She turned and started to storm out of the kitchen.

"Don't walk away from me, Shell. We're not done here."

"Oh, we're done, Copper. We're so fucking done." With that, she stomped out of the kitchen and up the stairs, ignoring Copper's irate voice as it followed her. She marched past Beth's room without a word to her daughter. She needed a minute to calm herself so she wouldn't pass her mood on to Beth.

Once she reached the room she shared with Copper, Shell's anger turned to profound sadness. With an unsteady breath, she sank down on to the bed they'd purchased together after buying the house. With closed eyes, she forced herself to breathe and level out. This wasn't the first time she and Copper had fought. One didn't get involved with the president of an outlaw motorcycle club without expecting a strong personality, but this was by far the ugliest.

He'd come upstairs soon. Copper was the one who never let tension sit between them. As a big fan of makeup-sex—not that Shell wasn't—he tended not to let problems fester, but to work them out quickly. Any minute now, he'd come walking up the stairs, and they'd come to some sort of understanding even if it was just to table any talk of babies until they'd both had time to process.

The slamming of the front door made her jump.

Shell pressed a hand to her chest as it ached with a vengeance. He'd left.

Walked away from their home in anger.

Something he'd never done before and had told her he'd never do.

That just left one question.

Was he coming back?

"Mommy," Beth said as she appeared in the doorway.

"Yes, honey?" Shell turned her face to the side and quickly swiped the tears away. Her daughter didn't need to see her in such a messy state.

"Are you and Daddy yelling at each other?"

"Uh, no sweetie," she said, keeping her face averted. "We weren't yelling at each other. Just talking about some grown-up stuff. Sorry, were we talking too loud?"

She nodded, but didn't seem remotely concerned. "Can we finish the cookies now?" Her little face was so bright with eagerness. The kind that only came once a year. The Christmas kind.

The last thing Shell wanted to do was put on a happy face, pretend everything was rosy, and decorate cookies. But she stood, smiled at her daughter, and nodded. "Yeah, baby. We sure can."

Hand in hand, they headed back down the stairs and into the kitchen.

She could do this. She'd been alone before and survived.

One big difference, though; this time, she'd know what she was missing.

Chapter Thirteen

LITTLE JACK

"Holy shit, babe! What the fuck are these?" LJ yelled with a full mouth after shoving a cookie in his trap. A box of them sat open and beckoning to him on the counter. He had another between his teeth before he'd even swallowed the first.

"What?" came the muffled reply. He heard something he couldn't make out, followed by the word shower. No worries, he had plenty to amuse himself while he waited for Holly to get out of the bathroom.

A few seconds later, she appeared in one of his T-shirts with a towel wrapped around her head. Damn, that sight got his dick hard every time. "Woman, you look—"

"What are you doing!" she shrieked so loud he couldn't believe the windows didn't crack as she rushed him.

There went his happy cock.

Holly ripped the half-eaten cookie out of his hands, giving him a deadly scowl. "How many did you eat?"

She looked like the most adorable angry person in the world, and LJ couldn't help but laugh at the exaggerated scowl on her normally cheerful face.

"Excuse me," she barked. "There is nothing funny about this. How many of these cookies did you eat?"

"Uhh, three?"

"Three?" Her eyes bugged.

"Well, three and a half. You gonna give me my cookie back?"

"LJ!" she whined, pinching the bridge of her nose as though dealing with a difficult child. This time he wisely cleared his throat to cover his laugh. "These aren't for you. They're for Izzy. She specially requested them."

"What?" he said with a laugh. "What does she need cookies for? She's fat enough as it is."

Now her hands were on her hips, making his T-shirt ride up enough to give him a peek of his favorite creamy thighs. This was too fun.

"Excuse me? Fat? She is not fat. She's nine months pregnant."

He shrugged. "It's not like you can put it back in the box."

Her forehead wrinkled. "What?"

He pointed to the piece of cookie she still held in her hand. "That cookie. I ate half of it. It's not like you're gonna give it to her now. So can I have it back?" He blinked his eyes, shooting for an innocent and pleading look. "Please."

"Ugh." She rolled her eyes as she held out the partial cookie, one hand still propped on her hip. "You're such a child."

"Maybe," he said as he stuffed the half cookie into his mouth. "But you love that I love your cookies."

That had her smiling. "Well, that's true."

"Why are these so amazing? They just look like sugar cookies with white chips."

With a sheepish look, Holly stole one out of the box and took a bite. "They're blizzard cookies. Made with cream cheese."

"Look at you, you little hypocrite," he said with a laugh as she took another bite of her cookie. Her cheeks turned a light shade of red.

"What? I can't give them to her without making sure they aren't poisonous first."

LJ crowded her against the counter. "Pretty sure I took care of that for you already." He yanked the towel off her head, letting the heavy wet strands of hair tumble past her shoulders. "I'd be dead on the floor if you'd poisoned them."

"One day…" she said with a wink.

LJ threw back his head and laughed. "Fuck, I love you, Holly Lane."

"Love you too, Jack," she said on a gasp as his hands slid under the T-shirt and over her bare tits.

He kissed her, reveling in the taste of the sweetest woman he'd ever had.

His woman.

"Mmm," he said on a groan against her lips. "Almost as good as those cookies."

"Hey!" Holly whacked him on the arm, but her laughter let him know it was playful. But then she grew serious. "LJ, how worried do I need to be about the Chrome Disciples?"

He rubbed at his beard. It'd be easy to lie to her, tell her nothing was wrong, and set up protection behind her back, but that's not how they worked. "We're not totally sure yet, sugar." Holly fiddled with the hem of his shirt. "So far, all they've done is show up where they aren't wanted and throw some words around. No clue if they've got the stones to back them up. But we aren't taking any chances, so when you and your girls are out or when you aren't with me, someone will be on you. Okay?"

Face solemn, she nodded. "Yeah."

At a time like this, she probably wished her father was still in her life, but the version of the man who she missed didn't exist. It'd been an illusion to cover up for a dirty cop who planted evidence and sent innocent men to prison. Still, LJ's efforts to keep Holly from falling into a pit of despair had been working. If this fucker Crank sent her on a downward spiral, he'd kill the guy for that alone.

"Don't want you worrying though, sugar. You'll be covered. Safe. All I want you to worry about is making more of these cookies for your man and enjoying the holidays with our family."

Holly snorted out a laugh. "I see what you did there."

Just as he went to dive back in for another taste of her lips, the doorbell rang.

Holly yipped and ducked under his arm. "I'm not dressed! Don't get it until I'm out of sight." She scurried down the hallway toward their bedroom.

LJ was still chuckling as he pulled the door open. "Welcome to the Sugar Shack! How can we—fuck me running."

Standing on the opposite side of the open door was a man he'd recognize anywhere but had never actually met. A man who Holly had admitted to thinking about numerous times over the past few months. The man she'd been dying to meet again, yet terrified to come in contact with. His story had made national news just months ago.

"Holly Lane live here?" The raspy, somewhat ruined voice didn't match the look of the man. LJ's gaze immediately landed on the thin pink line rimming the man's neck like a short necklace, only it was a scar indicating a brutal strangulation attempt.

Self-inflicted while in prison? Or perhaps an attack.

"You hear me?" he asked again.

LJ shook himself out of his head. "Sorry, man, yeah, this is her place. Sugar!" he called out.

"I'm coming," Holly yelled back followed by the sound of her bare feet hitting the wood floor as she ran toward the door. "Who is it?" She'd covered her lower half in a pair of ass-hugging jeans. LJ's favorite pair, to be precise.

LJ kept his body in the doorway. This guy may have been cleared of his crime and released from prison, but that meant shit as far as his intentions toward Holly.

"Uh, babe, I can't see through your giant body." Holly tried to wedge herself between him and the door with an unsuccessful hip-check. "Seriously, scoot that muscled ass over and let me see who it—oh, my God," she said as she finally caught a glimpse of the man on their doorstep. "Curly." His name was uttered in a barely audible whisper.

She couldn't possibly have a great view of him since LJ still blocked the doorway, but Holly had managed to peek around him. Most likely, Curly's image was burned into her brain, even if it'd been more than a decade since she'd laid eyes on the biker.

Curly snorted. "Ain't been called that a in long time." He pointed to his buzz cut salt and pepper hair. Back when Holly had met him, he'd had long, curly hair, hence the handle. "Mostly go by my given name now, Travis."

He couldn't help it, LJ had to throw a little intimidation Curly—Travis's way. He folded his arms across his chest and glared down at the man who was no slouch at around six-feet, but still quite a few inches shorter than LJ's six-and-a-half feet. His body was hard, honed by hours in the prison yard, no doubt, but without the bulk LJ had. He'd guess the guy to be in his mid to upper forties. Maybe even early forties. It was difficult to tell. Doing hard-time aged a man before his years.

Did that little growl come from him? Whatever, this fucker knew the world, knew the game better than LJ did. He'd expect some skepticism strutting into another MC's town, calling on an ol' lady.

"LJ, what the hell is wrong with you?" Holly said. She finally managed to worm her way in front of him. "Please ignore his guard dog routine. Especially since the actual guard dog can't seem to be bothered to come to the door." Her laugh sounded forced, strained.

His girl was nervous.

Travis chuckled. "Woulda wondered what kinda man you had if he didn't act like this." He met LJ's gaze. "I ain't here to stir up trouble. Just want to talk."

After another few minutes of posturing, LJ nodded, finally stepped back, and allowed Travis to enter their home, but he kept Holly's back to his front with an arm across her chest. A clearly possessive move, but who gave a fuck?

"Nice place," he said as he glanced around their home.

LJ and Holly had only lived in the rental house for about a month, but it had already become a cozy home, thanks to Holly's efforts.

"Thank you." Holly pulled out of LJ's hold. "Please, come have a seat. "Can I get you something to drink? Coffee, beer, soda?"

"Uh..." Travis cast a look in LJ's direction. Almost as if asking for permission to move further into his space and take his woman up on her hospitality. The respectful gesture killed any lingering doubt LJ had about Travis's motives. Without Holly being aware, he gave a slight nod. "Yes, ma'am, I'd love some coffee, thank you."

"Okay, great." Holly clasped her hands at waist level, started at Travis for a moment, then jumped as though startled by her own stillness. With a shake of her head, she said, "Oh, uh, sorry, let me go get that. Right. LJ can you take Cu—Travis into the living room?"

Watching her trip over herself with nerves had him wanting to jump in and take over the task, but he had a sneaking suspicion she needed to take a moment to regroup in the kitchen. "Want me to get it, sugar?"

"No, no, I got it. Thanks." She cast him a sweet smile as she walked backward toward the kitchen, wide-eyed gaze bouncing between him and Travis.

"Watch o—" LJ winced as her back connected with the corner of the wall.

"Oof." An uneasy giggle bubbled out of her as she bounced off the wall and stumbled into the kitchen.

Damn, she was flustered.

Instead of going after her like he wanted, LJ showed Travis to their living room. The former MC president settled on the two-cushioned love seat while LJ sat across a coffee table from him on their sofa.

"I've freaked her out," Travis said after LJ's ass hit the cushion.

He grunted. "You sure as fuck have. Not sure I've ever seen her so nervous she's crashing into shit."

"Wasn't my intention to throw her off her game. You either. Just…" He shrugged. "Sat through enough touchy feeling meetings and shit in prison, I've gotten to the point where I don't like to let shit go unsaid. Got a lot to say to her."

"I get that." Fuck. Twelve years the man spent in prison for a crime he didn't commit. Holly's father, who'd sent Travis away knowing his innocence of the accused crime, claimed the man deserved to be behind bars for a shit load of other wrongdoings. He'd felt justice had been served when Travis received a life sentence for the murder of Holly's sister.

What a load of horse shit.

"You been in contact with my president?" Curly wore a leather jacket, but no MC colors. Seems as though he either hadn't joined up with a club since being released from prison or he'd kept his colors off out of respect for the Handlers MC.

"I have. Going to introduce myself and pay my respects later today."

Holly burst back into the room, carrying a large tray with three mugs of coffee and a heaping plate of the very cookies he'd been scolded for swiping just moments ago. LJ hid his smirk. Of course, Holly would mess up her own plans to make Travis comfortable. Now she'd probably be awake half the night re-baking cookies for Izzy.

His woman was too fucking sweet.

"Here we go." Before LJ even had a chance to hop up and take the tray from her, she was placing it on the coffee table. "I have fresh coffee, sugar, milk, French vanilla creamer, and sugar substitute. There's also cinnamon. Some people like that. I had no idea how you take your coffee. Um, these are some cookies I made earlier today. No nuts. In case you're allergic to them. I'm a baker. Not that you care about that, but it's why I had the cookies." She spoke so fast, she had to inhale a huge breath at the end of that ramble.

"Sugar," LJ said, grabbing a hand from where she wrung them in front of her. He tugged her down onto the couch next to him. "The man's been in prison for twelve years," he whispered in her ear. "Pretty sure you could give him yesterday's coffee, and it'd be worlds better than what he's used too."

"LJ!" she said in the cutest stern tone he'd ever heard. "Don't be rude."

Travis just chuckled. "He's got point, ma'am. I'm not picky." He picked up a mug of coffee without doctoring it in any way and took a sip. Then he bit into a cookie.

Her desire for approval stemmed from so much more than a cookie. Holly harbored an enormous amount of guilt where Travis was concerned. Once her father's evil actions had come to light, she'd become convinced she could have kept him out of jail had she only stuck to her gut feeling of his innocence. If it had been up to LJ, this meeting would have happened when the man got out of prison a few months ago if only to ease Holly's misplaced guilt, but Travis had been near impossible to track down. The air needed to be cleared.

Travis swallowed the last of a cookie. "That being said, ma'am, these cookies are phenomenal."

"Please, you do not need to call me ma'am. Holly is fine, or you can call me Little Miss." She slapped a hand over her mouth as though shocked by her own words. "Oh, my God, I can't believe I said that. I'm so sorry." Her voice broke and tears filled her eyes.

Fuck, nothing gutted him more than the sight of his woman in pain. She'd gone through a fuck-ton in the short amount of time they'd been together, and he'd vowed to himself to make this Christmas season her the first one full of love and laughter she'd had since her sister died. And here she sat bleeding out painful emotions all over the place.

"I'm sorry for it all. I know it means nothing, and I can't imagine what you've gone through. The fear, and the anger, and the injustice of it all." She shook her head. "I'm just so sorr—"

Travis held up a hand. "That's enough," he said in a cutting tone that had LJ glimpsing the no-nonsense MC president for the first time since he opened the door to the man. "I'm not here for an apology, and I won't accept one from you because you don't owe me a fucking thing. Least of all, an apology."

With his gaze still on Travis, LJ pressed a kiss to the side of Holly's head as he ran his hand up and down her arm. She leaned heavily into his side. If the comfort of his touch helped soothe her in any way, he'd keep his hands on her for the rest of her life.

"But I knew," she said as she lightly pounded her fist against her chest. "I *knew* deep down you hadn't murdered my sister. Something had always seemed off. A gut feeling, but I let them sway me."

LJ wasn't the only one gravely affected by the agony in Holly's voice. Travis placed his mug on the table, then rested his elbows on his knees. "Holly, you were fucking twelve," he said in his ruined voice. "And if I remember correctly, you did tell the cops you thought I was innocent."

She had. Or so she'd mentioned to LJ. When interviewed by the police, she'd been asked if she'd ever had an interaction with the MC president. Holly told a story of the man's kindness toward her when he found her bleeding in the street after falling off her bike. He'd seen her home without harm, hell, without so much as a four-letter word, then repaired her bike on the sly. When he'd been suspected of murdering her twin sister, Joy, Holly had confessed the story stating the man who'd had so many chances to hurt her but didn't could not have been the man to kidnap and murder a twelve-year-old girl.

"But I should have done more. Been more adamant. Not let them influence me." She shook her head, eyes red, lashes clumped together from crying.

Travis' laugh was ugly and bitter. "Wouldn't have made a lick of difference, Little Miss. There was hard physical evidence. Planted by the cops, but I'm sure every murderer claims the cops planted evidence. It was enough to convince twelve members of a jury I was a child killer. They wanted me behind bars, and they got it. You could have thrown an epic fit in the courtroom, and you'd have just been patted on the head and looked at with pity."

LJ flinched right along with Holly at the disturbing visual. But… "He's right, sugar. It's time to let go of the guilt."

"I'm all right, Holly. I'm out. I have my freedom," Travis said, but the shadows in his eyes told a different story. The man might be free now, but he'd suffered through his years in prison. As though thinking along LJ's lines, Travis absently touched the scar at his throat. "If anyone owes someone here, it's me who owes you a debt of thanks I can never repay. I had a life sentence without the possibility of parole. I've done plenty in my life to earn me a spot behind bars. Sure as fuck never hurt a kid or a woman, but I saw the conviction as karma come to kick my ass for all the other shit I got away with. You coulda let me rot. You had no obligation to free me."

"Yes, I did," Holly said simply. She straightened and wiped her eyes. "And if you won't accept an apology from me, I won't accept thanks from you. It's Christmas. Almost a new year. Time for new beginnings."

LJ smiled. Damn, his woman was something. "I don't know what your plans are," he said to Travis, "but my club does Christmas in a pretty big fucking way. You're welcome to stay here with us and join us for the holiday."

Holly beamed up at him. "Thank you," she mouthed before laying her head on his shoulder.

With a nod, Travis lifted his mug in salute. "Thanks for the offer. If you mean it, I think I'll take you up on a place to crash. Maybe the holiday offer too."

Holly beamed. It was as though the sun shone straight out through her smile. Clearly, offering their home to Travis had been the right decision.

Yeah, mission accomplished. This was gonna be a great fucking Christmas for his girl.

Chapter Fourteen

MAVERICK

"You got plans for New Year's Eve, brother?" Maverick asked Zach as he handed him an uncapped bottle of beer. Been a while since the two of them had time to sit and chill together.

After taking a long drink, Zach looked at him with a scrunched face. "I look like I run our fucking social calendar? You gotta ask Toni that shit, man."

Mav laughed. "Social calendar? Sounding a little yuppy there, brother."

"Fuck you."

"Sweet offer, but Steph's got me covered." Mav stretched. His back had cramped up after being in a few interesting positions earlier that morning. Been bothering him off and on all day. Not that the uncomfortable twinges weren't well worth the mind-blowing way he'd shot his load—twice.

"Jesus," Zach muttered with a roll of his eyes. "You're on fucking fire tonight. What's up with the New Year's question? You guys having a party or something?"

"Nah. Well, kinda." Maverick took a moment to revel in the rush of excitement he experienced every time he thought of marrying Stephanie. Fuck, he loved that woman. It was beyond

Joy

time to lock that shit down and officially tie her to him for life. Make sure all the motherfuckers in his life knew she was well and truly off-limits.

"What's that mean?" Zach took another pull of his beer. The clubhouse was uncharacteristically quiet. Most of the guys were busy with some kind of holiday obligation.

"Means there'll be an after-party."

"This is like pulling fucking teeth, brother, but I'll play your game. A party after what?" Zach asked in an overly interested voice.

"Party after Steph and I get hitched." Mav did an internal backflip as he dropped the bomb, waiting for Zach to react.

His best friend didn't disappoint. Zach froze with the beer bottle halfway to his lips. "Come again?"

"Not sure I could right now. Steph's already wrung two outta me today."

"Christ, can you stop thinking about doing your woman for two minutes? Did you just tell me you and Steph are getting married on New Year's Eve?"

With a nod, Mav lifted his beer as though toasting. "That's the plan, brother. Asked her a few days ago. At first, she said she wanted to wait until her pops got out of prison, but the old guy flipped his shit when she told him that. He wouldn't hear of it. If he's on board, why the fuck else would we wait?" Thank Christ, because the thought of delaying years for Steph's father to get out of prison sucked ass. He'd do it, of course, but he wanted them married and as soon as possible.

"Son of a fucking bitch," Zach said as he slapped Maverick on the back. "Congratulations, brother. Man, I'm happy for you guys." The cheek-splitting grin he wore conveyed the truth of his words.

"Thanks." Mav took a sip, cleared his throat, and cast his friend a side-eyed look. Zach still had a goofy smile plastered across his face. "Wanted to ask you something."

"Sure, anything."

Insecure wasn't a word often used to describe Mav. Yeah, he was a confident guy. Why not walk through life with a high head and a King Shit attitude? Beat self-doubt and uncertainty any day. *Been there, done that shit.* But at that moment, when he was about to ask his best friend such a significant question, nerves had Mav's tongue lying limp in his mouth.

"You good?" Zach asked with a frown.

"Yeah." Christ, his voice sounded stiff and strangled. "I, uh, was wondering if you'd…uh…"

Zach smiled then and pulled Mav a into spine-snapping hug, slapping is back once again only this time he nearly knocked the breath of Mav. Damn gym owner. "Mav, I'd love to be your best fucking man. I'da kicked your ass to Kentucky if you'd picked someone else."

Well fuck, now he was gonna go and get all choked up. Instead, he cleared his throat, shoved Zach away, and said, "Christ, you turn into a pussy with stuff like this, don't you?"

Zach laughed, but their gazes met, and he saw the understanding in his friend's eyes. They were brothers every sense of the word but DNA. Both had been through some serious shit on their own, for the club, and with regards to their women. Forged some unbreakable bonds.

"So, what're you guys planning?"

"Keeping it small. Just here at the clubhouse. Brothers and their families."

"Sounds perfect to me."

They tapped the necks of their bottles together. "Anything new on the Chrome Disciples?" Mav asked after a few moments of comfortable silence.

A scowl appeared on Zach's Mark-Paul Gossilier look-a-like face. "No. I got eyes and ears out there, but these assholes don't seem to be making many waves besides occasionally popping up to annoy us."

"Maybe it means they're mostly shit-talkers with nothing to back it up."

"Hope so." Zach sighed and ran a hand down his face.

"My turn to ask. You good?"

"Yeah. Got some shit going on with Toni."

Mav's stomach dropped straight to the floor. "Fuck, you guys having trouble?"

With a wave of his hand, Zach said. "Nah, nothing like that." He finished his beer and set the bottle down. "There's this girl, teenager, been coming 'round the diner for the last week or so. Real sweet kid, according to Toni. I haven't met her yet. Anyway, she was looking for a job but is too young to legally employ, so Toni has been giving her little tasks and compensating her with meals and some cash. Pretty sure she's homeless."

"Well, that's fucked up, brother." Mav's own childhood was pure shit. Always made him a little sick in the stomach to hear of kids sharing a similar fate.

"Yeah, it's ripping Toni's heart out. You know my ol' lady. Thinks it's her job to save every lost kid out there."

Mav let out a light chuckle. That was the damn truth. Toni had a massive heart and gave chunks of it away to all the kids she helped set on the right path. She was a damn good woman and perfect for Z.

"Let me guess, she wants to adopt a stray."

Zach blew out a breath. "Hit the nail on the head. She wants to offer the girl, Lindsey is her name, and Toni wants to offer her a place to stay…indefinitely."

Mav whistled. "Big commitment, brother." Better Z than him. Mav may want to keep Steph forever, but he was too selfish a dude to start taking in kids. At least for the time being, he wanted his free time to be spent with Steph and only Steph. Having kids was something they'd talked about exhaustively because he was pretty certain he didn't want them any time soon, and he'd needed Steph to know that if they were going to move forward. Surprisingly, Steph seemed to be of a like mind. At least for now. Perhaps a topic they'd revisit in the future, but neither was anywhere close to ready for that kind of responsibility. "You on board?"

"You know," Zach said as he stood and rounded the bar. After fetching both of them another beer, he turned to Mav. "It's fucking crazy, but I am."

"If anyone could take in a kid and not fuck them up worse, it's you two. Marriage and fucking kids, man," Mav said with a laugh. "When did we grow the fuck up?" They clinked their bottles again.

"You two assholes are in your mid-thirties. Not sure you should be proud of the fact you're just growing up now."

Mav glanced over his shoulder to see Jigsaw strolling into the bar. "Hey, brother. What the hell are you doing here? Shouldn't you be home staring at your woman, waiting for her to pop or some shit like that?"

With a snort, Jig took a seat on the other side of Mav and waved away the beer Zach offered him. "Iz wanted some time to work up a few sketches she's behind on. Just grab me a soda if you don't mind."

"Meaning she kicked your ass out for hovering and driving her batshit?"

One of Zach's blonde eyebrows climbed up his forehead. "Pretty sure she went batshit the moment she peed on the stick." He slid a can of Dr. Pepper to Jig, then returned to his seat next to Mav.

Jigsaw took a long drink of his soda, swallowing three gulps before he said, "I'd watch your mouth, brother. She may not be able to do much now, but she'll kick your ass clear across the state once the baby comes. Don't think Louie can save you either."

"Wouldn't dream of taking her on, man. I've watched her beat ass in the ring one too many times."

"Bet all that aggression makes for some serious kink between the sheets," Mav said, wagging his eyebrows up and down.

Never one to broadcast his shit, Jig just glowered at Mav.

"What?" Mav said shooting Jig the most innocent grin he could muster, which he admitted was more of a cocky smirk than anything resembling purity. But what could he do? He was who he was.

"Mav, tell him your fucking news already, brother," Zach said. Christ, he practically bounced with excitement.

"What, are you a fifteen-year-old girl?" Mav tossed at his friend.

"Just fucking tell him."

"Tell me what?" Jig asked as he did a quick phone check. For the past week, any time Jig had been more than twenty feet from Izzy, he'd checked his phone nearly every sixty seconds on the dot.

"I—"

"He's getting married!" Zach blurted.

Both Mav and Jig stared at him.

"What?"

"Seriously, brother?" Mav asked. "Thunder stealing, much?"

"You were taking too long." Zach shrugged and chuckled. "I'm excited for you guys. What? Fucking sue me."

"I ain't gonna sue you, but I might staple your fucking trap shut. It's my news!"

With a snort, Jig shook his head. "Why the hell don't you two just get fucking married? You already sound like you are."

Mav raised a brow at Zach, who scowled like he'd sucked back a mouthful of sour milk instead of beer.

"Fuck no!" Zach said. "I couldn't put up with your ass night and day."

"No worries then because I'd be the one taking your ass, not the other way around."

"Jesus," Jig muttered. "Wish someone had stapled my trap shut."

"What?" Mav said with a shrug. "I'd be a shit bottom. Let's be real."

"The fuck?" Screw's voice came from behind the trio. "Who's bottoming?"

"Zach," said Jig, completely straight-faced, which wasn't hard for the guy since he wasn't the most jovial of the crew.

Screw stopped dead in his tracks, mouth hanging open. "How did I not know this?"

Mav snickered as Zach opened his mouth to respond.

Jig beat him to it. "They're getting married."

With his brow wrinkled, Screw said, "Who? Z and Toni?"

"Nah, Mav and Z."

"What?"

"Jesus Christ," Zach said on a groan as Mav burst out laughing.

He couldn't help it, he loved this shit. It fed the jokester inside of him. "What can I say?" Mav said with a shrug. "He's got a big dick."

"Seriously?" Zach said as he threw his hands in the air. "This is your fault." He pointed at Jig. "And when the fuck have you seen my dick to know its size?"

As his mouth turned up in a slow, teasing grin, Mav lifted the bottle to his lips. "You saying I'm wrong? You don't got a big dick?" He took a drink.

"No, it's fucking huge. Just saying you've never seen it."

Screw's gaze bounced between the three of them like a spectator at a ping-pong match. "You three are hurting my fucking brain."

"Maverick proposed to Steph. She said yes. They're tying the knot on New Year's Eve." Zach said as he smirked at Mav.

What? That little shit.

"Hey! Congratu-fucking-lations, brother," Screw said, whacking Mav on the back.

The words and gesture barely registered. "Again, thunder-stealer?"

"Yep, dick-looker." Zach shot him the shittiest grin. Any other time, Mav would have been damn proud of his friend for his shit-giving abilities. Of course, when the joke was on him, it lost some of its appeal.

"All right, enough with the bullshit," Zach announced, lifting his bottle. In his left hand. "We all love that girl of yours, Mav."

"Oh, hold up!" Screw jogged around the bar and grabbed a beer for himself. After popping the top and ignoring the fact it flipped onto the floor somewhere, he said, "Okay, I'm good. Continue."

Mav chuckled. He couldn't ask for a better fucking family than this group of shit-talking fuckers.

"As I was saying. Steph makes a fantastic ol' lady, and she'll make just as good a wife. We're all glad you found one who's willing to take you on for life. And this club needs all the happy events it can get. Love you, brother." Zach lifted his bottle as he finished speaking.

"Love you, brother," the other three parroted.

Mav cleared his throat and blinked. Some fucking time to develop allergies. "Thanks. I—"

The door to the clubhouse flew open, and a tornado of red hair, muscle, and unintelligible grunts blew through the bar and straight into Copper's office. Their prez stomped with so much force the liquid in Mav's bottle rocked like a choppy ocean. Two seconds later, the office door slammed shut, and the Hell's Handlers' placard popped off its nail and crashed to the ground.

"The fuck was that?" Jigsaw said at the exact same time the other three held a finger to their nose. "Not it!" they all chorused, staring at a slack-jawed Jig.

"Oh, come the fuck on," Jig said as tossed his hands up. "No. No fucking way. I'm not doing it."

"Oh yes you are," Mav sing-songed.

"Nuh-uh. Find some other jerk-off. Not happening. He's liable to tear the fucking head off the poor asshole who walks in there."

"Sorry, brother," Zach said with a laugh. "You were too fucking slow."

Jig looked at Mav with the most pitiful pleading expression on his bearded face.

"Sorry, man," Mav said as he raised his hands. "Rules are rules."

With a snort, Jig stood and walked behind the bar. He grabbed a bottle of Scotch and speared Mav with a death glare. "Like you've ever followed a single goddammed rule in your life."

"Aww, don't be a sore loser, Jig," Mav called as Jig headed off to Copper's office, walking like a man going to his doom. Copper in a good mood proved a formidable man. Copper in a bad mood…Mav shuddered.

No thanks.

Jig gave the door a light knock. "The fuck you want?" Copper bellowed.

Without turning around, Jig held his middle finger up to the three of them left laughing their asses off at the bar.

What could Mav say? He was getting married, and it was his favorite time of year. Fate was on his side.

Chapter Fifteen

COPPER

A baby.

A fucking baby.

The words replayed again and again in his head as though on a repeat loop. Shell was having a baby.

His baby.

My baby.

Nothing else penetrated his mind but those words. Not the freezing air as he'd ridden his bike in the thirty-seven-degree weather. Not the business with the Chrome Disciples. Not the burn of the Scotch he'd pulled from his desk drawer. Not the look of complete devastation on Shell's face as he lost his shit and screamed at her.

Nothing but the baby made it through his skull and into his neurons.

A sharp rap on the door jerked his attention away from the nothing he'd been staring at. "The fuck you want?" he yelled.

A second later, Jigsaw appeared in his line of sight, dropping in the chair directly across from Copper's desk.

"Thought you might need this," Jig said, setting a bottle of Scotch on the desk. "But I forgot you keep a stash of the good shit in here so you don't have to share it. Selfish bastard. Guess you don't want this piss." He shoved the bottle to the side.

With a grunt, Copper pulled two glasses out of the same drawer he'd unearthed the Scotch. After pouring himself three times as much as he'd usually drink, he held the bottle over the other glass and cocked his head at Jig.

"None for me, brother," Jig said a with wave of his hand. "Izzy can go at any second. You know what that woman will do to me if I show up tanked?"

Fuck, he was really off his game if he'd completely forgotten Jig's kid was past due to be born. "Shit, wasn't thinking. Sorry."

With a shrug, Jig leaned back in the chair and propped his ankle on his opposite leg. "Ain't a thing. You and Shell get into it?"

Copper leaned back and swallowed half the liquid in one healthy gulp. Finally, the burn registered, waking some of the nerves that had gone into shock at Shell's announcement. "Something like that," he said. One more swallow polished off the drink, then he poured more. Just as much as the first time.

From across the desk, Jig stared at him with a raised eyebrow. "You crashing here tonight?"

"Planning on it."

Jig nodded, then he smirked. "You musta fucked up good. Didn't think Shell was the type to kick your big ass out. And so close to Christmas." He chuckled.

"Didn't. I left."

The grin slid off Jig's face. "You left?" He dropped his leg, straightening in the chair.

He took another drink. "Yep. Shell's pregnant."

Jig's eyes nearly fell out of his head. "Wha—uh, let me get this straight. You're saying Shell told you she was pregnant, so you left her?"

For the first time since walking out of the house, unease replaced anger as his primary feeling. "You don't know what you're fucking talking about."

"I know your woman is one of the best I've ever met."

Copper narrowed his eyes, causing Jig to laugh and raise his hands in surrender.

"That look doesn't scare me, prez. I also know your woman loves you more than you fucking deserve."

That drew a snort out of Copper. Who could argue with that statement?

"Know she's a phenomenal mother. She and Iz are tight. Even tighter since I knocked Izzy up. Shell's the only one of Iz's friends with a kid. She's been a lifesaver for Izzy through the pregnancy and planning. Iz told me how much Shell wants another kid."

Christ, he'd failed his ol' lady. First, telling her he didn't want kids, then flipping his shit. Even knowing how royally he fucked up, it didn't change his feelings on the matter. Having another child scared him to death. "You looking to have my fist in your face, Jig?"

As he lowered his hands, Jig shook his head. "No, brother. You're the one who needs some sense knocked into him. Wanna hear the last thing I know?"

Like he had a choice. "Spit it the fuck out."

"I know that there ain't a goddammed thing in this world better than holding your kid for the first time."

Jig met his gaze, a mixture of sadness and determination in his eyes.

Fuck.

Copper tossed back the last of his second drink, only this time the burn of the alcohol made him want to vomit. If anyone should understand his reservations, it was Jigsaw, whose first wife and child had been brutally murdered. Yet there he was, condemning Copper for his actions.

"Wanna talk about what happened?"

"No."

"Man, you're a hardheaded fucker, prez," Jig said with a snicker. "How about this. I'll guess. Shell told you she was pregnant. You freaked the fuck out. Thought only about yourself and what *you* need and want. Then you said some stupid shit that probably has your woman crying by herself at home. Last but not least, you stormed out."

Why the fuck couldn't he just kill Jigsaw with his glare?

Another of those damn laughs, and Jig was dead. The guy was better as a surly fuck. This happy and sensible version of Jigsaw didn't make sense.

"Shit's heating up. The Chrome Disciples are gonna be a big fucking problem, Jig. I can feel it in my bones. I got enemies. Men who'd love to piss on my grave. Men who'd have no problem targeting my family. It's irresponsible to add to it."

"You think you can't keep your woman safe? Can't keep Beth safe? Think the club won't have your back? Keep you breathing? Protect your family?"

"What, no, that's not it. I have full faith in the club, but we can't always prevent the bad shit, Jig. You of all people know that. This whole club knows that. How much shit have we gone through? I wasn't able to stop any of it." All of a sudden, fatigue hit him hard. Be it the large quality of alcohol he'd consumed in a short time or just life in general, he needed a fucking break.

"You know, you were one of the people to convince me life went on after a tragedy and that it was okay to live again. To be with my woman. Have a family."

"I don't have fucking dementia, Jig. I remember."

"Then maybe you should stop being a chickenshit and take your own advice."

"You're getting on my nerves, Jig."

The other man smiled, making the scar on his face even more pronounced. "I know it. Tell me the rest."

"That's it."

"Nah, brother. That's not all. Tell me the real fucking reason you're freaked the fuck out."

"The real reason." Copper reached for the bottle again, but Jig was fast, snatching it out of reach.

"Yeah. The one you're burying so deep, you're afraid to even admit it to yourself. The one that made you react like a fucker instead of a man who loves his wife and wants nothing more than another strawberry-haired, blue-eyed baby to dote on."

A bone-rattling, blood-chilling, heart-stopping fear snaked its way to the forefront of Copper's mind. Shell was his fucking world. He *loved* that woman. For some reason, she loved and wanted him as well. Despite him being sixteen years her senior. Despite him being the president of an outlaw MC. Despite him being an ornery motherfucker. Despite the fact there were details of his club he could and would never share with her. None of it mattered when it was just the two of them.

The thought of plodding his way through the rest of his life without Shell by his side had Copper feeling something he was wholly unused to.

Fear.

Dread so great he could breathe through it, so he shoved it down and refused to allow the thoughts to penetrate. Fear so consuming, it made him act like a complete and utter asshole, yelling at his pregnant woman and leaving her alone and crushed.

Fuck, if any one of his men had acted this way toward their ol' ladies, Copper would be the first to beat their ass.

"She had an emergency C-section with Beth. Everything was great through the entire pregnancy, until it wasn't. Until she was bleeding so bad, she nearly died. It was close, Jig. Closer than she'd even admitted to me. I saw the records."

With a snort, Jig shook his head. "Don't want to know how you got your hands on those."

"I had to know. Won't apologize for that. But it was bad. And she's at a high risk for it happening again. Too much is out of my fucking control. I can't..." He cleared his throat as it tightened, and an unfamiliar tingling buzzed in the corners of his eyes. Fuck, when had he become such a pussy? He could barely get the word out without wanting to curl up in the corner and cry.

"I get it, brother," Jig said, not a trace of humor or disgust on his face. "As you said, I get it more than most."

"Sorry if this stirs shit up for you."

"I'm good," Jig responded. "I had to embrace my own fear, or I'd have been howling at the moon these past nine months."

Copper grunted in response.

"You know the doctors will keep on her, right? They'll monitor the fuck outta your woman and your baby. Won't be the same this time around." Some of the other men wouldn't' understand. The ones without women, mostly. Even some of the men with ol' ladies had never experienced the threat of something happening to them.

"Almost lost her before I had her," Copper said.

Jig didn't respond. Just a nod. Then he slid the bottle across the desktop.

Fuck the glass. Copper lifted it, taking three long swallows straight from the bottle. By now, the liquor had dulled some of his senses, taking away the immediate panic he'd felt on Shell's admission. This chat with Jig was partly responsible, as well. Now, he was left with a sickening feeling of shame and guilt.

"Pretty sure I fucked up, royally."

Jig's head fell back as he let out a hearty laugh. "Yeah, I'd say you did. Luckily that woman will forgive you pretty much anything. Though you may wanna practice your grovel a bit."

Yeah, he'd be getting on his knees all right. Hopefully, he could stay down there once Shell forgave him. Lick her till she screamed. None of this erased his fears or the very real problems facing his club, but Jig helped him realize he still had to live his life. Had to allow his woman to live hers. He'd just make sure he did anything and everything in his power to keep his family safe.

"She's gonna be just fine, Cop. Her and the baby. You know that, right? Every man in this club has your back. This isn't on you alone. We're a team. A fucking family."

"Up here," he said, pointing to his head. "Sure, I know it."

"Too bad that organ doesn't run the show most of the time, huh?"

"You ain't kidding. Hey, can you give me a ride home? Pretty sure I'd attract every cop in the state at this point," he said, indicating the near-empty bottle.

Before he had the chance to answer, Jig's phone chimed with an incoming text. He had it read in record time. "Oh, fuck me," he said.

"What's up?"

"You might as well stay here, brother. Izzy apparently sent out an SOS to all the girls. They're gathering at your house to do some kinda workout DVD in the hopes of getting the baby moving."

Part of him felt relieved. The distraction would do Shell good, but now that he'd dislodged his head from his ass, he wanted to see his woman. Setting the bottle down, he pushed back from the desk. "Guess we're settling in here for a few hours."

"Looks like it. But I'll take you when you're ready to go. Long as I'm not at the hospital."

"Thanks brother. Rode here."

Jig laughed. "You fucking crazy? It's freezing."

"I know. Just needed it. Hate this time of year."

"I hear you, brother. Let's go hang with the rest of the jokers while our women are doing squats and shit." Jig stood and headed for the door.

"Hey."

Jig turned.

Copper walked to him and held out a fist. "Thanks, brother. Proud to have you at my back."

After bumping his fist, Jig nodded. "I owed you one. Don't fuck up again cuz I'm done."

Finally, Copper laughed, and the feeling of dread left him. He hung back as Jig made his way to the bar.

A baby.

Shell was having his fucking baby.

A grin split his face. Damn, the next few months were going to be amazing. Watching her change and grow with his child. Just the thought of her rounding out had his dick plumping.

He was a lucky bastard.

One who had a shit load of apologizing to do.

Chapter Sixteen

IZZY

Izzy adjusted her over-the-belly maternity workout pants as she stood waiting for direction.

Apparently, her girls had grown tired of listening to her complain about still being pregnant, so they took matters into their own hands. Viper and Mamma V had taken Beth for the night. Shell had called about twenty minutes ago, ordering Izzy to her home with instructions to be dressed and ready to workout. Then she'd climbed in Thunder's truck and made him pick up all the girls. Their ol' men would grab them later.

Izzy snorted to herself. Workout. Ha. Her belly was so damn big she could barely walk, let alone exercise. But she'd do just about any damn thing to get this kid rocking and rolling. Nothing else had worked. Not spicy foods, not sex, not membrane stripping. Figures, the kid of a biker being stubborn even before birth.

"Okay!" Jazz clapped her hands together, getting the attention of the group. "Listen up, girls."

Tonight, their group consisted of Toni, Shell, Jazz, Steph, Chloe, and Holly. Pretty much all the ol' ladies and Jazz. The usual gang. The women Izzy loved like sisters. Something she didn't often admit out loud, but certainly felt.

"I've got Steph coming around with a tray of tequila shots. There's two for each of you."

"What?" Toni said with a laugh. "You serious?"

"Yes. Shoot 'em back to back, okay?" Jazz said as she scanned the group.

"You're joking," Holly said, wide-eyed. "Are we doing a naked workout? Because that's what'll happen if I down two shots of tequila in ten seconds."

Really, was she serious? She had to be kidding. As Steph walked by Jazz with the tray, Jazz grabbed two shots and swallowed them one after the other to the gasps of all the other women.

Guess she wasn't kidding. Izzy chuckled.

"Told you, I'm serious. Now, drink. This isn't a naked workout, but some of you prudes might need the liquid courage."

"Guess Steph can skip them," Toni said as she picked two shot glasses from the tray.

"Har, har," Steph said. "For that, you get to do three."

Toni's eyes grew so wide, Izzy burst out laughing. "What about me? What the hell am I supposed to do?"

With a grin that had a chill running up Izzy's spine, Jazz said, "We all know you want that baby out of you more than you want to save face, so you'll be fine without the liquid courage."

"Okay," Holly said, a shot in each hand. "Now, I'm officially scared."

"You should be." Jazz winked at her friend. "Drink up, babe."

Looking at the shot glass like it contained a cockroach instead of tequila, Holly did as commanded. Who knew Jazz wielded such an iron fist?

"You ever think about being a dominatrix, Jazmine?" Izzy asked.

She winked again. "Who says I'm not?"

The 'ohhhs,' and 'get it girls' went around the room faster than the shots.

"Shh, shh," Jazz said as she laughed. "We all lubed up?"

Chloe hiccupped then covered her mouth with her hand. "Think I'm good." The words came out muffled.

"All right, here we go." Jazz hit play on the remote then backed up to join the rest of the group spread out around Shell's basement. The large sectional sofa had been separated and shoved to the wall as had a coffee table. Aside from that, the room was empty, mostly used as a playroom for Beth.

The screen of Copper and Shell's massive eighty-two-inch television lit up with the face of a prominent reality television star. One particularly known for the size of her rear. Suddenly, in neon purple letters, the words "Twerk Out" started flashing on the screen.

"Oh, fuck, no," Izzy said as she started to back away from the group

Her new enemies all started laughing. Except for Chloe. "I'm with her," Chloe said. She patted her ass. "This thing does not move separately from the rest of my body."

Spinning around with her hands on her hips, Jazz shot a deep scowl Izzy's way. "Do you or do you not want this baby to come out of you?"

"Uh, I do."

"Then come up here, shut your trap, and shake your damn booty." As she spoke, she wagged her finger in Izzy's direction.

Shit. Who knew Little Miss Skinny had such a bossy side. "All right, all right. I'm coming. I'll shake. Just don't hurt me."

The workout started pretty tame. Some stretches, lunges, squats, hip rolls and circles. All things to loosen up the hip area. Izzy struggled her way through it, ashamed of how far she'd fallen from fit. Returning to her pre-baby body would be a feat.

"Okay, this isn't so bad," Chloe said. "I'm down with this so far. Wait—uh oh. What's she doing?"

"She's just bouncing, Chlo. You got this, girl," Toni said with a laugh.

The on-screen coach continued with her squats, instructing them to 'get low', but this time added a bounce at the bottom. Izzy snorted, she might never get back up if she went down that low. But what the fuck, if the activity got the spawn moving, it was well worth it.

So she squatted, as low as possible, which wasn't very low, then bounced a bit before rising.

"Damn, Iz, how are you in better shape than I am when you're forty-six months pregnant?" Holly asked with a distinct whine her in her voice.

"Seriously, this is actually a workout, isn't it?" Shell asked.

"Down," the instructor said. "Now, bounce, bounce, bounce."

"Why the hell is she so perky?" Chloe grumbled.

Izzy bit her lip to keep from laughing. As ridiculous as this was, and even if it didn't send her into labor, this night with the girls was exactly what she needed. Some fun to take her mind off swollen ankles, a sore back, and peeing way too often. The night also served to take their minds off the new MC and the worry they'd all been seeing on their men's faces.

Ten minutes later, Izzy and her girls were all bent over, hands on the ground in a sort of downward dog position. With alcohol coursing through their veins, Izzy's girlfriends no longer had any problems shaking their booties with gusto. They giggled and laughed, though their twerk game was seriously lacking.

"What the hell are you doing, Jazz?" Izzy asked as she looked under her armpit at her friend.

"Look, I wasn't gifted with a round bubble butt, okay? I'm working it the best I can. You just worry about yourself over there, mommy."

"I think I'm fucking stuck in this position for the rest of my life," Izzy said as she rocked her pelvis back and forth, trying get her ass to pop. She had to admit, the movement felt great and loosened the sore muscles of her back.

"What the fuck are you crazy bitches doing?"

"Thunder!" Stephanie screeched as she stood straight up. "What the hell are you doing here?"

"Oh, my God," Jazz whispered under her breath. Her face had turned so red, Izzy couldn't help but throw a little shade her way. She had organized this whole thing, after all.

"Hey, Thunder, can you watch Jazz twerk? Maybe give her a few pointers."

The death glare Izzy received was well worth the laugh that almost made her pee herself.

"No, seriously," Thunder said, glancing around the room at the no longer dancing ladies. "What the fuck are you doin'? I thought I was bringing you all here to braid each other's hair and watch sappy movies and shit."

"We're trying to twerk Izzy's baby out of her," Holly said, then dissolved into a fit of giggles. Steph joined her, followed by Jazz, and soon the whole lot of tipsy girls were laughing their asses off instead of shaking them.

Only Shell remained standing with an amused but sober smile. Huh, now that she thought of it, had Shell taken the shots like the others did? Or had she slyly avoided them?

Interesting. Hopefully, she'd remember to ask her friend about it later.

"No, no, no, no, no," said Thunder with a wave of his hand. "Just, no. You ladies need some serious help. Let a pro show you how it's done." He pulled his shirt off, then walked to the front of the room amidst Stephanie's whistling and Holly's shriek.

"Oh yeah, take it off," Jazz yelled at the same time Toni muttered, "Damn, boy."

Izzy arched an eyebrow at Jazz.

"What? I don't have an ol' man. I can ogle the prospect all I want."

"What are you doing here, Thunder?" Shell asked, her voice laden with suspicion.

He lifted his hands, revealing an impressive flex and play of abdominal muscles. Damn, the boy was a looker for sure.

"Prez sent me to just check in. No biggie."

A good idea, something Izzy would have thought of herself was her mind not clogged with worries about labor, delivery, and turf wars. She was tough, but come on, who wasn't a little scared their first go-around? First and last, that was. As someone who'd never described themselves as maternal, Izzy was pretty sure they'd be a one kid family. That was if she didn't screw this kid up so bad, they ran away from home before age one.

"All right, ladies, watch me." Thunder held his hands up in front of himself, palms out. "Now turn them, so your fingertips face three and nine o'clock, got it?"

"Yeah, sexy, we got it."

Izzy burst out laughing. Jazz was fun, but not usually mouthy or sexually aggressive. This was a side of her none of them had seen. And it was hilarious.

"How many drinks did you have?" Izzy whispered.

"Uhh, perhaps four shots of tequila. Oops." She bit her lower lip in the phoniest sheepish face Izzy had ever seen.

"Now, keep your hands like that and place them on your thighs, somewhere above your knees. You with me?"

"With you," Holly yelled out.

"Arch your back?" Thunder demonstrated, getting a deep curve in his back before he stood and checked everyone's posture. "Come on, Steph. You can do better than that. Stick that ass out."

"Jesus," Steph grumbled, but she did as Thunder asked, sticking her butt out more.

"Good." Thunder resumed the position. "Now, curl your spine up, then arch it again, fast, throwing your booty out as you do it. Like this." He demonstrated a few times.

Izzy had to admit, the guy had moves.

"Keep practicing, and soon you'll be able to do this." Thunder sped it up, bouncing his ass over and over again as all the girls started to whoop and cheer.

Before she knew it, Toni had pulled her phone out, cranked up a playlist, and started a full-on dance party. Izzy shook it as best she could, laughing and generally having a blast with her girlfriends. Thunder was in his element, showing off moves that might earn him a beat down later if the men caught wind of how he'd been dancing with their ol' ladies.

This had been an awesome evening. Hopefully, Jig also had a good time chilling out with his brothers at the clubhouse. They both needed a night off from the stress of becoming new parents and Jig's worries in general. Though, now that she thought of him, she couldn't wait to crawl into bed with him.

Soon.

After wiping a few escaped strands of sweaty hair off her face, Izzy snuck off to Shell's kitchen. "Water," she said when she saw one of her best friends standing at the counter. "Must have water." She moved toward the fridge.

"Sit," Shell said, pointing to a barstool at the end of the island. "I'll get it. You've gotta be exhausted after all that activity."

"Thanks, girl." The refrigerator was covered in colorful papers with drawings of rainbows, butterflies, and people. Beth's creations all displayed by an amazing mom. Shit. Would Izzy have even thought of that? She'd probably put the pictures on the counter, then accidentally spill coffee all over it.

Shell strolled over with a cold bottle of water in her hand. "Of course."

The cold liquid felt fantastic as it slid down her throat, cooling her. "Whew, I didn't realize how sweaty I was getting in there. It's gonna take me forever to get back into shape."

With a snort, Shell leaned her hip against the island. "I know you think you're the biggest pregnant woman to ever walk the earth, but trust me, you look fantastic. I think I was at least twice your size when I was pregnant with Beth."

A cloud moved over Shell's expression, and she grew quiet, sitting on the stool next to Izzy.

"Hey." Izzy bumped her friend's shoulder. "You okay?"

"What? Oh yeah, I'm good."

"Hmm." After another drink of water, Izzy said, "You didn't drink."

"Uh, what? Don't know what you're talking about."

"You didn't have any shots."

"Oh, yeah, uh, well, that's because…"

Izzy met her friend's gaze. She smiled. "Holy shit, Shell. Congratulations." She drew Shell in for an awkward hug considering the belly between them. "I always figured you'd be bouncing off the walls with excitement when you got pregnant again. Oh, shit. What'd I say?"

Tears ran in rivers down Shell's cheeks. She shook her head. "Nothing. It-it wasn't you."

"What is it, sweetie?"

"C-c-copper doesn't want a baby." Her lower lip trembled.

Goddammit, if this baby would just come out, she could kick Copper's ass for Shell. "Oh, bullshit."

Shell's head snapped up. "What?"

Okay, so maybe this was the reason most didn't choose her for a heart to heart. She tended to be far too blunt and not very touchy-feely as far as her emotions went. But whatever. Shell knew how she was, and if she wanted to open up, she'd get raw Izzy. "Copper is king of all these macho, alpha, walking testosterone factories."

Shell's face scrunched in confusion. "Okaaay…I'm gonna need a little more than that."

Rolling her eyes, Izzy winced as her belly tightened. No pain, nothing regular, just lots of random uncomfortable tightening. If this was the warmup, the real thing was going to be a bitch and a half. "The desire to knock up their woman is in their DNA. The more alpha they are, the more they want to impregnate you. It's basic science. Look it up."

Shell barked out a laugh. Then another. And another until she was bent over with her hands on her knees hysterical. "Oh, my God, Izzy. You're the freakin' best. I didn't realize how much I needed that. And I'm pretty sure your science is bunk."

Izzy shrugged. "Well, maybe, but trust me on this. That man wants you to have his babies."

"He flat out told me he didn't. Quite adamantly stated he wants a vasectomy."

"He's just freaking out. Scared about something and all that testosterone makes it so he can't have a normal human reaction to something that scares him. It makes him act like a stupid beast first. He'll come around."

"Hmm." With her lower lip between her teeth, Shell sighed. "I don't know. And I don't want to talk about this anymore. Let's get back in there before Jazz tackles Thunder. Pretty sure Screw would murder him if that happened."

"What's going on with those two, anyway?" Izzy had been wondering about that for the past few months, but Jazz staunchly refused to discuss anything Screw related.

"Who knows. He's sniffing after her pretty hard, but Jazz says she has no interest."

With a snort, Izzy slid off the barstool. "I'm gonna have to call bullsh—oh, fuck."

With a gasp, Shell rushed over. "What's wrong? Are you okay? Contraction?"

With a shake of her head, Izzy looked down at her soaking wet maternity yoga pants. "No. I think I just pissed myself. Like seriously pissed, not a little I-sneezed-and-pee-came-out. Holy fuck, here comes some more. I've lost control."

Shell's face lit up, and she jumped up and down while clapping her hands.

"Why the fuck are you clapping? I'm gonna need fucking Depends."

Still beaming like a maniacal clown, Shell rolled her eyes. "You didn't pee yourself. Your water broke! The baby is coming!"

Izzy froze. What? The baby was coming. No, that couldn't be right. "I'm not having regular contractions." Nope. No way. No how. She wasn't ready. She'd only had nine months to turn herself into a maternal creature, and she was pretty sure she'd failed.

Shell shrugged. "Sometimes your water breaks first. Come on, let's get you to the hospital. I'll have someone call Jig for you."

Izzy shot her hand out and grabbed Shell's forearm, preventing her from walking away. "What? No. Shell, the baby can't be coming. I'm not ready. I can't do it."

With a soft smile, Shell stepped close and cupped Izzy's face between her hands. "You're the toughest woman I've ever met, Isabella. You're gonna rock labor."

Shaking her head, Izzy tried to ignore the wet pants, now turning cold and extremely uncomfortable. There were far more pressing matters at hand. "I'm not scared of labor," she whispered. "I'm not sure I can be a good mom."

"Isabella Monroe, you listen to me and you listen good," Shell said in a commanding voice Izzy had no choice but to focus on. "You're an amazing friend. And amazing ol' lady. And a fucking stellar all-around person. You can rock any goddamn thing in this world. Including being a mom. Are you gonna be queen of Pinterest and head of the PTA? No, but who the fuck cares about that. There's not a single doubt in my mind you'll be a kick-ass mom."

Izzy swallowed down a lump of emotion. Since she'd been pregnant, they'd been running rampant. Mostly impatience and anger, which surprised no one, apparently, but the warm-fuzzies came much more frequently as well. It was past time to get her body and personality back.

And add a tiny human to her little family.

Joy

With a nod for Shell, Izzy said, "Thank you. I love you too. Now, let's go. I'm ready to rock this labor shit."

Chapter Seventeen

TONI

"Honey, you have to try to relax," Jazz said as she pointedly stared at Toni's fingernails drumming on the counter over and over and over again.

"Huh?" Toni flattened her palm against the cool surface. "Sorry." Problem was, now she could feel her pulse hammering out of control. At least when she'd fidgeted, she had something to focus on besides the rapid pumping of blood through her system.

"You okay?" Shell asked as she came up behind Toni. Her friend rubbed her back, soothing away...well, nothing. Toni was too far gone down the tension rabbit hole to for a simple touch to level her out. Not that she didn't appreciate the gesture. Her girlfriends were the best. Neither would judge her for becoming overly involved with a teenage girl she might not be able to save.

"Sorry, guys. I don't mean to make you as batty as I feel. It's just been two days since Lindsey has come around. I'm really worried about her."

"Maybe she really does have a family," Shell suggested softly, still rubbing Toni's back. "I know we were all skeptical and didn't really believe her, but maybe it's true. And maybe they had plans or went somewhere for the holidays."

"Uh-huh. I'm sure you're right." Toni said, though none of them really believed it. The words were empty platitudes by a friend trying to keep her from going out of her mind. With a nod, she ground her heel into the floor, keeping her leg from bouncing. "I need to chill out. Besides, it's early. She might still show today." The clock on the wall read nine in the morning, the day before Christmas Eve, and the diner was the quietest it had been in ages. Tomorrow they'd be open, but Toni planned to spend Christmas morning in bed with Zach rather than at her place of business. Since her staff more than likely felt the same— about their own families, not Zach—she planned to close for the entire day. "One of you distract me with some juicy gossip." Anything to keep her mind from spiraling further.

"Well, I talked to Jig about five minutes ago. Izzy just passed twelve hours of labor," Shell said with a sympathetic grimace.

"Oh, man, poor Izzy." Jazz shook her head. "I do not envy her."

"Yeah, it's no fun," Shell said with a dramatic shudder.

"Oh man, poor Jig is more like it," Toni said as she mimicked Shell's wince. "Can you imagine being trapped in a room with a laboring Izzy for twelve hours? Think I'd rather be the one in labor."

The three women laughed together behind the counter until a family of four walked in and sat at a table in Shell's section.

"Looks like I'm up," Shell said as she pulled her order pad out of her pocket. She patted the shoulder of the prospect assigned to babysit them as she passed by his table. Tex was what the club called him. Toni wasn't sure if he actually hailed from Texas, but he sure looked like it. Cowboy boots, wranglers, hell, sometimes he even wore a Stetson. Usually made her chuckle to see him in all that getup while wearing a prospect cut as well. Today, having him in a booth all morning only served as a reminder of what was out there. The potential dangers for Lindsey.

"I'm gonna go get that dry goods order in so I'm not stuck waiting until after the holidays," Jazz said. She lightly squeezed Toni's shoulder. "You good, hon?"

No. Far from it, but what could she do? She knew nothing about the girl beyond her first name and age. If they were even real. "Yeah, yeah, I'm solid. Go. Work. Earn me money."

With a sassy grin, Jazz said, "I'm about to go spend your money." With that, she sauntered off into the back of the diner where she and Toni's offices were located.

For what had to be the twentieth time that morning, Toni glanced at her phone. Nothing. No calls or texts unless she counted the one from Zach telling her he loved her. On a normal day, his customary text lifted her spirits no matter how chaotic the diner might be. Today, she couldn't get out of her own head no matter what.

Where was Lindsey?

Was she hurt? Scared? Cold? Alone? Hungry? Being abused? The questions went on from there, growing in severity until she could barely stand herself. Over the last year, since she'd started hiring at-risk youth for part-time weekend work, Toni had encountered dozens of kids in situations as bad or worse than Lindsey's. For some reason, this gangly, redheaded, freckled teen had wormed her way so deep under Toni's skin, she couldn't get the girl off her mind. Something about her called to Toni. A sadness representative of a difficult, possibly even traumatic life without the accompanying bitterness so often found in these teens. Lindsey was sweet, respectful, hardworking, and even funny when she let her guard down.

Bottom line, Toni had fallen in love with Lindsey and wanted to give her everything a thirteen-year-old girl should have, starting with a safe and warm place to lay her head at night. When Zach had agreed to the idea of opening their home to the lost soul, Toni had been floored. Not that she hadn't thought Zach would do something so generous, but she'd dropped the bomb out of the blue. Anyone would be skeptical of such a huge undertaking at first.

But not her ol' man. He'd seen straight into her soul to how important Lindsey had become. Zach knew Toni wasn't a frivolous woman prone to flights of fancy. So he'd listened, let her lay her heart on the table, then he'd wrapped it in silk and agreed to keep it safe.

Too bad nothing could keep it protected from the fear she'd had since Lindsay vanished two days ago.

"Bye, Miss Toni. Thank you for the holiday meal. You have yourself a good Christmas, ya hear?"

Toni glanced up, forcing herself to smile at the gentleman who was in her diner at least three hundred days of the year. She'd taken care of his bill today as a little holiday treat. "Thanks, Earl. You too. See you the day after Christmas?"

"Yes, ma'am," he quipped as he used his cane to slowly shuffle toward the door. Shell beat him to it, holding the door open for him to exit.

That was Toni's staff. Willing to do small, simple things that went above and beyond for their customers. Not because they were trying to earn more business or tips, but because they were a great group of individuals who cared about the people in their community. Toni was so proud of her little diner family. And proud of her big, loud, crazy biker family as well.

All right, time to snap herself out of this funk and get with the program. By now, the diner was a pretty well oil-machine, running with little to no supervision necessary from her. Especially since she'd hired Jazz on as manager. As often as possible, Toni jumped in to help in any way she could, most frequently taking on the role of hostess. But she'd done it all. Waitress, bus tables, wash dishes. Only thing she didn't venture into was cooking. Her one attempt at helping their chef Ernesto nearly had him in tears. Martha Stewart, she was not.

But Tex, well that guy apparently loved to cook. He'd asked a few times since he began prospecting three months ago if he could hang in her kitchen with Ernesto. Toni was more than happy to feed his desire to learn. Hell, maybe she could even employ him as a cook someday.

To keep her mind occupied, she wandered over to Tex's booth with a fresh pot of coffee. Poor guy looked bored out of his mind, playing on his phone. "Refill?" She asked the baby-faced blond who couldn't be much older than twenty-one. He might look like a boy, but from Zach told her, the guy had life experiences that would turn her hair gray.

"No, ma'am, I'm all good, thanks."

The ma'am got her every time. So freaking polite. "Hey, there's absolutely nothing going on today, and no one has had so much as a whiff of the Chrome Disciples in the last few days. Why don't you go on back to the kitchen and work with Ernesto. He'll have plenty of time to show you some tricks."

The prospect's face lit up then fell. "I should probably stay out here."

"You'll be twenty feet away. If someone comes in, you'll hear. Seriously, it's all good. And if Zach or Copper get on your ass, I'll take the blame."

He tilted his head as though assessing the truth of her words. Prospects weren't exactly used to someone having their back on something like this. "Yeah?"

"Cross my heart," she said, making an X over her chest.

"Huh?" His brow scrunched.

"Yes. I promise."

"Sweet. Thank you, ma'am," he said as he shot out of the booth and headed for the kitchen.

It wasn't until he'd disappeared behind the hinged doors that she allowed herself to check her phone again, which was stupid because she'd have heard or felt it should anyone have tried to get ahold of her.

With a sigh, she reached to her back pocket only to frown as she encountered the empty pouch. "What the..." Toni glanced around the dining area, then peeked under the last table she'd worked at. "Where did I..." She scratched her head, then cursed out loud. "Shit. I left it by the coffee maker."

What the hell was wrong with her.

A balding man in a wrinkled T-shirt, eating alone, stopped her as she tried to rush by his table. "Excuse me, miss?" he asked.

Though she wanted nothing but to ignore him as irrational worry for Lindsey threatened to consume her, she slowed and gave the man her attention. "Yes, sir, is there something I can get for you?"

"I want some hot sauce."

"Coming right up." She shot him a smile then rolled her eyes as she turned away. "Wouldn't kill you to say please," she grumbled under her breath as she darted behind the counter.

First things first... Her phone rested screen down, right next to the brewing pot of coffee. Toni snatched it up. "Shit!" she yelled. Of course, of fucking course, there'd be a missed call from an unknown number in the three minutes she hadn't been paying attention. Normally, she'd never answer or return one of those, but with Lindsey who knew where, she didn't think twice about calling back.

The phone rang. And rang. And rang five times before generic voicemail picked up.

"Dammit!" Toni yelled. She blew out a breath, closed her eyes and counted to ten before trying the number again.

With each ring, Toni's gut twisted tighter. As it rang for the fifth time once again, she began to lower it from her ear when she heard a whispered. "T-Toni?"

The phone was back at her ear in the blink of an eye. "Yes! Yes, it's me! Lindsey? Oh, my God. I've been so worried about you. Where are you? I can barely hear you. Are you okay?" A rushing sound dominated the noise, hitting her ear.

Wind? Water? Where the hell was she?

"I-I need...um, is there any way you can come get me?" in a timid voice.

God, she sounded so small. So scared. She should never have let Lindsey leave the last time. This was exactly what she'd been afraid of. "Of course I'll come. Where are you?"

"Uh…outside somewhere. I think it's a campground. I saw a sign. Something about a river." A repetitive clicking made her words difficult to follow.

Shit, were her teeth chattering?

Campgrounds. Her brain ticked through the ones she'd heard of or been to when she was younger. God, there had to be dozens through the Smoky Mountains. Was she even in Townsend? As the possibilities ran through her mind, the noise coming through the phone registered as rushing water.

There was campground not too far, set right on the river.

"Little River Campground?" There were a few areas of dangerous rapids along that river. The kind that claimed the lives of a few foolish and overeager tourists each year. Why would she be there? How had she gotten there? All questions she could quiz the girl on later. None of it mattered more than getting Lindsey to safety.

"Y-yes, I think that's it."

This time of year, the place would be deserted. Toni cast a quick glance out the window. Gray clouds rolled by, tumbling over each other in an ominous dance of impending precipitation. Snow was expected to start by noon, making for a picturesque white Christmas, but a nightmare for a thirteen-year-old girl without shelter in the mountains. "Okay, sweetie. I'm coming for you, but first, tell me if you're hurt."

"N-no. N-not really. I'm okay. J-just very cold."

Not really? Shit, they didn't have time to get into exactly what had happened right now. Not if Toni wanted to get to her as fast as possible. The longer they stayed on the phone, the worse Lindsey's shivers sounded. "I'm on my way. Try to find some kind of cover where you can get warm. And keep this phone with you. I'll call when I get there."

"T-thank you, T-to-ni," she whispered, then the line went dead.

She'd known something was wrong. Felt it deep in her bones. The feeling remained. That sense of doom, but she ignored it. "Shit, shit, shit," Toni said as she darted to her office. "Jazz!" she called.

Two seconds later, Jazz appeared in her doorway. "You okay, boss? You sound panicked."

"Lindsey contacted me. She's at Little River Campground, in trouble," Toni responded without glancing up at her friend and employee. Instead, she searched the top of her desk for her car keys, scattering papers and pens to the floor without care. "Shit! Where the hell are my keys?"

"Didn't Zach drop you off this morning? Maybe you didn't bring them," her manager said as she also scanned the desk.

Nooo. Her heart sank as her anxiety skyrocketed. "Fuck, you're right." She fisted her hair on either side of her head, resisting the urge to pull until the sting overrode her helplessness.

"I'll drive you," Shell said from the doorway. "It's practically dead in today. Jazz, can you handle my tables?"

"Yes, of course. You two go. I'll hold down the fort. Go. Go!" Jazz ushered them out of the room.

Hey! What about my hot sauce?" wrinkled-shirt called out.

Neither Shell nor Toni paid him any mind.

Without even thinking of their coats, Toni and Shell ran for the car. "What about Tex?"

Shit! She'd forgotten all about the prospect who would most likely be kicked out for letting them leave without protection. That was a worry she'd have to tackle later. Running back in for him would waste precious minutes.

"There's no time," Toni said as she reached the vehicle. "We need to go before the snow starts."

For just a fraction of a second, Shell hesitated. Then nodded. "Where are we going?" Shell asked as she yanked the driver's side door open.

"Little River Campground." Cold immediately penetrated her long-sleeved T-shirt. Shell had to be feeling it as well. Both wore jeans and fashion sneakers. Nothing to prevent the cold or wet from seeping in.

Though whatever she was experiencing, Lindsey had to be feeling it ten times worse.

"Geez, what's she doing out there? That place is a ghost town in the winter. There's nowhere to take shelter." Shell started her car and peeled out of the lot, heading onto the highway with far more speed than the law permitted.

"I don't know." Toni grabbed the *oh-shit* bar as Shell whizzed around a particularly sharp turn.

"Sorry."

"No worries. I'm good. Just get us there fast and in one piece. Maybe Lindsey picked the campground because it's deserted," Toni said in a vain attempt to distract herself from the treacherous trip. "I'm pretty convinced she's a runaway. An isolated campground seems like the perfect place to hole up until the temp drops too low. Maybe she has a tent. I don't know. I'm just trying to keep my mind from going to the worst case, which would be someone forcing her there for who knows what reasons."

Toni stared out the window, hundreds of possibilities rolling through her head. When was the last time Lindsey had eaten? Did she have a warm jacket? Some kind of blanket? Had someone hurt her? Taken advantage of her? She shuddered as she recalled the strung-out men under the bridge where she and Zach had searched earlier in the week. God, why hadn't she offered Lindsey a place to stay when she'd had the chance? She'd been so worried about coming on too strong, but maybe they could have prevented this.

"Hey."

The feel of Shell's hand closing around hers had Toni pulling her gaze away from the scenery hurtling by. Not that she'd actually seen any it.

Shell cast a quick concerned glance in Toni's direction. "Don't even go there, Antonia. There isn't a single thing about this that is your fault. I can feel your guilt ramping up from here."

With a sigh, Toni leaned her head back against the seat, then closed her eyes. "I know. You're right. I just…"

"You're an incredible woman who cares about everyone and wishes she could save the world."

Toni huffed out a self-deprecating laugh. "Yeah, something like that. Maybe not the incredible part."

"I'm serious. We're almost there. You wanna give her a call? See if we can pin down exactly where she is. This is a pretty big place."

"Okay, this is my first time here, so I'm clueless as to where to go," Toni replied as she dialed the number Lindsey had called her from. They passed a rundown cabin with smoke billowing from the chimney. One lone house next to the campground's entrance.

"I haven't been here since I was a kid." As she slowed the to a roll, Shell scanned all around the car." If I remember correctly, the road makes a big horseshoe shape, coming back out on this road a half-mile or so up that way. She tilted her head to the left.

With the cell pressed to her ear, Toni did the same. Five rings later, an electronic voice rattled off the phone number and once again encouraged her to leave a message. "Lindsey, it's Toni. I'm here and looking for you. Call me."

"No answer?"

Shaking her head, Toni tapped out a text with the same message she'd left by voice.

"Okay…" Shell glanced in the rearview mirror before focusing on the road again. "Shit! It's starting to snow. I'm just going to keep going forward, slowly. I think there are bathrooms up ahead. Maybe she's in there. You scan and keep calling. Yeah?"

"Yeah," Toni said, phone already to her ear. Once again, five rings and the voicemail message. "Fuck! Do you think something happened?"

When Shell didn't respond, Toni's stomach rolled. The chances of something happening to the girl were high. Especially now that the snow was falling in a thick white blanket.

"Shit, it's really getting heavy."

"You doing okay?" Toni asked.

With her hands clenched on the steering wheel so hard, her knuckles had whitened, Shell leaned forward for a better view. "Yeah. It's just us on the road, and I'm going so slow. Once we find her, we may have some trouble getting out of here, though."

Toni didn't say anything. They could cross that bridge when they got there. At least at that point, they'd all be in the car with heat and the ability to dry off.

Five minutes later, they'd probably only gone a few hundred feet. The snow was so thick, seeing beyond the curtain of white had grown near impossible. Any other time, Toni would have enjoyed the breathtaking and beautiful scene, but now all she saw was a dangerous barrier to finding Lindsey.

Both women leaned as far toward the windshield as they could manage. With her eyes squinted as though that would magically help her see through the veil of falling snow, Toni scanned every inch of the park. Shell did the same, as best she could while trying to stay on the rapidly disappearing road.

Something flickered at the very edge of Toni's peripheral vision. "Stop!" she yelled. Shell instantly slammed on the breaks, causing the car to skid forward about ten feet. "Go back a bit. I think I saw something!"

Shell put the car in reverse and rolled at a snail's pace. "Tell me when."

"Stop, stop, stop!"

Practically mashing her face against the window, Toni squinted. "I swear I saw something."

"Take your time Toni. And take a deep breath. You're breathing like you ran here from the diner."

She was. Her heart slammed against her rib cage and her skin felt too tight for her body. As best she could, she ignored the discomfort and forced herself to calm. This wasn't about her. It was about finding Lindsey and ensuring her safety from here on out.

Toni held her breath as she continued to search through the snow. The rapid rise and fall of her chest, combined with the sound of her own breathing caused too much of a distraction. "There!" she yelled as she made out the form of a person. "There's someone out there. It's gotta be her." She whacked her forehead on the window as she tried to get a closer look. "I think she's sitting on a picnic table or something."

Shell threw the car in park. "Okay, let's go. I'm gonna leave the car on with the heat cranked."

"Good idea," Toni replied as she opened her door. "Fuck! I didn't even think to grab my jacket and it's freezing."

"Yeah, I didn't think of it either. We won't be long at all."

The cold hit Toni like a slap to the face. Didn't matter that she'd just been toasty in the car; none of the warmth lingered when she stepped out of the vehicle. Almost instantly, snow soaked into her long-sleeved T-shirt. Within seconds she was the kind of cold that reached her bones and brought on full-body shivers.

"God, I hope she's dressed for this weather," Shell said as she scurried around the car to Toni's side. She grabbed Toni's hand. "Stay close. Last thing we need is to lose sight of each other."

Hand in hand, they jogged forward.

"Why isn't she running to us?" Shell asked.

"Not sure."

"This feels wrong."

Without voicing it, Toni agreed. But they'd come this far and would not be leaving without Lindsey.

"Lindsey?" Toni called when they were within twenty feet. The girl sat on top of a picnic table, huddled in on herself. With her legs drawn up and her arms wrapped around her shins, it was easy to see she was dressed in a similarly inappropriate manner as Toni and Shell. The girl must be a block of ice. She'd probably need a trip to the hospital to check for hypothermia and frostbite.

"Lindsey?" Toni called as they drew even closer to her.

The girl lifted her head from her knees. Tracks of tears were easy to see, streaming down her face. "I'm sorry," she said on a broken sob.

"It's okay, sweetie. We're just glad we found you." Toni let go of Shell's hand and took one tentative step forward, bringing her within touching distance of Lindsey. The teen's gaze darted around as though skittish. Despite her urge to lurch forward and gather the frozen child in her arms, Toni resisted. Scaring the girl into running would be disastrous. "Come on, we have the car just over there. It's still running and toasty warm. We'll get you to the diner and get some food and hot chocolate in you. How does that sound?" She held out her hand.

The girl's sobs only grew. Toni glanced at Shell, who shrugged and shook her head, seeming as confused as Toni. "Lindsey, can you walk?"

"I'm sorry," she said again.

"It's all right. I'm so happy you called me. You made the right choice."

"No, I didn't," Lindsey said in a voice so low, Toni almost missed. "I'm sorry. I had no choice."

The words had an icy chill running down Toni's spine that had nothing to do with the intense and biting cold.

Shell walked forward until she was at Toni's side once again. "Toni…" she whispered.

"I know." She glanced around, seeing nothing but white and trees as unease slithered through her stomach.

"I didn't have a choice," Lindsey said again as she sobbed and rocked back and forth, her slight body wracked with visible shakes.

"What do you me—"

The sound of clapping had both Toni and Shell whipping their heads to the right. Crank strode into their line of site, seeming to materialize out of the falling snow.

"Two heroes, excuse me, heroines, come to save the damsel in distress. So noble of you. So very fucking noble." He punctuated each word with a clap. As opposed to the rest of them, he had dressed appropriately for the weather with a thick leather jacket, heavy boots, and that goddammed Santa hat.

"Oh shit," Shell whispered.

Toni couldn't get her throat to vocalize. She stood there so stunned, she didn't even blink. The whole time? Was this a ploy the entire time?

They were screwed. They hadn't told Tex, and hadn't called their men. Ton had been so focused on getting to Lindsey, she hadn't given a single thought to her own safety.

Or Shell's.

And now she'd gotten them into a situation that seemed impossible to survive. Her entire body trembled, and she couldn't tell whether the terror or cold was getting to her more.

Crank walked forward, climbed up on the picnic table, and put an arm around Lindsey, who visibly recoiled from him. That had Toni wanting to lunge forward and claw his eyes out, but the cold had her muscles feeling sluggish, and he would probably swat her away like a pesky fly.

"I'm s-sorry," Lindsey said again.

"I-it's okay, sweetie," Toni said. She'd have cried if the tears wouldn't just freeze on her face. Beside her, Shell took her hand. Her cold fingers curled around Toni's and tightened to the point of pain.

Both Toni and Shell had been in shit situations before, but this? In a deserted campground in the middle of a snowstorm with a dangerous man? She swallowed as dread filled her.

This made her blood run cold even, without the outside temperature.

"Aww," Crank said. "Isn't that kind of her, Linds? Even after you tricked her for weeks, she still says it's okay. You know what we call that?"

When no one responded, he gripped the girl by the hair and yanked her head up. She let out a yelp then fell silent again. Toni began to lunge forward, but Shell grabbed her arm. "Don't be stupid," she said in a harsh whisper.

"I asked you a question," Crank said, shaking Lindsey by her hair.

"N-no," she said, her voice cracking. "I don't know."

"We call that a sucker." He laughed as though he was the funniest person in the world. Suddenly, Toni no longer registered the cold. Instead, a hot rage fired through her system.

"Okay, ladies. Come have a seat here next to my friend Lindsey." He glanced at a thick black watch on his left wrist. "We're gonna be taking a trip in about ten minutes here."

What should they do? Follow his orders? It was a horrible idea. Same as getting in a car with a madman. She couldn't run and leave Lindsey. Maybe Shell could make it to the car on her own…

"Toni," Shell whispered so low, Toni had to lean her head closer to her friend to hear.

"What?"

"Any chance you thought to let Zach know where we were going?"

"No. You?"

Shell shook her head. Any hope she'd had fled.

"I said come have a fucking seat!" Crank yelled, making them jump and Lindsey cry out again. He pulled out a gun and waved it in their general direction.

There went any hope of escape. No chance of Shell getting away now. Not with a weapon in the mix.

Toni met Shell's gaze and saw the same hopelessness she felt. They were in serious trouble.

Joy

With a stuttered sigh, Toni squeezed Shell's frigid hand, and the two started toward the picnic table. She looked to the sky, no longer feeling the snow as it pelted her frozen face, and sent up a little prayer that Zach or Copper would somehow know something was wrong.

Chapter Eighteen

ZACH

"Prez still passed out?" Zach asked Maverick as he sat at the bar sipping the morning's second cup of coffee. The first had come from the diner. A parting gift from Toni, along with a few muffins as she'd sent him on his way after he'd dropped her off. That coffee had been rich, piping hot, and full of flavor. This java was thick, burned, and tasted like liquid tar. To make matters worse, it barely could be called lukewarm.

But the sludge was chock full of caffeine, and that's what counted. Someone had to go wake Copper's hung-over ass up and Zach had drawn the short fucking straw. So, he needed to be on his game to survive the hibernating bear.

Last night, after about a bottle of Scotch, the prez had confessed his fight with Shell. Actually, the confrontation couldn't really be called a fight. It was basically Copper acting like a stupid fucking shithead. Something Zach took great pleasure in informing his president. Wasn't too often the guy screwed up so royally his men got to razz him about it. Zach would be lying if he didn't admit he got a little pleasure—okay a fuck-ton—out of watching the big guy squirm. Around two in the morning, after hours of guzzling booze, Copper had decided it was time to go home.

Thankfully, Zach had called Toni early in the night and let her know he'd be sticking around at the clubhouse to babysit their fool of a president. Took nearly an hour to convince the prez he wouldn't make it home alive. And even if he did, Shell would accomplish what the drunk drive home hadn't, and end his life for barging in wasted at three in the morning.

Jig had rushed off to meet Izzy at the hospital, and Mav offered to drive Toni home from Shell's where he'd set up a prospect to watch the house.

Now, it was nearing ten am and past time for Copper to head home to face the music. Shell would be off work in the next hour or so, giving Copper time to shower and prepare to grovel. Zach had also shot her a text last night, letting her know her ol' man was blitzed and crashing at the club, but she didn't need to worry. His brothers had his back. Even if that included telling him what a dumbass he'd been.

"Dead to the world," Mav said with an evil smirk. "You gonna wake him with a kiss, Prince Charming?"

Zach raised both middle fingers. "For that, I'm eating the chocolate chip muffin Toni boxed up for you."

With his panicked eyes wide and his mouth in a perfect *O* shape, Mav shook his head rapidly. "I take it back. I take it back. Don't eat my muffin!"

Stephanie strode over with her brows raised. "Hmm," she said, tapping her chin. "Do I need to leave you boys alone so Zach can 'eat your muffin,'"? she asked, making air quotes.

Mav slipped an arm around her waist and drew her close, placing a kiss on her neck. Then another. And another.

"Wow, never thought I'd rather wake a sleeping and hungover Copper, but it's gotta be better than watching you two slobber all over each other."

Giggling, Stephanie shoved Mav off her. "Boy," she said as she slipped her hands in her back pockets and rocked on her heels.

"I sure am hungry. Didn't get to eat anything before this one made me get out of bed and come here." She thumbed her hand in Mav's direction.

Stephanie could be so fun. "Oh, well, here you go!" Zach tossed her Mav's muffin. "Bon appetite."

"Ooooh!" Steph's eyes lit. One-handed, she caught the muffin, then took a giant bite, right in Mav's face.

Zach compressed his lips to keep from laughing.

"Oh, Zach, that's delicious. Thank you so much. Really hit the spot."

Mav narrowed his eyes. "You are an asshole," he said, pointing at Zach. "And you're going to be punished at home. Severely."

With a waggle of her eyebrows and a mouth full of muffin, Steph said, "Can't wait."

Ugh, time to go. Zach made a mock retching sound that had Mav giving him the finger this time. "I'm out. You two are gross."

Last thing he caught as he walked away was Maverick's low, "Come on, baby, give me a bite." Sounds of laughter followed him as he made his way up the stairs to Copper's room. Halfway there, his phone rang from his back pocket. Tex's name appeared on the scene.

Fear snaked down Zach's spine. There was only one reason the prospect would be calling, and it wasn't to shoot the fucking shit.

"Tex?" he barked as he lifted the cell to his ear.

"We got a problem, Zach." His voice was clipped, all business.

Instantly on alert and ready to jump into action, Zach said, "Give it to me."

"Toni got a call from the girl. She and Shell tore the fuck outta here while I was in the kitchen." His volume dipped at the end as though he was nervous to admit he'd been slacking on his job.

Rightfully so. He should be nervous as fuck and would be dealt with once Zach was sure Toni and Shell weren't in any danger.

"Fuck! Where'd they go?"

"Little River Campground is what they told Jazz."

Fuck, fuck, fuck. "I'm waking Copper now. When did they leave?"

"Five minutes ago."

When he found Toni, he was gonna tan her ass so bad she'd be sleeping on her stomach for a fucking week. Probably nothing in comparison to what Copper was going to do to Shell when he found out his ol' lady went charging off without telling him. While pregnant. With a new MC in town. With snow in the forecast. Yeah, that shit wasn't gonna be pretty.

"Want me to go there?"

No, he wanted the guy to toss his cut on the ground so Zach could piss on it before after he found his woman. "Stick with Jazz. Cop and I will head there now."

"Jazz says, don't be too rough on them, Zach. Toni's been a mess all morning worrying over Lindsey."

He snorted. Sure. He knew that. He'd gotten home around six that morning, with just enough time to witness Toni in full-on stress mode before he drove her to work. Lindsey's disappearing act had her in a tizzy like he'd never seen. Didn't excuse her or Shell from making such a stupid and reckless decision. It was supposed to snow for fuck's sake. Hard. Those campground roads hardly ever saw a plow.

"Fuck off, Tex. I'll call Jazz when I find them. You better keep her ass safe unless you want to be eating your Christmas dinner through a straw."

"Got it," Tex said, sounding appropriately chastised.

"Fuck!" Zach shouted after hitting end.

His chest tightened, and his mind ran wild as horrifying scenarios bombarded him. Using every ounce of strength he had, he forced himself to keep his shit together and take a fucking breath. Memories of a time Toni had been in danger from a madman made him want to tear the clubhouse apart, but he fought the urge. Hard. She'd been a badass then, and he had to keep faith she could handle whatever she and Shell encountered.

Sprinting now, he hit the top step then ran to Copper's door. After pounding five times without a response, he grabbed the door handle. "Fuck it." With far too much force, Zach shoved the door open and burst into the room.

Copper slept on his stomach, wearing only a pair of black boxer briefs in the exact same position he'd fallen when Zach finally put him to bed about six hours ago. They guy would be hurting today for sure, but it was his own damn fault and didn't matter for shit now that they had to get to the girls before they ended up stuck in two feet of snow at a deserted campground.

I'm gonna kill her.

Right after he fucked her into submission.

"Wake the fuck up, Prez," Zach said as he flipped on the lights then pulled up the shades on the two windows in the president's large room. Light flooded in, eliciting a groan from Copper. The man had to have a beast of a headache.

Before returning his attention to the prez, Zach spared a glance out the window.

Snow fell in a steady cascade of white already coating the ground.

Shit.

"The fuck, Z?" Copper grumbled as he struggled to sit at the edge of the bed. He had one hand on his head as he squinted his eyes against the harsh light.

"Cop, we gotta get the fuck outta here. Toni got a call from Lindsey, you know, the girl she's been helping out?"

"Uh...yeah, I think so." Copper nodded as he dragged a hand down his face. Bloodshot eyes met Zach's gaze. His brain hadn't quite caught on to the urgency in Zach's tone.

"Well, Toni and Shell took off from the diner to pick her up at the campground. And it's fucking snowing. Hard. Don't know what this girl is into, but Toni thinks she's been hanging or maybe living under that bridge where all sorts of nasty shit goes down. Have no idea what kinda state our women will find her in or if they're equipped to handle it."

Instantly awake, Copper jumped to his feet and yanked on the jeans he'd been wearing last night. He grabbed his phone then scowled at the screen. "Why the fuck didn't they call?"

"Don't know. Probably thought it was simple as picking the kid up and bringing her home. Plus, your woman probably wouldn't call you right now if you were the last man on earth."

"Fuck you." The look Copper shot him would have scorched a man unaccustomed to the president's ways.

"Last one. Promise."

"Tex?"

"In the kitchen when they ran out. Probably jerking himself off to the sight of Ernesto cooking."

"His ass is mine," Copper growled, buckling his belt.

Normally, Zach would let Copper have it, but he might fight him for this one.

"Something ain't right," Copper said. He jerked a T-shirt over his head at the same time he stuffed his socked feet into his giant boots.

Falling serious once again, Zach said, "I know. Feels all wrong. How the hell did a thirteen-year-old girl get all the way to the campground, and why the fuck is she there in the first place? There ain't shit up there this time of year. My gut's fucking screaming over this."

"I hear ya. You drive."

With a nod, Zach sprinted out of the room after his president.

Thank Christ for Copper, who barked orders and let everyone know what was happening as they ran through the main level of the clubhouse. Had Zach been the one in charge, everyone would have been left confused as fuck because he was useless at that moment, his mind consumed with worry for Toni.

Hadn't been that long since he'd seen her in the hands of a club's enemy. The stark memory of fear, rage, and fucking helplessness as he watched the woman he loved nearly lose her life hadn't faded in the least over the past year. In fact, as his feelings for Toni strengthened, so did the recollection of how easily she'd been put in harm's way.

"Your head in the game, Z?" Copper's gruff voice snapped him out of the past.

Zach blinked. Fuck. Somehow, they'd ended outside in the snow next to Zach's Ford F150.

Keep your head in the game.

"Yeah, prez, I got it. Let's roll."

They rode in silence for the first five minutes until Copper said, "Thank fuck this truck is a beast. Tomorrow I'm getting Shell a goddammed four-wheel-drive SUV. Can't believe I didn't do that shit before now."

Those two hadn't been a couple last winter, and Shell refused to accept shit from the club or Copper before that. He'd had to get pretty crafty to help her and Beth out. The moment Shell thought she was getting charity, she refused it. No way in hell would she have accepted the gift of a vehicle.

With a growl, Copper tossed his phone on the dashboard. "Neither is answering."

"They'll be okay, Prez," Zach said though his gut rejected his own words. "They're not stupid."

Copper snorted. "Think this little stunt proves otherwise." With a roar of frustration, he slammed his clenched fist on the dashboard. "She's carrying my fucking baby, Z." His voice dropped. "If anything happens to them…"

"It won't. We're fifteen minutes behind them max. Probably less because I'm driving like fucking Mario Andretti. We'll get there, collect them, raise a little hell, then head home and spend the rest of the afternoon fucking them."

Copper's lack of response did nothing to quell Zach's nerves.

He choked up on the wheel as the snowfall thickened. Dropping his speed wasn't an option despite the treacherous road conditions. At least he'd only passed one other idiot out in the storm.

Another seven minutes of icy mountains and snow passed before they turned into the campground. Together, they searched through the wintery landscape for any sign of their women.

"God, fuck!" Copper yelled the longer they came up empty. His hands gripped the dash so hard, his knuckles turned whiter than the snow. By now, his fingers had to be aching, but he never let up, as though he needed to hold the dash to keep from coming out of his skin.

A sentiment Zach echoed. With each passing minute, fear clawed at his back like a beast bent on tearing him limb from limb.

"Wait! There," Copper finally said, pointing straight. "Think that's Shell's car up ahead."

Miracle of miracles, the snow finally appeared to be letting up as Zach pulled up behind what was, in fact, Shell's little sedan, still running.

Zach kept the truck idling as well as both he and Copper stared out the passenger window. Seated on a picnic table were Toni, Shell, and between them, a girl who had to be Lindsey.

In front of that fucking table paced none other than Crank, gun in hand, phone at his ear.

"Send out an SOS," Copper ordered as he opened the door and stepped down from the truck. His boots crunched, and frigid air immediately flooded the cab of the truck.

"Done." Zach fired a message off to Rocket and Screw. They'd organize the cavalry. All he and Copper had to do was keep shit from going south for fifteen minutes or so. "How do you wanna play this?"

"Fuck if I know," Copper said. "Weapons?"

"I got Louie and one pistol."

"Bring 'em both," Copper said as he slammed the truck door shut. Zach didn't miss the gun he shoved in the back of his pants for easy access.

Zach scrambled out after his president, catching up to him when he was halfway to the picnic table. His thick leather jacket and motorcycle boots kept the worst of the chill at bay, but the biting cold stung his hands and face like a swarm of angry bees.

The desire to charge forward and rip Crank's head from his body with his bare hands burned a fiery path through Zach's body. His hands curled to fists as he imagined pounding the guy into the earth. Painting the snow red with his blood.

He'd die for this. For the fear written across Toni's face. For the way she shuddered and shook in the cold with her damp shirt and no jacket. It would be sweet, Cranks death. Zach only hoped Copper would let him have a piece of the action.

"Fucking hell," Copper said.

Zach echoed those sentiments in his head. The women sat on either side of Lindsey, huddled together shivering. Not one of them had any protection from the cold, not even so much as a fucking mitten among them.

His gaze immediately sought out Toni's. Her nose shone bright red as did her cheeks, no doubt chapped and stinging from the biting cold. She'd sucked her hands into the sleeves of her shirt, bunching the fabric to keep them inside. The effort couldn't have been worth much. Her shirt had soaked up the falling snow, appearing wetter than wet, and Toni visibly shook with the force of her shivers.

As did the other two.

Shell's arms crossed protectively over her midsection as though she could somehow keep the baby safe and warm while poor Lindsey hugged her knees to her chest.

"You boys got here fast," Crank said. The fucker still wore that stupid Santa hat the women had reported. "Wasn't expecting you here. Was just about to give these ladies a ride to our next destination. Blade is looking forward to meeting them." As he spoke, a white panel van rumbled down the road, slowing to a stop behind Zach's truck.

Wasn't one of theirs, so it had to be more Disciples.

Now they were fucking boxed in from the front and back.

By now, the snow had slowed to a light flurry, but the air remained popsicle cold.

"Went to a lotta trouble to get me here," Copper said. "Coulda just asked me for a fucking meeting."

With an unrepentant grin, Crank shrugged. "Talk is so very fucking cheap, as they say. I'm a man of action."

Copper grunted. Though he appeared calm on the outside, Zach knew his prez was anything but beneath his skin. His pregnant wife suffered, and Copper would make Crank suffer far worse.

The familiar weight of his bat dangling from his right hand provided Zach with a measure of comfort. Even though he couldn't hit bullets with it, he could inflict some serious fucking damage.

And he planned to.

"So that's what this was? A little demonstration to show me what you can do? Show me how easy it is to snatch what's mine?"

Another casual shrug. "Worked, didn't it? You're taking us fucking seriously now, ain't ya?"

"The girl one of yours?" Copper asked, pointing to Lindsey.

Crank's head fell back as he let out a loud laugh. "What's the matter, Copper? Your woman getting too old for you already? You the kind who likes 'em *real* young? Because you know, I can provide that if we come to an arrangement. You could even have this one right here." He thumbed his hand at Lindsey, who quivered and shook her head.

Toni wrapped an arm around her, whispering in the girl's ear and, hopefully, informing her Copper would never lay a fucking hand on her. None of the Handlers would. His woman was a fucking rock star. Terrified, frozen, yet more concerned with

Lindsey's wellbeing than her own. Just what he'd come to expect from her.

"Whatdya say to a little joint venture?" Crank asked. "Any idea how much we could make together moving weapons through these mountains? Fuck, man, we could all retire in a few years."

"Already told your president what I say to that."

Crank laughed again. "Did you? Hmm, you'll have to remind me. Not sure he passed on the message."

"Love to. I say, fuck you."

"That's how it's gonna be, huh?"

Zach could feel the tension and fury rising in Copper. It flowed off him in waves. Shell's gaze remained riveted to her man while Toni stared at Zach. He hated this shit. There they were, stuck with no real moves. Who the fuck knew how many guys were in that van behind them or how much artillery it held. Copper had his pistol, and Zach had Louie and one gun as well. Not much to go on. It wasn't as though they could start firing in the direction of the picnic table.

Crank held all the power. At least until the cavalry arrived.

"Let's cut the bullshit," Copper said, taking a step forward.

Crank's gun leveled on him. "Far enough."

As though he didn't have a deadly weapon pointed at his chest, Copper continued. "You're good. We can all see that. You fooled us for weeks then lured our ol' ladies here by tugging on their heart-strings like a fucking puppet master. Big man, you are. We don't want a piece of your business today, and we won't tomorrow or next year. My club doesn't deal in guns. All you're doing is setting yourself up for an ending like Lefty. One where your body fucking rots in a hole, and no one gives a shit you're gone."

The longer Copper kept them talking, the better chance of Rocket and Screw mobilizing help.

"They had fun with it too," Zach said, shooting a grin Crank's way. Toni's eyes widened at his words, but he couldn't worry about shocking her now. "Rocket sliced that fucker up real good. Starting with his dick. Messy shit, but fucking satisfying." He rested Louie on the ground, leaning his weight on the bat.

A flash of something, discomfort, maybe disbelief shone in Crank's eyes. "Bullshit," he said.

Copper just smiled, and if the prez hadn't been one of Zach's closest friends, he'd have trembled in fear, because that smile held a promise. A promise of pain. A promise of retribution.

A promise of death.

A faint buzzing sound could be heard from Copper's pocket.

The boys had arrived.

Game fucking on.

Chapter Nineteen

JAZMINE

Why did all the damn hallways have to look exactly the same? Maybe she should have turned right at that last split. She'd made a left, but now was totally lost and probably as far from Labor and Delivery as she could get. With a frustrated sigh, Jazz continued forward. Next desk she encountered, she'd ask for some help because her normally stellar sense of direction had done shit for her today.

Problem was, she couldn't concentrate worth a damn. Ever since Shell and Toni had practically flown out of the diner, she'd been on pins and needles waiting to hear from them.

Did they find Lindsey?

Did they even make it to the campground?

The moment they left, panic set in. Who the hell went to a campground alone in the middle of winter?

Trouble, that's who.

She'd stood in the office, freaking out for about two minutes before remembering Tex in the kitchen. The girls hadn't even alerted him to what was going down. From there, she'd run into the kitchen yelling like a lunatic. Tex caught her as she slammed through the swinging doors. After giving her a good tongue lashing for letting them leave, he grilled her with a million questions then called a justifiably irate Zach.

Not long after her girlfriends left, snow had begun to fall in buckets, and the few diners enjoying a late breakfast opted to take their meals to go rather than get stuck in town for the afternoon. At that point, Jazz made the executive decision to close up for the remainder of the day. She sent the employees home before the roads got too bad. She couldn't concentrate for shit anyway, her mind firmly on her friends.

Something was wrong. She felt it deep in her gut.

After Tex told her he'd been ordered to stick to her like glue, Jazz decided to head to the hospital to keep her mind from spiraling to every horrible scenario she could dream up. Izzy had to have that baby sometime, right? There weren't any cases of women being pregnant for the rest of their lives. At least not that she knew of. Some tabloid somewhere probably ran an article on that very thing.

As luck would have it, she'd pulled out right behind a plow, and had a fairly smooth trip to the hospital.

And now she was freakin' lost because she couldn't focus on anything but the worry for her friends.

As Jazz rounded the corner, she finally saw a clinic waiting room with less than a handful of waiting patients. "Radiation Oncology," she muttered as she read the sign. Whatever, as long as they could point her in the direction of the Labor Deck, she didn't care where she ended up.

"Excuse me," she said as she approached the blond twenty-something behind the window, staring at her electric-pink nails. "Um, excuse me."

The woman jumped then dropped her hand. "Sorry! Slow around here today. Holiday and all that. How can I help you?"

"Can you tell me how to get to Labor and Delivery. My friend is having a baby, and I made about ten wrong turns somewhere along the way."

With a wide, glossy smile, the woman pulled out a paper map of the large hospital. "That's so exciting! I just love babies. Congratulations to your friend. Here." She pulled a yellow highlighter from a cup with some kind of complicated drug name printed on the side. "We are right here," she said as she put a big circle around a little box labeled two-oh-two. "And you want to go here." She pointed to another spot on the map, one long, vibrant nail tapping the paper. "Easiest way is to follow this hallway to the end, then make the next two rights. Boom, you'll be there in just a few minutes." As she spoke, she traced the route with the highlighter. "Got it?"

"Yes, thank you. Happy Holidays." Jazz sent her a warm grin then turned, holding the trusty map. As she walked back to the hallway, past rows of vinyl chairs in the waiting room, someone let out a squeak of a sneeze. "Bless you," she said on instinct as she glanced in the direction of the sneezer.

Her eyes popped wide, and she stopped walking so fast, she nearly pitched headfirst onto the linoleum floor. "Mama V? Viper? What are you…"

She glanced over her shoulder at the receptionist who'd resumed the fingernail inspection. Right above her desk was a sign reading "Radiation Oncology." Okay, she hadn't read it wrong the first time. That meant…

"No," Jazz whispered as her legs seemed to lose all their support. She sank down on a chair opposite the couple who'd come to mean so much to her since she'd moved to Townsend. "Who…What…" She swallowed around a lump in her throat as tears immediately came to her eyes. Back and forth, she glanced between the two until her gaze finally settled on Mama V. She'd thinned, almost too much, and her face had taken on an ashy tone over the past few weeks. "Oh, God," she whispered.

How had she not known something was wrong? How oblivious could she possibly be?

"I made sure no one knew," Mama V said in a voice full of sorrow.

"Huh? What?"

The compassionate smile Mama V sent Jazz's way had guilt wrapping around her like a rope. Here she was, obviously suffering through something significant, and Jazz was the one requiring comfort. Selfish much?

"I can practically hear the questions bouncing around in your head. You couldn't have known. I was very careful to hide it from everyone and made sure Viper knew to keep it quiet." As she spoke, she lifted a frail hand to her head, brushing her long hair behind her ear. "Won't be able to hide it for much longer, though."

Her hair had thinned, the thick silvery locks Jazz loved looking stringy and sparse. Life could be so cruel.

"So, um, are you okay? I guess I'll start there."

Viper, who'd remained silent though the tough man looked ready to cry himself, threaded his fingers through his wife's. Cassie tightened her hand around his as she smiled at her husband.

Jazz's heart clenched. Cassie would make it. She had to. She and Viper deserved to live through their golden years together until they reached the end far, far in the future.

After a heavy sigh, Cassie said. "I have lymphoma. The doctors have been positive about my prognosis, and we've chosen an aggressive treatment course." She winked. "Don't worry, Jazz, this old bird isn't ready to fall from the nest just yet."

"But how are you feeling?"

"I'm feeling all right."

Viper snorted as he rolled his eyes, making his wife chuckle.

"Okay, fine. I feel like crap ninety percent of the time, but I'm tough."

"Yes, you are, beautiful," Viper said. "You make Izzy look like a kitten."

All three of them laughed, though Jazz had to force the sound through her lips because it's what Viper expected.

"Well, uh, what can I do? Do you need food? I can't cook for shit, but I can have a prospect start bringing you meals from the diner. Do you need rides to treatment? Someone to keep you company when you're not feeling well? Do you want me to take over watching Beth for you? Maybe I can—"

Cassie reached out and covered Jazz's hand with her own. Had it always felt so small? Delicate? Breakable? Was her mind now weakening the woman due to her diagnosis? Or was she just that fragile now?

No. As Cassie said, she was tough. Strong. And seeing her as anything less did the remarkable woman a disservice.

"Just seeing your beautiful face makes my day so much better, sweetie," Cassie said with the wonderful way she had of making everyone feel special and loved. "But I'd never say no to visitors if you'd like to swing by the house from time to time."

"You got it. I'll come the day after Christmas."

With a smile, Cassie patted her hand. "Good. Now you run off and find Izzy. I imagine she's a bit...cranky by now."

The laugh that bubbled out of Jazz this time as genuine and felt damn good. "I know. I'm thinking I should have worn a helmet and body armor."

As the three of them shared a laugh, Jazz rose. Using a gentle touch, she wrapped her arms around Cassie. "Love you, Mama V."

"Oh, sweetie, I love you too. Like you were my own."

After hugging Viper and promising to bring him some of Holly's pastries from the diner when she stopped by, Jazz headed out to find Izzy once again. Only this time, the excitement of the new baby had been dampened by Cassie's news. With a heavy heart, Jazz rounded the corner as instructed and ran smack into a brick wall. Or what felt like a brick wall.

It wasn't, of course. It was worse.

It was Screw.

God, why did the man have to be so damn built? More than once, she'd fantasized about all those hard muscles pressing her into the bed. Or the wall. Or her kitchen table. Hell, they'd feel good any damn place. Too bad they came along with a man who viewed it his mission to make the Guinness Book of World Records for most sexual partners.

"Hey, Jazz," he said, without his usual flirtation.

She narrowed her eyes at him. Was this part of the game? Throw her off with sincerity? He hadn't made his pursuit of her a secret, not by any means, and everyone in the club assumed she wouldn't give in because she didn't want to be a notch in his bedpost.

It wasn't entirely true. The number didn't matter. Nor did the fact that he slept with men and women alike. His cavilier attitude toward the people he bedded is what gave her pause. They were nothing to him. Names were forgotten seconds after he came, if he'd learned them in the first place. Faces weren't remembered for much longer. He straight up didn't give a single shit about any of the people who shared their bodies with him.

Maybe if her life had taken a different direction, she'd be able to relax with regards to her sex life, but she didn't have the luxury. To Jazz, the vulnerability that came with baring herself to another made it impossible to sleep around. Being with a man who'd brag to his friends, tease, and not care how she felt during and after the encounter wasn't possible.

No matter how much pleasure it'd bring in the moment.

"Jazz?"

She blinked. Screw wore a frown now. They hadn't spoken since he decorated her house, and if she was honest, she'd been feeling guilty for her treatment of him that day. But between her worry for Toni and Shell, newfound worry for Mama V, and concern for Izzy, her brain didn't have the capacity to fret over one more thing today.

"Sorry, did you say something?"

"Just hello. You all right?"

Was she all right? Fuck no, she wasn't all right. One of her favorite people in the entire world was suffering from a potentially incurable disease. She was very far from all right. But the news wasn't hers to share. Cassie clearly wanted to keep it close to the vest for a while, so Jazz would honor those wishes.

Before answering him, she took a second to study his face. Nothing but sincerity stared back at her. No snarky quip. No attempt to get her naked. She had to admit, running into him filled her with relief. Even without unburdening her worries onto him, she felt a little less alone with her troubles.

The feeling made no sense since he wasn't at all privy to what went on in her mind. She'd held herself back from people for more than a year. Even while making friends and enjoying time with the Handlers, she hadn't let any of them see her. Physically or emotionally. There were reasons for that. Deep, personal, painful reasons, but for some reason coming across Screw at that moment soothed her.

She cleared her throat. "Uh, yeah. I'm good."

Even though their last encounter hadn't ended well, Jazz had to admit she'd been touched by the way he decorated her house. Of course, he had to go and spoil it by trying to get her into bed again, but the gift had still been one of the sweetest given to her in a very long time.

Screw stepped close. Too close. Close enough, the woodsy scent his cologne or aftershave or whatever it was permeated her senses and made her knees wobble. A good smelling man was her weakness, and right then, Screw smelled incredible. She wanted to lean forward, plant her nose against that hard chest and inhale. But instead, she took a step back.

He followed.

Then another step back.

He followed.

The pattern repeated until she collided with the wall of the quiet hospital hallway.

Of course, he moved right on into her personal space.

Joy

"You're too close." Instinct had her almost pushing him back, but at the last second, she dropped her hand. Feeling that chest under her palms would be a foolish move.

"Liar," he whispered, right against her ear. So close his breath tickled her skin, sending a shiver down her spine

Damn him. She wasn't at her best today.

Somehow, she found the strength to resist. "I'm not lying. You're too close."

He didn't move his body but drew his head back and looked her in the eye. "I'm talking about you telling me you're okay. It's bullshit. Something has upset you."

God, along with smelling good, he looked downright edible. A light stubble covered both cheeks and his chin, making her palms itch to feel the scratchy sensation. His hair was slightly mussed, as though he'd been running his hands through it at some point. There was a reason both women and men shed their clothes and hopped into his bed without a second of thought. The man was a walking sexual temptation.

One she'd become very adept at resisting, but today she felt off her game. With so much stress and worry running through her mind, she stayed where she was instead of rebuffing him as she'd normally do. He was warm and strong, exactly the opposite of how she felt at that moment, and for just a second, she wanted to absorb those traits. To have someone hold her up instead of relying on herself all the time.

"They're gonna be fine. You know that, right?"

He tilted his head, studying her, and she felt the need to avert her gaze from his curiosity but forced herself to maintain eye contact. "Shell and Toni. Their ol' men won't let them be hurt."

Jesus, Cassie's news had completely scrambled her brain. How could she have forgotten about her friends?

"So, Zach caught up with them?"

Screw's face clouded. "You didn't hear?"

Her heart started to pound out a nervous rhythm. "Hear what? No, I haven't heard anything since Tex talked to Zach. He's out in the parking lot."

"Shit." Screw ran a hand down his face. "It was a trap. A set-up by Crank."

Sagging against the wall, Jazz gasped. "No. Please tell me they're okay."

"They will be. Z called in for help."

Shit! And here she was taking Screw's time and thinking about how much she wanted to lick his neck. "Oh, my God, am I holding you up? Go! Go!"

If he wasn't going to rush off, he needed to move back. The feel of his rock-hard body pressed against hers had quickly reached the point of too good. Bad-decisions good.

"I was actually heading out to the diner to pick you up and bring you either here or to the clubhouse."

"What? Why? Shouldn't you be helping Zach? Isn't that what you do?"

Screw shrugged. "He's covered. Cop wants eyes on all the ol' ladies so I took over for Tex. That boy is in some hot water."

"But I'm, not—"

With a roll of his eyes, Screw chuckled. "Fine. Cop wants eyes on all family. That better?"

No, but it killed her argument. She saw the Handlers' men and women as family, so it shouldn't be surprising they felt the same.

"Is this going to get ugly?" She tried to sidestep, but he placed his palms on the wall next to her shoulders.

Boxed in.

But instead of the cocky grin and swinging-dick attitude Screw usually portrayed, he stared at her with an expression so serious, Jazz's blood ran cold. "Yes. I think it's gonna get pretty fucking ugly around here pretty fucking fast. In fact, I'd say it's already ugly."

Jazz swallowed as she nodded. He was right. Today crossed a line the club couldn't come back from. Now they had to retaliate. Had to show they were a force to be reckoned with. Had to let the Chrome Disciples know they couldn't fuck around in Townsend.

"You worried?"

"About Shell and Toni? Yes, very." About herself? Maybe a little. She came to Townsend for a fresh start, never anticipating she'd hook up with an MC. She'd worked as the receptionist in a garage where she came from. The place was owned and operated by the members of an MC. The No Prisoners had been much like the Handlers. Maybe that's why she'd gravitated toward the club here, the familiarity. The feeling of belonging. Of being home. That being said, she knew what could happen when clubs went to war.

Ugly wasn't a strong enough word.

Screw leaned in again. "We'll keep you safe, Jazzy. *I'll* keep you safe."

She watched his face for the telltale signs this was another come on. Just one more invitation to his bed for a night of screwing Screw. But once again, only sincerity registered on his face. "You smell good," he whispered.

Not as good as you.

"Screw…" She tried for a warning tone but feared it came out needy instead.

"Yeah, baby?" He shifted so his lips were a breath away from hers.

"Don't."

His lips twitched as though he was fighting back a grin. "I have to."

Before she had a chance to process his words, his large hands cupped the sides of her face, holding her exactly where he wanted her as he kissed her.

And holy shit, it was a kiss like no other. Sweet and gentle. So unlike what she'd have expected from the cocky biker who talked about sex like it was nothing more intimate than shaking hands. Her head swirled as he sampled her mouth with small flicks of his tongue and light pressure.

She went soft and gooey all over as though she could just melt into Screw. The longer his tongue teased hers, the more heat flared throughout her until *she* was the one who tried to deepen the kiss. But he didn't let her, maintaining a grip on her face and keeping the kiss feather-light.

She'd never been kissed this way before, as though she was a treasure to be savored and worshiped. And it was exactly what she needed at that moment when the world as she knew it was spiraling out of control…again.

Exactly what she needed…

The thought hit her like a bucket of ice water, cooling her insane lust in an instant. She didn't *need* any man. Couldn't allow herself to. She shoved Screw away with both hands. He stumbled back, not expecting her violent outburst. "Get the fuck off me."

How could she have been so stupid? Of course, he was giving her exactly what she needed. It was all part of the game. He was a master at getting people out of their clothes, and she knew it. After resisting for the better part of a year, she'd almost succumbed in a moment of weakness and mental anguish.

A state he'd shamelessly taken advantage of.

Asshole.

"What the hell, Jazz?" He said as he swiped his thumb across his bottom lip.

"I've had enough, Screw. Enough of your fucking games. It's done. I'm done. I'm not going to sleep with you, and if you think you can take advantage of my worry over my friends, you're not only stupid, you're a piece of shit." Her chest heaved as she plastered herself against the wall. Her face had to be a thousand degrees and red as blood.

Anger flashed across Screw's face. Not the first time she'd seen it, but the first time it'd been directed at her. But it didn't last long. Within seconds, the scowl had been replaced by an arrogant smirk.

"Busted," he said with a shrug. "Can't blame a guy for trying. I'll get between those thighs yet. In fact, I'll have you begging me for it." He winked.

Jazz shoved off the wall, flipped him off, then stomped down the hallway toward the labor deck. At least she hoped she'd gone the right way because she'd die before turning around and walking past Screw again.

"So freakin' typical," she muttered as she turned another corner. Even as she said the words, a little seed of doubt sprouted in the back of her mind. Something had seemed off. Screw's voice at the end, had lacked his normal playful tone. The kiss couldn't possibly have been genuine? Could it? An honest desire to give her what he thought she needed.

Jazz huffed out a laugh. "Of course, it wasn't," she said out loud. "He's just thinking about his dick."

The words sounded hollow as they echoed through the quiet hallway.

Chapter Twenty

SHELL

Copper was there. He'd come for her.

Violent shivers racked Shell's body with so much force, she expected to bounce right off the picnic table. More concerning was the fact Lindsey had stopped quaking about a minute ago. Toni must have noticed as well because the moment Lindsey's body stilled, they shared a look and both crowded closer to the girl. At this point, Lindsey needed to be seen at a hospital, and Toni and Shell would be right there with her if they stayed out in the harsh winter elements much longer.

Actually, Shell probably required a hospital visit no matter what. The moment she'd sat on the unforgiving picnic table, she'd hugged her arms across her middle in a desperate attempt to provide warmth and protection for the tiny baby growing inside her. She couldn't let herself think about what might happen. Couldn't wonder if this prolonged time in extreme cold was harmful to the fetus because if she allowed her mind to wander in that direction, she'd literally curl up in a ball and sob.

Instead, she focused on Copper and Zach.

Her husband hadn't so much as glanced her way, and while Shell understood he couldn't afford the distraction, her heart bled with the memories of their last encounter. If things went south today, if one of them was injured, or God forbid worse, her last memory of Copper would be the nastiest fight of their relationship.

Copper and Crank went back and forth, trading hatred and barbs. Following the conversation grew more difficult, the colder she got. As did thinking in general. It felt as though her brain slowed, processing the words as though trudging through thick honey. Or maybe it was the thunderous drum of her pulse in her ears, causing difficulty hearing the conversation. Probably a combination of the two.

"Y-you girls h-h-hanging i-in?" Toni asked. She trembled and shook with near-violent shivers. Her lips held a blueish tinge while her cheeks and nose shone bright red.

Shell's tongue felt thick in her mouth, so she nodded instead of answering. When Lindsey didn't respond, Shell nudged her.

"Sleepy," the girl slurred as she uncurled, letting her legs drop down to the bench seat.

Shell met Toni's fretful gaze once again. Her friend's alarmed expression matched her own level of concern.

"S-sweetie," Shell said, fighting a losing battle against the chattering. "T-rry to s-s-stay a-awake, o-okay?"

Even as she nodded, Lindsey laid her head on Toni's shoulder.

"L-lind-say," Toni said, shrugging her shoulder, trying to nudge the girl conscious.

"I'm awake. Just resting my eyes." Her speech had slowed, and the words ran together, but her teeth no longer chattered. Shell might be the furthest thing from a medical professional, but even she knew it was bad news when the body stopped trying to warm itself with shivers. They needed to get the girl warm. And fast.

Shell shifted her gaze back to Copper to find him finally staring straight at her. Gone was the anger he'd shown her yesterday. All she saw reflected back at her was love and deep-seated fear. Maybe regret too. Without tearing his attention away from her, he called out, "Not shitting you, Crank. Second best day of my life was the day I gutted Lefty."

The first was the day I married you.

Though he didn't say the words, Shell heard them loud and clear, cutting across the distance.

Crank snorted. "Fuck off. That shit supposed to scare me? Been up against bigger and badder than you and lived to tell the fucking tales."

The man was a fool if he doubted what Copper had done to Lefty or the Handlers' ability to do the same to him. Shell hadn't learned specifics, she wasn't ever privy to the nitty-gritty details, but she'd known Copper and Rocket had killed Lefty in a spectacular fashion. Maybe it made her heartless, or evil, but she'd only experienced one emotion when Copper had confessed that deed late at night while she laid in his arms.

Pure fucking relief.

The same thing she'd feel once he did the same to Crank and his president. And he would. Because men like those who made up the Chrome Disciples MC didn't stop. As their hunger for money and power grew, so did their atrocities.

"Enough fucking around," Copper said even though it had seemed he was the one stalling a few moments ago. "Here's how this shit is gonna go. I'll give you one minute to walk the fuck away from the women. If you haven't moved, you'll be taken out. If you have a lick of sense and leave, what happens after that will be up to your president. If he's lookin' to get bloody, stick around town. If he wants his men to live, get the fuck off my turf."

Shell sucked in a breath. She'd seen Copper in president mode enough times to know the threats weren't idle. Her ol' man meant every word out of his mouth. If the Chrome Disciples stayed in Townsend, there'd be hell to pay.

Handler's style.

Shell could only stare at the back of Crank's head, but she imagined he wore quite the sinister grin, if the evil-sounding laugh coming from him was any indication. Now that the gauntlet had been thrown down, she strained to hear every word said. She needn't have bothered. Words weren't necessary. The man's actions gave a pretty clear indication of his intentions.

"Or, I could just end this right now." Without so much as glancing behind him, Crank extended his right arm and aimed a pistol directly at Shell. She froze as though her blood had finally dipped below thirty-two degrees. Not breathing, not even daring to blink as though the tiniest disturbance in the airflow would cause him to pull the trigger.

On the other side of Lindsey, Toni stilled, then sucked in a sharp breath. Lindsey didn't react. Not even a twitch. The teen's eyes remained closed, her head resting heavily on Toni's shoulder. If this continued much longer, it wouldn't be a bullet that took the girl out.

When she shifted her eyes front again, Shell's heart rate skyrocketed. As though they were magicians pulling weapons from thin air, both Copper and Zach had guns out and at the ready.

Chances were high, this showdown would end in a bloodbath. Had she any idea how to defuse the situation, Shell would have spoken up, but she couldn't think. So she placed her trust in Copper prayed her man would get them all through this.

He had to. Shell refused to leave her daughter this way. The hug and kiss she gave Beth as she sent her off to preschool would not be the last. She uncurled her aching and wind burned fingers, stroking them over her tiny stomach bump.

Daddy will protect you.

"Sure you wanna do that?" Crank asked.

The telltale *chick-chunk* of a rifle being cocked split the air. The barrel of the rifle extended from the passenger window of the van. Another biker in a Chrome Disciples cut now loomed outside the van, aiming a shotgun at the back of Zach's head. Then there was a third emerging from the back of the van, a second shotgun at the ready and trained on her man.

Suddenly the cold was no longer anyone's biggest concern, and Shell found herself simultaneously sweating bullets and freezing her ass off. With each passing second, their chances for survival grew bleaker.

"Seems as though you're outnumbered, boys. Maybe I should just kill you right now. Claim the town for my men."

Copper didn't respond, but his eyes narrowed to focused slits. Shell could barely breathe. Between the icy air burning her lungs and the terror of what could happen, she was more focused on watching the scene unfold than drawing in oxygen.

"Or," Crank continued, his voice taking on an almost giddy edge, "maybe I off your women. Watch you flop around for a few weeks then kill you anyway."

"You sure we're outnumbered?" Copper asked then.

Shell's eyes fell closed. He had a plan. Brothers at his back.

Crank made a big display of glancing around then laughed once again. "You hallucinating, old man? Pretty sure it's four guns to two."

"Don't need to be able to spot the sniper for him to kill you."

Rocket. Rocket was out there ready, willing, and able to take Crank and his buddies down.

All of a sudden, the whoop-whoop of a siren sounded from afar, but not nearly far enough away. Immediately following the shrill blare, a voice called, "Anyone in the campground needs to vacate immediately. If you need assistance, it can be provided. This road will be shut down." The words were loud and harsh, as though announced through a bull horn.

Another sharp bleep of the siren, closer than before.

Faster than a bullet could have burst from one of those guns, Crank's men were back in the van. The enforcer himself charged forward, all thoughts of turf wars and violence forgotten.

At the same time, Copper and Zach rushed toward the picnic table.

The sound of the panel door sliding open on the van had Zach's body jolting. "The fucker's gonna get away!" he shouted to Copper, as he reversed direction and took off running after Crank.

A gun fired, making the snow explode much too close to Zach's body. Being unable to do anything but stare at the scene unfolding would forever haunt Shell's dreams.

"Zach!" Toni screamed. She sprung off the picnic table as though shot from a cannon.

"Toni, don't!" Shell grabbed Lindsey, who toppled over when Toni ran, catching her just before her head hit the table.

"Got her!" Copper snagged Toni around the waist. She fought, kicking and screaming as she tried to get to her man. "Settle down!" Copper growled.

Another shot rang out, and Toni screamed as Zach's body jerked. He didn't fall, but the impact slowed him enough to allow Crank to dive headfirst into the rolling van. It peeled out, door open, throwing wet snow behind its wheels in an arc of slush and dirt. The whole thing happened over a total of ten seconds, but it felt like hours of slow-motion as Shell watched in horror, keeping Lindsey in her arms.

"Zach!" Toni screamed, as Copper finally released her. She sprinted toward her man, who was on his way back, his movements slow and sluggish.

"We gotta move, ladies," Zach said, voice thick with pain. "Can she walk?" He jutted his chin toward Lindsey.

"I t-think s-s-she's p-p-passed out." Shell's arms ached from holding the slumped teen.

"I got her, babe," Copper said as he scooped Lindsey into his arms. She went with ease, one arm flopping down and swinging back and forth. Shell immediately lifted it and tucked it between Lindsey and Copper.

The siren blared again, this time not in a short burst, but a continued whine.

"Shit! Pigs musta heard the shot. Move!" Zach said as he grabbed Toni's hand then hustled toward his truck.

Shell scrambled off the table as best she could with her limbs frozen solid. She slogged along after Copper, who'd jogged ahead toward Zach's idling truck. Her heart raced in contrast to the slow movement of her legs.

"You hit?" he yelled as he reached the truck.

"Shoulder. Flesh wound. I'll live."

Copper settled Lindsey in the front seat of Zach's truck as Zach and Toni reached the vehicle. They had a two-second argument over who would drive, then a grumbling Toni climbed in next to Lindsey and gathered the girl into her arms. Zach slid behind the wheel.

"Take off. We'll be right behind you. Circle through the park so you don't have to explain shit to any fucking cops."

"Meet you at the hospital," Zach called before Copper slammed the passenger door. Zach sped off at a pace way too treacherous for the road conditions. Especially since he was losing blood in the process.

The siren grew scarily close. Shell tried to run but her legs just wouldn't obey. "C-copper."

"It's okay, babe, I got you." He swung her into his arms and ran toward her car. Immediately warmth diffused from his body to hers and she wanted nothing more than to burrow into his strong body and sleep for hours. Days.

But they weren't out of the woods yet. No longer in danger from the Disciples, they now had to worry about the cops.

The siren shrieked so loud, Shell was floored she couldn't see the police vehicle yet.

With efficient but gentle movements, Copper deposited Shell into the warm car. Heat immediately penetrated her ice-cold limbs and she groaned at the amazing sensation. Not more than two seconds later, he dropped into the driver's seat. Shell tried to buckle herself, but her icy fingers refused to cooperate. Copper grabbed the belt, secured it, and took off just as the headlight of a police SUV came into view.

Shell held her breath once again. "Did they spot us?"

"Don't think so," he said, eyes on the rearview mirror.

"They can follow our tracks."

"Rocket is out there. He'll lead them on a wild goose chase."

Rocket, right. Shell blew out a shaky breath. They'd made it. They were safe.

We're safe.

Might take a few hundred more repetitions to actually believe it.

"That was too close."

Copper grunted.

As he navigated his way through the snow-covered park, Shell remained quiet. Her car wasn't exactly built to handle unplowed roads, and he'd need to concentrate. Even if she'd wanted to chat, her body might not have let her. The longer they drove, the heavier her eyelids grew until they remained closed for about ten seconds with each blink.

"Keep 'em closed, baby. Rest. I got you."

"Copper?" She blinked and forced her eyes open.

"Yeah?"

"Do you think the baby is okay?" she asked in a tiny voice both afraid to breathe life into the question and worried about his reaction.

One massive hand lifted hers then placed it on his thigh before returning to the wheel. "Yeah, Shell. With a tough mom like you and a mean sonofbitch like me for a dad, our baby is swimming around in there like an Olympic champ."

That was it. Her eyes refused to remain open any longer, but she squeezed Copper's thigh in response. Of course, he wasn't a doctor. Had no idea if his words were accurate, but the confidence and acceptance in them bolstered her.

"Love you so much, Shell."

A smile tilted her lips as her ol' man's words warmed her more than the heat of the car.

"Love you, too," she said right before sleep claimed her.

Chapter Twenty-One

ZACH

Even though his woman was safe, warm, and insisting she felt fine, Zach found it impossible to be more than one foot away from Toni's side. Actually, he refused to remove his touch from her body.

It'd just been too damn close. And now they had Lindsey, someone connected to the Chrome Disciples in a way they'd yet to determine. No way in hell was he letting his woman out of his sight long enough to blink. Even with a prospect shadowing their every move.

"You good, babe?" he asked, probably for the hundredth time in a few hours.

With a roll of her eyes, Toni huffed. "Zach, stop fussing. I'm good. You're the one who was shot for crying out loud. I can't believe you wouldn't even take any damn pain medicine."

"What? For this tiny scratch?" He shrugged his shoulder. A sharp stab of pain nearly took him to his knees.

Okay, maybe it was more than a scratch, but he'd refused medication all the same. First, he wasn't a pussy, and second, he needed his wits about him.

Again, she rolled her eyes. "Come on, tough guy." She threaded her arm through his uninjured one, giving a light tug. "Let's check on Lindsey. This is her room." She pushed the door open and quietly stepped inside with Zach right at her back.

Toni had been treated for mild hypothermia in the emergency room, given scrubs to replace her wet clothing, then released. Lindsey hadn't fared as well, having been out in the elements far longer than either Toni or Shell.

She'd been treated in the emergency room as well, then admitted for a night for observation, per the physician. Now, she lay in bed with electric blankets and an IV of warm saline working to heat her blood.

"Hey, sweetie. How are you feeling?" Toni sat at the edge of Lindsey's bed. The girl's tearful eyes immediately went to the bulky bandage on Zach's arm, and her crying went from soft tears to full-on snotty hysteria.

According to the medical staff, Lindsey was progressing nicely except for one thing. She hadn't stopped sobbing. The team wanted her calm, and so far, they'd failed at that task in a spectacular way, so they'd come to find Toni. Maybe it hadn't been the best idea.

"I-I-I'm so s-sorry," Lindsey said for what had to be the millionth time since she woke up on the drive to the hospital. They were the only three words she'd uttered to him or Toni. And she said them over and over again in the car, ER, and now. Toni, his amazing fucking woman, had the patience of a fucking saint. She sat at the bedside, Lindsey's hand in hers making cooing sounds and uttering nonsense sentences to get the girl to calm.

Zach wasn't quite as patient, and though his heart broke for the girl, they needed information, and they needed it yesterday. They now had someone the Disciples most likely considered their property. Finding out how much blowback they'd suffer became number their one priority as soon as everyone was deemed out of the woods medically.

"Lindsey," he said in a sharp, but not harsh tone. Enough to snap her attention his way and cut off her babbling, but not to upset her further.

As predicted, the plan worked. She jumped then shifted her gaze his way as the apologizes ceased. "Y-yes, sir?"

Toni laughed. "Oh, God, don't call him that. It'll go straight to his head."

The girl gave the tiniest wide-eyed, watery smile.

"There we go," Toni said. "That's better." She stroked a hand over Lindsey's damp hair.

"Can you tell us what happened?" Zach asked. "Is your father in the club?"

Lindsey shook her head. Her red hair, no longer wet, hung limp past her shoulders. Tears continued to roll down her chapped cheeks, but she no longer blubbered and sobbed. "My parents are dead. They died about six months ago, and my brother was given custody of me. He was a prospect for the Chrome Disciples."

"Was?"

"Uh, yeah, Blade kicked him out when he was found, um… you know…with an ol' lady," she whispered that last part as though Zach and Toni weren't way too familiar with the concept.

Shit. Caught fucking someone's woman. That'd do it.

"He didn't take you when he left?" Toni's mouth turned down.

Zach didn't need to hear the answer to that question to know the club had kept Lindsey as payment for time and trouble.

"Uh, n-no. Blade said I had to stay because I was club property."

Beside him, Toni froze, her mind no doubt going to worst case scenario.

"I'm so sorry," Lindsey said again. "I didn't want to keep tricking you. You were so nice. All of you at the diner. The nicest people I've met in a long time."

Toni opened her mouth, probably to tell Lindsey all was forgiven, but Zach squeezed her shoulder. When she glanced his way, he gave a single shake of his head.

Now that the girl was on a roll, it'd be good for her to purge the toxic experiences and good for Zach to hear exactly what went down.

"He made me." Her sobs kicked up again. "I-I told him no. I wouldn't do anything to h-hurt you. But Crank said I had to or he'd give me to the brothers. And I know what that means. Right now, the club uses me to clean the clubhouse and get them stuff they need. Uh, sometimes they made me sell drugs or help with the guns." She shrugged. "They said I wouldn't be hurt as long I did everything they ordered me to. But if I didn't help them trick you and Shell they'd let this guy Louco have me. It means crazy in Portuguese. He's insane. I couldn't...I had to do what Crank said. I was s-s-so s-scared. I'm s-sorry!"

"Shhh," Toni said as she climbed into the bed next to the girl. Zach resisted the urge to pull her back into his arms. Lindsey needed Toni at that moment more than Zach needed to keep his hands on his woman. But just slightly.

Toni wrapped the girl up in her embrace. "Shh, it's okay, Lindsey. You did what you had to do to survive a horrible situation. No one will hold that against you." Stroking the girl's head, her gaze met Zach's. Written all across her face was the love she'd developed for this troubled girl after such a short time. "Sweetie?" Toni asked.

"Y-yes, ma'am?"

Zach snorted. "You think calling me sir is bad, for Christ's sake, don't call her ma'am. She'll be ordering everyone around in no time."

"Hey!" Toni said, nudging him with her socked foot, but she laughed. "Seriously, sweetie, we're Zach and Toni."

"I can do that." Finally, she settled against Toni without tears.

"Did anyone hurt you while you were with the club?"

Lindsey fell silent. "Not too bad."

With a clenched jaw, Zach waited for her to finish her thought. If one of those perverted fuckers so much as laid a hand on the girl…

"They hit me a few times when I didn't do something right. I got a couple black eyes and a busted lip once. But once I learned how they liked things and didn't mess up so much, that mostly stopped."

"So they didn't…I mean, no one…"

Toni shot him a pleading look. Like he knew a sensitive way to ask a thirteen-year-old girl if she'd been raped? Christ. "Uh, I think what Toni asked is if they ever touched you… inappropriately."

Her eyes widened as the light bulb went off. "Oh, no! No, no, no!" She shook her head back and forth, bumping Toni's chin. "No, never. They just looked at me weird and made threats. I think they liked using me to sell drugs. I could go places without the cops or anyone thinking much about it since I'm not a big scary biker."

Maybe they hadn't touched her yet, but it would have come. Probably sooner rather than later.

"Lindsey," Zach said as he leaned forward and curled hand around Toni's calf beneath the scrub pants. Despite all the measures to warm her, her skin still felt chilled to the touch. "What do you think about coming to stay with us after you're released from the hospital?"

The girl's bloodshot eyes widened. Her chapped and peeling lips had been slathered in ointment, as had her bright red cheeks. Right then, she looked younger than her age. Truly like a child in need of a home.

"Y-you mean like for the night?"

"No, sweetie," Toni answered. "We mean for as long as you'd like to stay. Forever even."

"So you'd be like my parents? Do you want to adopt me?" Her shocked gaze shifted between the two of them.

"We'd be whatever you want us to be. Any role you need us to play, we'll do it," Zach said.

Toni met his gaze. "Thank you," she mouthed. "I love you."

He shot her a wink. Though he'd do anything for his woman, this was no longer just about granting Toni's wish. Lindsey was a sweet kid, given the rawest of deals. Were she to say in the Chrome Disciples grasp, her life would be complete and utter shit. She'd be whored around like nothing more than a common street hooker, no matter how hard she fought it. Any hopes and dreams she had would never come to fruition. After meeting her and seeing the way she interacted with Toni, Zach knew in his bones she'd be the perfect fit for them. She'd help make them into even more of a family than they already were.

He looked forward to making Blade and Crank pay for the terror and pain they caused this sweet girl.

"Is this for real?" she whispered, tears for a new reason now.

"It's very for real," Toni whispered back.

"Yes! Yes, please! I'd love too." Her arms came out from under the heavy blankets and hugged Toni back.

"But wait, what about the MC?"

"You just let us worry about them, okay?" Now that she had the Handlers at her back, he'd do everything he could to lift the burden of constant fear off her shoulders. Though it might not be easy. Chances were high, the club would try to get their property back.

Lindsey nodded, then seemed to sag into the bed as though no longer having to worry took all the air out of her.

"You think they'll try to come get you back?" Toni asked.

Lindsey shook her head. "I don't know. Probably not. Mostly they just always seemed annoyed by me. Blade threatened to kick me out on the street a lot. I think he just kept me around to mess with my brother's head. Pete is always trying to get back in with the MC."

"Will your brother come for you?"

The girl snorted. "Uh, no. He hates me. He was so mad when my parents died. Not because he cared about them either, but because he got stuck with me. Nah, he won't care."

"All right, then it's settled," Toni said with a smile. "You'll come home with us when you are released."

Hopefully it would be just that easy.

What started out as a grin, quickly morphed into a yawn as Lindsey's eyes began to droop.

"Come on, baby," Zach said to Toni. "Let's go home. She needs to rest."

Toni glanced down at Lindsey, who'd already fallen asleep. "I don't know," she whispered as she gently extricated herself from Lindsey's arms. As she dropped her feet off the side of the bed, Zach tugged her up to stand with him, ignoring the deep ache in his shoulder. "I think I should stick around while she sleeps."

"Babe," he said as he pulled her flush against him. "We'll come back. Give me two hours. You can take a warm bath and a nap."

One of Toni's eyebrows arched. "A nap, huh?"

With a playful grin, he glided his hands down her back to her ass, where he gave a sensual squeeze. "That's right. A nap."

Toni bit her lip as she glanced over her shoulder at Lindsey. "I don't know. What if she wakes up and she's scared?"

"Thunder is right outside her door. We'll be back in two hours, I promise. And if she wakes, Thunder can call and hand her his phone, so she can talk to one of us."

Toni still looked doubtful. "I'm just worried about—"

He cut her off with a soft kiss. The kind Toni melted into. Breaking it off before he actually wanted to, he brushed his lips against her cheek on his way to her ear. "Please," he whispered. "I need this. I need you, naked and in my arms...well my good arm. I know you're safe, but it was way too fucking close, baby. Please come home with me now."

By the time he drew back to gaze at Toni, her eyes had changed to a warm melted chocolate. She pressed her lips to his, and he let his eyes drift shut as he absorbed the wonderful feeling of his woman in his arms.

Whole. Safe. Unharmed.

Just as the kiss began to grow a little too heated for a hospital room, Toni drew back. "I'll come home with you now on one condition?" she said with a seductive smile.

Zach tilted his head, holding her against his erection. "Oh yeah? What's that?"

"You join me in the bath."

Fuck yeah. "Baby, you couldn't keep me outta there if you tried."

"Well, why would I do a silly thing like that?"

"Beats me."

Taking his hand in hers, Toni said, "Come on, Z, let's go home."

Home. The word sounded so damn good.

And hopefully soon, Lindsey would feel the same.

Chapter Twenty-Two

COPPER

Copper stared at the black and white image in his hand. He couldn't tear his eyes away from the tiny curled up bean in the center of the paper.

His baby.

His and Shell's baby.

Christ, the thing was beyond tiny. So vulnerable and not even recognizable as a child yet. But it would be. That little ball would grow and change into a child. One Shell would protect and carry for the better part of the next year. Then their lives would change yet again as the baby joined their little family.

The weight of responsibility nearly crushed him. Copper considered his club family and had always thought he protected each man and woman as though they were his own. But now, he knew different. Shell, Beth, and the little bean actually were his. And the need to keep them safe and happy felt different. Vital. Imperative to his very survival. Should something happen to any of them, he wasn't sure how he'd continue. Even though they hadn't been together that long in the grand scheme of life, Copper had no doubt he'd self-destruct should any harm come to his girls. Or his baby.

"Well, she's finally down," Shell said as she padded into their bedroom wearing black sweatpants, a gray hoodie, and wooly socks. She looked fucking adorable. Like a cute little stuffed animal.

After being treated for mild hypothermia and having an ultrasound confirm the baby was thriving, they'd gone to pick up Beth. The little girl had chatted almost non-stop, blissfully unaware of the harrowing events of the day. The distraction had been welcome, but her incessant chatter left little time for him to talk to Shell.

For him to apologize.

And, Christ, did he need to apologize.

"She was wound up tonight."

With a small chuckle, Shell nodded. "Happens every Christmas. Kids become crazed for a few days. It's fun to see her so excited, though."

It sure as hell was.

An awkward silence fell between them, making Copper's gut clench. He'd done this to them with his disgusting reaction to Shell's news. And now it was time to fix it.

"You still cold?"

She nodded, shuffling further into the room. "It's like the chill went all the way to my bones. I can't get warm enough. Even with all these layers. Is that the sonogram?"

Copper set the picture down on the bed beside him. "Yeah. Come sit with me."

It only lasted for a fraction of a second, but Copper saw the hesitation in her gaze, and it fucking slayed him. That he'd brought her to the point where she faltered before getting close to him nearly killed him.

"Please."

With a nod, she walked toward him. Instead of letting her sit on the foot of the bed next to him, as she'd tried to do, he scooped her up and deposited her right onto his lap, straddling him. The moment her weight settled on his thighs, Copper blew out a breath. He felt like a pressure cooker that had finally been set to release. All of a sudden, the tension and stress of the day began to fade. Though he still had a shit-ton to make up for, the closeness they shared now let him feel confident in their status once again. Shell wouldn't be tossing his clothes out on the lawn and changing the locks.

He wrapped his arms around her and buried his face in her neck. "I'm sorry," he said against her skin.

Shell's arms closed around his upper back. "I know. And I'm sorry too. I shouldn't have blurted it out to you that way. I blindsided you."

"Fuck, baby, please don't apologize to me for anything. This is all on me. I fucked up. I almost fucked us." He lifted his head. "There was no excuse for the nasty shit I laid on you."

There was no denying his claim, no telling him it was all okay. Shell didn't let him get away with shit. She challenged him to be the man she deserved. And he loved her all the more for it. Even if it made him dig deeper into his feelings than he was always comfortable with.

"Why?" she asked. "You aren't one to lose it like that. I know this isn't exactly what you wanted—"

"Stop," he said, placing a finger over her mouth. That was the first misassumption he needed to correct. "I want it. The idea of you growing our baby...Shit, Shell, there's nothing I want more."

A frown appeared on her pretty makeup-free face. "But..."

"But it scares the piss outta me."

There. He'd said it, and no one came to confiscate his man card.

"Because of what happened today? Things like that?" Shell tilted her head and looked deep into his eyes.

"Yes," he nodded. "That's part of it. Shell, Crank got to you despite having a prospect on you. So much is out of my control. Makes me feel like I can't protect you. Makes me feel like a

fucking failure as both your man and the Handlers' president."
His voice dropped as he admitted his biggest shame.

"Baby," Shell whispered, gazing up into his eyes. "You are the
furthest thing from a failure. I trust you with my life. So does
every man in your club. Today was at least partly on Toni and
me. We broke the rules. We ran out without Tex. I will not do
anything like that again. I promise. No one expects you to carry
us all on your back while fighting off the bad guys. We are all
adults, responsible for ourselves. And together, we are a family
who will protect each other."

"Shell…" Words fled him, so he pressed a soft kiss to her
Chapstick coated lips.

"What else? You said things like what happened today was
part of it." Her forehead scrunched. "You can't be worried about
being a good father, Aiden, because you already know you are
that. Beth worships the ground you walk on, and you're
absolutely incredible with her."

"No, it's not that."

"Then what? I'm trying to understand." Frustration tinged her
words.

Copper looked between their bodies, to the place covered by
layers of clothing where their child grew. He placed a hand over
her lower abdomen. "Your first pregnancy almost ended very
differently. I can't lose—" He stopped as an invisible hand closed
around his throat, stealing his air.

"Oh, Aiden." Shell placed her soft hands on either side of his
face. Did she even realize she stroked his beard as though he was
a cat? It was something she seemed to do unconsciously every
time she touched his face. He'd been keeping the beard a little
closer cropped than usual since they got together. Just the way
she liked it. "I'm fine. You heard the doctor today. Everything
looks perfect."

"Yeah, and everything was perfect last time, too. Until it
wasn't. Until you hemorrhaged and almost bled out." She'd
suffered a placental abruption shortly before Beth's due date,

causing a life-threatening amount of blood loss and an emergency C-section. "You told me a few months ago that you wouldn't want to automatically schedule a C-section if there was a chance you didn't need to. It scares the fuck outta me, Shell."

"Is that where this entire thing stems from? The whole wanting a vasectomy and the crazy reaction to hearing I'm pregnant?" She wore an expression of disbelief.

"Yes. That and the very real fact shit is going downhill with the club."

"I can't believe it." She huffed out a laugh as she shook her head.

"What?"

"I just never even realized you'd worry about that. Or even think about it."

Was she crazy? "You didn't think I'd worry about something that almost killed you the first time happening again? Jesus, Shell, you're fucking all I think about." He slipped his hands under her clothes, resting them against the cool skin of her back. She practically purred as the warmth of his hands seeped into her. "You, and Beth, and the club are it. Everything. And you're at the top of that fucking list. No matter my vow to my men. You're fucking number one."

He tried to pull back, but her hands tightened on his face, forcing him to make eye contact. "Aiden, I love you. And I'm not going to take any unnecessary risks with my life or our baby's. My doctor here knows all about what happened last time, and she's keeping a close eye on me. I'll be seen more frequently than I was during Beth's pregnancy. She said for now, it's safe for me to plan to have the baby the natural way. Well, natural with a lot of drugs. If that changes, we'll discuss our options with the doctor, and together, we'll make a smart plan. I'm not going to do something foolish, Copper. I have way too much to live for."

He blew out a breath as relief filled him. "Like a cranky ol' man who flips out on you?"

With a chuckle, she said, "Yeah, he's at the very top of my list too. But you know, maybe next time we have this conversation before the freak-out. I hear good communication is one of the keys to a lasting relationship." She shrugged and winked. "Just sayin'."

Shell was so much better than he deserved. For so long, he'd feared she wouldn't want to be with a man his age. Yet sixteen years his junior and she was the one schooling him on relationships.

"I'm sorry," he said.

"I know."

"You didn't deserve any of the ugly I threw at you."

Another little chuckle. "I know that too."

"It won't happen again, baby. The way I felt after...and the look on your face. It won't happen again."

"I. Know," she said, punctuating each word with a kiss. "Guess what?"

He stroked his hands up and down the smooth skin of her back. "What?"

"I'm not cold anymore," she whispered against his mouth. "In fact, I'm starting to get a little too warm."

"Is that right?" Now his hands went down the back of her sweatpants, cupping her round ass.

"Yep."

"What do you think we should do about it?"

"I was thinking we should get rid of some of these layers."

That was all it took to have him hard as steel and ready for her. In an awkward shifting of hips and legs that had Shell giggling, he managed to divest her of her sweatpants and panties.

"Forget the rest," she said, breathless, between deep, drugging kisses. "Just fuck me."

He reached between them, prepared to work her to a frenzy when she grabbed his hand, stilling him. "Not tonight. I need you inside me so bad. Just fuck me."

Goddamn, the command in her tone had his cock leaking behind his boxer briefs. He couldn't even manage to stand and shove them down because Shell was attacking his mouth and grinding down on him. He barely managed to pull his cock out when Shell was sinking down onto him, engulfing him in the hottest pussy on the planet.

"Yesss," she hissed, head thrown back. "This is what I needed. You are now officially forgiven."

With a chuckle, he arched his hips off the bed, driving even deeper inside her.

"More," she cried, working her pussy up and down his length. Almost frantic in the way she rode him, Shell moaned and gasped with every bounce.

Three minutes couldn't have passed before Copper felt the telltale tightening in his balls. "Shit, shit, shit," he said as he ripped his mouth away. "Baby, slow down, or I'm gonna fucking bust already."

"Yes! Me too. Please, Copper, give it to me. I want it."

How was he supposed to resist the raw need in her voice?

Wasn't possible.

With a groan, Copper grabbed Shell's ass in a tight grip as he pumped his hips up into her. She shouted his name once then locked her arms around him as she shoved her face into his neck. Just as she started to tremble in his arms and clench around his cock, he felt the prick of Shell's teeth sink into his skin.

Made him fucking crazy when she lost it like that and got rough with him. With one hand, he braced on the bed behind him as he pounded up into her hard.

"Aiden," she screamed as he fucked her through the orgasm.

The sound of his name ripping from her throat in the throes of a powerful climax had him filling her with his cum. With one last thrust, he held her hips against him and pulsed into her again and again.

"Well," Shell said in a sleepy voice. "If I wasn't pregnant before, I certainly would be after that."

She wasn't kidding. The entire encounter couldn't have been more than five minutes total, but fuck if they weren't five of the hottest minutes of his life. And knowing the woman with her arms and legs woven tight around him was carrying his son or daughter deep inside her only made it that much better.

They stayed like that, wrapped up in each other until their hearts no longer raced and their breathing evened out. Shell's head rested on his shoulder, not moving.

"Hey," he whispered. "You asleep, baby?"

"Yes," she mumbled, causing him to laugh.

"Come on, let's get in bed."

With a groan, Shell unwound her arms and legs, then crawled up the bed and beneath the thick covers. Copper preferred one thin blanket, and usually, that was enough for Shell if he kept her close, but tonight she'd probably require the whole shebang, so he didn't bother moving anything.

The moment he slipped in next to her, he pulled her back flush against his front. Shell sighed a sleep, contented sound that reflected exactly how Copper felt.

At peace for the first time in more than twenty-four hours.

"Oh," Shell suddenly said, sounding more awake than she should. "Speaking of babies. Do you think Izzy finally had hers? I know Toni inquired while we were at the hospital, but there was no news."

"For Jig's sake, I fucking hope so. If not, she's been in labor for an entire day, but I can't imagine no one would have called us if she did."

"Poor, Izzy."

"Poor, Jig."

With a giggle, Shell elbowed him in the gut. "Be nice, or I'll have Izzy coach me on how to act during my pregnancy."

Shit!

"Don't even think about it," he growled in her ear, eliciting another giggle from her. So much for being a big intimidating one-percenter president.

"Love you."

"Love you, baby," he whispered as he settled his hand on her stomach.

All it took was one curly-haired woman to turn him to fucking mush.

Chapter Twenty-Three

IZZY

"Looks like you've finally made it to ten centimeters," the nurse said as she aimed that perky grin Izzy's way.

Fuck, if her legs weren't numb as shit, she'd hop off the bed and slap that happiness right off that woman's face. This nurse with her bubblegum pink scrubs, platinum blonde hair in a bouncy ponytail, and life-is-grand attitude couldn't be farther from Izzy on the personality spectrum. And who the hell had that much energy at two in the morning?

Not women who'd been in labor for more than thirty hours. That was for fucking sure.

"About fucking time," Izzy mumbled.

Nurse Sunshine's mouth dropped open. What? She couldn't honestly say she'd never heard a woman in labor cuss before. Izzy had just assumed swear words flew around in the place about as much as they did in Jig's clubhouse.

Speak of Jig, the man deserved a medal. Maybe a monument. Or a month of daily blowjobs or something. She knew she'd been…testy during the pregnancy. Most of it had stemmed from fear of motherhood, not that she'd admit that out loud to anyone but Jig. The man had taken it all in stride. Her moods, her cravings, her frustration. No matter what she threw at him, it seemed to roll off his back.

He'd been exactly what she needed. Even when the guys teased him about her, he never wavered.

Good fucking man.

Actually, the best fucking man.

The man in question squeezed her hand. "Doing okay, babe?" he asked. "Any pain?"

Izzy shook her head. She'd tried, really gave it her all to have the baby without an epidural, but after twenty hours of labor, she'd caved. The contractions had been coming hard and fast for so long, but aside from that, things had progressed slowly. After watching her groan and grimace for hours, Jig finally convinced her to get the epidural, which allowed her a few hours of rest. "No pain, just feeling some pressure."

"That's because the baby is *right* there," Nurse Sunshine said. "Doctor Nichols is on her way in." As she spoke, she bustled around, draping the floor and area around Izzy with what she assumed would be used to keep the room from becoming a bloodbath. "So," she continued, practically bouncing around the room. "On a scale of one to ten, how excited are you?"

Izzy scowled and shot Jig a death look. He just chuckled and pressed a kiss to her cheek. The tickle of his beard, so familiar and comforting, worked wonders to keep her from snapping at Nurse Sunshine. "I don't know. Maybe a four."

"What?" The nurse stopped dead in her tracks as she pushed a cart with a bulb syringe, blanket, and other birthing necessary items. But then she grinned again because nothing seemed to keep her lips down for long. "Pretty sure the baby won't come out until you're at least an eight."

As she turned away to grab some more supplies, Izzy flipped the annoying woman off. A snort coming from the door had Izzy whipping her head around.

Shit! Had the doctor caught that?

Joy

Dr. Nicholas, a short and slender woman, probably somewhere in her fifties winked. Yep, she'd caught Izzy giving her nurse the middle finger.

Lovely.

"Great," she murmured to Jig out one side of her mouth. "Now she's probably gonna report me to CPS." Beside her, Jig shook with silent laughter.

The traitor.

The next few moments were a whirlwind of medical staff setting up, adjusting her bed, and getting her legs into position. Jig held her right leg as he'd been instructed to and still somehow managed to hold her hand in a tight, reassuring grip. The pushing didn't scare her, but she was completely terrified of that moment they'd place her child in her arms for the first time.

Her child.

Her and Jig's child. For him, almost more than for the kid, she wanted to be a good mother. Izzy loved her ol' man so goddammed much. Giving him the family he'd been robbed of earlier in his life had become extremely important to her no matter how scared she was of the tiny person about to bombard his or her way into their lives.

On her other side, a patient care assistant held her left leg.

"Would you like the mirror?" Nurse Sunshine asked as she began to pull an extendable mirror down from the ceiling.

"I'm sorry, what?"

"The mirror. Would you like me to position it for you?"

Izzy blinked. "What for?"

The nurse gave her one of those are-you-stupid looks. "So, you can watch the baby being born."

Was she for real? "So I can watch the baby come out of my cooch? All bloody and stretching me to shit? Do people do that?" She looked at Jig.

With a shrug, he said, "Don't ask me. It's your choice."

"Well then fuck no, I don't want to watch that. Jesus, it sounds horrifying."

From a stool between Izzy's spread legs, the doctor chuckled. "Okay, Izzy, I want you to take a deep breath and push as hard as you can. I'm going to count down from ten. When we get to zero, you relax. Got it?"

"Think I can handle that."

The doctor nodded. "Okay, push."

Izzy sucked in a breath and began to push.

"Ten, nine, eight…"

She shifted her gaze to Jig to find him staring at her with an intense expression of awe and adoration she'd never seen on his face before. It bolstered her, chasing away some of her unease.

When they got to one, the doctor glanced up at Izzy. "Okay, take a few breaths, then we go again."

Five…*five* times, they went through that routine before the baby was finally born in a whoosh of pressure relief. A sharp cat-like cry split the air. "Oh, my God," Izzy said as she flopped back on the pillows. "So much for TV where the baby slides out with one little push."

The physician laughed and then might as well have disappeared because nothing registered except the tiny slippery baby resting against Izzy's bare chest. On instinct, her hands came up to cradle the tiny body. Immediately the crying stopped, and two dark eyes gazed up at her.

"It's a girl," someone in the background said.

A girl.

A girl.

"Jig," Izzy whispered. She couldn't tear her gaze away from the tuft of black hair plastered to the cutest head she'd ever seen. "Jig," she said again.

"I see her, baby," he whispered before placing a kiss on Izzy's head. "I see our daughter. Just as beautiful as her momma."

"Our daughter…I—" Izzy swallowed around a softball sized lump in her throat. All around her, people worked in the room cleaning the supplies they'd laid out, but none of it registered. "She has your nose."

"Mmm," he said, the sound full of wonder. "And we already know she has your stubborn personality. Why else would she have stayed in there so long?"

The tip of Izzy's nose began to tingle. Her chest felt tight, but not in a bad way, in a way that meant it was full of warmth and love. Something she'd only experienced since meeting Jigsaw. "Oh!" she said, watching every move her daughter made.

Her daughter.

"What's she doing?"

A nurse peered over the top of the baby's head. "She's rooting. Your little girl is hungry. Feel free to feed her. You're planning to nurse, right?"

Blinking, Izzy glanced up. "Um, yes, but…now? She's all messy."

"That's all right. We can certainly clean her if you'd like, but we like to leave parents alone for a while to bond with the baby. And by the looks of it, this one would love to eat."

"Okay." She could do this. She'd read the books, even watched a few YouTube videos on nursing. No problem.

Suddenly, it was as though everything she'd read and studied fell out of her head. She couldn't recall a single thing such as how to position the baby, how long to feed her for, how to get her to latch. With fake-it-till-you-make-it in mind, Izzy shifted the baby's puckered mouth toward her breast.

Within seconds a strong suction sensation occurred, and the baby was happily drinking away. "Holy shit," Izzy whispered. "She did it. Jig, she did it!"

"Pretty and smart. Definitely like her momma."

Without tearing her gaze away from her hungry baby, Izzy snorted. "Pretty sure we both know you're the brains in this relationship."

The bed shifted, finally causing her to look up from the baby. Jig had lowered the railing on the bed and settled himself down at her side. His dark head lowered as he kissed their daughter for the first time. In that instant, Izzy knew she'd never experience a more perfect moment.

A soft click had her scanning the room. At some point, all the hospital staff had cleared out, leaving their little family in the room alone.

As though it'd been hours instead of seconds since she'd peeked at their daughter, Izzy brought her attention back to the baby, still sucking away. Together, they watched her eat until she drifted off to sleep, her soft weight against Izzy's chest the best thing she'd ever felt.

"So beautiful," Jig whispered in her ear before pressing a kiss to her temple. He once again kissed the top of their daughter's head.

"I didn't believe them. I heard them all say it, but I didn't believe it." Izzy said so low, it was barely even a whisper.

"Didn't believe what?" Jig placed his large hand on the baby's back, and she let out the most adorable sigh to ever have been breathed. The sound brought a gorgeous smile to Jig's face.

"That it'd be this way for me. That I'd feel it."

"Oh, Iz, I knew you'd feel it."

"How?"

"Because you're you. You love as fiercely as you fight. There was no way you'd have a baby and not feel the instant connection. The immediate bond and love."

She gazed into the dark eyes of the man she loved. "Thank you for having such faith in me."

"Always."

He kissed her until the baby made another one of those sleepy noises. "It's a girl."

Jig chuckled. "So I've heard."

"And you're okay with that? Even with…everything." *Even with the fact you once had a daughter and a wife who were both brutally and senselessly murdered.*

"I'm fucking amazing with that. I'd have been pretty worried for my son's sake had we had a boy. You're a bit rough on men."

Joy

"Hey! I just had your baby. You're supposed to be extra sweet to me." She gave him a half-hearted elbow to the gut.

Jig wasn't looking at her. His gaze stayed trained on the sleeping infant. "How are you feeling?"

"Good. Great, really. My legs are starting to tingle." Izzy wiggled her toes. "Getting some movement back too."

"How are you gonna top this Christmas present next year?" He wore a grin full of mischief.

"Oh, no, don't even think about it. Having a baby will not be our family's Christmas tradition. No way, no how. You're gonna have to do some serious negotiating if you think I'm doing this again anytime soon."

"I'm kidding, Iz." He reached back and pulled a folded piece of paper out of his pocket. "Actually, I was hoping you'd be willing to give me a second present this Christmas," he said, holding it out to her.

"Can you open it. My hand are a little full." Her heart raced as he unfolded the paper. What could it possibly be?

He'd said it was a gift for him.

As more of the paper was revealed, Izzy gasped. "Jig," she whispered. "It's beautiful. Where…"

"I had Rip design it. I was hoping you'd ink it on my left thigh."

Her hand trembled as she reached for the paper with a sketch of a gorgeous flowering tree with two bright blossoms.

One for her.

One for their daughter.

On his right leg, Jig had a tattoo memorializing the lost life of his wife and daughter. A huge, dead tree with blood-red leaves falling. Each year, on the anniversary of their deaths, he added two falling leaves. This new design, so alive with life and vibrant colors marked his new life.

His life with her and their daughter.

This time, Izzy had no hope of preventing the tears that coursed down her cheeks.

"Babe." He wiped them away with the pads of his thumb.

"I'd be honored to ink you with this, Jig. So, so honored." To know she not only laid the ink but was responsible for bringing him out of such a dark place in his life made every bit of struggle she'd experienced well worth it.

"Good. Merry Christmas, baby," Jig said right before kissing her.

"Merry Christmas."

Jig rested his forehead against hers, keeping them connected. "Thank you," he whispered.

The seriousness in his tone had a lump forming in her throat. "For what?" she asked as low as he spoke so as not to disturb the peace of their sleeping infant.

"For you. For her." He stroked a finger over the baby's head. "For so many years, I'd been alive but not living. I existed in a state of anger and bitterness. Not once did I even contemplate the idea of having a second chance at…well, at being happy. And you've made me so fucking happy, Iz. You gave me a second chance at a damn good life."

"Jesus, Jig," she said as two fat tears rolled down her cheeks. Were he anyone else, she'd have forced those drops to remain in her eyes even if she went blind. She was Isabella Monroe, tough, snarky, and all-around badass bitch. She was not an emotional crier.

Until Jig.

Until the man made her feel things she'd thought didn't exist. But it was all right for her to break down in front of her man. All her secrets were safe with him. As was her heart.

She cleared her throat. Just because she'd shed the tears didn't mean she was comfortable talking about it. Jig knew how much his words meant to her, and he knew she felt the same. "So, uh, you're happy with the name we picked?"

The indulgent smile he gave her let her know he was on to her topic change. "Yeah. I think it's perfect."

Joy

After he kissed her forehead, Izzy stared at their baby once again

Perfect. Yeah, that was a damn good way to describe life at that moment.

Chapter Twenty-Four

HOLLY

"Maybe we should have just waited until they were discharged to see the baby. What do you think?" Holly asked as she fiddled with the neatly wrapped baby gift, she'd purchased about six weeks ago. Two sets actually, one in purple—because no way in hell was Izzy a pink kinda gal—and one in blue in case the baby had been a boy. Since the grapevine informed her the baby was a girl, Holly only wrapped the purple.

With a hearty laugh, LJ slung his heavy arm across her shoulders and tugged her to his side. "Dontcha think it's a little too late for cold feet?" He pointed to a door about ten steps away, well maybe only five for his enormous stride. "That's their room."

Holly stopped dead, causing LJ's arm to slide off her as he continued forward. He spun and planted his hands on his hips, legs spread. "Sugar…" The twitching of his lips was an obvious and poor attempt to hide his amusement. "Why are you still clinging to this notion that Izzy hates you?"

Staring at the ground, Holly toed a chipped corner of a linoleum tile. "I don't know," she said with a shrug."

"Sugar, she's flat out told you she likes you," LJ said as he used one finger to lift her chin.

So maybe she was acting irrationally, but she'd just always gotten this from Izzy. These vibes of dislike, or maybe, distrust was a more accurate description. She shrugged again. "She watches me a lot with this suspicious look like she thinks I'm going to go search out my father and bring him back to arrest everyone."

LJ's head fell back as a boisterous laugh left him.

"Hey!" She whacked his stomach only to end up shaking out her hand. "Ouch."

Damn washboard abs.

Okay, she loved those rippling abs, but come on, the man could at least pretend to be wounded by her. Boost her ego a bit. "Don't laugh at me. I'm serious. I get this impression that she doesn't like me. It might be stupid, but I'm just not confident in our friendship."

"Oh, sugar…" He reached out, snagged her wrist, and pulled her to him. "That's just Iz. She's a tough cookie, but I promise she likes you. If she didn't, she'd flat out tell you."

Holly screwed up her mouth and rolled her eyes. "No, she wouldn't. She wouldn't want to offend you."

"Ha! You think Izzy gives two shits about offending anyone? She's gone toe to toe with Copper. And won. Trust me, if that woman didn't like you, you'd know it. For certain. None of this 'maybe she doesn't like me' nonsense. You'd be sleeping with one eye open."

That finally had her laughing and relaxing. "I'm sure you're right. Besides, she just had a baby. I'm sure she'd be nice right now even if she didn't like me."

"You're nuts. Come on." It was LJ's turn to roll his eyes as he tugged her toward the open door of room four-eighty-seven. "Knock, knock," he announced, rapping his knuckles on the door frame. "Favorite uncle here!"

Holly suppressed a giggle as they entered the room together. Izzy sat on the side of the bed, cradling a sleeping baby all bundled in fuzzy blankets while Jig sat in a high-backed recliner next to the bed.

"Hmm," Izzy said. "Copper just left so…"

This time Holly did giggle.

"Whatever," LJ said as he flipped Izzy off.

"LJ! You can't do that in front of the baby." Holly bumped him with her hip.

"The baby is sleeping. And don't you think with parents like those two, the poor kid's first word is gonna be fuck?"

"All right. Get out of our room. You're now relegated to worst uncle," Jig said, moving his hand in a shooing motion.

"What if I told you we come bearing gifts? Does that bump me back up?" LJ pointed to the package Holly held, so she lifted it and jiggled the gift around.

With a tilted head, Izzy tapped her lip as though giving the question some serious thought. "Guess it depends on how good it is."

"Oh, it's good. Tell her it's good, sugar."

"It's good," Holly parroted in a robotic voice making the other three laugh. She'd missed half of what they'd been saying as she couldn't tear her attention away from the sleeping baby. God, she was so stinkin' cute. A little button nose. A tuft of fuzzy black hair. Chubby cheeks. Just new baby perfection.

"Wanna hold her?" Izzy asked in a soft voice Holly had never heard from her before.

"What?" She lifted her gaze.

"Do you want to hold her while I open my gift."

"Yes." Her answer was immediate and forceful. Without looking, she shoved the gift at LJ and approached Izzy, who shifted the baby to her as though she'd been doing it for years instead of hours.

Entranced, Holly absorbed the weight of the soft and warm newborn in her arms. The baby let out a soft sigh, then her lips moved as though sucking a bottle twice before she settled back into steadiness. "Hi, beautiful girl," Holly whispered. "Aren't you just perfect?" She couldn't resist. Holly leaned down and took a long inhale before kissing that soft as silk hair. The scent of baby lotion filled her senses. Without any actual evidence, Holly was convinced the makers of the stuff put some kind of drug into the baby lotion. A drug that made women's ovaries go bonkers with just one sniff.

"Uh oh, LJ," Izzy said with a teasing voice. "I can practically hear Holly's uterus begging you for a baby."

LJ's eyes went wide. His gaze ping-ponged between Holly and the baby. "What? Uh…really. I…um…"

Both Izzy and Holly laughed. "Settle down there, big guy. I can appreciate the cutest baby in the world without needing one of my own. Your sperm is safe…for now." Her voice had grown unnaturally high while she said the words cutest baby in the world, and she'd bounced the little bundle gently in her arms.

LJ was staring at her as though she had three heads. Clearly, the man hadn't had much baby time in his life.

Time to steer this conversation back to something that wouldn't give her man hives or have him running for the hills. "So, what time was she actually born?" Holly asked.

Jig smiled a cheesy, beaming grin Holly wouldn't have thought possible from the typically serious man. Maybe it was the scar, but something about Jig had always had her keeping her distance. Just seemed as though the man had an ever-present scowl. Or it had until his baby girl was born. "Two forty-one in the a.m. A Christmas Eve baby," he said.

An invisible fist squeezed Holly's heart, stealing her breath and causing a pang in her chest. Duller than usual for this time of year, but still there. She had LJ to thank for lessening the pain, though it'd probably never fade entirely.

"Oh," Izzy said. "That reminds me. Happy Birthday, Holly. The big two-five, right?"

Yes, in just a few hours, Holly would turn twenty-five, which meant she'd officially lived more years without her twin than she had with her. Were this last year, the grief would have consumed her. Her biological family hadn't been worth much when it came to providing comfort. But this year, LJ and her new family had done a fantastic job of keeping her too happy and satisfied to wallow in the tragedies of the past. Plus, she had someone new in her life. A man who was very quickly becoming important to her. Travis refused to let her feel guilty over his past imprisonment. Rather, he felt he owed her a debt of gratitude for his recent release. Holly didn't want his thanks, and he didn't want her guilt, so they'd settled on giving each other something they were both lacking in their lives.

Family.

"Yes. Twenty-five today." Holly smiled, though the lump in her throat made it difficult to speak. "And thank you." She cleared her throat as the room grew quiet. Everyone knew of her past and how her twin sister had been brutally murdered at the age of twelve. "Anyway, uh, you haven't even told us what this cutie's name is. Please tell me it doesn't say "Baby Girl" on her chart."

Izzy's face softened as her attention fell to her daughter. As with Jigsaw, this gentle easiness was a side of Izzy she hadn't witnessed yet. It was nice, knowing the woman so often hard and fierce had a special side reserved just for her man and her daughter.

"No," Izzy said. "We gave her a name."

"What is it? No, no, let me guess," Holly said. "Xena? Or is it Shera? Maybe Lagertha?"

A loud snort came from Jig, followed by a terrible attempt at hiding his smirk.

"Seriously? Those are your guesses?" Izzy rolled her eyes. "I think I should be offended."

The baby stirred, letting out another of those adorable squeaky sighs before conking out once again. Man, Holly

238

couldn't get enough of this. She foresaw a lot of babysitting in her future. "What? Those are all badass females. Nothing wrong with those names."

"I bet you went with Izzy Jr.," LJ said, laughing as Izzy flipped him off.

"You two are a barrel of laughs," she said.

"Okay, I'm serious now. What's this princess's name?" Holly asked. "What's your name, princess?" She couldn't stop the high-pitched baby talk to save her life.

"First of all, if you ever call her a princess again, I'll kick you in your teeth."

Ahh, there was the Izzy they all knew and…feared. "I'm not sure I want to know what the second thing is."

"The second thing is her name, which is Joy Mary Miller." Izzy stared straight at Holly as she spoke the words.

The moment the word Joy left Izzy's mouth, time seemed to slow. The rest of the words flowed from her as though traveling through thick mud. Holly blinked. "Joy?" she whispered. "You named her Joy?"

LJ moved in behind her, wrapping his arms around her, careful not to disturb…Joy.

"We did," Jig said. "And Mary is the name of my daughter who was taken from me."

Izzy had yet to add anything. Holly turned her attention to the woman. With her hair in its customary Dutch braid, she appeared ready to go to battle, not like a woman who'd just suffered through hours and hours of labor. Though the dark rings residing under each eye gave away her fatigue.

Holly's hands began to tremble, so she stepped out of LJ's embrace and returned Joy to her mother before leaning against LJ once again. If there was ever a time she needed his strength behind her, this was it. As though he sensed her inner turmoil, he wrapped her up tight and kissed the top of her head. "But why? You don't even—"

"Like you?" Izzy said with a smile. "Yes, I do, Holly. I don't know why you think I don't like you, but I promise you I do."

"It's the resting bitch face," LJ said, and he received another middle finger from Izzy. "Or it could be that," he said as he laughed.

"You're family. There is supposed to be a Joy in this world who was born on December twenty-fourth. Just like Jig is supposed to have an eleven-year-old daughter named Mary. All of us in this room here have seen how evil the world can be. And how often there is suffering and heartache. We're just trying to put a little joy back in the world." She extended a hand to Jig, who captured it with his then brought it to his lips for a lingering kiss.

Holly's insides had never felt so warm and gooey. For the first time in a long time, Holly truly knew she was loved. Not in the romantic way LJ showed her every day but cherished by her family. Sure, none of them were blood, but she'd learned over the past few months that blood meant nothing more than DNA and similar traits. It didn't guarantee loyalty, respect, or compassion. Her chosen family had given her all that and more.

They gave her Joy.

"I don't know what to say. This is the most incredible gift anyone has ever given me."

LJ's arms tightened, keeping her close and supported. With a slight tremor in her arms, she crossed them over LJ's.

"Thank you," she whispered. The words seemed so inadequate an expression of the wonder and appreciation she felt for what they had given her. But thank you was all she could muster without bawling like a baby. As it was, she had to blink about a million times to keep the tears at bay. Though they were tears of happiness, Holly refused to let them fall. Nothing that could be misconstrued as sadness would be allowed in that room today.

"There isn't anything to thank us for," Jig said as he held out his arms for the baby.

Izzy immediately passed Joy to her father. Holly's heart nearly stopped at the look of bliss that passed over the stern man's face.

Apparently, all it took to turn big tough bikers to mush was a tiny baby girl.

"Well," Holly said, suddenly experiencing the urge to lighten the heavy mood. "At the very least, you guys get cookies and brownies for life."

"And that's why we really did it," Izzy said as she held her hand up for a high-five from Jig. "Score, baby!"

"Well, now that we're out of the serious part of today's program, can we give them their gift, sugar?" LJ asked as he unwound his arms from her.

"Oh, right! Sorry, I forgot." Holly snatched the wrapped gift off the bedside table where LJ had set it before embracing her. "Here you go." She handed it over to Izzy.

"I think I'm supposed to say something like, 'you didn't have to do that,' but I'm kinda loving all the gifts you guys have been bringing by today."

"Well this one is the shit," LJ said.

"Oh, great, now the pressure is on," Holly said as she playfully pinched his nonexistent stomach flab.

Silence fell while Izzy went to work, tearing the elephant wrapping paper off the gift. Once free of the crinkled paper, she lifted the lid off the box, then began laughing. "Oh, my God," she said, gasping for breath. "Jig, look at this. You guys win best present, hands down."

"Let me see, babe," Jig said.

Izzy lifted the purple onesie from the box, holding it up so Jig could read the text. Printed across the tiny garment in bright white letters was the word "Fighter," along with a picture of a baby in a fighting stance. An arc above the image read, "Crib today," and an arc below read "Cage tomorrow."

Holly beamed as her gift was enjoyed. She'd searched for a while until she found something Izzy would truly enjoy. And for some crazy reason, the woman loved to beat on other people.

"Shit, you guys nailed that gift." Jig held out his fist and accepted a bump from both Holly and LJ.

They stayed for another fifteen minutes or so, oohing and aahing over Joy. When she woke up with a hungry wail, it was time to jet. Holly loved Izzy and all but didn't feel the need to stick around and watch her feed the baby.

The moment they stepped outside the hospital, Holly shivered. LJ pulled her close, sharing his ever-present heat. "Can you believe that?" she asked, staring up at his handsome face.

"I think it's perfect."

Perfect. Yes, that's exactly what it was. The most amazing birthday and Christmas present imaginable. Holly vowed at that moment to be the best aunt that child could ever have.

When they reached LJ's truck, he backed her against it and leaned down to steal a kiss. "You ready to go home and unwrap your first birthday present, sugar?"

"Hmm," she said, letting her eyes fall closed as she absorbed the feeling of LJ's beard tickling her cheek. "Does it come in six-and-a-half feet of wrapping paper?"

He chuckled against her ear. "How'd you know?"

With a shrug, Holly said, "Just figured you'd know exactly what I wanted for my birthday."

"Mmm, I do know exactly what you like, don't I?"

God, all it took was that sexy voice, and she melted like an ice cube on ninety-degree day. "Yes, you do."

"Come one, let's get home before I fuck you right here in a freezing hospital parking lot."

After one last quick kiss, LJ helped her into the truck. As he walked around to the driver's side, Holly rested her head back and let her eyes fall closed. For the first time in thirteen years, she felt true happiness on her birthday.

No wonder. She had so many fantastic people in her life this year. Her MC sisters. The men of the club.

LJ first and foremost.

Joy

And, what she'd never thought possible, now she had Joy back in her life.

Chapter Twenty-Five

ROCKET

"You know, you're allowed to actually have a good time today. What, with it being fucking Christmas Day and all," Copper said as he lumbered up next to Rocket at the bar.

Rocket grunted. Holidays had never meant much to him before joining the Handlers. It all seemed like a lot of pomp and circumstance for one day. But the MC made a big deal of Christmas each year, and ever since he'd patched in, he played along with the hoopla. Now that he had Chloe in his life, Christmas was an even bigger event. She'd nearly lost her mind when he told her he didn't bother putting up a Christmas tree and had no plans to this year either. Now he was saddled with a ten-foot fir taking up real estate in his cabin.

Though he had to admit seeing Chloe's eyes bright with happiness the first time they lit up the tree made the hassle of chopping that fucker down worth it. Since then, his kitchen had been used to make piles of Christmas cookies for the first time ever. The entire inside of the cabin smelled of Christmas pine, and decorations hung everywhere he looked. Chloe insisted she bought him the perfect present and practically bounced off the walls when she gave it to him.

Joy

She'd been right.

The vacation to South Dakota she'd booked them hit the nail on the head and then some. They'd hit Sturgis, ride to Mt. Rushmore, and cruise through a motorcycle-loving section of the country Rocket hadn't had the pleasure of visiting yet. Late spring couldn't come fast enough.

"Chloe with you?" Copper asked as he flagged down Thunder behind the bar.

"She's still at the house with her brother. Figured I'd give them some time alone. But he'll be tagging along, and they should be here soon." Outside of his brothers, Scott was the only man he trusted to keep Chloe safe.

One of Copper's red eyebrows arched. "Straight-laced Scott is gonna step foot in a biker clubhouse? The world ending, and I don't know about it?"

With another grunt, Rocket shook his head.

"You pissed about his visit or something?"

"Nah. He's a good guy." Though he'd nearly ripped Rocket's head off when Rocket gave him the heads up to remain alert at all times.

"So why the fuck you sitting here with a fucking glower when everyone else is eating, drinking, and being fucking merry?"

Behind them, chatter reached a dull roar as gifts were exchanged, drinks were consumed, and Beth made every biker in the club kiss her cheeks under the 'missy toe.' Even if he wanted to be just a little less antisocial today, Rocket couldn't bring himself to join the festivities. Hopefully, when Chloe arrived, she could drag him out of his funk

"It's nothing, Cop. Just got some shit on my mind." Shit that meant bad news for the club. Shit he came across while investigating the Chrome Disciples, but couldn't bring himself to reveal until Christmas had passed. Instead, he ruminated on the information alone.

"Bullshit."

"Scotch, Prez?" Thunder asked as he strode over.

Copper nodded but kept his attention Rocket's way. "Spit it the fuck out, Rocket. My woman's worried about you and fuck if I'll let anything bother her today. So open your fucking mouth and talk."

"Can we do this tomorrow? I got shit to say that'll likely fuck this day for you."

Copper's eyes narrowed, and he set his glass down, all attention on Rocket. "Talk."

Fuck. Looked like he wasn't getting out of it.

"Got some intel on Crank."

"Fuck." Copper downed the few fingers of Scotch in one large gulp. "Let me guess, you're not about to tell me he fled town, are you?"

Pointing to his glass for a refill of the straight vodka he'd been consuming, Rocket shook his head. "Not even close, brother."

With a heavy sigh, Copper shifted on the barstool until he faced forward. Two beefy forearms landed on the bar top before Copper let his head fall forward. "Okay, lay it on me."

"Found out Crank was in the army. Spec Ops. A Ranger for six years."

"Oh, fuck me," Copper whispered, shaking his head back and forth as it dangled. "So he's not just some cowboy who can't hit the broad side of a barn."

"No, boss. He's a highly trained and lethal operative. There's more."

"Of course, there is. All right. Give it all to me."

"He was other than honorably discharged about four years ago after an incident involving weapons in Afghanistan. Most of the files were buried fucking deep, but my contact was able to get his hands on a few. Crank, or Michael Ainsley, was accused of involvement with a weapons trafficking group overseas. Nothing could be proven, but not much of an investigation was done, either. The army offered him an out with the other than honorable discharge in exchange for foregoing an investigation."

"So basically, they pushed him out the door and swept the entire fucking incident under the rug?"

"Not basically, fucking exactly," Rocket said before grabbing a few chips from a bowl on the bar.

"Does this mean he has contacts in the fucking Middle East? Jesus, think he's supplying terrorists?"

"Worst case, yes, but I don't know for certain." He shoved three chips in his mouth. Shit like this was why he'd run away from that world. Too many men turned crooked and fucking evil with a mere taste of power and money.

"Christ. Merry fucking Christmas to me."

Rocket couldn't have said it better himself. If the Chrome Disciples were sending guns overseas, the operation was highly organized and much more lucrative than they'd realized. That meant the Chrome Disciples were not only dangerous but motivated to keep their business alive.

"We need to fucking end them."

"We do," Rocket said around a mouthful of chips. "The warehouse they claimed as a clubhouse has been dead since the incident at the campground yesterday."

"You think they left?"

"Not for good. No. Maybe restocking their supply or taking care of unfinished business wherever they came from. Don't know. But I doubt they're gone." He shrugged. "Think this gives us a little time to breathe, though."

Copper ran a hand down his face then nodded to Thunder, who filled his empty glass as he passed by. Once again, Copper sucked back the entire contents with two swallows. "Keep this tight for now. We'll address it immediately after the New Year. I want the men to have a few days with their families without worries before we dive into the next crisis. But keep eyes on the warehouse and let me know the moment they roll back into town."

With a nod, Rocket said, "You got it, boss." Hopefully, the invading club would keep away for the next week or so.

The door opened, allowing a rush of frigid air to flow into the clubhouse.

"Looks like your ol' lady made it. I'm gonna go track down mine. I've been informed dinner is at three, so if you plan to take Chloe off somewhere for a Christmas quickie in the hallway, be back by then."

Rocket snorted. "Think that's more Mav's style than mine. Plus, not looking forward to pissing off the Green Beret brother five minutes after he gets to town."

As he stood, Copper slapped Rocket on the back. "Point taken, brother. Think Scott would have come across one Michael Ainsley at some point?"

"Don't know."

"Might be worth looking into in a discrete way that won't have him moving in to protect his sister."

Fuck.

Easier said than done. Scott was a fucking mamma bear when it came to his baby sister. He also wasn't the most biker-friendly individual on the planet, though he'd been civil since Chloe ripped into him a few months ago. She'd informed him in no uncertain terms Rocket was there to stay, and he needed to either get on board or go fuck himself. And yes, she'd said it exactly like that.

God, he loved that woman.

"I'll see what I can do, Cop."

"K. Hi, sweetheart," Copper said as Chloe and Scott made their way to the bar.

"Merry Christmas, Copper." Chloe gave the president a cheerful grin and accepted a kiss on her rosy cheek. The tip of her nose wasn't too far off Rudolph's color, either. Both she and her brother still had on thick coats, scarves, and Chloe's long red hair hung out from below a gray knit cap with a ball on the top.

"Scott," Copper said with a nod.

Scott returned the nod and lifted his hand in greeting just before Copper went off in search of Shell. "Hey, man." He extended his hand to Rocket.

"Hey. You guys all caught up?" Rocket asked as he gripped Scott's hand. He'd been trying to be a little more conversational and a little less…himself around Chloe's beloved brother.

"Think so." Scott shrugged, his gaze already scanning the bottles behind the bar.

"Hey, babe," Rocket said as he pulled Chloe close. "Cold out there?"

"No, it's a balmy seventy-five." She shot him a slightly scary grin as she snuck her fingers under his T-shirt.

"Shit! Oh, fuck!" He jerked back as her icy digits made contact with his warm skin.

"Ohhh, that's nice." She burrowed her frozen nose into the crook of his neck.

"Jesus, woman." His body temperature had to have dropped ten degrees in two seconds.

Her chuckle tickled his skin. "You're so warm."

"Not anymore." A shiver raced down his spine as heat leeched from his body into hers. Oh, fuck it, he was man enough to take a little cold. He circled his arms around her and crushed her to him.

"Mmm, thank you for warming me up." Chloe lifted her head, and before she had the chance to say anything else, he stole a scorching kiss that would melt an igloo.

Chloe moaned into his mouth, returning the kiss with gusto. Her tongue delved into his mouth as though trying to steal a taste of the vodka he'd drank. His cock filled, irritated with the confinement of the ridiculous Rudolf briefs Chloe forced him to wear after he'd lost their little bet over the sex of Jig and Izzy's baby. He'd been so damn sure it'd be a boy.

A loud throat cleared, causing Chloe to jump out of his arms. Now her cheeks were flushed for an entirely different reason. A much more pleasurable but frustrating reason. Maybe Copper had something with the quick fuck in the hall comment.

"Watching my baby sister try to climb down some biker's throat doesn't do much for the Christmas spirit," Scott said as he tossed back a shot of whatever Thunder had delivered. "Another," he said to the prospect. "Gonna need a bunch to scrub the image of my sister sucking face from my brain."

"Sorry, man," Rocket said while Chloe rolled her eyes and smacked her brother's shoulder.

"Please," she said. "It's the least you deserve after I walked in on you and Missy Haberfield when I was fifteen. Talk about scrubbing your brain. I still have nightmares from that shit." As she spoke, she shifted to Rocket's side, sliding an arm around his waist. Her clever fingers slipped back under his shirt, a much more tolerable temperature this time.

With a neutral expression, as though he wasn't suffering from a raging hard-on, he listened to Chloe chat with her brother as she ran her fingernails up and down Rocket's back. Every scrape of those damn nails sent a surge of lust straight to his already straining dick. If he didn't get his woman somewhere private in the next thirty seconds, he was likely to bend her over the bar and fuck her right there, brother be damned.

"Hey, Scott, let me take your coat. Chlo and I'll drop it up in my room so it'll be safe," he said, not caring that he'd interrupted a conversation between the two. "Come on, babe, help me out?"

Chloe shot him an innocent grin as though she had no idea he was about to crawl out of his fucking skin. "Sure, let's go."

As Scott shrugged out of his bomber jacket, he narrowed his eyes Rocket's way. The guy probably wasn't fooled in the least, but at least he had the foresight not to interrupt this sister's inevitable fucking. With his lips pursed, he held out the jacket.

"Great." Rocket said. He grabbed Chloe's hand and towed her toward the stairs.

Joy

"Geez, Rocket, slow down, will ya?" Her voice was full of laughter as she practically ran to keep up with him.

"Where ya going, Rocket?" Mav called out when they were halfway up the stairs.

Rocket didn't give a fuck if the entire clubhouse knew he was heading upstairs to fuck his woman, and he let them know it by flipping Mav off without breaking stride.

Chloe laughed again but kept pace with him.

The very second he had her in his room, he slammed the door and moved to box Chloe in.

"Nuh-uh," she said, wagging her finger as she slipped under his arm. He was turned around and the next thing he knew, Chloe was shoving him against the door, hard. "I've spent most of the morning driving to and from the airport. Didn't get a chance to stop for a snack. I'm hungry. And I need to thank you for warming me up downstairs."

She dropped to her knees, and his head fell back against the door. "Babe…"

"Yes?" she asked all innocence as she worked his belt open. Just knowing her hot mouth was on its way to his cock had him leaking in those fucking briefs. "Something you want to say to me?"

Huh? Was there? Who the hell knew?

Once she'd removed the belt, she slid the zipper down. "Kinda testing the limits of this thing, huh?" One finger took a journey up the ridiculous underwear, straight over his dick.

"Kinda testing the limits of me, Chloe."

She giggled. "One of my favorite things to do."

Fuck it.

Rocket shoved the jeans to the ground the stuck his fingers in the sides of the briefs.

"No!" Chloe barked. "So impatient. That's my job."

"I hate these fucking things."

Another giggle. "I know. But I love how they mold to your cock. And how I can do this." As she lowered the band, his cock sprang out, nearly hitting her in the face. "Damn, that was a snug fit."

She had no fucking idea.

"Think we should make these a Christmas tradition. Don't know why, but knowing you were wearing these things has made me want to suck your cock all day."

"Christ, woman. You're fucking killing me." He flattened his hands against the wall and willed himself not to come from her words alone. Not that he wouldn't love to see that pretty face bathed in his come as he shot off, but he really, really wanted to feel her sucking— "Jesus, fuck!"

She sucked him to the back of her throat. The room spun, and his knees went fucking weak as she worked him. Her hands curled around his bare thighs, holding him in place. Up and down she went, using just the right amount of suction with each pass. Every few seconds, she paused to pay special attention to the head of his cock, his favorite thing in the fucking world. When that sexy little tongue of hers worked the underside of his cockhead, he saw fucking stars.

"Fuck, that mouth."

"Mmm," she hummed, the vibrations traveling straight up his cock and landing in his balls. As though following the path, her soft hand cupped him, and his eyes rolled back in his head.

There was no way he could keep his hands from going to her head. As he held her in place, the silky strands of her hand sliding through his fingers, he punched his hips forward. God, he hoped that wasn't too much for her because he didn't think he had the power to keep still.

Chloe moaned again, and he thrust forward, fucking her mouth in a steady rhythm now. She took it all, playing with his balls as he lost his mind. The next time he hit the back of her throat, she tightened her hand on his balls and gave a gentle tug. "Fuck, Chloe," he shouted as spurt after spurt of hot come flooded her mouth.

The sight of Chloe's throat reflexively swallowing his load never got old. All the energy seemed to leave his body with the orgasm, and he sagged against the wall.

"Merry Christmas," Chloe said with laughter in her voice.

Rocket pried his eyes open and stared down at his woman, still on her knees. She licked her lips, causing him to groan. She was a fucking goddess.

"Get up here, baby." He hauled her to her feet and sealed his mouth over hers. Didn't matter that he could taste himself on her tongue. All that mattered was her flavor on his lips. He spun them, pressing her back to the wall.

"When do we have to be downstairs?" she asked, panting as he kissed his way from her jaw to her earlobe.

A quick glance over his shoulder at the clock revealed it was two fifty-five. "Five minutes."

"Shit," she said with a groan. "Not enough time."

Rocket chuckled. "Challenge accepted," he said as he slid his hand down the front of Chloe's leather leggings. No way was she going to give him such a monster orgasm and not get hers in return. "All I need is three."

"Oh, shit," Chloe said on a breath when his fingers slid through her wetness. Her head fell against the door, and heavy-lidded eyes stared at him.

"You ready?"

A slightly drunk looking smile appeared on her lips. "Do your worst."

Chloe's brother was gonna skin him alive him after he caught sight of her floating down the stairs with mussed, post-blow job hair and a satisfied grin on her face. Not that he cared. Years from now, he wanted Chloe to look back on their first Christmas together with a big fucking smile.

A screaming orgasm right before dinner ought to take care of that.

Chapter Twenty-Six

COPPER

As Copper rose from his chair, he took a moment to soak up the atmosphere. His family sat around multiple tables in the clubhouse, seconds away from digging into a feast the ol' ladies had outdone themselves creating. The aroma of crispy-skinned turkey, sugary ham, and a host of sides wafted around the space making his mouth water in anticipation of the meal. A giant Christmas tree took up one corner of the clubhouse, decorated by none other than Maverick a few weeks ago.

His brothers and their women chatted, laughed, and drank as they waited for him to announce it was time to dig in. As of yet, no one had noticed he'd stood. On his right, Beth bounced in her seat as she nibbled on a roll she'd stolen from the kitchen a few moments ago. Shell sat on the other side of her chatting away with Izzy, who held a sleeping infant in her arm. How the baby managed to sleep through the boisterous excitement of their family would forever be a mystery to him.

Even Mama V looked her best today, sitting beside Viper with a smile on her face. Her battle was far from over, but knowing she'd made it to both breakfast at Copper's house that morning and dinner at the clubhouse was a positive sign she was feeling well today at least. On the other side of her, Curly sat next to Holly. He'd proven to be a polite and respectful addition to dinner. One Copper was considering extending an offer to join the club too.

For today at least, every person in the room was happy. Merry. Full of bliss, alcohol, and soon to be stuffed to the brim with delicious food. It appeared as though the Disciples had left town. He wasn't fool enough to believe it was permanent, but it meant a safe and drama-free Christmas. Tomorrow it might all change, would all change as shit ramped up with their newfound enemy, but for today?

Today there was joy.

He glanced at the newest member of their family. Her sweet round face snuggled into her mother's chest. It'd be him soon. Him and Shell. Copper fully considered Beth his daughter, but he'd not even met her until she was three years old. He had no experience with something so small. Something he could literally crush with his mitt sized hands.

As he turned away from the baby, he caught Shell watching him with a soft smile on her face. She practically glowed today. Since they'd made up and he'd embraced her pregnancy, the smile hadn't left her face. Now, she stared at him with a bit of wonderment in her gaze. This baby experience would be entirely different for her, as well. She hadn't had a man in her life the first time around, and Copper vowed then and there to be the best goddammed husband and father he could possibly be.

He winked, loving the way after all this time, her cheeks still pinked when he flirted with her.

"Daddy, I'm still hungry," Beth said, pulling at the hem of his shirt. Her roll had disappeared, and now she eyed a massive bowl of mashed potatoes with a predatory lick of her lips.

"K, princess, just let me say a few things, then we'll eat."

"All right," she said with a huff as though he told her should wouldn't be eating again until tomorrow instead of in two minutes.

"Listen up!" he shouted as he clinked his fork against the side of his whiskey glass.

It took a good thirty seconds for all conversation to stop, but eventually, the room fell quiet, and all fifty or so sets of eyes fell on him. All the men wore their cuts as was required in the clubhouse, but most had stepped up their game a bit with the rest of their clothes. Black jeans, pressed collared shirts, a few polos. His crew looked pretty damn sharp. The women, especially. They all brought their Christmas A game with dresses, glittery shoes, and fancied-up hair.

"Guess I should start with a Merry Christmas," he said as he lifted his glass.

A chorus of Merry Christmas was repeated back to him before a hush fell over the group again.

"Promise I won't ramble too long, but this has become somewhat of a tradition, me reviewing how shit went over the past year. As you know, we've had some pretty sweet highs and some pretty fucking crushing lows. We added a lot of members to our family. Some patched brothers," he said, lifting his glass to Screw then LJ. "New prospects," he said to Thunder, who raised his beer bottle in return. "Quite a few ol' ladies."

Maverick stuck his fingers in his mouth and whistled as others clapped and hooted. The girls ate that shit up, beaming at their men.

"I want to welcome our visitors, and of course, the newest addition, the most badass baby to ever be born," he said, facing Izzy and Jig. The entire room erupted in cheers and applause.

"All right, all right. Give me two more minutes."

Beside him, Beth picked up her fork and whacked it on her plate so hard, he couldn't believe the thing didn't crack. "Hey!" she shouted. "Listen to my daddy so I can eat!" Her outburst had a round of laughter circulating the room as Shell snatched the fork from their daughter's hand and shushed her.

Once the attention was back on him, Copper said, "We dealt with some serious fucking shit this year."

Shell huffed and covered Beth's ears.

"Sorry, babe. We handled some rough stuff this year. Wish I could tell you it was over, and every day would be like today. Full of laughter and cheer. But we all know this life can be more thorns than roses. That being said, I'm so goddamned proud to call you my brothers, my family. I couldn't ask for a better group of men riding at my back."

"Fuck yeah!" Zach yelled as the rest of the men stomped their boots and pounded the tables.

Copper held up a hand. "To whatever comes next. The good, the bad, the ugly, and of course…the fucking sexy."

"Here, here!" the men yelled, lifting their glasses as they waited for Copper to take the first sip.

"I got one more thing to say, then we're gonna eat till we burst." He turned to Shell, whose eyes widened.

"Now?" she mouthed as she lifted her hands to her cheek.

He nodded.

Shell stood and walked behind Beth's chair until she reached his side. Then she slid her hand in his and squeezed. Pure happiness radiated from her as though she'd been lit up from the inside by a thousand-watt bulb.

"What's going on?" Toni called out.

"Yeah, Mommy, what are you doing?" Beth asked, craning her neck straight back to watch them.

"Got an announcement to make."

"Oh, my God!" Steph yelled. "Are you…"

Copper nodded. "That's fucking right! My woman is knocked up! Gonna be another little terror running around here in about seven months! Now let's fucking eat!"

Everyone went nuts, shouting congratulations, sipping downing their drinks, and digging into the spread.

Copper kissed his wife, patted her on the ass, and let her go back to her seat. If his size was anything to go by, she'd need to eat a helluva lot to keep his baby satisfied.

Two hours later, dinner had been devoured, dessert consumed, and about half the contents of the bar sucked down. Some of the brothers had left, having other friends and family to visit for the holidays.

Zach, Mav, Jig, Rocket, LJ, and Screw remained along with their women and Jazz, who seemed to be working extra hard to avoid Screw. Cassie and Viper had taken off shortly after dinner, but the fact that she'd made it at all meant the world to Copper. Shell still wasn't aware of Cassie's diagnosis, and though she'd be pissed when she found out he'd been keeping it from her, the news would have ruined her holiday for sure. His woman deserved this day without the sadness of Cassie's illness casting a long shadow.

The lingering group sat around the clubhouse, most of the men with their ol' ladies on their laps. They chatted and had another few drinks. More likely than not, most of them would be crashing there that night. Shell and Izzy would take him and Jig home, but the others couldn't drive for shit at this point. Beth had passed out about twenty minutes ago in Copper's bed upstairs wearing the brand-new Elsa dress Mav and Stephanie gifted her.

"Man, you ladies outdid yourselves this year," Mav said as he rubbed his stomach then let out a loud belch.

"Oh, that's lovely." From her perch on his lap, Stephanie rolled her eyes. "But I have to agree. We really rocked that meal."

"I'm not sure I'll be able to eat again for a week." Toni groaned and let her head fall back on Zach's shoulder. "Someone should have stopped me before that second piece of pie. I was out of control." She shot Holly an evil glare.

Holly giggled. "Hey, don't blame me," she said in a sing-song voice while she cooed at Joy, who rested in her arms, awake for the first time in a while. "She shouldn't blame me, should she? No, she shouldn't. Oh no she shouldn't."

"Telling you, LJ, that uterus is begging." Izzy pointed a finger at Holly.

LJ cast Holly a wary look. "Sugar, maybe you should give the baby back to Iz now."

"Oh no, I shouldn't. No, no, no," she continued to babble with the baby talk.

Copper laughed right along with the rest of them.

"So, how are the wedding plans coming?" Chloe asked.

Steph smiled. "Great. It's gonna be super chill. New Year's party here at the clubhouse. Then, right before midnight, we'll say our vows and have our first kiss at twelve. Then more partying."

"Awww," both Jazz, Toni, and Shell said at the same time.

"Holy shit, that's cheesy," Izzy said, looking like she just drank some sour milk.

"Hey, fuck you!" Mav laughed as he spoke. "It was my idea."

"Ahh." Izzy nodded. "Makes sense now."

"Makes sense now," Mav mocked in a ridiculous tone.

"Aiden?" Shell whispered.

The rest of the room faded away as he focused on the most important person in his life. "Yeah, sweetheart?"

"Thank you."

He wrinkled his brow. "For what?"

"For this amazing life you've given Beth and me. For our family, crazy as they are. For loving us. For loving me."

He slid his hand up Shell's back until it tangled in her curly hair. "Listen to me, Shell, and listen good."

Her eyes flew wide and she nodded as best she could with her head being held captive.

"I don't know how to do anything but love you. And Beth." He placed his other hand over the slight swell of her stomach. "And the bean. Don't thank me for it. Loving you is the greatest pleasure of my life."

He kissed her. A gentle press of his lips against her. Shell let out a soft sigh and melted into him.

"Next year's gonna be an adventure," she said as she drew back.

"This year was an adventure."

"Good point. Guess they're all gonna be, huh?"

"With this club? Yeah, baby, pretty fucking sure life will never be dull."

Shell hummed her agreement. "Let's get out of here. I've got one more Christmas present for you." She winked.

Well, who was he to look a gift horse in the mouth?

It was Christmas, after all.

EPILOGUE

STEPHANIE

"Holy shit, girl, Mav is going to lose his fucking mind the second he lays eyes on you." Izzy stood in the doorway of the room Stephanie had claimed as a bridal suite of sorts. "That dress is fucking hot. If I ever lose this baby weight, can I borrow it?"

"Can you borrow her wedding dress?" Shell asked, looking at Izzy like she had two heads.

Stephanie laughed. "Sure, Iz. You're right, this dress is hot. Too hot to sit in the closet for the rest of its life."

"See." Izzy stuck her tongue out at Shell, who rolled her eyes.

It was eleven-thirty on the dot on New Year's Eve. The entire club and some additional invited guests had been partying their asses off for the past four hours. Steph and her girls had snuck away about two hours ago to prepare for the short and sweet wedding ceremony, which would take place in about fifteen minutes.

The girls had curled her blonde hair, now hanging halfway down her back. For a while, she'd considered wearing it up in a fancy updo, but Mav liked it best down, and she wanted him to *lose his fucking mind* as Izzy had said. They'd also done her makeup, giving her a sexy smoldering look she'd never have been able to accomplish on her own.

After slipping into the extremely tight and extremely short strapless white leather dress, Steph was nearly ready to go. All she needed were the sky-high sparkly white shoes that actually made her legs look long, and she was ready to rock and roll her way to her man.

Her soon to be husband.

Butterflies took flight in her stomach. A year and a half ago, if someone had told her she'd no longer be an FBI agent but working as a private security consultant for a biker owned company, and engaged to said biker, she'd have laughed in their face. But here she was. In love with and about the marry a man with more inked skin than not. Who was a professional snark artist and innuendo-maker. Who teased and joked more often than he was serious. A man who'd saved her from a horrible fate at a great personal sacrifice. A man who'd taught her the world was so much more than black and white, right and wrong.

A man who loved her a much as she loved him and who made each day better than the one before it.

"Hey," Toni said as she walked over, wearing a short denim skirt and Handler's tank top like the rest of her girls. "We're gonna give you a few minutes by yourself to take it all in. See you at the top of the steps in five."

After squeezing Steph's shoulder, Toni began to turn toward the door.

"Wait," Steph said as she grabbed her friend's wrist. "Thank you. I know you all thought we were a little crazy for planning a wedding in about ten days, but you guys jumped right in with so much excitement."

With a shrug as though she hadn't worked her tail off for this since Christmas, Toni said, "We love you guys." Then she kissed Steph's cheek and followed the rest of the women out of the room.

After blowing out a breath, Stephanie finally stepped in front of the mirror and gazed at herself for the first time. The girls hadn't let her peek the entire time they were jazzing her up.

"Holy shit," she breathed as she stared at the nearly unrecognizable woman in the glass. Her hair curled down her back in thick, glossy waves. Her cheeks had a rosy glow and her eyes smoldered with a definite come fuck me vibe. Right up Maverick's alley.

But they were right, the dress would drive her man insane. The poor guy would be marrying her with a hard-on for sure. It hugged her body so tight, breathing was difficult, but she had the rest of her life to make up for those missed breaths. Riding high on her thigh, the skirt combined with the shoes made her legs look miles long. Quite the optical illusion.

Her tits looked great too, encased in the leather dress that gave them a little lift. With her shoulders and back bare, but tanned thanks to the salon Toni made her visit, she truly looked better than she ever had.

Screw waiting the full five minutes.

It was time to see her husband.

MAVERICK

"You ready, man?" Zach asked as he slapped Mav on the back with a little more force than necessary.

Bracing his hand on the wall so he didn't stumble forward from the blow, Mav nodded. "Very fucking ready, brother."

"No cold feet? No second thoughts?"

Not a one. From the moment he asked Stephanie to marry him, he hadn't had so much as a flicker of doubt. "Nope."

"Lotta women weeping tonight." Zach's shit-eating grin had Mav flipping him off.

"Pfft." Screw strode overlooking sharp in the same black leather pants, white Henley, and cut the rest of the wedding party wore. "No one is weeping. I'm keeping them too occupied to shed any tears. Unless they're crying for more of my dick." He winked.

"Fuck, did I used to be that annoying?" Mav asked, but he couldn't keep the smile off his face. Nothing would break his fucking spirit today. Not a goddamned thing.

"Yes," Jig, Rocket, and Copper all answered at the same time.

"Well, fuck you all. I was gonna apologize, but now you can all shove it."

"Hey!" Izzy shouted from the top of the stairs. She wore a baby carrier on her front with Joy snoozing away. "You jokers ready?"

Fuck, Mav loved this. His family just acting themselves on his wedding day. No prissy fluff everyone would forget the moment they woke the next day. No flowers that cost a mint and would wilt and die before the ink dried on their marriage license. Just good friends, good food, good booze, and him promising to love Stephanie for the rest of their fucking lives.

Perfection.

"Fuck yeah, we're ready," Screw answered. "Bring on the ball and chain."

Mav smacked him on the arm. "You fucking upset my woman and you'll be partying with my boot up your ass."

"That mean I'd get to be there when you fuck your wife for the first time?"

Jesus, of course Screw would go there. Mav thought he was bad, but Screwball took it to another level.

"Fuck no, brother. I'd cut that boot off, foot and all before I'd let you watch."

"Oh please," Screw said as he rolled his eyes. "You guys are the first family of public fucking. Nice try."

Mav shot him a wolfish grin as the music kicked up. Steph had picked a country mix to play in the background as her girls walked down the aisle—or down the stairs and across the clubhouse to where Mav and the boys lined up in front of the bar. Zach had agreed to get ordained online and would be the one marrying them.

Joy

Izzy walked down the steps first, looking fierce as usual, even one week out of having a baby. Holly followed, then Chloe, Shell, and finally Toni. Once the ladies were in position, the music changed, and Ed Sheeran crooned out the lyrics to *Perfect* as Stephanie appeared at the top of the steps.

Mav's jaw dropped and he swore his heart stopped beating. Everyone else disappeared. They might as well have been the only two people for miles around. The entire clubhouse could have exploded around them and Maverick wouldn't have noticed.

"Fuck," he whispered an exhale as the vision in white leather descended the steps toward him. Her hair was curled, but not in a neat style. More as it would look had he been running his hands through it as he kissed her stupid. And her eyes...fuck those eyes begged him to follow her to the bedroom.

But it was the dress—if one could call it that—that had his dick rising to attention. Not that he cared, the entire room could point and laugh at the groom with a tent in his pants and he wouldn't give a fuck. Not when he'd be peeling her out of that thing shortly. And peel he would have to do because it was goddammed tight. So tight, it'd be an effort to work it off her. But so worth it. He bet she had something even more sinful on underneath. Something he'd tear off with his teeth seconds before he ravaged her.

His wife.

It didn't take long for Stephanie to reach the bottom of the stairs. He'd been instructed to wait for her to make her way to him, but fuck if he could make it another second without touching her. Mav strode forward, meeting her halfway to the small podium Zach stood on. He took her hand, brought it to his lips, and pressed a lingering kiss to her palm.

So sue him, he may have tossed in a quick lick that had her gasping and her eyes dilating.

"You're so fucking beautiful," he whispered.

Stephanie beamed. "So are you," she said, smoothing a hand down the front of his shirt.

"Ready?"

"So ready."

"Let's do it." Mav guided her to Zach, who pecked her cheek before addressing the crowd.

"Welcome, everyone. We're gonna make this short and sweet so we can all get back to partying, and these two animals can go and find a corner to consummate their marriage in."

Steph giggled right along with everyone else. How much more perfect could she get? Finding a woman willing to forgo a princess wedding with all the trappings was one thing, but to find one who actually seemed to love this causal shit as much as he did was a rare prize.

"I'm not gonna say much. These two want to just dive right into what they wrote. Ladies first."

"Yeah, Steph," someone yelled, making her blush an adorable shade of crimson.

When she looked up into his eyes, he got the same punch to the gut he always experienced gazing into her baby blues. Mav wasn't one to believe in fate or soulmates, but he swore on all that he had Stephanie was put on this very earth just for him. No woman had even tempted him to give up his swinging bachelor ways before, and now, it was as though other women didn't even exist.

"Maverick, my Mav," she said, then cleared her throat. "Everyone knows you're the life of the party. You're the fun in a room full of people. You're quick with a joke, always inappropriate, and you make everyone laugh and roll their eyes at the same time. But not everyone gets to see just how incredible you are. How brave and selfless. How loving, supportive, and comforting you are. I'm the luckiest woman in the world because I've had all those parts of you for more than a year. And now I get them for the rest of my life. You saved me," she whispered.

Joy

Mav's heart slowed to a strong, steady pound as he listened to his woman's words. She thought far too much of him, but to know he'd made her feel that way about him was a gift he'd cherish for the rest of his life.

"You saved me and paid a terrible price because of it." She grabbed his arm and stroked a finger down his forearm where the Hell's Handlers brand had once been. Now, the logo was inked over horribly charred skin from where his and Stephanie's captors had burned the fuck outta his arm. "You're the most incredible man I've ever met. Both the way you look, the way you act, and the way you make me feel. I love you, Maverick, more than I've ever loved anyone or anything in my life. I promise to keep your heart, mind, and body safe until my last breath and beyond."

God, she'd torn him inside out with her words.

Now it was his turn. How did he follow that? How did he express the depth of his feeling for Stephanie with just words. His hands shook as he reached in his pocket for what he'd prepared to say, but as he drew the paper out, he found himself crumpling it and dropping it to the floor.

Stephanie cocked her head and gave him a crooked grin.

"What I have to say is simple. I love you, Stephanie. Before you, I'd never said those words to a living soul. They are yours and yours alone. I'll never give them to another, Stephanie. It isn't even fathomable." A lump rose in the back of his throat as strong emotions swamped him.

Stephanie's eyes filled with tears, and one spilled over. He cupped her face and wiped away the little bugger. "You're my everything, baby," he whispered as his own eyes began to prickle and the tip of his nose twitched. "I promise I will spend every day of my life worshiping the ground you walk on."

"M-mav…" Steph said with a hitch in her voice. "I love you."

"Love you too, baby. For fucking ever." He turned to the crowd. "Y'all mind closing your eyes so we can get down to business here?"

Stephanie snorted out a laugh through her tears as most everyone groaned.

"What?" Mav shrugged, totally unrepentant. "Had to throw a little of my patented flavor in there somewhere."

"Yeah, yeah," Zach said as he clapped his hands to get everyone's attention. "Almost done here, folks. Keep your pants on. Especially you too." He pointed to Mav and his beautiful bride. "Okay, do you, Stephanie, take Maverick to be your husband. Through sickness and health. In good times and bad. Even if he wants more ink. Until death parts you?"

"Hell yes, I do!" Steph said with the biggest smile he'd ever seen from her. She practically bounced on the balls of her feet in those sexy as fuck shoes.

"And, Maverick. Do you take Stephanie to be your wife? Through sickness and health. In good times and bad. Until death parts you."

"Fucking A," Mav said. He burst out laughing when Steph put a hand on her hip and jutted it out. "Sorry. I do."

"Well then, by the power of the motorcycle gods, I pronounce you man and wife. Mav, you can kiss that woman in 10…

"9…

"8…

"7…

"6…

"5…

"4…

"3…

"2…

"1…

"Happy New Year!" Everyone screamed as Maverick crushed his mouth to Stephanie's. Noisemakers blared through the room. Something, confetti maybe, was thrown at him from all angles, and balloons bounced off his head. Mav didn't pay attention to anything except his wife and her amazing lips. She opened without hesitation, kissing him back with as much desperation as he felt. The kiss went on and on, neither of them willing to break the connection. In the back of his mind, he could hear the party resume. His brothers drinking, shouting, and generally being rowdy as fuck.

He didn't care. All that mattered was the woman devouring his mouth was now his for the rest of their lives.

Mav had everything he wanted. So did the majority of his brothers, and they'd do anything necessary to keep and protect it.

Please read on for **Viper**, a short story from the Twisted Tales of Mayhem Anthology.

Chapter One

1985 Burien, Washington

He was a legacy.

The makings of the Devil's Tribe Motorcycle Club literally coursed through his blood. Started by his great grandpop back in nineteen thirty-one, every man in his bloodline had their chance to lead the club. Right now, his pops ran the show. The old man had been president for the past ten years, give or take.

As long as he didn't fuck up and land his ass behind bars, Viper's shot at top dog would come. He'd head up the rough and raw group of men he'd idolized since the first time his diapered ass rode on a motorcycle. Rumor had it, his old man had made a trip into town with a ten-month-old baby Viper strapped to his back, ignoring the blue streak his mother had cussed from the porch. Young Viper had laughed and squealed the entire ride, solidifying his place in the pack.

Or so the story went.

Being heir to the throne might mean he'd be the prez one day, but as a prospect, it hadn't meant shit. No one cared who or what he was. He'd suffered like all prospects before him. He'd had to prove himself and his loyalty like all the others if he'd wanted to receive that patch.

And he'd wanted it more than anything.

270

Finally, last night, he'd earned it. Best moment of his life. Proudest for his pops too.

But, right now? Well, now he wanted to take his rifle and mow down each and every man he'd considered a brother until five minutes ago.

Shit could change in a fucking instant.

Even the core of what made Viper a man wasn't safe from the universe's fuckery.

"So, this is really fucking happening?" Sarge, the other brand spanking new patched member, muttered under his breath. "We got a problem, brother. I sure as fuck didn't sign on for this shit."

Less than twenty-four hours ago, after thirteen months of abuse and scut work, both Viper and Sarge received their official patches. At twenty-eight, Sarge had a few years on Viper's twenty-one. The guy served time in the Army, discharging at the rank of Sergeant, hence the nickname. They'd prospected together, and forged a bond, toughing out the torture the brothers loved to dish out.

"Shut the fuck up," Viper whispered back, his gaze fixated on the rusted-out van starting up the long dirt road that led to the shack owned by the DT's. His entire life, he'd been told the rundown two-room abode was a safehouse of sorts. Used by guys looking to lay low for a while.

The truth was entirely different than that bullshit.

"You telling me you ain't freaking the fuck out, V?" Sarge spoke out of the side of his mouth, so low Viper had to strain to hear him. To the others, it'd look like the two were merely standing guard, waiting for the van to arrive. "Come on, man, we got tight over the last year. You told me all about your high school sweetheart. You cannot be okay with this shit."

Viper's stomach clenched as it always did when Vanessa was mentioned, which wasn't much anymore, but it still happened on occasion. They'd been young, stupid, and head over fucking heels wild for each other. Double V, as everyone nicknamed them. In their youthful ignorance, they'd made plans to marry the summer after high school graduation.

A week before school let out, Vanessa was raped. Brutally raped. A random act of senseless violence, or so the useless pigs claimed. The assault destroyed a beautiful and vibrant girl. No matter what Viper did, and he tried every fucking tactic he could think of, he couldn't drag her out of the dark pit her mind descended into. She'd become so consumed by the trauma, she committed suicide three months after it happened.

So, no he wasn't fucking okay with this. Truth was, he was okay with a lot of illegal and even amoral shit, but this was not one of those things.

"Shit, brother, you know I'm not fucking on board with this." He kept his voice a notch above a whisper. Nudging his chin toward their president, vice president, and enforcer, he said, "They'll have your ass if they catch wind of what you're saying, though."

Sarge scratched the side of his clean-shaven head. The guy had been cue-balling it ever since some skirt he'd been chasing told him she had a thing for bald men. "So you're just gonna let this play out?"

Was he? Could he live with himself?

Viper ran a hand across his unshaven chin. "Fuck," he mumbled. "How did we not know about this? Can't believe they managed to keep the fact they're trafficking women a secret from us for an entire year."

"Too risky when we were just prospects," Sarge responded. "Now that we're patched in, we're committed. No choice but to be loyal. Well, I guess we could choose to die." He snorted out a soft laugh.

"Goddammit." Never in a million years had Viper imagined his dream turning into a shit-pile.

"We gotta do something, V," Sarge said. The guy's moral code was looser than a whore's twat. If he had a problem with this, the situation was pretty fucking bad.

"Can't do shit right now, brother," Viper said as the van rolled to a stop. "Meet me at my place when this is done. We'll come up with a plan."

The club had its fingers in just about every illegal pot in three counties. Drugs, guns, money laundering, even prostitution. They owned two cat houses full of women selling themselves on a daily basis. Viper never so much as blinked at any of it. Difference was, each and every one of those women came to the club willingly looking to work.

This shit? The chick supposedly in the back of the van? Yeah, she was being sold to the highest bidder and Viper was pretty fucking sure she didn't want to be.

A short, stout man with a cheap rug and a stash that rivaled a seventies porn star climbed down from the driver's side of the van. He walked with an exaggerated swagger befitting a cocky teenager trying to hang with the men. With the gold chains and tuft of chest hair peeking from the collar of his shirt, the man was practically a cartoon pimp.

"Hey, Fox. Long time no see." The man greeted Viper's father with a limp handshake.

"Yeah, sorry about that, Wayne. Had a cop sniffing around for a few months. Had to lay low with this shit," Fox replied. His shoulder-length hair had gone gray a few years ago, but even at fifty, Fox managed to maintain a hard and intimidating physique.

Wayne played with the longest of his necklaces. "Heard about that. Glad it's all cleared up." He sent a smarmy smile Fox's way. "Got you a beaut this time, boys. Rich little princess. Virgin too." He whistled. "She'll be fun as shit for your buyer to break."

Vipers stomach turned as his father, and the rest of his cronies, laughed. Viper grew up in the club. Not a single day went by where he wasn't at the clubhouse for some reason or another. He'd spent thousands of hours around the men. From the time he was twelve, he'd caught snippets of club business he never should have been privy to. Never once, did anyone let slip that they trafficked women.

"This is fucked," Sarge muttered, cracking his knuckles.

"Keep it in check, brother," Viper whispered back. "We can't do shit right now. Save it for later."

"Bring her on out," Fox said. "My guy is looking for something real specific. I'll check out the goods. She passes muster, we'll pay."

Wayne's beady eyes lit up. The motherfucker was practically salivating. Whoever the unlucky lady was, she must be going for a mint.

Viper and Sarge stood about fifteen feet from the van, arms crossed, taking it all in. They'd been invited along as extra security on a "sensitive transaction." Viper hadn't thought twice about it. He trusted his new brothers implicitly.

Or he had. Until he realized his old man was involved in the one criminal act Viper couldn't stomach. Hardest part to swallow was that Fox fucking knew what happened to Vanessa and what it did to Viper. He fucking knew Viper would never go for this shit.

As though knowing he was in Viper's thoughts, Fox turned his way. Viper shoved down the newfound hatred for his father and gave the man a nod. A false show of support.

Fox grinned. He was proud as fuck of his son for approving of the buying and selling of women.

Fuck.

Wayne fished a keyring out of his pocket. The thing made him look like an apartment super. After sifting through about thirty keys, he stuck one in the lock on the back door of the van and twisted. After pulling the heavy door open, he climbed in.

Despite the near freezing temperature, sweat beaded across Viper's forehead. He idly wiped it away. With each second that ticked by, tension coiled tighter. Where the fuck was she?

After a few more seconds, Wayne hopped out of the truck with what could only be described as a leash in his hand. He paused, then reached out and roughly grabbed ahold of a woman. After yanking her out of the van, he shoved her toward Fox.

She wobbled then fell to her knees at Fox's feet.

Viper's father arched his back, and let out a loud booming laugh that had Viper's fists clenching. "Appreciate the sentiment, darlin', but I'm not the one you'll be on your knees for." Struggling to rise, she shivered. Viper swore he could hear her teeth chatter. When she rose to her full height, which couldn't be more than five foot five, Viper let his gaze scan her body. Clad in nothing but bikini panties and a bra, it was no wonder she was so fucking cold. Bruises marred her upper arms, and her amber-brown hair was a tangled mess, as though she'd been struggling for hours. A leather collar ringed her neck, attached to the leash Wayne controlled. Despite the dirt and bruising, it was clear the woman had a body made for long sleepless nights of passion.

Sarge moved, as though he was going to charge forward and take Fox out. Viper shot his hand out and caught his brother's arm before the idiot got them both killed.

"Rein it the fuck in," he rumbled so low no one would hear.

"Shit. Sorry. I'm cool," Sarge muttered back, rubbing his hand over his head. "Just…"

"Get it, brother. I really do."

Sarge nodded and scanned the area around them.

Viper should be doing the same, but at that moment, the woman lifted her head, and he couldn't do a damn thing but stare at her. Green eyes, full of defiance stared up at his father. Even with black tear tracks marking her cheeks, and her caramel-colored hair a rat's nest, she was the most gorgeous woman he'd ever seen. With that face and that body, it was no wonder some sick fuck was willing to pay big bucks for her.

Viper felt a stirring below the belt. Shit, he was just as sick as the fucker who'd purchased her.

"Hmm," Fox hummed, the sly grin he was named for curling his mouth. "Not bad, Wayne. Pretty much exactly what I asked for." He reached out grabbed the woman's breasts. She jerked back, but with her hands bound, wasn't able to end the unwanted fondling. Tears spilled down her cheeks, and she trembled, but held her head high and toughed it out.

She was strong.

Viper growled, he couldn't help it. Watching his father paw the unwilling woman was making him rabid.

Sarge's elbow connected with his gut.

Fuck, he'd been too loud.

Fox shot him a look then laughed. "See something you want, Viper, my boy? Sorry, this one's not for the taking. At least not by you." He stepped back and stared at her. "She is your type though, ain't she? Don't worry, I'm sure we'll find you one just like her for the night."

Viper grunted in response. He didn't trust himself to speak. Not without calling his father out on being a rapist piece of shit.

"Excellent find, as usual, Wayne," Fox said as he handed the slimy bastard a thick envelope. "There's a little something extra in there for you. I know this one was hard to get."

Wayne's smirk was more snake-like than Viper's name. "Always good doing business with the Tribe," he said as he took the envelope. As though this routine was rote, which Viper supposed it was, Wayne gave Fox a two-finger salute, slammed the back door of the van, then climbed in the driver's seat. Without another word, he was off, leaving the victimized woman alone with five bikers.

Fox rubbed his palms together, then blew into his cupped hands. "Fuck, it's cold." He chuckled. "You'd know, wouldn't you, girly? "Legs," he said to the club's enforcer, a muscle head with quads the size of tree trunks. "Take her in, chain her to the bed. Her buyer is flying in on Tuesday to pick her up, so she'll be our guest until then." He narrowed his eyes. "Hands off, okay? Or at least keep them on the outside of her body. The buyer was very specific. Rich, twenty-one, virgin, green eyes. Ain't risking the two hundred grand pay off cuz your dick's twitching. Get me?"

Two hundred thousand dollars? Beside him, Sarge whistled.

"Got it, boss." Legs bent down and picked up the lead Wayne had dropped. "Let's go, bitch." He yanked the rope, jerking her forward, chuckling at her yelp of pain.

Viper growled again. This time Fox missed it, but the girl didn't. For just three seconds, before she started for the shack, her gaze collided with Vipers.

It was like a punch to the gut and a stroke to the dick all at the same time.

Terrified, but absolutely stunning green eyes stared into his as though pleading for mercy. He clenched his teeth so hard his jaw screamed for relief. Steeling his expression, Viper returned her stare with a hardened, impassive one.

The tiny flare of hope his growl must have sparked died, and her shoulders slumped in defeat. Another tug on the rope had her jerking, and following Legs into the ramshackle house.

Viper wanted nothing more than to rush forward, grab the girl, and toss her on the back of his bike. But they wouldn't make it two miles before Fox had the whole club hunting their asses.

He settled for trying to send her a telepathic message

Hang tight, baby. Viper's coming for you.

Chapter Two

No matter how tightly Cassandra huddled into herself or how vigorously she rubbed her arms and legs, she couldn't warm up. The house wasn't frigid, at least not compared to outside, but it certainly wasn't toasty. And after what had to be nearly a day of being unclothed, she was chilled to the bone.

Not that these men cared about something as trivial as her comfort. No, most kidnappers weren't overly concerned with their captives' contentment.

God, she'd been *kidnapped*. And sold to the highest bidder like some kind of auction item. Straight out of a fucking movie, only she couldn't walk out when it sucked.

The overwhelming panic hovering all around threatened to overtake her again. Cassie rested her forehead on her bent knees and fought to steady her breath. It'd worked this far to keep her from losing control of her emotions. Who knew how long it'd be before she freaked.

God, she was so stupid. The reason stereotypes about naïve rich girls existed. Apparently, she was precisely what some sick piece of work was looking for. A dumb, spoiled, sheltered rich girl who'd never had sex, and had no clue how the real world worked.

Well, whoever he was, he'd gotten her. Or these asshole bikers had snagged her, and the *buyer* would get her in a day or so.

And he'd break her. Or so the bikers kept saying as they laughed and pawed at her mostly naked body. Wouldn't take much, she was so near broken already.

Maybe whoever purchased her would be disappointed if she broke too quickly, and he'd return her. Was there some kind of trial period? A trade-in credit if she didn't work out? A harsh laugh escaped into the quiet room. She was going crazy.

"The fuck you laughing about?" an impatient voice asked as the door flew open.

A beefy guy with a flaming red mohawk and freckles galore stood in the open doorway. He was one of the ugliest men she'd ever seen, with a clearly deformed nose and cauliflower ear on both sides of his head. A long scar ran straight across his forehead. Whoever he was, his face had been through the mill. Looked like this guy had replaced Legs at some point in the hours she'd been there.   How many hours, she had no freaking clue. The men didn't exactly leave a clock. Or a phone. Too bad the bikers were smarter than they looked.

"Nothing," she mumbled, keeping her eyes trained on the enormous booted feet standing in the doorway.

The biker, whoever he was, grunted. "You ain't got much to be laughing about right now, bitch."

Why the hell did they use the term bitch like it was some kind of common pet name? She'd been called bitch more in the past twelve hours than in her entire life.

"Nothin' to say?" He snorted out a laugh. "That'll change fast. You'll be saying yes, sir and no, sir all day long." She glanced up just as he smirked. "Mostly yes, sir."

A run of terror skittered up her spine. Clenching her teeth, she tried to give him a formidable stare. She wouldn't let him know how each and every word he spoke was a lightning strike of fear directly to her heart.

"W-why are you doing this to me. I don't want to be here. I'm not a willing participant. It's kidnapping. And it will soon be rape." For some reason, the why mattered to her. Was he in some sort of financial crisis? Struggling to feed a horde of children? Was this a desperate attempt to save his family? It certainly wouldn't justify his actions, but it'd give her some hope that she had at least a snowball's chance in hell of being set free.

The ogre cocked his head and grinned. "That's an easy one. Money, baby doll. It makes the world go 'round."

"You in some kind of financial trouble? I have money. I can help you out if you let me go. You could do hard time for this." Hard time? Who was she, Olivia Benson?

"Nice try, but nah. Club's got money. We do real well." He shrugged. "Just want more of it. And we'll only do time if we get caught." With a snort, he stepped into the hallway. "Don't plan on getting caught. Get comfy, princess, you'll be here for another day or so before your master comes to collect his new pet."

Any hope she might have had seconds ago burned up into ash. Greed, straight up money-hungry business was driving this bus. And that meant she had no chance of convincing him to let her go.

For one fleeting moment, while that smarmy asshole Wayne was delivering her to this piece of shit shack in the woods, she'd thought she'd glimpsed a man who didn't approve of what was happening to her.

An angry-sounding growl had come from the hunk in leather who seemed to be some kind of guard dog for the bikers. Something about him struck her as different. An energy he projected drew her to him.

Now she was trying to read biker's auras? She really was losing it.

She'd given the guy her most pleading *save me* look, but all she'd received in return was a cold, hard stare.

He'd been a gorgeous man. Tall, lean but not skinny with a leather jacket and jeans hugging his firm thighs. A floodlight had shone in her direction, blocking her view of his true eye or hair color, but both appeared some shade of brown. Maybe on the lighter side. A few days' worth of stubble obscured his cheeks. Cassie had had the insane desire to rub her own face against his, and find out it if was scratchy or silky soft.

Hot was too mild a word to describe him. Incendiary more like it. Had she run across him at her parent's country club, she'd have swooned and stammered like a school girl.

Another bark of laughter left her. That man wouldn't set foot inside a country club. And not just because security wouldn't let him, but because he was way too badass.

Too bad he was as evil as the rest of them.

"You good with the plan?" Sarge asked as they sat astride their bikes.

Viper stared straight ahead at the quiet shack. Legs was back on duty, had been for the past six hours. Viper and Sarge were set to relieve him for the rest of the night. Their orders were to keep the girl alive and a virgin, but were given the green light to "play a little" as Fox had said. Never before had Viper actually considered murdering his father.

Until that moment. He'd had to walk away because he couldn't trust himself not to wrap hands around the old man's throat.

Since making eye contact with the woman the previous night, Viper felt like a live wire dangling from a power pole, snapping and popping with dangerous energy. Every man in the club had suffered from his mood at some point over the last day. Fox was so fed up with him, he assigned "bitch sitting" duty and ordered Sarge along to babysit the babysitter.

Mission accomplished. Now they both had a reason to be back at the shack.

"Yeah. I'm good."

Sarge nodded. "Okay, the body should be arriving in about two hours. I've got the Scoundrel's cut all ready to go."

Nodding without taking his attention off the shack, Viper said, "You never told me how you managed that one."

"What? Swiping one of the Scoundrel's cuts?" Sarge said with a chuckle. "Remember that bar fight Legs got into with one of those fuckers last year?"

"Yeah."

"Before the fists started flying, both of 'em took their cuts off. Legs tossed his to Fox. The Scoundrel was stupid enough to leave his on the bar. I straight up walked out with it. Figured it'd come in handy someday. I was right."

Viper grunted. He'd actually heard the story before, but his brain was only half in attendance tonight. Most of it was dedicated to the woman they were about to rescue. The plan was simple. Frame the Scoundrels, an MC from a neighboring town.

The Devil's Tribe's one and only enemy.

Sarge had a contact who worked at a funeral home. Actually, he had a woman he banged on the regular who worked at the funeral home. A good fucking and five hundred dollars was apparently what it took to purchase the dead body of a homeless man. Not much, all things considered.

"All right, let's review one more time. We bullshit Legs until he leaves. Body comes in two hours. We wait one hour after that just to make sure someone ain't coming around to feed us or some shit. I'll make a trail in the woods for the club to follow, you place the body then grab the girl and scram. I'll burn the place to the fucking ground." Sarge sounded almost gleeful, as though they were planning a party instead of an escape. "It'll look like one of he Scoundrels didn't make it out, but the rest took off through the woods."

"What if the cut burns up, and they can't tell it was the Scoundrels?" Viper asked.

They'd been over it a hundred time since Sarge devised the plan last night, but he seemed to understand Viper needed to hear it one more time. "If you put the body where we discussed, it should be far enough to get charred but not fully cooked. The club will tell the cops the place was empty, which will hopefully keep the search to a minimum. If all goes well, they'll just assume we're dead."

The plan was risky. Fox wouldn't just let his son's death go unretaliated. He'd bring war to the Scoundrels door. At some point though, sooner rather than later, it'd come out that none of the Scoundrels actually burned up in a fire. The jig would be up, and Viper and Sarge would be enemy number one as far as the club was concerned. There'd be a manhunt. The club's reach was far and wide. The only hope they had was getting away far enough and fast enough before that happened.

"I'll take the girl to the motel in Oregon. No stops along the way."

"Right," Sarge said. "And I'll meet you there."

The trickiest part would be getting out of town without being seen. They planned to stay at a motel a few hours out of the state and lay low for the next few days before heading east.

"And this place we're heading, what's it called again?" Viper asked.

"Townsend. It's in Tennessee. At the base of the Smoky Mountains."

"How'd you hear about it."

"They've got a club. One percenters, but definitely not into this kinda shit," he said pointing toward the shack.

Easy to assume, but he'd have said the same about his own club two days ago. Never again would he walk into a situation blind and stupid. "So you say."

Sarge grunted. "True. When I was getting out of the army, I almost prospected there. Came here instead to be closer to my folks."

"All right, brother, let's do this shit." Viper held his fist out.

When Sarge bumped his against it, their gazes collided. Neither was comfortable with the decision to flee the club, but they'd come up with no other viable option. Viper couldn't remain loyal to a club involved in the kidnapping and selling of women. That was the bottom line.

The fact that he'd be leaving his family, leaving the only life he'd know hadn't exactly sunk in yet. His entire life, he'd been preached to about loyalty, brotherhood, club family. He still believed in all those things even if he'd be labeled a traitor. A disloyal deserter who the club wouldn't hesitate to kill.

Legacy or not.

Thing of it was, he saw the situation differently. He and Sarge weren't the disloyal ones. The rest of the club earned that title. They'd kept secrets, tricked their prospects, and pulled Viper into something Fox had known his son would object to.

Fox knew Vanessa's rape and death tore Viper up like nothing else.

And the fucker had been committing similar acts all along.

"Eyes open, watch your six the whole time," Sarge said as they started toward the shack. He'd be on the lookout outside. Viper felt he'd connected with the woman, and probably had the highest chance of convincing her to leave with them. Worse came to worse, they'd knock her out, but he hoped it wouldn't come to that.

He'd watch his six all right. Especially once there was a gorgeous woman nestled against it on his bike.

Chapter Three

Cassie had thought through every possible escape scenario she could drum up, and each one ended in failure.

She'd never be able to overpower whoever was on guard.

She couldn't break the wrist bindings securing her to the bed —she'd been trying for hours.

When they released her for a bathroom trip, she couldn't outrun the long-legged man watching her.

Screaming would be fruitless. She'd noticed the lack of neighbors when they pulled in.

Offering the men money had been a flop.

Threatening them with her parent's wrath hadn't worked either.

That left one option. A sickening one, but considering what was in store for her, she'd have to get used to the idea.

Seduction. Maybe if she offered a blowjob or even sex one of them would let her go. Her stomach twisted and turned at the idea.

Though not completely innocent, she was a virgin, and wasn't exactly planning to cash in her V-card as a bargaining chip. But if it would work to get her out of here?

She might just have to.

What waited for her on the other side would be far worse than one romp with a biker.

So, she shored up her courage and ignored the internal voice screaming at her not to do this. Just as she was about to call out to whoever was babysitting, the door to her room opened up.

"You," she said on a gasp as the man from the previous night stepped into the room. As if by instinct, some of the fear dissipated. Despite his scowl, and the authority radiating from him, she knew deep down, this man wouldn't hurt her.

"What's your name?" he asked, not moving from his spot.

"C-Cassie," she said. "Cassandra." She held as still as possible as if not moving would somehow make her safer.

"Will anyone be looking for you?"

She studied him. He might not harm her outright, but he was one of them. Wouldn't these guys die before betraying their motorcycle clubs? Or was that just in the made for TV version? Something compelled her to tell the truth. "Um, I'm not entirely sure." She cleared her throat and fought to hold his intense milk-chocolate gaze. "Normally, I'd say yes. But I had a falling out with my family. Which was why I was at that bar and distracted. Your guy slipped something in my drink and…"

He nodded, face tightening as though he didn't approve. Then why was he with them? Could he be an undercover cop?

"Your folks rich? Powerful?"

Ahh, so one of them was willing to take money. Not an undercover cop. "Yes! They'll pay." Would they? Her father had cut her off, told her she was no longer in his will. Not that she'd taken a dime from him in ages, most of her money came from a trust set up by her grandparents. They'd known what controlling assholes her parents were. Throughout her schooling, she lived off that money but planned to earn her own once she graduated and began working. "Or I will if they won't. I have money."

He tilted his head and stared at her. He really was attractive. Not like any man she'd ever felt an interest in before. Raw power radiated from him. She bet there wasn't anything in the world this man was afraid of.

Must be nice.

His gaze heated her unclothed skin, eliciting a tremor from her.

"Shit," he said, shrugging out of his leather vest. He tossed it on the bed then drew his hooded sweatshirt over his head.

Cassie flattened herself against the headboard. Gone was the bravado of a few moments before. Now that the opportunity to sex her way out of this was upon her, the concept was repulsive, despite how hot he was.

But instead of getting naked and coming for her, he tossed her the sweatshirt, making her jaw drop.

"Um, I can't..." She held up her right arm which was bound to the bedpost.

"Fuck, sorry," he said, stalking toward her. He didn't stop until he was right up in her personal space. The scent of tobacco and some kind of manly deodorant surrounded her. God, that was an arousing smell. Beneath her bra, her nipples peaked.

Terrified one second, aroused the next. What the hell was happening to her? Some kind of Stockholm syndrome? That had to be it. There was no other reason for her to be drawn to the man whose true intentions were unknown to her.

"W-what's your name?" she asked more to distract herself from the inappropriate lust than to really learn his name.

"Viper." He drew a long blade from a sheath on his belt. "Just gonna cut the ropes off you, babe? Okay?"

Babe? What? And how on earth was someone so hard able to hold her arm so gently? "Okay," she whispered, emotion clogging her throat. She'd managed to keep it together through slaps, drugging, and groping, but a caring touch was nearly her undoing.

"Won't cut you, I promise."

"Okay," she said again, at a loss for anything more substantial. The blade sliced through the tight ropes with just a few vigorous back and forth saws. The moment her hands were free, she sighed and rotated her sore wrists. "Why do they call you Viper?"

"I'm mean as fuck and strike fast."

Okay then. Her eyes widened then almost fell out of her face when he started to work the sweatshirt over her head. Once she'd pushed her arms through the very long sleeves, she swallowed and said, "Thank you." Warmth immediately surrounded her like a comforting hug. The fabric smelled just like him, and the metaphorical hug became a little more intimate. And arousing.

"You're free," he said.

Cassie's heart stuttered. "W-what? Are you serious?"

Viper nodded. Yeah, the man was serious. She had a feeling he was always serious. "You have anywhere to go? Anywhere I can take you?"

Did she have anywhere to go?

No, she did not. Not two days ago, she'd found out her married father was screwing her best friend and had been since she turned eighteen. And how did she find out? Well, that would be because her four months pregnant ex-friend showed up at her apartment sobbing and begging for advice. The entire story spilled out in a torrent of tears and hysterics. Cassie supposed if she'd been a better person, she'd have felt some compassion or even pity toward her friend, but she didn't. She'd felt rage, hatred, and betrayal.

After kicking her bawling friend out, Cassie had turned her fury on her father. All that accomplished was being told she was acting like a child and to grow up. Excuse her for thinking her fifty-three-year-old father knocking up her twenty-one-year-old best friend was fucked up.

She'd threatened to go to the media if he didn't support her friend financially and stop seeing her romantically. He'd laughed and said his lawyers would handle it and her "gold-digging" friend would never see a dime. He'd then threatened to cut her off if she went to the media. So she cut herself off and stormed out of the house determined never to return. Maybe had this been the first twisted offense her father had committed, Cassie would have considered forgiving him, but her father's sexual proclivities had him in hot water on more than a few occasions.

He was part of the wealthy, corporate, high society elite, yet he was far trashier than the man sitting beside her. The man her father would consider the lowest of low. She wanted no part of that life anymore. It was chock full of lies, manipulation, and greed.

"No, I don't." Absently, she rubbed her sore wrist. "Have anywhere to go that is."

Viper took hold of her right forearm. Lifting it to his eyes level, he studied the angry red gouges she received struggling against the ropes. "Shit. I didn't think to bring a first aid kit. There won't be anything here." Once again, his touch was so gentle she'd have never thought it possible.

"It's okay. It can wait until we, uh, I get somewhere."

With a heavy sigh, he pressed his lips to the raw marks. Cassie gasped as electricity shot straight up her arms and to her nipples.

Before she had a chance to say anything, he repeated the gesture with her other, un-harmed wrist then lowered them to her lap. "I'm heading to Oregon tonight to hole up for a few days. When it's safe, my buddy and I are driving out east. You can come with us tonight then decide what to do from there. You just can't ever tell anyone what happened here tonight."

Her head spun with the new information. "But, wait, you're leaving your club?"

He nodded, solemn as ever. "Won't be welcome once they realize we let you go."

Wide-eyed, she shook her head. "We can come up with a lie. I'll say I knocked you out or something. You can't give up your life for me."

The smile he gave her was sad, almost defeated. "You think I could stay with those men knowing what they're doing to women? Knowing what they were doing to you?"

Their gazes locked in a stare that felt far too intimate considering they'd met ten minutes prior. "I don't know you," she whispered.

Another sigh. "No, you don't, do you?" The words were as sorrowful as his eyes. Rising, he moved to the door. "We leave in two hours. You're free to roam about, but I wouldn't recommend going outside. Don't want to risk anyone seeing you. Think I got some sweatpants in my saddle bags. I'll go check."

The moment he was gone, the left side of her chest started to ache. Rubbing it with her palm she rose. A few trips around the room worked the kinks out of most of her leg muscles. Her stomach made a very unladylike growl, sending her into the hallway in search of food. What she found had her once again surprised. Viper stood at the stove, cracking eggs and flipping bacon.

"Pants are on the table. You hungry?" he asked, back to her.

How had he known she was there? She'd been virtually silent tiptoeing down the hallway. "Um, yeah, I really am." She slowly started into the room uncertain of how to act. This entire situation as way beyond bizarre. Five minutes ago, she'd had the feeling she'd offended him by insinuating he'd stay with his club, and now he was cooking for her? "Can I help?"

"Nah, just sit that pretty ass down. I'll be done in ten minutes."

Almost exactly ten minutes later, he slid a plate in front of her. It was piled high with fluffy scrambled eggs, crisp bacon, and two pieces of dry white toast.

"Sorry," he said. "No butter."

She laughed, a small giggle at first, but it morphed into an uncontrollable belly laugh.

Viper watched her with a look of fascination on his face. "Oh my god," she said, struggling for control. "I'm losing my mind.

No butter. Sure do wish that was my biggest problem right now."

He gave her a genuine smile. "You're something else, you know that?"

Her mouth turned down. "What do you mean?"

"You're tough. Not once have you cried, freaked out, yelled, panicked. And you're smart. I can see you assessing every situation before you speak. Plus, you're gorgeous. The whole goddamn package."

Warmth filled her. Finally, after hours and hours in the shack, she was pleasantly warm. Almost too warm.

"I'll come with you," she said, heat rushing to her cheeks.

Fork halfway to his mouth, he said, "Huh?"

"I'll come with you to Oregon. If the offer's still on the table."

For the first time since he walked in her room, he smiled. "Fuck yeah the offers on the table. Get your shit packed," he said like she was on vacation. "We leave in under two hours."

Cassie smiled, and for the first time in days, it was genuine.

All thanks to this biker who was giving up his entire life to rescue her.

Chapter Four

"Ready?" Viper asked over his shoulder.

Cassie's soft laugh had him smiling despite what was about to happen. "To get out of here? Hell, yes, I'm ready. To ride on a motorcycle?"

He could feel her body move as she shrugged behind him, dragging her tits along his back.

She laughed again. "I'm not so sure."

"You're ready. Just hang on."

Her death grip around his waist tightened even further. Viper couldn't help but chuckle. The woman had guts. She was practically trembling behind him but hadn't voiced a peep of protest. He respected her for doing what had to be done despite fear, and without bitching. It was an admirable quality not everyone possessed.

"Oh, my God." She gasped and pointed toward the house. "Viper, look, it's on fire!"

"I know, baby, that's our cue to leave. Just wanted to stick around long enough to make sure Sarge lit the place up. We're out." He hit the throttle and peeled out, spraying dirt in an arc behind him.

He'd warned her they wouldn't be making any stops on the three-hour trip to Beaverton, Oregon. Long ride for someone who'd never been on a motorcycle, but as he'd expected, she didn't so much as divert his attention away from the road once. In fact, at one point he worried she'd fallen asleep, but when he placed a hand on her thigh and gave it an affectionate squeeze, she threaded her fingers through his and squeezed back. Guess she'd gotten more comfortable riding as time wore on.

Around midnight, they pulled into the sparsely populated parking lot of what could only be described as a no-tell motel. The place was cheap, known for being discrete, and unfriendly toward local police. All things they needed, depending on who came sniffing after them.

By now, the club should be well aware the shack burned up. Viper figured his pops was losing his mind trying to determine if Viper had died, been taken prisoner, or went AWOL. A pang he could no longer ignore hit his heart, and he pressed a hand to the left side of his chest. Not only was he leaving his life behind, but he could never return. Not unless he was looking to die. This decision was life-changing and permanent.

"You okay?" Cassie's sleepy voice asked in his ear.

"Yeah, babe. I'm good. You must be beat."

"I could be persuaded to sleep," she said, humor in her voice.

And just like that, his mood lifted. He liked this woman. Genuinely liked what he'd learned of her and seen from her so far. Maybe he could convince her to join him and Sarge on their cross-country adventure. She'd said she had nowhere to go.

He climbed off the bike then turned to help her down as well. Drawing her into his arms, he smiled at her drowsy face. "Then let's get you into a bed."

Immediately, a blush pinked her cheeks, and she stared at his chest instead of his face. He'd meant the bed comment strictly in reference to sleep, but, huh, look at that, the little virgin had a dirty mind. He groaned as she burrowed into his embrace. A dirty mind and a body that fit perfectly in his arms. Like he'd been custom built to absorb her softness.

His dick hardened against her stomach, something she couldn't possibly miss. Instead of jerking away or acting like he was a lecherous jerk, she sighed and snuggled closer, clearly enjoying her effect on him. "Babe, enough of that or you're gonna be getting an education you didn't bargain for, right in this damn parking lot."

Her eyes were wide and full of disbelief as she took a tentative step back.

He chuckled. "Thought so. Here, put your hood up." Even though he gave her the instruction, he tucked her long caramel-colored hair into the hood of the borrowed sweatshirt himself. He shouldn't have, but he couldn't resist brushing his fingertips along the baby-soft skin of her neck. A subtle tremor ran through her at the contact. Damn, she may be inexperienced, but her body responded as though it knew exactly what it wanted.

Turning away before he got a glimpse of those lust-filled eyes, he grabbed a crumpled ball cap out of his saddlebag, and shoved it on his head, pulling the brim low. Best they had as far as disguises. "Don't make eye contact with the guy working the desk if you can help it. We want to be as forgettable as possible."

"Got it. I bet they have one of those displays with pamphlets of things to do in the area. I'll browse through them while you check us in."

"Good thinking." For someone so obviously rich and sheltered, she sure rolled with the punches well.

Hand in hand, they walked into the lobby of the motel, checking-in with cash as Mr. and Mrs. Dickerson from Wyoming. The clerk handed them an key with a large rectangular plastic keychain. A peeling number seven sticker indicated their room. Cassie played her part perfectly. As soon as they entered the lobby, she kissed his cheek and moseyed on over to the brochure display. Try as he might, Viper couldn't stop the rush of blood to his cock as her soft lips brushed his stubbled face.

The clerk was slow as shit, but Cassie had managed to look interested in what the area had to offer the entire fifteen minutes it took to get a damn reservation. After securing a room, Viper moved his bike, parking right outside the room so Sarge could find them easily. He should be rolling into town within the next few minutes.

Once they arrived at their room, it took a few seconds to work the key into the rusted lock. Once he finally had the door unlocked, Viper opened it to reveal a very unimpressive motel room. He suppressed a chuckle. In her most terrifying nightmares, Cassie probably never imagined herself staying in a place with stained yellow walls, the distinct odor of stale cigarettes, and faded bedding.

"After you, m'lady," Viper said, sweeping his arm in a grand gesture.

With a giggle, Cassie marched on into the room. Slowly, she spun. "Nice place." Her eyes sparkled, and playfulness was evident in her voice. "Though it's about a thousand times better than where I was headed, so I'm pretty damn happy to be here with you." The teasing expression turned into one of sincere gratitude.

Damn, she kept surprising him. He'd at least expected a wrinkled nose or a shudder at the accommodations. Looked like he had a lot to learn about the rich girl he'd rescued.

As though driven by an invisible force, he walked to her. He'd only had the barest of touches, yet his hands itched to feel her skin once again. "You don't need this anymore," he said, sliding his hands into her hood and drawing it off her head. She kept her mesmerizing green gaze locked with his as he worked her long hair out of the sweatshirt. This time, he didn't even try to pretend he wasn't touching her on purpose. He stroked the pads of his fingertips along her neck, tracing her hairline.

A soft puff of air left her lips, and she quivered as she'd done in the parking lot.

"That tickles," she whispered.

"Yeah?" He took a step closer. All he had to do was bend a few inches forward, and those gloss-free lips would be his. For the first time since he started having sex at fifteen, he hesitated. She was a goddamned virgin. A virgin who'd been kidnapped, roughed up, and sold. He might have saved her before they raped her, but still, she probably wasn't feeling too great about men at the moment. "Want me to stop?"

Her eyes drifted shut. "No. Definitely don't stop. It tickles in a good way. In a tingly—"

"Well, shit, didn't think I'd be a third fucking wheel."

Cassie's eyes flew open as she jumped away from Viper.

Shit. Viper turned to find Sarge standing with his shoulder propped against the door frame, arms crossed, and a shit-eating grin on his face. Viper sent an apologetic smile Cassie's way before running his hand down his face. Nothing he could do to hide the damn boner tenting his jeans.

Christ, he hadn't even closed the damn door. Whatever fascination he was developing with Cassie was causing him to lose sight of the big picture.

Safety and protection. He couldn't neglect simple shit like closing and locking doors. At some point, the club would realize they'd been played. He and Sarge needed to remain vigilant at all times.

"Hey, brother," he said. "Any trouble getting out of town?"

Sarge shook his head, but his focus was squarely on Cassie, whose face was an adorable shade of red.

"Sarge this is Cassie. Cas, Sarge."

"Hi, Sarge," she squeaked. "I know it's not nearly adequate, but thank you."

With a nod for her, Sarge strode into the room. He made a big production of closing and locking the door. Viper rolled his eyes at his brother. If possible, Cassie's face turned an even deeper shade of red.

"Ain't a thing, doll," Sarge said with a wink for Cassie, as though they'd helped load her groceries in her trunk instead of rescuing her from sex traffickers.

"So everything went as planned?" Viper asked. Cassie took a step closer to him. Then another. And one more until her shoulder bumped his. And, damn, if he didn't like the fuck out of that. Meant she felt safe with him. Wanted to be near him. Maybe it was just the high stress of the situation, but he had the distinct urge to puff out his chest and beat his fists against it, Tarzan-style. Instead, he wrapped an arm around her shoulders and tucked her against him.

"Yeah, it's all good," Sarge said, eyes shifting between Viper and Cassie. "Place burned fast. The body burned too, but not enough to be unrecognizable. Should buy us enough time to get across the country before the coroner IDs the guy."

"Where are you going?" Cassie asked.

"Tennessee," Viper answered.

"Oh, wow, that's far."

"That's the point," Sarge said. He scratched at the back of his neck then met Viper's gaze. After prospecting together for a year, they'd developed a sort of non-verbal communication. It'd come in handy, saving their asses a few times. Tonight, though, Sarge didn't seem to be picking up what Viper was putting down. And that was to keep his ass in the motel room.

"Okay, kids, I'm all amped up. Need to find a place to have a drink. Wanna join?"

Damnit, could he be more obvious? Leaving Viper and Cassie alone was a bad fucking idea. He could only resist so much temptation.

"Oh, um, I don't think I'm up for it now," Cassie said, twisting the ends of her hair. She gave a little chuckle. "Especially in this outfit. Plus, I need to shower." She stepped out of Vipers hold. "But you guys go."

She was crazy if she thought they'd leave her alone and unprotected. Viper scowled at his brother. "I'm staying."

"Okay," Sarge said with a shrug. "Don't wait up, I'll be a few hours." He winked at Cassie then started for the door.

Viper clenched his teeth. With his luck, Cassie would be terrified he was gonna be on her like a starving mutt on a steak the second Sarge closed the door. "Here. Take this." Viper tossed the oversized keychain to Sarge who caught it with a downward swipe of his hand.

"What the fuck?"

Cassie giggled. "Think of it as an accessory."

"Whatever. Be good, kids." The door snicked shut, leaving Viper and Cassie in charged silence.

"Well, um, I guess I'm going to take a shower." She seemed to be looking everywhere but at him.

"All right. Take your time."

Without another word, she scurried into the bathroom. He didn't miss the distinct click as the lock engaged. Guess that was that. She didn't want his company.

With a sigh, Viper dropped onto one of the beds. After kicking off his boots, he hefted his feet on the bed and flopped back. Damn, as shitty as the bed was, it felt good to be horizontal.

The shower rushed to life, a comforting sound that lulled him into a pensive state. Just one day had changed everything. Instead of rising to the top of a club he'd always felt was part of his soul, he was on the run with only one friend and a girl who was worming her way deep under his skin.

He didn't regret leaving. It had to be done. Even at just twenty-one, Viper knew himself. He couldn't take part in what was going to happen to Cassie. Not with his history. He'd never be able to look in the mirror again. The only potential regret was leaving without speaking to his old man first. Fox would grieve the loss of his only son fiercely. It'd be a wound that would never heal. Although, Fox would probably prefer Viper's death to his abandonment of the club. What he and Sarge had done would be seen as the ultimate betrayal. The greatest act of disloyalty.

If he was honest, Viper was starting to feel disloyal. When he'd patched in, just two nights ago, he'd sworn to do anything and everything asked of him by the club. He'd sworn in blood, to shed more blood to protect his brothers if necessary. He'd vowed nothing would ever come before the club. He'd keep no secrets from the club. He'd love nothing or no one above his brothers.

And at the first test of that commitment? He'd bailed like the boat was fucking sinking.

A soft throat clearing jolted him out of his head.

Cassie stood next to the bed wrapped in the thin hotel towel. Jesus, it barely covered her from tits to snatch. Both hands clutched the terrycloth where it was tucked to hold closed. Her damn hair hung even longer with the weight of the water. God, he loved long hair. Then there were those innocent green eyes, peering down at him, uncertainty clear as day.

"You okay?" he asked when he found his voice.

Her chin dipped in a nod. "W-Will you have sex with me?"

If she'd asked him to slit Sarge's throat in his sleep, Viper wouldn't have been more shocked.

"What?" He said, struggling to sit up.

Her throat worked as she swallowed. Viper could practically see her shoring up her courage. "We're on the run. I may have been sheltered for much of my life, but I'm not stupid. If we're caught, I know exactly what will happen to me," she whispered.

He frowned. "You don't think we can protect you? You don't think I can protect you?"

She shifted, biting her plump lower lip. Viper groaned. Why the fuck did she have to be so sexy?

"That's not it. It's just…" She sighed. "There are two of you against a whole club out for your blood. I just want to be prepared if something goes wrong. If they get me, I want to have the knowledge of what good sex is. I want to know that it's not just what they'll do. I want to be able to remind myself what it's like to lose my mind from pleasure."

Shit. He was going to cave. "Cassie."

She held up a hand, keeping her elbow tucked to hold the towel in place. "It's not just that. I want you. You have to know how hot you are. I feel safe with you. Drawn to you. When you touched me—"

Fuck it. He wasn't even anything nearing a goddamned saint. Cassie was an adult. She'd asked for it. Asked for him. Viper rose to his knees, grabbed a handful of her gorgeous wet hair and crushed her mouth to his.

Chapter Five

This wasn't a kiss. Cassie had been kissed before. She'd even been kissed well. But this was an entirely different experience.

Viper owned her mouth. In the minutes he spent sliding his tongue against hers, nipping at her lips, and controlling her head, she lost awareness of anything but the man making her crave more. His taste flooded her mouth, hot, spicy, and more delicious than her favorite candy.

This wasn't the first time Cassie had been aroused either. She'd felt desire, want, lust. But, holy crap, never to this extent. Her breasts literally ached. Her nipples were tight points of need. If she'd had more experience, maybe she'd have begged him to touch her, but as it was, she had no idea what she was doing. Between her legs, a dull ache formed making her aware of how empty she was. And how wet she was becoming. All she knew was that if he walked away from her now, she'd crumble.

"Fuck, you taste so sweet," he muttered against her lips. "Give me more." He dove back in, tightening his fist in her hair as he plundered her mouth again.

Cassie couldn't help it, she moaned shamelessly into his mouth and wrapped her arms around him. When her body came in flush contact with his, she pressed her chest into his, finding just a tiny bit of the pressure her nipples demanded. She moaned again, and it seemed to douse Viper with cold water.

"Shit," he growled as he tore his mouth away.

She stood, eyes wide, holding up the towel, panting just as hard as he was. Her head spun.

"Jesus, Cassie. For the love of God, cover your tits." Viper groaned, running a hand down his face.

With a quick glance at her chest, Cassie realized she was all but flashing him. After adjusting the towel, she peered up to find him staring at the ceiling. Uncertainty and embarrassment filled her. Had she misread the situation? Was he not as into her as she was him?

"Baby, I'm not first-time material," he said, still gazing up.

Cassie frowned. "Why not?"

Finally, he gave her the gift of eye contact. "I have no idea how to make it all…" he waved a hand in her direction, "perfect for you."

Her heart melted at the softly spoken words. So, it wasn't that he didn't want her. Quite the opposite. He was afraid he couldn't give her what she needed to make her first time special. She hadn't realized he could be so sweet.

Yet stupid.

"Do you know how to make me come?"

He chuckled, folding his arms across that firm chest. "Yeah, babe, that I can do." He winked. "More than once."

"Well, then, I think that's a pretty good place to start, don't you?" Somewhere, she found the courage to be bold and demand what she wanted. Actually, her words might have come from fear, not bravery. Fear that they'd be discovered, and she'd be sold off to some sicko who'd rape her, and make her his toy for the rest of her life. If that were to happen, at least she'd have the memories of this night. She'd have the knowledge that her first time was with a man of her choosing at the time of her choosing. And her choice was Viper.

Now.

She had no doubt it would be absolutely perfect.

So, she straightened her shoulders, swallowed her nerves, and dropped the towel as she stepped forward.

Viper's eyes widened, gaze immediately going to her breasts. "Cassie," he said on a groan. "You're playing a dangerous game."

She rested her hands on his chest. Damn, the man was hard everywhere. "I'm willing to risk it. Seems to me like the prize might be worth it."

"I'm too rough, baby." He whispered the words.

She spoke just as low. "I think I've proven over the past few days that I'm not a china doll. Takes a lot to shatter me. Give it your best shot."

He looked up, straight into her eyes.

She almost squealed in delight at what she saw there. She won. He wasn't going to be able to resist her.

"Oh, I'll make you shatter, sweetheart," he said right before he nipped her lower lip. "I'll make you shatter all over my cock."

Cassie shivered. No man had ever spoken to her with such raw sexual intent.

She liked it.

Loved it.

Viper cupped her breasts in his large hands. Just the heat and rough feel of his palms on her skin made her knees wobble. He kept his gaze on her face as though gauging her enjoyment of his efforts. When he pinched both nipples with firm pressure and gave a little twist, she cried out and grabbed his forearms.

"Like that?"

"Uh, yes." Was she expected to say anything more intelligent?

"How about this?" He bent his head and sucked a nipple into his mouth, keeping his fingers on the other.

"Oh, my God," she whispered. "Yeah, that's good."

He chuckled then sucked harder. Cassie grabbed his hair, unsure if she was trying to drag him closer or push him away.

The sensation was so new and intense, she could barely process it.

He increased the suction. A shot of heat streaked from her nipples straight to her clit. "Viper," she shouted.

"I got you, baby. Just feel me. Enjoy it. I promise I'll make it so good for you."

Yeah, she was pretty sure if he stopped right then, it'd be the best sexual experience she'd ever have. The next thing she knew, he was spinning them. Before she had the chance to adjust to the shift in position, he pushed her down to the edge of the bed.

Standing before her, he stripped his shirt over his head, revealing a smooth, tanned chest with a snake tattoo curled around one pec. His cut abs rippled their way into his jeans along with a trail of fuzzy brown hair.

Next, he lost the jeans. Black briefs held a bulge that had her licking her lips.

"Damn, baby, you want it, don't you?" He reached into his underwear, stroking his hard cock.

"I want you," she whispered, transfixed by the sight before her. Watching him touch himself was so erotic, she almost told him to forget about her and keep going.

Almost.

Viper swiped his thumb over the tip of his dick then brought it to her lips. A wet streak of precum coated the finger. Without needing to be told, Cassie took his thumb into her mouth, cleaning the salty digit with her tongue. Viper groaned.

He yanked his thumb from her mouth and roughly shoved her back onto the bed. Before her head hit the mattress, he was on his knees, pushing her thighs wide. With her legs dangling over the edge of the bed, he had an up-close and personal view of her saturated pussy.

Viper wasted no time diving between her spread legs. When his tongue stroked through her folds, she cried out and fisted the scratchy comforter in her hands.

"And I thought your mouth was sweet," he said against her sex. "It's got nothing on this delicious pussy."

"Viper," she yelped as he swiped her clit with his tongue.

"Ready to come?" he asked.

"Uh-huh," she said.

"Here we go." He buried his face in her, licking, sucking, and nibbling everywhere his mouth could reach. Two minutes couldn't have passed before she was thrashing on the bed, and begging for relief. He showed her no mercy, plunging his tongue into her, and fucking her with it. Thank God she was lying down. She'd surely have collapsed otherwise.

Two thick fingers breached her, making her back arch which only pushed her clit harder against his tongue. "Fuck, you're tight," he said, though it seemed he was talking more to himself than to her.

He stroked the front wall of her pussy, and she saw stars. When his lips wrapped around her clit, Cassie swore she died a little at that moment. Her world shrank down to the pleasure between her legs before exploding into a sensation so intense, she screamed. Screwing her eyes tight, Cassie gave herself over to the wonder of it.

When she joined the world again, she realized he'd moved her farther onto the bed. Now, her head rested on the pancake-flat pillow. Viper hovered over her, propped up on his elbows.

"Hey," he whispered.

"Hey," she said. She was far to sated to feel embarrassed about the way she lost control and screamed.

"You ready for me?"

"I'm ready."

He winked down at her. "You sure you can handle all this?" As he spoke, he nudged her opening with the thick head of his cock.

Cassie gasped. "I'm sure. Do your worst."

He chuckled then grabbed one of her hands. Guiding it to his cock, he wrapped her fingers around him.

Without waiting for instruction, she stroked her hand up and down his length, dying to discover all there was to learn about his body, and what made it feel as good as hers did. He was long, thick, hot, and hard against her palm. The grunts that came from him had her smiling and stroking harder, faster.

"Stop," he ground out. "I gotta get inside you, baby."

Cassie nodded. She needed that too. Though he'd satisfied her only seconds before, her body was already craving more of the pleasure. Keeping her gaze on his, she guided him to her pussy.

"Tell me if you need me to stop," he said in a strained voice as he began to push inside her.

There was an immediate burn and stretch that had her gasping and biting her lower lip.

Viper froze. "Too much?"

"No, no. Please keep going."

He slowly thrust his hips forward. He didn't stop until he was buried to his balls. Cassie breathed through her mouth, panting as her body adjusted to the forcing sensation of having a man—a large man—inside of her.

Viper held still. He seemed to be waiting on her before he made another move. It only took a minute for her body to soften and relax around him. Feeling playful, she squeezed her pussy muscles, clenching hard around his shaft.

"Shit," he yelled as his hips jerked. The action pushed him even deeper inside her sending the most incredible pleasure through her entire body.

She laughed and wrapped her legs around his body.

"You trying to tell me something, minx?"

"Think it might be time for you to move."

"Happy to oblige ma'am." He drew back at a maddening pace. Her pussy clung to him, pulling and stretching as he dragged himself out her. It was so incredible, her eyes rolled back in her head.

When just the tip remained inside her, she stared at him. Sweat beaded across his forehead. His arms shook with the effort of holding himself in check. Well, it was time to put an end to the restraint. "Viper," she said in her most authoritative voice.

His lips curled, and he raised an eyebrow.

"Fuck me."

Now, he gave her a full-blown sexy smile. He powered forward, no longer concerned with going slow or being gentle. Cassie absorbed every thrust, every moan, every grunt that he poured into her. It went on and on, the pleasure driving higher each time he rammed into her.

Her body coiled tighter and tighter until she teetered on the edge of another explosive release. "Viper," she said, losing her grip on reality. The sensations were so powerful, they were almost scary.

"I got you, baby," he said. "Keep your eyes on me and come. Come with me."

She stared into his deep brown eyes, shocked by the depth of emotion shining back at her. There was something there. A connection that went beyond the mind-blowing physical pleasure. Something she hoped to have the opportunity to explore after tonight.

She came, riding a wave so high, it was nearly impossible to keep her eyes locked with his. But she did it, and it made the orgasm even more intense than the last. Plus, it gave her the opportunity to watch him come as well.

And what a sight it was. He shouted through his release, throwing back his head and thrusting into her with a powerful slam. His body tensed, muscles straining before he went limp, collapsing down onto her.

"Jesus," he whispered into her neck. "You okay?"

"I'm perfect," she said, stroking his damp back. "So, so perfect." Even though he'd softened, he could still feel him in her oversensitive channel.

He grunted then rolled to his side, taking her with him. He slipped from her body. The sense of loss was startling. Two strong arms wrapped around her and snuggled her back against his chest, reestablishing the connection. Even though they were in legitimate danger, she'd never felt safer or more content in her life.

At her back, his heart beat a rapid rhythm. As the minutes ticked by, and their bodies relaxed, she found her heart matching the beat of his. A startling thought hit her. She could fall for this man. This rough, tough, biker who risked his life to save a woman he'd never met.

She had no idea what the morning would bring. Would they drop her somewhere along their route? Would they leave her in Oregon? She couldn't go back to Washington, living every day of her life terrified someone would find her and take her again.

Was there a chance they'd allow her to tag along?

She closed her eyes and willed herself to sleep with the hope of joining them on their trip Tennessee in the forefront of her mind.

Chapter Six

Viper woke with a start as the door to their hotel room creaked open. He glanced over his shoulder keeping Cassie shielded with his body in case of a threat.

"Just me," Sarge said as he shut the door behind him.

There was an audible click then the lamp next to the empty bed turned on. It flickered a few times before finally casting a dim light into the room.

"What time is it?" Viper asked.

"'Bout two thirty." Sarge smirked. "Guess you and the used-to-be virgin had a good time, huh?"

Viper grunted. No way was he about to tell Sarge what a wildcat Cassie had been in bed. He wasn't sure what had happened there at the end, but it wasn't like anything he'd ever experienced. If it wouldn't make him sound like such a pussy, he'd swear their hearts became one.

"You still good with the plan?" Sarge asked, sounding vulnerable for the first time since Viper met him.

He cast his brother a narrow-eyed look. "Yeah, of course. You think I'm gonna bail now?"

Sarge's gaze landed on the sleeping Cassie before he shrugged.

Shit. Viper made sure she was fully covered before propping himself against the headboard. "I'm not gonna flake out on you, brother."

Sarge removed his boots then lined them up at the foot of his bed. He was the neatest fucker Viper had ever met. Leftover from his Army days. Apparently, some shit got drilled so deep into his head, he'd never dropped the habit. Once Sarge was boot-free, he rested back on the bed, curling an arm under his head. "This more than a fuck?" he asked.

Viper glanced down at Cassie. She was on her stomach, face turned away from him. He couldn't resist stroking his hand up and down the gorgeous slope of her back. If the warmth in his chest was any indication, this was definitely more than a fuck. At the very least, he wasn't ready to walk away from her. "Not sure. Think it might be."

"Viper?" Cassie's sleepy voice had him smiling. "You okay?"

"Yeah, baby. Sarge just got in. We were talking. That's all."

"Oh." Cassie rolled over. She propped up on one elbow, taking care to keep herself covered with a sheet. "Hey, Sarge." Between the sex and falling asleep shortly after a shower, her hair was a wild mess around her shoulders. Instead of looking crazy or scruffy, it was sexy as fuck. Viper shifted his hips to avoid giving Sarge an eyeful of tented sheet.

"Hey, girl. Damn, now I'm kinda wishing I was the one who got to give you a ride out of Washington," he said with a wink.

Cassie laughed and scooted back until she was sitting up, the sheet still around her. Her face was flushed, and Viper wished they were alone. Wrapping his arm around her, he dragged her to him and kissed the hell out of her. When he finished, her eyes were glassy and lust-filled.

"Looks like I'll be at that bar a lot over the next few days," Sarge said with a laugh.

Cassie frowned. "The next few days? Thought you were going to Tennessee."

Joy

"We are," Viper said. "We're gonna lay low here for a few. Just to make sure no one is on to us. Then we'll head out." He held her gaze wanting to ask her to come with them, but afraid she'd burst out laughing.

The whole idea was insane. They'd just met days ago. Now he wanted her to uproot her entire life and move across the country. If she did, she'd never be able to contact her family. The club would surely be monitoring them for communication from her for a while.

A small snore came from Sarge's bed. Cassie peeked at him then laughed softly "Guess that's the end of that conversation." She rested her head on Viper's shoulder. Damn, she felt good there. Better than good. She felt right. Like she belonged in that very spot. When she sighed and melted into him, it gave him the confidence to breach the subject.

"You can't go home, Cas," he said, running his fingertips up and down her spine.

"I know. I don't want to anyway. I was walking away from them when I was kidnapped."

"What do you want to do?"

She played with the sheet for a few seconds before looking up at him. "Well, I was, um…I was thinking, maybe…well…"

"I'd like you to come with us," he said, keeping his voice low to avoid waking Sarge. "It'll be a long trip, and rough at first. We'll need to lay low, stay off the grid for a while."

Her gaze met his, eyes hopeful. "Why Tennessee?"

"Sarge knows of a motorcycle club there that'll let us prospect. They're called Hell's Handlers, and they're good guys. Not into the shit the Tribe is into."

She tucked her lower lip between her teeth as though deep in thought. "I don't know much about motorcycle clubs, but my one experience hasn't been good."

He nodded. "It's in my blood, baby. It's all I know. All I want. But I'll promise you this, I will not get involved with a club that hurts women. I don't stand for that shit. Neither does Sarge. I was lied to my whole life about what the Devil's Tribe was. I will be not played again. It won't be an easy life, not like you're used to, but it'll be a good life."

"So you want me to go with you guys?"

"I want you to go with *me*. I want you to be with me. Take a chance that we could become something pretty fucking great."

A huge smile lit her face. "I've been hoping you'd ask me to go with you. Yes, Viper, I want to go with you. I want to be with you. And I'm pretty sure we're already something pretty fucking great."

He couldn't believe the feeling of relief and elation at her declaration. It eased nearly all the tension inside of him. He bent down. "Thank you," he whispered against her lips. "Thank you for giving us a chance."

"Thank you for saving me," she whispered back before kissing him. Her slender arms wrapped around him, pulling him with her as she lie back on the bed. Viper groaned into her mouth as her sweetness flooded him.

"You two start fucking, and I ain't leaving this time. In fact, I'll probably watch the show," Sarge called out.

Cassie inhaled. "Oh, my god," she whispered. "I totally forgot he was there."

Viper laughed. "Guess that's a pretty good sign, huh?"

They gazed into each other's eyes for a moment before Cassie said, "What if they find us, Viper? What if they come for us?"

"Then we'll handle it, baby. We'll handle anything Hell sends our way."

Join my Facebook group, **Lilly's Ladies** for book previews, early cover reveals, contests and more!

Thank you so much for reading **Joy**. If you enjoyed it, please consider leaving a review on Goodreads or your favorite retailer.

Other books by Lilly Atlas

No Prisoners MC
Hook: A No Prisoners Novella
Striker
Jester
Acer
Lucky
Snake

Trident Ink
Escapades

Hell's Handlers MC
Zach
Maverick
Jigsaw
Copper
Rocket
Little Jack
Joy

❄ ❄ ❄

Join Lilly's mailing list for a **FREE** No Prisoners short story.

www.lillyatlas.com

About the Author

Lilly Atlas is an award-winning contemporary romance author. She's a proud Navy wife and mother of three spunky girls. Every time Lilly downloads a new eBook she expects her Kindle App to tell her it's exhausted and overworked, and to beg for some rest. Thankfully that hasn't happened yet so she can often be found absorbed in a good book.

Made in the USA
Middletown, DE
28 May 2021

40617387R00186